GIVE ME YOUR TIRED, YOUR POOR

"If the true facts are there, if fearless advocacy
is properly presented and the cause is
fundamentally just, jurors can, will, and do
respond positively. This case is an
example of what can happen when the law
operates in all its magnificence."

Jim Hogan

The individuals and incidents portrayed in this novel are fictitious. Any resemblance to actual incidents, or individuals living or dead, is purely coincidental.

Library of Congress Catalog Card Number: 98-92303

ISBN: 0-9672979-0-7

Presidio Publishing
239 East Commerce Street
San Antonio, Texas 78205
1-800-247-7694

12 11 10 9 8 7 6 5 4 3 2

Purpose of Life

Lives of great men all remind us
We can make our lives sublime,
And, departing, leave behind us
Footprints on the sands of time;

Footprints, that perhaps another,
Sailing o'er life's solemn main,
A forlorn and shipwrecked brother,
Seeing, shall take heart again.

Let us, then, be up and doing,
With a heart for any fate;
Still achieving, still pursuing,
Learn to labor and to wait.

Henry Wadsworth Longfellow, "A Psalm of Life"

"Where law ends, tyranny begins."

William Pitt, Speech, January 9, 1790

Let Me Win

But If I Cannot Win,

Let Me Be Brave

In The Attempt.

(Special Olympics Oath)

Dedication

Over the past fifty years of a very active trial practice, to all of the courtrooms, lawyers, judges, and most of all, to my family of five children, all of whom are lawyers, my wife who is a lawyer, my daughter-in-law who is a lawyer, for all of the trials and tribulations, the sadness and the joy, the ashes and the tumult of victory. Justice sometimes has square wheels, sometimes is lost in confusion and perversion, and sometimes is gloriously equitable. Paraphrasing Churchill, it has many infirmities, but it is still the best system the world has ever devised.

Give Me Your Tired, Your Poor

A great many lawsuits involve only money, and there is greed on both sides. There is none of that in this litigation. It does involve a matter of life or death, but underlying all of this is the principle of the strength and the depth and the wisdom of the jury system.

In these days, when it is met with assault on every side, many believe its elimination would be a great boon to the country. There is much to be learned from the vicissitudes of this case and the strength of the system.

Principle, honor, dedication, and testing -- all of these to the extreme are fomenting throughout these turbulent times and have a message for many that could have, or should have, lasting effect.

There is much to be learned if only we listen.

Chapter One

July 29th, 1979, late evening

There were six shots in all. They formed a small ring in the back of a man named Billy Joe Hardin of San Ignacio, Texas. He was a big man, and in the hot coastal night he pitched forward like a felled tree.

The pistol was held by a small Vietnamese man of only twenty years. He ran down the dock in the dim evening and threw the weapon into the waters of the bay. It was never recovered. His name was Cai Van Nguyen.

The killing sent the town into a rage. There were firebombings, boats were burnt to their keels, and Vietnamese trailer homes were set ablaze. The Vietnamese immigrants became the target of the Ku Klux Klan and the Nazi Party. A violent reaction seized the Gulf Coast area of Texas and spread far beyond the tiny town of San Ignacio.

Chapter Two

July 10th, 1979, afternoon

In the dusty coastal town of San Ignacio, the local fishermen gathered in the Flores bar to drink and pass away the lengthy days of bad weather, or the long hours when they were not fishing.

"They are taking every crab out of the Gulf," complained one man. He was young, and thickset, with net-scarred fingers in crisscrossed lines and an oil-stained T- shirt.

The dim bar seemed to give the men license to speak their thoughts. The place stank of beer and the upholstery of the bar stools was cracked and discolored. Dust lay thick on the floor and the heat was held at bay by dark plastic sheeting over the windows.

Beer signs lit the interior. 'Open 48-Hours a Day' said one, and another read 'Unattended Children Will Be Sold As Slaves.'

"How many Vietnamese does it take to shingle a roof?" the young man asked. He sat with two others at a corner table. When the others couldn't think of an answer he said, "Ten, if you slice them real thin."

The others laughed and looked around to see who had heard the joke. The man beside him said, "We need to organize. We got to look out for ourselves, and I know the people who know how to organize. You know, grass roots stuff, door-to-door. People's voices need to be heard and you got to organize. To take care of these guys. They should all be on reservations, like we handled the Indian problem." He seemed to be a man who knew how to organize, how to get things done, make people listen.

The men at the corner table nodded and seemed to agree and looked at one another. There were four or five other fishermen in the bar and they looked over at the group uneasily, then drew back and bent to their own conversations.

Chapter Three

July 21st, 1979, late evening

At the trailer park, the local women, tired and worn from the relentless heat, hung out clothes in the evening wind from the gulf and the T-shirts and permanently stained overalls flew out, filled with the stiff breeze. Dogs ran in packs through the oyster shell streets.

Father Dominic, the Vietnamese priest, stood a long moment in his church. White paint was peeling off the wood frame structure and rubber buckets were scattered about to collect water dripping from the leaky roof. Two stained glass windows behind the altar remained miraculously intact and were the only suggestion that the building was a place of worship. He switched off the only light bulb in the place and then went out, locking the thick slabs of wooden doors at the entrance to the church. Then he started for the trailer park to visit Judy, the wife of Billy Joe Hardin.

Judy was twenty-eight, going on forty-eight. She married in her early teens and majored thereafter in hardship, babies and poverty. She was too young to be so overburdened with constant fear and financial worries, concern about Billy Joe and the trouble that might be ahead. She was in a state of anxiety about how she could keep her small family going.

The children were ages five, three and one. They had a lot of health problems, asthma and ear infections, and the oldest needed glasses. Judy had once been a high school beauty with natural blonde hair, a cheerleader shape, and a gaiety that made everyone a friend and neighbor. That gaiety had been abraded now to a thin edge.

Life before the Vietnamese came was hard enough. But when three hundred of them, all excellent and indefatigable fishermen, came into the bay area waters, making a living became tougher and tougher. It was sparse before they came, and now the resources of San Ignacio Bay were disappearing.

Her husband Billy Joe had been the loudest and the most boisterous in opposition to the influx of Vietnamese immigrants. He was the local leader of the various groups who approached everyone in town with a petition that said the Vietnamese had to go. It was a cause that got Billy Joe's mind off all the problems that had troubled him before the Vietnamese arrived, and it was his only moment of glory in an uneventful life. In the past, Billy Joe had been a popular, outgoing, and

3

kind man under most circumstances. At one time he had been a man who was good to know. But weather and drink and hard times had changed all that.

The one-time high school athlete was at least a hundred pounds overweight. He had a beer gut of impressive proportions and his self-esteem was in bad need of repair. And his recent obsession against the Vietnamese had made him a hard and intolerant individual.

Judy had tried to understand her husband's situation. But she was a Catholic and a close friend of the local Vietnamese priest, Father Dominic. She tried to attend his services when Billy Joe would permit her to do so, which wasn't often. Judy had come to think there was no other solution to the growing tension than that the Vietnamese must pack up and leave San Ignacio, even though she would have had it otherwise. The Americans were not going to tolerate the Vietnamese presence, and she reluctantly accepted that.

Father Dominic came walking through the trailer park, making once again the futile and tiresome trek to where most of the locals lived to see if he could find Billy Joe and hold another fight at bay temporarily. He hoped he had found the solution.

There were flourishes added to some of the trailers, such as picket fences and potted plants, toy wind machines, the Roadrunner forever pursued by the Coyote. Billy Joe's had none of these things. The screen needed mending, and the accumulated trash in the front yard needed attention. The air conditioning unit in the window dropped a steady stream of water and rust stains down the walls on either side, and the entire trailer urgently needed painting. Babies' cries greeted him at the front door as he tentatively climbed the stairs.

"Mrs. Hardin, can I see you a minute?" Father Dominic called from the second stair. He was hesitant to go any further.

Underweight, a baby hoisted on her hip, Judy answered the door. She looked as if she'd been crying. "Father, he's down at the Flores bar this evening, or maybe the dock, but you're welcome to come in."

Father Dominic accepted the offer. He stepped over a pair of work boots, and tried to ignore the stench of dirty diapers in the corner.

"Father, if you're here to talk about the Vietnamese, you know it won't do any good," Judy said. "What do you expect us to do? We barely made a living before you brought those people here. Now they're setting traps where we used to fish, and, my God, they're out there twenty-four hours a day!"

The baby began to fuss and she jiggled it on her hip. "Are we supposed to pack up and leave and let them take everything away from us? I know you're a good man and you mean well, but what were you thinking when you brought them all here?"

Father Dominic nodded and sighed. "I know," he said. "But Mrs. Hardin, I will relate to you good news now." Father Dominic's English, absorbed in classrooms in Vietnam and the United States, was very formal. "Tomorrow Cai and his brother have promised to leave town. When they do, that will be the start of many others. I think this will relieve all the pressure and tension over the fishing."

Suddenly Judy smiled, and the smile made her worn face almost pretty. "Oh, Father, that's great news!" She bounced the baby to keep it from crying. "That's going to change things!"

Then they heard someone running through the hard-packed, dusty streets of the trailer park. Someone was yelling.

"There's been a shooting!"

Screen doors flew open, women and unemployed men looked out into the dimming evening.

"Who?" Judy demanded as she joined the onlookers, pressing past Father Dominic. "Who was it?" A small tow-headed boy in shorts and runners ran past them, beside himself with excitement.

"Billy Joe's been killed!"

Judy nearly dropped the baby. "No! No!" She stood in the oyster shell path with her mouth open. A woman from the next trailer ran to her and took the baby from her but she didn't notice. Judy started running toward the dock. She didn't notice where Father Dominic went to; nor did she care.

Chapter Four

August 2nd, 1979

Jim Hogan sat in his office looking out over the downtown streets of San Antonio and wondering when he was going to stop wanting something to drink. They said it took a while. Deep down he felt he would never lose that thirst. They said it depended on what you did with your time. The long hours he used to spend in bars, eight hours at a time, had now to be spent elsewhere. He had discovered there were just so many A.A. meetings that he could abide. He told himself surely there was a life in recovery. A life after the last drink.

August in San Antonio was white-hot and dusty. The streets below his window swarmed with tourists heading toward the Alamo, coming up from the River Walk, drifting from El Mercado and the Spanish Governor's Palace to the riverside bistros. The great cypress trees stood up out of the river, reaching to the fifth stories of the buildings around them. And the hell of it was, he owned the greatest bar in town—right next to his law office. He couldn't bear to look down at his haven of so many years.

Despite blackouts, paranoia, self-pity, anxiety and lost memories, he miraculously still had twenty-five people working for him, his law practice was completely intact, and he was head of one of the most successful law firms in the country. He was aided by his secretary, a woman named Sabine from Louisiana. For the last five years he had not been able to imagine life without a stiff shot in the morning, and drinks paced through the day, and then eight hours of oblivion in bars. Neither had he been able to imagine his life going on the way it had. It was hell if he did, and worse if he didn't.

Jim Hogan was in his late fifties, dark red hair now going gray. He was five foot nine with a boar neck, a deep voice that mesmerized juries, and clear gray eyes. He had the build of a middle linebacker, and even the whiskey couldn't put fat on him, but he looked ten years older than he was. His face was craggy and weathered, but his alert expression reflected a deep interest in people. He had both a whiskey face and an affidavit face. Hogan was from a long line of ordinary working people — Irishmen with the gift of talk and a love of whiskey and all of it showed. Juries felt as if they knew him and they listened to him. He would push the rules all out of proportion when he could on behalf of a client. And with each passing year he became more conscious that his drinking and the miscreant life he led were destroying his health. He feared loss of memory. And lately he'd become far too aware of his own mortality.

His magic with a jury had always been that he liked them and they liked him in return. But now he wondered if he would ever try a case again.

He used to say rehab was for quitters. Now he was just confused. His staff tiptoed around him, and his secretary Sabine was always letting him know she had just put on yet another pot of coffee. Lately, in sympathy, she had been offering him exotic teas, some sort of witches' brews of orange spices and mint.

He had a tape player going with some of his favorite music, Scott Joplin's ragtime. It was supposed to be soothing. He was supposed to expand his interests to something other than the legal world. The daily paper was laid on his desk and sometimes papers that told him of the work his law office was doing. It was going along without him as if he were no longer needed.

Hell, maybe he wasn't. Maybe he would just sit there at his desk and look out over San Antonio like a brass statue, doing nothing, thinking of the glorious days of yesteryear.

Hogan reached for the tea; it smelled like candy. First, the sports page. After that, the front page. One day at a time. One *moment* at a time. He had to accept hardship as to some kind of peace. If this were so, he was going to have a hell of a lot of peace. He damn sure had a full plate of hardship.

On the front page was a photograph of something ablaze. It was a burning fishing boat, and the faces of Vietnamese women. He wondered briefly if he had been so out of it for so long — the extended blackouts, the years that seemed to be a series of bizarre and disconnected events — that he hadn't known the U.S. Army had returned to Vietnam.

He took up the newspaper and read the cut-line. It was that trouble down on the coast. Vietnamese immigrants had moved into a small town and started fishing and eventually clashed with the local fishermen. The Catholic church had sponsored them, since most of them were Vietnamese Catholic. But they'd been foolish, thought Hogan, to resettle so many in one place. Now somebody had been shot. A local guy shot by a young Vietnamese man. The shit was really going to hit the fan. Damn good thing he was an alcoholic cripple and not available to take the case. It was going to be a big media event if nothing else, and then the jury would send the Vietnamese kid off to life in prison, the maximum available sentence.

A few years ago, Hogan had been unstoppable in the courtroom. Now he knew the word in the world of trial lawyers was that he was a failure. Many said he was a broken-down drunk with little hope of returning. And it was true; he wouldn't presently make anybody's short list as a candidate for a successful recovery. In fact, at rehab he had been voted most likely to fail.

The law had been the cornerstone of Hogan's life and now he was afraid he had lost it. In every one of his cases he had always felt his charisma would get him through. His deep voice had carried conviction and compassion, and his rather shambling demeanor and a slight clumsiness with his thick hands — he was always dropping papers — endeared him to jurors. He knew how to build the case into a kind of magic carpet that would carry a jury away.

He wondered if he could reach that pitch again without walking out of the courtroom and straight to a bar. He was especially worried about his memory. Things faded in and out. He would vapor lock in mid-sentence. If he ever returned to a bar, he didn't expect to ever leave until he was escorted out by a minion or one of his kids. They were grown now, and lawyers themselves, and big enough to take him by the elbow to a car.

Hogan loved being a trial lawyer. Probably he loved it too much.

He had graduated from the University of Texas Law School and got his first job in the D.A.'s office. He began trying cases as a young prosecutor immediately and was very good at it. He started winning cases and kept on winning them. He loved it. He came to love the world of trial lawyers in San Antonio, and elsewhere, for he tried cases all over the state. He especially enjoyed the courtroom work; all the drama and turmoil that South Texans could create for themselves was often enough played out in the old red stone courthouse of Bexar County, in San Antonio's ancient Hispanic heart.

He had never dreamed of being a lawyer when he was a kid. Before law school he had never seen a trial. His dad had been an alcoholic shoe salesman, and the extent of Jim's ambition before he became a lawyer was to be as good a shoe salesman as his old man. When he was sent to the South Pacific in World War II as a Marine infantryman, his goals had been to win the next battle, or get drunk on liberty and find a good fight.

Hogan was discharged from the Marine Corps after serving his last campaign on Iwo Jima. When the decision was made to drop the bomb and not invade Japan, Hogan and thousands of Marines had risen cheering to their feet. There was no philosophical hang up with them about dropping the bomb. They figured it saved their lives. There had been so many terrible campaigns; they all felt they were living on borrowed time.

Back then it was not acceptable to talk in terms of psycho-neurosis or lingering mental disabilities, or even nightmares. For more than a decade Hogan couldn't get through a night without living over again some grim event from the war -- a flame-thrower burning out Japanese in a cave, or a Browning automatic rifle jamming when the drunken enemy was charging, or a mortar shell exploding in a covey of fox-holes. Being plunged into battle on a sandy, shattered island was an other worldly experience, it was as if he were in the center of hell or an exploding star. When a friend he had gone through basic with was hit with a mortar, the red fragments and rags were not anything he had ever met or known before, nor did he want to. The worst was a grenade exploding in his face. Hogan had been blinded for weeks.

Hogan relived all of these secret terrors with increasing bitterness, thinking of all the Marines he knew returning to civilian ranks with the medical advice: "'There's nothing wrong with you, it's all in your head." So he *drank the memories away.*

He came home and went to the University of Texas in journalism. He met his wife when he was at the university; she was in law school, something women didn't attempt in those days, but she was bright, hardworking, a lovely young woman, and he was smitten. He'd gone to law school to be near her, and she'd talked him into going into law himself. She'd been one of the first women to graduate from that law school, and Hogan hadn't taken long to get his law degree or to propose.

He went to work for the district attorney. In three years he rose to the rank of first assistant and trial chief. He tried over one hundred jury trials to verdict, including all major felonies in a three-year span.

When he left, he was hired by a premier personal injury firm in the state of Texas. As a young plaintiff attorney he adapted quickly to civil trial work and loved it. He loved seeing the little guy win. It utterly absorbed him and he poured his energy into it, early in the morning and late at night.

It was an almost exclusively male profession. The lifestyle was hard drinking and hard work.

Hogan had no real goal other than winning. When he was in the military he had learned you won or you died. He won often. He was able to quickly certify for membership in trial organizations. In a short five years he tried one hundred cases to verdict. Then came invitations to prestigious trial organizations. After the meetings Hogan, in his carelessly worn suits, drink in hand, spent the hours in talk and whiskey. He won more cases, and then headed up his own trial firm. The settlements were more than good and at a relatively early age he had hit a pinnacle.

When the children were half grown, his wife died suddenly from a heart attack. He knew she'd rarely seen him entirely sober. He knew he'd rarely given his undivided attention to anything unrelated to try-

9

ing law suits. She and the children had deserved better from him, but it had been too late.

His contribution to domestic tranquillity and family unity had been eighty to twenty. Hogan knew he was being generous to assign himself the twenty per cent.

He had five children. Two daughters and three sons. He loved them dearly, but he had been a stranger most of their formative years. He'd been available if a crisis presented itself or if money was needed, but family days at school or Scouts went by without him. He'd come home late to cold leftovers from Thanksgiving dinners and barely made it through Christmas midnight mass at San Fernando Cathedral.

Why people held him in respect and friendship was not of his own making or credit, but they did. Perhaps they realized that with all of his shortcomings — and there were so many — he had deep love and compassion for them. Hogan was a sucker for anybody down on their luck. He was a formidable opponent and a good friend, complex and mercurial. He could be acerbic and cruel often enough and sentimental as well. Hogan loved laughing.

Then something went wrong with Hogan himself. The armor that he'd built up to protect himself from the stress and anxiety of handling as many as two hundred personal injury trial cases at one time was beginning to show. As the years and cases went by he found he was drinking more and enjoying it less. He didn't like to be alone but felt lonely inside even around friends and family. He didn't understand what was wrong and hoped staying at top speed in the fast lane was the answer. Looking inside himself would mean slowing down.

When a trial ended he was sometimes ambushed over a drink by terrible thoughts -- that this was all there was, these endings where he was left adrift and reaching for the next trial.

He came to see himself only one way. A lawyer. A special kind of lawyer. A trial lawyer. His profession came first, before everything else, even above family and friends. As time went on, he found he couldn't turn it off at the end of the day. He'd pull his tie loose and try to shake loose, but he'd had to rely on alcohol more and more to relax in the evening. He felt out of place and uncomfortable in any area other than the courtroom, or working with lawyers, or drinking.

He found himself cross-examining his wife or others in routine discussions. After she was gone, he was determined to be a good father, even if a single parent, and he'd treated family situations in a lawyer-like manner, with analysis and logic applied and what he thought as rational approaches. He cross-examined the housekeeper, the nanny and the man who came to keep the front yard in shape. He was a modern-day warrior wearing an imaginary suit of armor, a man who'd stopped dealing with his own feelings.

Memories hovered at the edge of blackouts. He recalled suddenly, one Sunday that he had been drunk at his wife's funeral. He told himself it was a real Irish wake and that he'd had no way to deal with his children's grief. He found out later that they'd spent most of the grieving hours with their grandparents, not him. Despite his lack of attention to her, his wife had been important to him. And now it was too late to make amends.

Few women had come into his life after that. Only one had caught his interest, but he'd been too afraid of rejection to pursue her.

When his children were grown and had moved out of the house, he lived alone in a downtown condominium at the Casino Club. Sometimes in the morning he felt like crying, but little boys and successful trial lawyers don't cry, and so he had a drink instead.

Most of his colleagues did not recognize his deterioration. He never missed a day of work and he didn't drink during the day when he was in trial, but he drank heavily every night to help get himself to sleep. He would wake at three or four in the morning in a chair, with Scott Joplin's ragtime playing over and over on the stereo.

After two decades of drinking and trial work, Hogan had reached the stage where he had only to take one drink and he was gone. Hogan knew he was killing himself; the loneliness, the blackouts and strange episodes of paranoia had won. He didn't want to look inside himself because it was terrifying in there. An interior jungle of unquenchable fire and perhaps death.

One day, when he was drinking in the dark and comfortable recesses of the Esquire Bar, he was struck by the remark of his closest lawyer friend.

"No man on his death bed ever said, 'I wish I had spent more time at the office'."

"So we'll just spend our time here, boys," Hogan had replied. They'd all laughed, but deep down Hogan knew he needed to get in touch with himself and his soul. He just didn't know how.

That was when the blackouts started.

Hogan had established a prestigious local Trial Lawyers Association, when he was a rising young lawyer. He'd become its first president and mentor.

To his pleasure, two decades later, his son was elected President of the same organization. It had been a night of ceremony and personal satisfaction for him to inaugurate his son into the office. A night of talk and laughter -- and drinking.

Two days later he'd asked his son when they were going to have the inauguration and where it was to be.

"Dad, we already had it," his son had replied. "You were there." His son had looked at him with caution and then turned away, embarrassed. Paul was an instinctive gentleman, at ease in almost any situation, but for a moment the young man had been dumbfounded and had not known what to say.

Hogan had been stunned into silence.

The second time had been in the Deep South. It was the incident that finally did him in.

It was a very serious tobacco litigation case in Mississippi, and Hogan had told himself that he would wait until five o'clock every day for a drink. In the mild Mississippi winter he would walk to a bar after the day's work and then, and only then, he would have a drink. He had told himself that again and again, but every morning he'd found some reason to break his resolution. That particular morning he had started the day with not one whiskey but two, and by the time they had taken a short recess he'd taken another.

Sometime during the afternoon he'd stood up to make an objection and found he'd forgotten what he was going to say. He'd wanted to say, 'I need a drink,' but his mind was blank. Vapor-locked. The jury had looked at him with shock and amusement. Then they'd turned and looked at the judge.

Hogan stood there unsteadily while the judge bent forward and said, "Mister Hogan, I will see you chambers immediately."

Once there, the judge continued. "Mister Hogan, I am almost certain that you are drunk again. I believe this is probably the fifth time, according to my recollection, that this has been the case. I am going to recess the jury and then ask the sheriff to put you in handcuffs and take you downstairs for a drunkometer test to ascertain whether or not my suspicions are correct. If they are, you are an outstanding candidate for disciplinary action."

Hogan could hardly believe he was going to be led out of the courtroom in handcuffs. Within seconds, with the snapping of the steel around his wrists, every shred of dignity and respect had been stripped from him. He heard gasps from the jurors still in the hall and low laughter from others. He knew he had hit bottom.

He failed the drunkometer test. The trial judge granted a mistrial. He'd been referred to the Bar Association, who subsequently put him on six months probation with a private reprimand.

Chapter Five

Hogan hoped there would be something in the day's mail to distract him, and sure enough, there was a note to call Father Daugherty. This was not going to be just a distraction, it was going to be trouble. Hogan hesitated to return the call.

His friend Father Daugherty was an expert in the field of alcoholism. Daugherty had been twice to Hazelden himself. After the public humiliation in Mississippi, Hogan unsteadily got Father Daugherty on the phone and said he wanted to take the alcoholic test to prove to himself that he was not an alcoholic. The whole thing, he said, was a misunderstanding and he just needed this assurance.

Father Daugherty handed it to him, and Hogan filled it out. How many drinks he had, at what time, if he could remember, and a lot of other things Hogan cringed over as he answered them.

Father Daugherty said, "You passed it with flying colors, Hogan. You are the most A+ candidate that I've ever tested."

Then Hogan hung up his trial lawyer clothes and found himself on the way to Hazelden, a world-famous rehab center for alcoholics in Florida. It was tougher than he had ever imagined. The party was over and the lights were out.

During his thirty day's drying-out, he found himself unpopular. He was unsuccessful as a leader or associate or friend. He insisted on giving advice to this venerable institution, which had been in existence for fifty years, about how best they could achieve sobriety for their members. Hogan felt sorry for all of those drunks, so pale and weak, who tottered around the place. He felt grateful that he wasn't one of them.

His counselor was a charming woman, an extremely attractive redhead. Every recovering alcoholic in the place fell in love with her -- including Hogan. But she was both professional and reassuring, keeping them all at arm's length. Sheila Ryan finally managed to break through to him, to make him understand that he was on the brink of disaster. Slowly he came to grips with the acknowledgment that he was an alcoholic. He came to accept that one of his life's greatest achievements, forty years of drinking with gusto and great fun, was no more. He was Jim Hogan, alcoholic, and his life had become unmanageable.

Now, he was like an old lion, marked and scarred, coming out of the bush, glancing here and there, and condemned to walk in solitude.

That's the way he often felt in the trial of lawsuits, and he felt it now. He would not take a drink. There was an old Texas expression from the days of the Sutton-Taylor feud down in the Gulf coast counties; 'I'll die before I run.' It was his way -- to do or die trying.

Hogan tried to pretend that the A.A. meetings were a lot of fun and sometimes they were. At least they were the only thing that gave him some serenity. With all of his desperation to quit drinking, Hogan had faith in only one thing, and that was his A.A. program. He thought it was a long shot, but it was the only hope he could see.

He had quit looking for substitutes. He regarded therapy as no substitute for the program. Nor were religious doctrine, words, intelligence, or heroic acts a substitute for the program.

'Easy Does It' was no substitute in his mind for the program. Hogan was just not an Easy-Does-It kind of guy. Education was no substitute for the program. Sex was no substitute for the program. A warm heart was no substitute for the program. Practicing law was no substitute for the program. Only action, only the Steps, were going to get it done for him. By action, he meant sharing the A.A. program with another drunk, and by Steps, he meant the Twelve Steps. There were no quick and easy answers, not even the redheaded woman with a ready smile who was far away at the end of a telephone line.

He continued to sit at his desk and gaze out his window to the busy, hot streets of San Antonio. The green trolleys filled with happy tourists dinged their bells. Airmen in basic training blues walked jauntily together to see the Alamo.

Chapter Six

Father Daugherty was a man deeply involved in good works. Hogan felt a little too shaky to go around doing good works right at the moment. Something told Hogan not to pick up the phone, but he did.

"Is that you, Jim?" He recognized Daugherty's voice. "Sure and it's good I caught you, because we are badly in need of your services for that mess down on the coast."

"Father, I need to take things easy for a while. I don't need a mess." Hogan pulled restlessly at his tie. "Ninety meetings in ninety days — meditation — the Steps. Right now every day is like seventy-two hours."

"Wait till you hear me out," said Father Daugherty. "It's that Vietnamese case down on the coast."

"Not now," said Hogan. "I'd think you would be concerned about my unlikely recovery rather than getting thrown into the grease. Hell, you know I haven't tried a serious lawsuit without a drink for the past fifteen years."

"I do know all of that," assured Father Daugherty. Hogan could tell he was in full charge. In the background he could hear the light walking bass and the graceful notes of Joplin's *Pineapple Rag*. "Don't you want to do something for those two poor defenseless Vietnamese boys who have been falsely charged with murder?"

"I'm not real strong right now," Hogan told him.

"God will provide the strength."

"God doesn't have to try a lawsuit without a drink," answered Hogan. "I do. Besides, I'm not a criminal lawyer. And furthermore, I think the church was wrong to resettle so many Vietnamese immigrants in one small town. This case is hopeless. From what I've read, that Vietnamese kid shot a local hero six times in the back! Where is the defense to that? And I'm sure the Church, as always, is not prepared to pay any kind of a fee."

"Sure and you shouldn't be expecting a fee!" said Father Daugherty. He was indignant. Then his voice grew persuasive. "That would detract from this great chance to serve these wretched unfortunates, Hogan; these people who have been so badly misunderstood. You are not that far removed from Irish immigrants yourself, are you now? I happen to know it was the Klan who ran your dad out of Dallas.

That's why you grew up in San Antonio. Jim, I am shocked and disappointed."

Nodding, Hogan said a mental *uh-huh, uh-huh* to himself. "I couldn't make it through without a drink, Father. That's the truth, and you know one drink and I'm through. I would never make it back."

Father Daugherty ignored the edge of despair and fear in Hogan's voice. He cried, cheerfully, "Of course you can! I am sending the wonderful man who is their parish priest up to see you. Will you at least speak to him?"

"How is he going to help with my drinking problem? If he'll cure that, I'll damn sure be his lawyer."

"We need a champion," said Father Daugherty. "Not a lawyer."

"All right, I'll talk to him," Hogan said with a sigh. "When can he come?"

"Now," said Father Daugherty.

"Okay." Hogan hung up and sat there and waited for the man to appear.

The small Vietnamese priest was rotund and pleasant, and Hogan could tell there was a shyness about him. He would probably rather be doing anything besides visiting with a lawyer. He sat down in the chair that Hogan offered him.

"Why in hell would the Catholic Church take such a big stake in the Vietnamese problem?" He tightened his tie. "We've got trouble enough with all of the other immigrants, particularly the migrant workers, who are much more sympathetic and a lot closer to home." Hogan shifted restlessly in his chair, impatient and mercurial.

"Yes," said the priest. He smiled and nodded agreeably. "We are few in this country and far from home. As you know, the trouble is great down there. But I know God will help us."

Hogan knew it wasn't that simple. He had been given that kind of assurance many times in the past and concluded that God rarely took sides in these matters.

"Well, this is very problematic," Hogan began. What he didn't say was that he had lost all confidence in his ability to return to trial work and had the strong premonition that, for the next few years, stress of any serious kind would surely pull him under. His friends and family agreed.

He knew his involvement in the case would be a disservice to an unsuspecting client. With him as a friend they didn't need any enemies. He was determined to resist the appeals of both Father Daugherty and this small Vietnamese priest with his round face, ready smile, short, stout body, and serene countenance.

"Father, you don't understand. I'm in no shape to take on a case like this."

Father Dominic smiled. "But the Lord often gives us strength where by ourselves we would fail."

His clerical collar was frayed and his black priestly suit was so worn it was almost blue. He nodded often, as if bowing. He sat at the edge of the large leather easy chair with his hands clasped together. He did not look around the office but kept his eyes directly on Hogan, who was easily twice his size. Father Dominic reminded Hogan of Friar Tuck.

Hogan shut off the tape with Joplin's entrancing musical structures so that he could concentrate. He would be polite to Father Dominic and get rid of him in a kindly way but with finality.

Father Dominic beamed at Hogan. "You are known for the defense of the working people. Here is something I would like to give you."

The Vietnamese priest laid a spiral-bound booklet on Hogan's nearly-clean desk. "It tells of the history of the Church in Vietnam. Very sad. Many martyrs. But not giving up. Faith and trust in God no matter the problem."

Hogan looked at the booklet. He hesitated.

"Father, here's what I'll do. I'll contribute to the fee of anyone who wants to step forward and represent the Vietnamese defendants. I'll give my best advice and recommendations, but count me out personally. I am not a criminal lawyer. I do civil law. Besides, I haven't been well."

Father Dominic stared at Hogan a moment, trying to assimilate the reasons for Hogan's reluctance. Hogan realized Father Dominic was running all that through some mental translation device, seeking the Vietnamese equivalents of legal involvement and Hogan's consequent reluctance.

"Ah, but you are known for helping others. You are very fortunate to be able to help!"

Hogan looked at the small man for a long moment. "I help myself in helping others, Father. You're not looking at a saint. These guys are penniless, and I'd probably do them a disservice in trying to help." Hogan paused, working up the nerve to make himself admit the truth. "You need somebody a lot younger and a lot stronger."

Father Dominic looked distressed. "I have spoken with the Archbishop and I understand." He clasped his hands together and nodded a kind of small bow. "You have had trouble. I know. I think it is you who needs God, and God also needs you. The boy who did the shooting, he is not a bad boy, nor is his brother. They are in jail in that town and the people want to lunch him."

"Lunch?" Hogan bent forward. Had he heard right?

"Ah, sorry, lynch! Lynch! Sorry! My English is not always perfect. They are very alone. All the Vietnamese people are leaving town. Some boats are burnt, and now there is this Kluck Klan--"

"Ku Klux Klan," Hogan corrected.

"Ah, yes, that's the ones. They want to lynch them. Please. Mr. Hogan, please. Don't let this happen."

"That's up to law enforcement." said Hogan. "They're supposed to stop lynchings." Did the man think he was going to go down there with a gun?

Father Dominic leaned forward politely and lifted his eyebrows. "Yes, yes, I know, Mr. Hogan. But they need you to defend them in the trial." He smiled, paused again, and asked, "You are educated in the church?"

Here it comes, thought Hogan. He nodded. "Grammar school with Incarnate Word sisters, high school with the Brothers of the Holy Cross. Then college at Georgetown, with the Jesuits."

"Very well. Maybe this will help you. Let me give you a little history of my country."

"All right," said Hogan, resignation in his voice. He could at least listen to that much. He remembered Vietnamese Catholics being mentioned during the Vietnam War, but he'd never been sure what role they played. Like most Americans, he thought of the Vietnamese as Buddhists.

Father Dominic pushed the booklet across the desk. "I have brought this for you, if you care to read it later. Let me tell you a little. Christianity came to Vietnam in 1615. Vietnam was then three separate kingdoms, under the Portuguese. The first permanent mission was opened at Da Nang that year, 1615. The Jesuits ministered to the Japanese Catholics, who had been driven from Japan."

Hogan nodded politely. The man knew his subject by heart.

Father Dominic explained that those of the Catholic faith had been persecuted, like the Irish, for nearly three hundred years. Sometimes they were suspected of playing politics, but always they were barely tolerated under all the various kingdoms that had been called Annan.

"The practice of the Catholic faith has not been without great cost to the Vietnamese, Mr. Hogan."

Hogan nodded, listening. The priest was very well-prepared and there was no stopping his flood of information or his enthusiasm for his cause. Hogan would hear him out and then excuse himself.

"And what about during the Vietnam War?"

"Yes. By 1954 there were over a million and a half Catholics. They were about seven per cent of the population in the north. Buddhists represented about sixty per cent. But then, you see, oppression was terrible. Never stopped. Then about 670,000 Catholics abandoned all lands, homes, all possessions and fled to the south. In 1964, there were 833,000 Catholics in the north but so many in numbers in prison. In the south, Catholics were enjoying the first taste of religious freedom in centuries. Many came from the north to join them. But now the whole country is under communist rule. It is an intolerable situation, for Catholics especially."

He tapped the booklet. "It may help you to understand, to think of Vietnam not only in terms of this recent war, but to realize that the cross has been part of the lives of Catholic Vietnamese people for centuries. As a Catholic, you ought to understand why the Church feels such an obligation to help with these immigrants."

Hogan fiddled with a pencil. He tried again. "All right. Here's what I'll do. I'll contribute to the fee of anyone who wants to represent the defendants. Count me out personally." Hogan knew this was a twice-told tale, but, in his mind, it became more reasonable each time he explained.

"Mr. Hogan, money is not the issue."

Hogan sighed. "Father, I've done my share ten times over, and I just can't go to the well one more time. I don't expect you to understand, but it just wouldn't be right for me to represent those boys."

Hogan remembered an immigrant case he had taken a few years ago. At the time he'd been looking for some kind of substitute to convince himself that he wasn't an alcoholic. He had hoped the heroics of saving a Mexican immigrant from deportation would help him recover his self-esteem. It had worked, but only for a short time. That's why the humble and desperate man before him could not appeal to Hogan's sense of the heroic or his love of the law to suck him into his hopeless case.

It was a loser, a total loser. Hogan had experienced the bias and prejudice against immigrants. He knew the feeling against the Vietnamese was even worse. The case would be tried down there on the coast and the jury would be full of steely-eyed locals, descendants of some of the most hardened, feuding outlaws and desperadoes in the great state of Texas. The Anglos of the coastal counties had learned in the chaos that followed the Civil War that hanging was the best way to stop trouble. A verdict of guilty was foregone, as well as the maximum sentence.

"Do you know how they came to the coast?" Father Dominic asked. There was an edge of anxiety in his voice. He was trying to keep Hogan's attention.

"Resettlement," said Hogan. "They were boat people, I suppose?"

"Yes," said Father Dominic. "Well, we tried. The ones who came to San Ignacio were fishermen. Most from the same villages. We thought they could make a living there. A restaurant owner from Baltimore set up a crab-processing plant there. We thought, 'this is great.' The women would work in the plant and the men would fish. Vietnamese people work very, very hard. They are used to scrambling for every grain of rice."

Hogan had read all the newspaper reports since the Vietnamese had come to the coasts. It seemed that the more Vietnamese fishermen were resettled on American coasts, the more trouble came.

Chapter Seven

Hogan found himself listening. The little Vietnamese priest was an expert storyteller, weaving a tale of conflict, of the most profound human emotions, of clashing with the enemy on starless nights.

He listened as Father Dominic told him how the protests grew stronger, not only on the Gulf coast but in other places where the Vietnamese had settled to fish. The gulf waters of Florida and the lakes of Wisconsin. At first, in San Ignacio, the abuse was only vocal, delivered by a core group of young men looking for trouble. But the Vietnamese didn't leave, so the protesters grew more and more strident.

Town meetings on what to do about the Vietnamese became more and more vitriolic. Invariably, the meetings were led by Billy Joe Hardin. Hogan had even seen him on television a couple of months ago. A big, loud man, violent in his words.

"There is no other solution!" he'd shouted. "They've got to go!"

After Billy Joe Hardin had been killed, several of the young white troublemakers had thrown firebombs at trailers. Vietnamese boats had been burned. Most of the Vietnamese families began to leave, sometimes abandoning all they had and taking only a few clothes and the children. It had been volatile before, now it was explosive.

Father Dominic explained that most of the Vietnamese couldn't speak English, and didn't have American social skills. They cooked in woks over open fires in the yards of the trailer court. They squatted on their haunches while waiting on Railroad Street for their wives to finish shopping, and their six-toned language sounded like Donald Duck to the locals.

The fishing industry was all the Vietnamese really knew. They didn't understand or care about television or what was on it. They didn't go to any of the local hangouts. They knew they were unwelcome almost anywhere, especially at the Flores bar, the main place to be.

Their urge to recreate their own country and culture was strong. They came eagerly to the small church that Father Dominic set up in a trailer, where they could speak their own language and be among friends.

All they knew to do, said Father Dominic, was to cling together and associate together. It was their only hope for common welfare, their only hope for survival. Here in this new country, life seemed so mysterious, so foreign and threatening. At the time of the murder, the Vietnamese community in San Ignacio was in desperate straits with little hope of recovery. They didn't want to leave, but didn't know how they could stay. They were finally beginning to understand what they were up against and many had been preparing to get the hell out of San Ignacio.

But Cai and his brother Tho had resisted. They so badly wanted things to work out. They had at last found a home if only they could avoid being run out of town. It didn't seem possible, but they wanted to continue trying. Father Dominic was strongly against their hope of staying.

To compound the situation, the Vietnamese had still not emerged from the trauma of the fall of South Vietnam to the Communists. Their homeland and their culture had been devastated, ground under the iron heel of the North Vietnamese Communist dictatorship. They had fled to live in a foreign land that neither accepted nor understood them.

"There were too many at once," Hogan said in his blunt way. "Couldn't anybody see that?"

"Yes, perhaps so." Father Dominic looked pained.

"And I guess very few of them speak English. How am I supposed to talk to the defendants?" He leaned back and looked at the priest. Hogan didn't even know the first thing about the language or the culture either.

"Do not worry about the language problem," the Vietnamese priest assured him. "We have a very good translator. Her name is Lillie May Van Dam. She is very good at English, much better than I. She will be at your side. A very able assistant. She is strong and courageous."

"What's her name again?"

Father Dominic took a piece of paper and a pen and spelled it out. "Lillie May," he said. "At least that will do. We have a tonal language, so we approximate."

Hogan began to feel the smallest bit of interest.

He leaned his broad frame back in his office chair, thinking of lawyers he could call to take on the case. "Let me find you somebody," he said. "I'll find you the best that is available."

"You personally can do it."

Hogan held up a hand. "That's where you are wrong for so many reasons," he said. "I'll find you somebody, if there is anyone available. Otherwise, the court will always appoint someone."

He saw the despondent priest to the door and watched him trudge down the hall to the elevator. Then Hogan turned back to his office and looked at the newspaper with the photographs of burning boats on the front page.

God, what a loser, he thought. Perhaps he would send his son to see if the case really was as bad as he suspected. He knew the children were just out of law school. Paul had only been practicing for two years, and he was filled with idealism. He would be thrilled to try to help. Maybe the D.A. would take a lesser plea.

At any rate, it would make Hogan's conscience feel better about the matter. The truth is, he felt he would take the damn case -- if he were younger and not alcoholic, dying daily for a drink. These people were aliens, aliens who'd landed smack in the middle of the most clannish area in Texas.

But Hogan knew that the simple truth was, he just didn't have enough left in him to rise to the occasion. He felt guilty that he had drank too damn much to be of great service to anyone, especially the pair of young Vietnamese men accused of murder.

Chapter Eight

August 4th, 1979

Hogan's oldest son, Paul Xavier Hogan, had been a lawyer for two years. He was considered ambitious, idealistic, and smart. When Hogan sat down with him to discuss the case, his son was reserved.

"Now wait, let's look at this," Hogan said. He pushed the booklet on Vietnamese Catholics and the newspaper clippings forward on his table.

"Yes, I've read about it," said Paul. "You can hardly avoid it."

He was so much like his mother, Hogan thought. He was tall and slender, and he had her dark brown hair and temperate nature.

"I've been watching this. Everybody has. I *knew* you were going to get into it."

"No," Hogan denied. "I'm not taking the case. I just said I'd look into it."

Sabine brought in a file of newspaper clippings. She was dark-haired and pretty, and she had the kind of light-heartedness about her that the office badly needed, especially now.

"Paul suggested I do a clippings file on it," she explained, placing the file on the desk and then moving back to stand with her hands behind her back like a proper schoolgirl. Hogan knew she was dying to go to law school. He knew she was saving every penny for the day when she could begin. And he knew, when her chance finally came, he'd lose a terrific secretary to the seductive world of law.

He hunched his beefy shoulders and thought a moment. He ran his hand through his hair and sat back, his hair sticking up in spikes.

"When did you guys decide this?"

Paul looked at Sabine before answering. "After that little priest came to talk to you. We just figured it out, Dad. It wasn't hard. Let me look into it, okay? I really am interested."

Hogan gave a wry smile. "You mean, you don't think I can get through it without a drink."

Again there was a pause, that kind of instinctive guardedness that the children of alcoholics often have, formed by years of trying to protect and cover for a parent, trying to stand between the parent and the next drink, hopeless as that might be. Hogan knew Paul, and all of his children, had been doing it for years.

"Don't worry," Hogan said. "I'm going to hang in. I'm okay. Besides, I told him I'm not taking this. I told him I'd find someone to refer it to."

"Well, I guess that's me," Paul said with a grin.

"Now, that's not what I meant at all," Hogan protested.

"We'll just go down and look it over," said Sabine.

"We?"

"I need her help," Paul quickly explained. "Just in case we decide to do something with this. She can prepare a deposition and interview people like you've never seen."

Hogan looked at both of them and said "*Hmm.*" He had been missing something here, along with all the other aspects and facets of life he'd been missing.

He decided to let them have a go at it. It would be off his desk. It would give them practice and, if they decided to really take the case, they would at least see that the young Vietnamese defendants might be given a fair trial and didn't get 'lunched.'

He threw up his hands. "All right then. Let's see what it looks like," he said.

The three of them spent the afternoon going over every aspect of the situation. It was an extraordinary case from the standpoint of publicity. It had made the New York Times and the Los Angeles Times, USA Today and national television. The television networks had covered the story with film clips of great dramatic impact, especially the Klan marches and the firebombs.

"Look at these news clippings," Hogan said. "You know what you'd be getting into?"'

They saw photographs of men wearing T-shirts, they had slogans like *Gooks, Get The Hell Out Of San Ignacio*. Paint dripped from the slogans on prominent walls in town. *We Stand For White Supremacy, All Pure White, Degenerates and Gooks Go, The Invisible Empire — Vietnam, and The Guilty Must Pay — This Means The Vietnamese.*

"Yeah, I know, Dad," Paul replied. "But they need help. You know that as well as I do."

"It'll be a fight," Hogan warned.

"I've never seen anything like it," replied Sabine. "But that's no reason to back out."

"This is Friday," said Paul, his mind obviously made up. "If we do a little local checking, we could get going by next week."

Hogan sighed and got up. "Go for it. I could probably spring all of you out of jail if I had to."

After they had gone, Hogan left his office and went downstairs and out the heavy front door. It was an old stone building, three stories high. It had once been a bank and it was a solid symbol of his erstwhile success. He paused in the hot street and wondered what to do with himself for another long evening, at least until an A.A. meeting started. His mind drifted away, briefly, to a woman with red hair and green eyes, but he put the thought away.

The newspaper box showed yet more headlines about the San Ignacio case. He bought a paper and carried it rolled up in one hand, walking west toward the Plaza de las Islas. He would go on to El Mercado and sit with a cup of coffee at Mi Tierra, buying time. He had always been told to make your last case your best one, and this was going to be more grief and worry and misery than he'd had since he quit drinking.

Chapter Nine

August 7th, 1979

The trip from San Antonio to San Ignacio seemed to be a journey to nowhere. Paul and Sabine took the five-year old blue Ford. They made their way through the noisy highway construction going on Interstate 10, and then onto the much smaller two-lane Highway 87, which snaked its way down to the coast. They drove through the high-brush country, and then down to the coastal counties, into the great standing live-oaks with their drooping beards of Spanish moss.

The town of San Ignacio was about 140 miles southeast, on the Gulf of Mexico. It was oil country and cattle country. They passed pump-jacks and the masses of piping that made up the expansion joints. The air was hot and muggy.

As Paul and Sabine approached San Ignacio, they passed chemical plants on either side of the highway, and the billowing white smoke and bleachy smell were indications they were nearing the coast.

The town itself was little more than a collection of sun-bleached buildings stripped to a clean gray color by the wind. The town looked out at the Gulf of Mexico from one end of a low promontory. There was a trailer park and a crab-processing plant at one end, and a group of modest homes on the other end. Paul and Sabine noticed the excessive number of cars in town. Some were State Police, but others were unmarked

"Media," said Paul.

"Looks like it." Sabine leaned out the window to look, and the hot air moving off the glittering water made her dark hair spring into curls. She looked back at Paul. "This is so cool. I am so glad to be along on this." She was wearing a pair of khakis and a bright tropical shirt splashed with parrots and palms. She put on her sunglasses.

Paul smiled back at her. "Aren't you from the coast in Louisiana?"

"Yeah, and am I ever glad to be out of the city!"

They parked in front of the Super S grocery store and walked down the street. Since the recent violence, there seemed to be more police and media in town than inhabitants.

They split up. Sabine went to locate the town council offices, the trailer park where the Vietnamese mainly lived, and the jail.

Paul first went to see the chief of police. His name was Cotton Wheeler, a man in his sixties, waiting for retirement in a year. He was bald, overweight, and less than six feet tall.

Chief Wheeler reluctantly pushed a chair toward his visitor.

The chief of police had two men under him and two police cars. He leaned heavily on the sheriff's department, which was twenty-two miles away in the county seat of Spanish Port. All investigative matters of any substance were done by the chief investigator of the sheriff's office, a man by the name of Larry Breece. Paul remembered gossip from other attorneys that Larry Breece always explained carefully to the people he interviewed which side they should come down on, always on the side of law and order and against the defendant.

"We got a full confession from both of them," said Wheeler. "No doubt about it."

"But they don't speak English," Paul objected.

"Like hell they don't. Wake up, son. It's what they always say, them and the Meskins both. But it don't matter anyway because we got a translator."

"Where is he?"

The chief shrugged. "I don't know. Around here somewhere." Wheeler continued. "This is a serious situation. But let's face it, American fishermen have been here for many, many years, and how do you think they have been taking this mess for so long, the Vietnamese living in San Ignacio?" The chief leaned back in his chair and crossed his arms. "Most of the problems are between longtime crabbers and the Vietnamese. They don't understand the unwritten rules of the fishing community here."

It was obvious to Paul. The chief felt the only real solution was for the Vietnamese to leave.

"I'm going to be retired in a year, young man," he said. "I don't want to go out on a bad note."

"Right," said Paul. "I can understand that."

Outside once again, Paul found Sabine walking down the street toward him. He took her arm, and they went into the jail to see the Vietnamese brothers.

As Paul and Sabine were standing at the front desk of the jail, they met their translator, Lillie May Van Dam. She and Father Dominic had just walked down to find them.

Lillie May was as graceful and slim as a flower, with blue-black hair, a faultless complexion and a mild manner. She seemed so fragile. Her manner was one of gentility and reserve, and she was impeccably dressed in a light summer suit of yellow linen and a white blouse. Paul was surprised how respectful the sergeant at the desk was to her.

"How good that you are here!" she said cheerfully. She had only the barest trace of an accent, and that accent seemed to be French. She held out her hand.

"Well, I am certainly glad to see you as well," said Paul. They all shook hands. Paul couldn't believe this fragile thing was going to be of any help to them. "Father Dominic told us about you. He's a great fan of yours. I guess we ought to see those boys and reassure them."

They walked back to the cells, their steps on the concrete floor ringing out loudly. The men in the cells lay back on their bunks lazily, like caged felines, and stared at them. One prisoner was making a belt out of chains of silver-foil cigarette papers, another was reading a Prince Valiant comic book.

At last they saw the two young Vietnamese men. Surprisingly small, the brothers were in cells side by side and they sat as in a trance, staring at the wall. Dressed in jail coveralls, they looked desolate and frightened to the point of hysteria -- convinced they were shortly to be shot. When they looked up and saw Lillie May, they burst into Vietnamese and, for the first time, Sabine and Paul heard the vibrant tones of the language.

Lillie May turned to Sabine and Paul. "They think they are going to be shot," she explained calmly. Her voice was clear, her English perfect.

"Tell them absolutely not," said Sabine. They stood in a defensive group in the hot, dank air of the cells and the gray-painted steel.

"Get them to tell us about themselves, and what happened," said Paul.

He looked around. On the walls was graffiti with desperate sentiment. The floor was gritty with sand and dirt, and the heat in the small building could not even be kept at bay by the thick concrete walls. It was sweltering. Even a short while was a long sentence in this place.

"I was a fisherman in Vietnam," said Cai, through Lillie May. Sabine noted how quickly she interpreted. She followed in English swiftly on the heels of his Vietnamese words. "I like living here in the United States." His voice was almost inaudible. "When I came here, I worked as a welder and I worked for another company in a grain elevator, but I love fishing. Many of us arrived in San Ignacio after many other cities. We felt we had found a home."

"It's going to be all right," said Sabine, quickly. "Lillie May, tell them they will have a fair trial."

"Yes, I will try," said Lillie May.

After getting the boys some small necessities, clothing and candy and shaving gear, as much as the police would permit, they went out to explore the rest of the town, what there was of it. Details could be obtained later from the boys when they were cleaned up. Lillie May had moved quickly and efficiently into her role as a translator.

Their goal was to find others in the town who would talk to them. Paul decided to head toward the docks.

"I'll meet you down there later," said Sabine. She put on her dark glasses. "I'm a sleuth! I'm a sleuth!"

Paul couldn't help but laugh at her. He shook his head and waved good bye.

Sabine ducked into a small restaurant. It was air-conditioned and quite homey. There were hand-made tablecloths on every table and Precious Moments dolls in a glass case. From the kitchen came the scent of sturdy cooking; hamburgers, potatoes in every variety, bacon. She sat down at the counter and by great good luck ran into a talkative insurance clerk. It turned out that the mayor owned the restaurant.

"Well, he's been in office about ten years," the insurance clerk told Sabine. "Nobody wants the job anyway. He's the only one that will do it. You don't get paid and it's a constant hassle."

"What about the guy that got shot?" asked Sabine. "I forgot his name."

"Billy Joe? Oh, he was nothing but trouble. He'd get in a fight and people would go call the mayor out of the house at suppertime and the mayor would go try to quiet him down. He was always hanging out at the Flores. All the guys out crabbing come in about noon and go over to the bar."

As soon as she stepped outside, Sabine jotted down some quick notes. Then she went in search of Paul.

The fishing area was composed of about fifty boats, thirty of them belonging to the Americans and the rest to the Vietnamese. The Vietnamese boats were much smaller and much older, easily identified as hardly fit for safe piloting.

Paul and Sabine visited the Flores bar and tried to talk to some of the local fishermen. It wasn't difficult to make a quick diagnosis of the local feeling — hostility. The trouble had been growing for three years, ever since the Vietnamese had arrived. Paul sat with a couple of men in the light of bubbling beer advertisements, the air thick with cigarette smoke. In self-defense, he lighted one of his own.

Crabbers told stories of Vietnamese fishermen stealing their catch or running their lines parallel with those they had already set, a clear violation of local custom. The Vietnamese didn't subscribe to such practice. They seemed to have the idea that the water belonged to all.

Another shrimper friend of Billy Joe's, a man who'd been a prominent crabber until the Vietnamese came, told Paul he believed that crabbers and shrimpers would begin arming themselves for future confrontations.

"It will probably get worse before it gets better," he said before turning to Sabine. "It was already overcrowded, even before the Vietnamese arrived. Can't you see that? It was bound to come to this."

Paul and Sabine left the lounge. Discouraged, they walked out to their car in the dusty parking lot.

Paul and Sabine gathered together their notes and their thoughts. They returned to the same motel with the same dusty bedspreads and broken window-blinds, their rooms at opposite ends of the small motor-court. For the next two days they worked in the immense, sweltering heat.

They went over the names they had acquired. Paul had listened to the talk about Billy Joe. The townspeople said Billy Joe was quick-witted, jovial, big on petitions and patriotic talk. He was a large man and apparently could be a bully. Paul realized that many fishermen had gravitated toward Hardin as the man who was willing to solve the conflict with the Vietnamese fishermen.

Billy Joe had apparently led the local people in inviting the Ku Klux Klan, the America First Party, and the Nazi Party to San Ignacio to parade. The Vietnamese provided the issue that these groups needed. The remnants of these groups were in the nearby county and they enthusiastically welcomed volunteers to their ranks. The purpose of the parades was to convince the Vietnamese that their departure was in their own best interests, and sooner rather than later. The marchers could be intimidating and they loved an unfair fight.

Each day was worse than the last. Paul wrote up a profile of the American fishermen in San Ignacio. He wrote quickly each night in the motel as he sat for a few hours rest. The evening wind from the Gulf battered the windows. If he opened them for some air, it blew his papers off the little bedside table, so he had to put up with the stale cold air from the air-conditioner.

The wind sanded and seared, the sunlight burning off the water ruined vision, salt water rusted everything. Even the people. Paul wondered about them and how the coast had come to be the way it was. He fooled with his ballpoint pen. San Ignacio was old history and old ways, but Paul's knowledge of Texas history was limited to a course in high school and one at the university. Eventually, he let it go and went back to his work.

In the hope of putting together some additional information, they drove down Railroad Street to the crab processing plant, where crabs were prepared for sale or immediate shipping. The plant was located in the area of the boats near the bay. A sign on the corrugated-steel wall of the plant bragged that the local crabs were noted as some of the best in the world. They met Georgia Cadwaller, who was in charge, and she gave them the name of the owner and some details.

Georgia was a huge woman, taller and stronger and bigger than most men. She was dressed in a calico shirt and blue jeans with suspenders and a large floppy hat. Her complexion long ago was destroyed by the seacoast weather. Her voice was as heavy as a man's but Georgia was good-hearted and open. She was immensely fond of the Vietnamese. She found them honest and hard-working, appreciative and loyal. They were deeply devoted to the sea and to the work of fishing. She bitterly resented the local opposition to the Vietnamese. She regarded most of the newcomers, especially Cai, as her children, for she had none of her own. She reported that the situation since the killing was impossible and that the Vietnamese were largely afraid to stay. Georgia explained that Eisenberg, a very successful restaurateur from Baltimore, was responsible for bringing many of the Vietnamese to San Ignacio to work in his crab packing plant.

That night Paul and Sabine sat in Paul's room and made a phone call from the motel to Eisenberg in Maryland. Sabine talked to him and made notes as she listened.

"We didn't intend to open the plant to get anyone killed. We wanted to run a good business that gives people jobs," Eisenberg said. "My operation supplies some of the finest quality crabs in the United States. We hope to keep it going, but we doubt that we can. Our reputation for being friendly to the Vietnamese is costly."

Sabine listened sympathetically and nodded as she continued taking notes.

On the second day, Sabine and Paul found Billy Joe's brother at the bar. His name was Charlie Hardin, and, like most of the family, he was big.

"They just don't understand our customs or give a damn," he said. "And that's all I got to say to you. Go talk to my sister. See if she'll give you the time of day. I hope not."

And so they kept on, doggedly.

They sat down in the office of a city councilman, a fisherman as well. He was about fifty, and worn and weathered with the salt wind. They crowded uneasily into his tiny office. There was a trash can filled with soda cans and a calendar on the wall from the bank in Spanish Port, a photograph of cool, snow-capped mountains. Like most of the town's officials, his duties were entirely voluntary.

"Look here," he said. "They moved those people in here and gave them loans and food stamps and I don't know what-all. This was our country first. What makes you so anxious to give away all our fishing grounds? Did anybody ask the people here in San Ignacio?" He pushed his ball cap back from his forehead. "Huh? Did they? Did they come along and say, 'We're thinking about moving three hundred families in here from Vietnam,' when the population of this town is a thousand? 'We're moving all these people in here from Vietnam, so what do you think?' Hell no. We're just rednecks, so we don't matter."

The hostility in the air was sharp as knives. Sabine smiled a bit nervously and asked, "So there's bad feeling ..."

"Bad feeling don't describe it. The Vietnamese are taking over the fishing industry. They have two hundred shrimp and crab boats up and down the Gulf Coast and they fish all day and fish all night. Either we drive them out or get driven out. Nobody listened to the American fishermen down here until some of these other organizations came along. Now you hotshot lawyers in San Antonio are listening, ain't you?"

Paul and Sabine sat and said nothing for a moment, and then Sabine said, "Yes, that's why we came to talk to you."

The city councilman shook his head. "You come on down here and support a family by fishing." He reached in his pocket and threw a set of keys on the splintery desk. "There's the keys to my boat. Go on. Lay a line of traps. You spend a day out there in a high wind and you're going to come back feeling like you been in a bathtub with an alligator."

Paul ignored the keys. "Then how do the Vietnamese take it for twelve hours?"

"Hell, I don't know." The man took his keys back. "But I am telling you, they want it all. Go and have yourself some crab pretty soon because there ain't going to be none left. But you ain't going to listen. Well, there's some organizations that listen."

Chapter Ten

August 9th

They found Billy Joe's sister, a Mrs. Edith Vance. They approached her with caution because she was not only hostile but recently bereaved. She had, after all, lost a brother and it was none of her fault. The two of them sat down to talk with her at the local restaurant. She was tall, like her brother, and grief had deepened the lines around her eyes. She was dressed in jeans and a T-shirt, and she was feeding bait fish to a black and-white cat.

"Some of these guys tried to explain local crabbing customs to them, but it was crazy. They give out this old thing of 'we no speaky no English,' but that's B.S. They're going to pay for Billy Joe," she declared. "I tell you, I am going to be right there every day of that trial and they are going to *pay*."

"Well," said Sabine, " I am so sorry. This is a terrible thing. A young man cut off in the prime of life." Sabine was sincere; it wasn't put on. She had an air about her of a small-town girl that Paul both admired and, cynically, knew was valuable here. "It's the most terrible thing."

"Is that your *real* feelings?" Edith smiled a wry smile. "Y'all can just put in an order for your feelings, can't you?"

"No," Sabine denied. "That's not true. And couldn't we talk to the widow, Mrs. Hardin?"

"You'll never get ahold of her," the big woman said grimly.

And she was right; they never did.

They located Lillie May again, at the jail talking to the Vietnamese brothers, and took her with them to visit with the Vietnamese community.

Lillie May walked with them through the trailer park where the Vietnamese lived. Amid crying babies and women cooking in the out-doors over open fires, they learned that the local crabbers had pro-voked the confrontation. With each passing day, the situation was get-ting worse. Language and cultural barriers compounded the problem.

Most of the people did not want to involve themselves, and they could find no one who actually saw the shooting who was willing to talk to them. But they did manage to find others. Lillie May listened, and then translated.

The Vietnamese women had found work at the crab-processing plant, removing the meat from the shells, while the owner had helped the men finance crab boats. These were relatively small twenty-foot power boats. The big shrimp boats with their powerful diesel engines and net booms, forty to fifty feet long, were initially beyond the means of the Vietnamese.

"How much?" persisted Sabine. She was wearing light summer khaki slacks, sandals and a loose Hawaiian shirt, but she was still sweating. Lillie May was as cool as lemonade in her pale yellow suit. She translated without a pause.

"Maybe five thousand for a crab boat," Lillie May answered, "but perhaps twenty thousand for a shrimp boat."

The owner, they said, was fair and supportive of the workers at the plant and the crabbers. The women worked for up to thirty-five dollars a day and were glad to get it. The men went out for days at a time. They would brave the most turbulent weather when the American fishermen stayed home. After three years of intense work, some had been able to buy trailer houses, one woman said.

Getting information was like pulling teeth, but Lillie May remained bright and cheerful, a ready smile on her face. Her blunt-cut black hair swung freely in the wind. She seemed so confident, with such optimism, that Sabine and Paul felt carried along by it.

Then they found the man who had helped Cai escape after the shooting. He was down at the docks, stripping paint from an old boat. He was a tall, skinny Vietnamese named Vinh Quang. He spoke English better than most, and very fast. He smoked a great deal and looked around every corner and obviously trusted no one. It was impossible to tell whose side he was on, except his own.

To Lillie May, he said, "It was very bad between the Vietnamese and the local people long before the shooting. Now we go shopping and people who knew us before don't want to fool with us. They don't trust us. They don't want to walk close to us even."

Vinh Quang said he and others came to San Ignacio in April, 1975, after the fall of Saigon. Several had served in the Vietnam Military Intelligence Corps, assisting the United States. There was something tough and streetwise about the man.

"When we came to this country, none of us had the proper skills to immediately get a job. We took any odd job and accepted any aid we could from the Catholic Church. Except for them we would all have starved. These people have as much animosity toward us as the Communists had." He smoked the last of his cigarette and then tossed the butt well away from the cans of paint-stripper.

"Someone told us we were qualified for welfare and food stamps, but we didn't accept it because we were willing to work and not be supported by the government. That is the way we wanted it. Pay taxes, work hard, be honest. But you know, Billy Joe didn't stop harassing people. Mainly he went after Cai and Tho. They were kind of the leaders of the Vietnamese fishermen."

Paul went to Cotton Wheeler and managed to get copies of the police reports about the shooting, and he and Sabine sat down to go over them at the motel room. They read and drank cold sodas while the air conditioner cooled the room with wheezes and whines.

It seemed that Billy Joe and others felt that the Vietnamese were crowding and stealing traps. Billy Joe pulled up the Vietnamese traps when he thought they were too close, and he complained to the chief of police and the sheriff that someone was going to get killed if the Vietnamese didn't learn the rules of the bay. He told the chief of police in a complaint that, "Two angry Vietnamese brothers left and got reinforcements and surrounded the boat occupied by me and my wife and small children. One of the Vietnamese carried a knife in his mouth, pirate style." The authorities had later arrested the men and then waited for Billy Joe to press charges, but, according to the eyewitnesses, he never had.

The evening of the shooting, Billy Joe met the Vietnamese at the dock and confronted them, saying, "You got a beef?" Cai had answered Billy Joe, saying "No beef, no beef."

Billy Joe then punched Cai twice, and three of the Vietnamese left, leaving the two brothers with Hardin.

After loud words, Billy Joe followed the brothers to their car. He hit Cai several times in the face and cut him on the chest, and stomped on his hand. According to the witnesses, the brothers got into their car and went to their home. At their trailer in the trailer park, Cai got a pistol and a rifle, and then he returned to their boat. Billy Joe was still there.

He saw them and turned and walked away toward his pickup. Cai crept up to Billy Joe, and shot him in the back before he'd gone more than two feet. Billy Joe turned and called out. "No, man!" and fell. When Billy Joe slumped to the ground, Cai stood over him and shot him again, five more times in the back.

Then Cai had panicked and driven away in the car, leaving his brother Tho. Cai's friend told the chief of police that Cai forced him at gunpoint to take him to Houston where Cai got off at the bus station. Three days later, Cai gave himself up to the local police in Port Arthur.

"Anything else?" Sabine looked up from the report.

"Looks like that's the bare facts," Paul replied.

He Xeroxed the reports and then returned the originals to Wheeler's office, under the glare of the sergeant. When he returned to the motel, there was a message waiting for him. Hope blossomed. Somebody was actually trying to contact them instead of the other way around.

He called the number and was surprised to hear Georgia Cadwaller, the manager of the crab plant.

"Listen, if you want to find somebody that will testify as to how dangerous Billy Joe really was, you call Slim Lambert. He was a Texas Ranger. He grew up here, and retired here after serving as local constable. He was the man who tried to make peace between the Vietnamese and the locals more than anybody. He was probably the only one in law enforcement who cared. Everybody respected him, even if some of the local people resented him."

"Where is he?" Paul asked. It seemed a bit like a fairy tale. A Texas Ranger riding to the rescue?

"I'm not sure," said Georgia. "It was just a thought. Don't tell anybody I told you." And she hung up.

"Well, that was a lot of help," Paul murmured to himself. When Sabine came in with some takeout sandwiches for supper, he told her about it.

"She's been watching too many T.V. programs," said Sabine. She tossed her dark hair out of her eyes. "Jeez, I'm turning into a poodle. What do you think?"

"I'll give you the assignment," Paul said, ignoring her feeble attempt at a joke. "See if you can track him down."

"I didn't know you could track down Texas Rangers," Sabine replied. "But I'll give it my best."

The last day, Sabine had breakfast with Lillie May. Lillie May Van Dam was small — five foot at most — weighing no more than one hundred pounds, if that. She was striking, with her coal black hair, deep black eyes, and oval face. She had porcelain skin and fine bones. She was in her late twenties or early thirties, but she could have passed for a teenager. They both carried cups of coffee back to a booth at a local fast-food restaurant near Spanish Port. Graceful as always, Lillie May sat down across from Sabine.

Sabine wondered if the Vietnamese woman, so cool and petite, would be able to stay with them for the duration of the case, if the Hogan firm were to take it. She was an accomplished translator; in fact, she was truly remarkable. That and her refined, graceful manner would make her impressive to any jury anywhere.

Smiling, Sabine pushed the sugar toward Lillie May. "Tell me how you got here," she said. "When did you leave Vietnam, and what brought you here?"

She listened as Lillie May explained that she had been educated by the Catholic nuns in Vietnam. After obtaining her degree, she had taught grade school and then served as an interpreter at the American Embassy before the fall of Saigon. She spoke English with a distinctly French accent that seemed far displaced among the local Texas voices.

She'd had a dangerous and difficult time finding her way to San Antonio. She was on the last plane out of Saigon. Her husband and children preceded her. Along the way, her husband, Chang, became dangerously depressed and had to be hospitalized. The children, ages four, eight and ten, were taken in by the nuns and Lillie May joined them a year later after stopping in camps at Michigan, Arkansas, Georgia, Philippines, and finally San Antonio.

She had moved from one place to another in the hope of finding a home. She hoped San Antonio would finally prove to be that. She had the equivalent of a Master's Degree in English Literature. She hoped to get a Doctorate in the English language and American History some day. San Antonio, with three major colleges, presented a real opportunity for her plans for her family.

Her first and only job was with the Catholic Service Agency where she assisted in the resettlement activities. Her employment with the Catholic Church was a godsend. She came to know San Ignacio and the Vietnamese brothers, Tho and Cai, very well. She was encouraged in her efforts by Father Dominic. The two of them became fast friends.

Lillie May's parents were still in Vietnam, she told Sabine. Her husband was seriously incapacitated by depression. For the first time Sabine saw the smallest indication of some inner pain in the young Vietnamese woman. A little reading between the lines verified that she was the cement and fabric of what was left of the marriage.

"I do what I can to make him more cheerful," she said, and then she gave a small shrug. "But it seems so hopeless." It was the only time she even alluded to her own problems, and she never did so again.

Lillie May had learned the art of being elliptical, of listening, cultivating. Her voice had a ringing quality that was an absolute delight, and her articulation and English were perfect. She spoke with authority and a conviction that portrayed the highest kind of credibility. For some reason, she had an optimism and serenity -- two traits that to Sabine seemed totally misplaced.

"The boys were in such a difficult position. The law and culture and traditions are so very strange to them. In Vietnam, they are encouraged to be strong and brave and stoic and to never show that their courage has deserted them, which it has, completely. The face they put on is very different from that which they feel inwardly. They are terrified and feel that they are going to be killed at any moment.

"They don't understand why the lawyer would go to all this trouble. They had been taught that if you kill someone you can expect to be killed. They expect such a fate. But Tho had nothing to do with the shooting. In fact, he tried to prevent it. Nobody will listen to him," Lillie May explained.

"They can't see how it could possibly be if they shot someone, as they did, that the law would give them any consideration or flexibility in this country," Lillie May said. "Are they not right?" she inquired.

"No," Sabine answered. "Absolutely not."

"The idea of self-defense makes no sense to them. You will have to explain this to me," she said. "It isn't a waste of time, is it?" The question was sincere. "It has to make sense to me before it can make sense to them."

Chapter Eleven

August 10th

The next day, Paul drove to the nearby county seat of Spanish Port to try to speak with the district attorney who would be handling the case. The county seat of Winfield Scott County was also on the long, indented coastline. The Texas late summer heat lay over everything, and the asphalt seemed hot as a forge.

The district attorney had several counties to look after. He had one office in Scott County, at Spanish Port, but his main office was in the next county, at the town of Stillwater. He shuttled back and forth between them, and on this afternoon the D.A. arrived at his office with the local deputy sheriff who was assisting in the Vietnamese trial preparation. He arrived just before Paul got there.

The D.A., Roger Davis, was a big man. He was three or four inches over six feet. He had the kind of deep voice that could be intimidating, or cajoling and persuasive to any jury, particularly when he talked to them of the flag and patriotism or law and order, and he inevitably spoke of those things.

His full head of hair was so blond it looked bleached. His complexion was bronze, and the ready smile with pearly teeth was practiced but still engaging. Davis believed he'd been thwarted in higher ambitions, not by lack of competence but by geography. The D.A. considered that part of Texas 'the pits,' economically and politically. He felt sure he should have moved to Houston years ago.

Anger rising, he glared at Paul. "If you are looking for any help from me, forget it. My very best advice is to stay out of this case. That is particularly true for that drunk ol' man of yours. His day is long gone, and these boys have got trouble enough." The D.A. reached for his cigarettes and lit up. "Let me tell you, son, the Archangel himself couldn't help these gooks. They're both going to get the max, and they should. Don't expect the time of day from us. Smoke?"

"No thanks," Paul answered.

"Good. These things will kill you." The D.A. laid the pack back on his desk. "Son, you're just out of law school, aren't you? You have that look. You're thinking about truth and justice and the American Way. I'm thinking about bigger things." He drew on his cigarette again and waved his hand at his office and the town of Spanish Port and south Texas in general.

"This is the case that I've been waiting ten years to come along," he said with brutal frankness. "It's my ticket out of here. It's got *every-thing* — headlines, law and order, America for Americans, and a very friendly media. They will eat this story up, and I will supply the salsa.

"I'm telling you, this town is so closed it's almost off-limits to you. The word is out that talking to the enemy — and that's you — is simply off limits and it ain't going to happen. Your best shot is to hit the highway back to San Antonio. Both boys will be indicted tomorrow, and we are asking the judge for a trial right here in Spanish Port within the month."

Paul said nothing. The D.A. smiled.

"You can go tell Hogan that his grandstanding and flamboyant ways are not going to do him any good down here."

Paul's face tightened with anger at this reference to his father, but he maintained his composure. It was all he had.

"The Viets are going to pay," Davis continued, "and I'm going to see to it. This is the day of their reckoning. You'll find that nobody has an unkind word for Billy Joe, and nobody has a good word for the Vietnamese."

Davis stubbed out his cigarette. He detested Hogan. He always suspected that men who were that successful had signed some kind of a pact with the Devil, had given away their firstborn or something. Hell, Jim Hogan was shorter than he was by six inches and his teeth weren't half as good. He'd languished in Pittsville while Hogan rode high. But Davis had heard about the fiasco in Mississippi, heard it with great glee. Oh, how the mighty had fallen.

"Okay, counselor," Paul said. "I'll tell him. But I want to ask you, can I see the confession?"

"Oh, sure! It makes great reading." Davis turned his back and tugged a file out of a stack of folders on his sideboard. He made sure he still had two copies of the confession, then put the folder back in place. "There you are. It's a copy; you can keep it," he said magnanimously.

"Thanks." Paul tucked the papers under his arm.

"I heard Hogan is on the wagon," said Davis. "Well, if he wants to stay on it, he'd better stay out of this case. If he doesn't, we'll make him as big a defendant as the Vietnamese brothers. You won't be able to tell the difference between them and him."

"I'll tell him," Paul said, his voice tight and controlled.

"Good," Davis replied, knowing the senior Hogan would view the statement as a thrown gauntlet. "As far as giving you any information, at the very most I'll only do whatever the judge makes me do. Have I made myself clear?"

"Very much so," replied Paul. He smiled slightly and nodded, trying to ignore the red flush of genuine fury inching up his neck.

"Fine. I'm very busy now, working with the prosecution and the media. Nobody is going to screw up this case for me. I've waited too long. So, if you will excuse me." Davis turned his attention back to the papers on his desk.

Paul cleared his throat and said nothing, then he walked out of the courthouse office with his ears burning.

Getting the case was the best thing that had ever happened to him, Roger Davis thought as he drove out that afternoon to visit Judge Barret. They were throwing a big to-do at the home place, the Barret ranch headquarters, for Barret's wife; she'd just snagged a big gallery show in Houston for her oil paintings.

Davis drove the small county road, passing live-oaks with swishing skirts of Spanish moss and fields of grass and black cattle. He barely noticed the Christmas-tree piping of the oil wells. Davis' wife and kids were off with a sick grandparent in Yorktown and he was just as happy to go alone. He had business. He had to lean on Barret, hard.

It was a case made in heaven. It had *Roger Davis, Congressman* written all over it. It had a media circus, a big city attorney to oppose, and a sure guilty verdict. The problem on his mind was that he needed more than token opposition. He could roll right over the young Hogan kid. What he needed was somebody who could throw punches. Hogan Senior would be the perfect answer. He knew Hogan hadn't tried a criminal case in decades. Hell, he had his own kid working on the case and the boy was hardly out of law school; the boy was still being sent to church with a nickel in his pockets. But Davis liked it. He could make Paul's old man a public enemy along with the Vietnamese.

He passed a cattle truck on the narrow black-top highway. "Get out of the way, cowboy," he muttered.

Davis had been born in the coastal area, the son of prominent physicians. His older brothers were as successful as Hogan was. Of the three brothers, he'd been predicted to finish a distant first. But it hadn't happened, and that had always baffled him.

The press was only interested in urban areas like Houston, Dallas, San Antonio. Nothing happened down here that would attract statewide attention -- at least not until Cai Van Nguyen shot Billy Joe. Davis was almost grateful to the little bastard.

Davis knew he needed to deflate the idea that Billy Joe was a crazed savage. Billy Joe and his family had been from the Gulf area for generations. He had to have witnesses testifying that he was a good family man. Upstanding. Hardworking. He also had to explain to the judge that the immigrants were on the public dole. They might have been fleeing from Vietnam, but it was perfectly possible that there were criminals and homicidal maniacs among them, one of which was, quite clearly, Cai Van Nguyen.

Tied to the gate posts at the entrance to the ranch were large bouquets of balloons and ribbons, jerking in the Gulf wind. Davis turned in, his tires racketing over the cattle guards.

Judge Barret was new to the bench and he was a bit soft, a little squishy. Davis knew he was the only thing that would give the guy some backbone. Barret was refined, him and his artsy wife. It was going to take somebody like Davis to keep the jerk on the road to town.

Chapter Twelve

August 12th

The next day, while Sabine worked at her motel-room table to put together what they had garnered, Paul once more turned onto the small two-lane highway to Spanish Port. This time he had an appointment with Judge Barret.

The judge was not friendly, but at least he wasn't as outspoken as the D.A. had been. In his mid-forties and several inches short of six feet, he was slim, with a florid complexion. He was known to be a man who was often bullied by the D.A. Paul almost expected him to say *'The court and the prosecution are announcing ready for the state.'*

After inviting Paul into his office and offering him a chair, Barret got down to business. "Well, you can see quite clearly, Mr. Hogan, the area's in a state of outrage over the shooting. I expect the D.A. to be clamoring for an early trial and maximum sentences." The judge had a mild voice, restrained and diffident. "I'll appoint someone to represent the defendants, if need be. At first glance, it looks like a formality. If you're asking me my advice, you'll find the turf very unfriendly and it's a poor case for which to expect any consideration from either the court or the prosecution. The people expect a conviction."

"Yes, sir," said Paul. The whole thing was looking worse and worse. He suspected — knew — that the judge had been talking with the district attorney. They sounded just alike, like they were reading off the same sheet of music.

"I hope I've made myself very clear, and I'd particularly appreciate it if you'd tell your dad just that." He clasped his hands together and leaned back in his chair. He seemed to be bracing himself for the onslaught of the wild Irish Hogans. "We don't need any flamboyance or pretty speeches about minority rights. This is neither the time nor the place, and it will only hurt — not help."

Paul thanked him and left. He was beginning to think that a guilty verdict and the maximum sentence were the foregone conclusion.

After four days of research, Paul and Sabine left the coast and returned to San Antonio. Lillie May went with them. Sabine sat in the back seat, chewing at a pencil and thinking. The petite Vietnamese translator sat in the front seat and looked out at the countryside.

Turning to Paul, she smiled happily and said, "I think it is so wonderful that Cai and Tho will be given a trial, and that they will be allowed to tell their story."

"Well," said Paul, "they'll sure be able to tell their story." He didn't know what else to say.

Lillie May insisted that he drop her off at the Benedictine Sisters' residence in the King William District where she was staying. Sabine and Paul saw her go through the cast-iron gates and through the front doors. They wondered about extended family or friends, wondered why Lillie May chose to stay at the convent. They suspected they'd never know the answers to their musings. Despite her cheerfulness, Lillie May had a reticence that discouraged such personal questions.

Paul and Sabine huddled in Sabine's secretarial office. They were hiding from the Old Man. They weren't ready to tell him how bad it was.

"She said she's so happy the boys can tell their story. What story?" Paul asked. "So far we have proof that Cai is an expert with weapons. He knew how to kill. He realized it was Billy Joe or him, and he fired six times to make sure Billy Joe was dead. I don't think there's much of a story to tell. Hell, once told, that story could send them up for life."

"What do you think?" Sabine asked. "What do you *really* think?"

"*Vraiment vraiment?*" Paul asked her.

Sabine crossed her arms and leaned back. "*Dit-moi the vrai* truth."

"It's one hell of a case. I'd get my face in the papers, but there's no way I could pull this off," he answered. "It's too much for us and it would drive the old man right over the brink. He'd start drinking again for sure. I think it's hopeless. How could a case this hopeless ever come out right?"

"*Dufois s'arrive* that the little guy wins," said Sabine.

"What?"

Sabine leaned forward and straightened his tie for him. "Dialect," she said. "Patois. Only true Cajuns can speak it."

He looked down at his tie and up at her again. "What would you do if you were a lawyer?"

"You wait," she said with a smile. "Just *wait* until I am and then I'll let you know."

"Really?" he teased.

Suddenly Sabine stopped being jokey and pert. Her shoulders slumped. "You're right. Those two guys, my heart just goes out to them, but it's an open-and-shut case. He plugged the guy in the back, confessed to it, and what else is there to say? And your dad — well, he's a little fragile right now."

"Well, we'll still have to tell him," Paul said with a sigh.

45

They all sat in Hogan's office drinking coffee while the old bank building around them hummed with the many people busy at their work.

"The prospects are that the only testimony for Cai will be from the defendant himself," Paul explained. He was taut and upset. Hogan could see it.

"We've got almost nobody," Sabine added. She had a pencil stuck over her ear, and she took it between her fingers and rolled it back and forth like worry beads.

"I could take it, as long as Sabine helped, but we can't do it alone," said Paul "It would be malpractice! The place is exploding, and what experience do we have? We couldn't even begin to get a fair shake for those two kids. They're scared to death. Someone's got to see that they get a fair trial. It isn't going to happen with the present plans of the D.A. and the judge."

Paul and Sabine glanced at one another. Just out of recovery, they knew the Old Man couldn't handle it.

Hogan listened. If it's hopeless, he thought, why should I get involved? He had spent his life in hopeless causes. He felt that it was someone else's turn. Someone without all the trauma and scars of trials gone by. It was time for him to start saying 'No.'

"We promised to bring back the facts, and the facts are that nobody gives a damn for the Vietnamese," Paul continued. He was wearing a light tan summer suit, and he looked even skinnier in it than he was. He shook his head. "It's clear as day that he shot the guy in the back, that he's guilty. He's an alien. The court, the prosecution, the community, the D.A. are just waiting to get the trial over with and send him up for life. What could we defend it on? Self-defense?"

Sabine appeared worried and depressed, twirling the pencil faster in her fingers. She was torn with the desire to do what was right. But she was intelligent enough to see the truth of what could actually be done.

Hogan bent forward and flipped the file with the newspaper clippings open and then shut it again. "You know, if I hadn't already wasted so much talent, I'd probably have no reservation. I feel so damn guilty that all my life I've been saying we have to help the helpless, and now I'm afraid I can't do the job. The first failure we run up against, I'd get drunk. The case would suffer and what's left of my professional career would go right in the can. I can't do it."

"Okay," said Paul. "Dad, I think that's the best decision, but, boy, it's going to be hard to walk away and leave those two guys with no word of hope. They look about as menacing as elves."

Chapter Thirteen

Hogan's reflections were so dark they were almost dangerous. He was furious, with the situation and with himself. He knew his son was ashamed he couldn't pull it together to take the case. That smart-ass D.A. needed a lesson. Bad. They were pushing his kid around.

If only he hadn't squandered his life. If only he had enough left. If only he weren't so eaten up with fear. If only he hadn't lost all of his nerve and confidence. If only he could have a drink.

Hogan wondered in the still and solitary night about his own demons. They were as lively and vigorous as he was not. He wondered again and again if he could take the case and get through it. He knew he had only one drunk left in him.

The only person he knew that would understand his dilemma was the redheaded counselor at Hazelden. Sheila Ryan. Fifteen years his junior and a recovering alcoholic herself. Sheila Ryan, the only woman he'd been attracted to since his wife died. She'd been attracted to him, too. He was sure of it.

Sheila would know what he was going through. She'd been there, and still was there, more than anyone else he knew. He had never told anyone so many secrets about himself. She knew him like no other human being -- and liked him despite his failings. She'd even laughed when he told her the Mississippi incident, enjoying it immensely when he'd imitated the judge's drawl. They'd talked a lot at Hazelden. He knew her story as well as she knew his.

She was from a poor rural family in southern Ohio. She had an overwhelming drive, a liveliness and energy that he admired. He admired even more her glossy auburn hair and green eyes, the clear, pale skin dotted with only a few freckles, the slightly turned-up nose.

In many ways their lives mirrored each other's. She'd gone to Atlanta, and worked her way through law school as a secretary and later worked as a paralegal for the largest law firm in the city. Hogan's career, although much longer, was an image of hers in its journey from ecstasy to ashes. Though he had more trappings and perhaps more talent, they each had hit bottom with a resounding crash.

Alcoholism killed people and destroyed lives and they both knew it. There was something very tender and fragile about the feeling that sprang up between them, as if they had survived some terrible shipwreck. It was spring, after Florida's brief winter, and the grounds were lavish with oleander and hibiscus blooms.

As they went for walks, she told him that she had met and married a young lawyer destined to become a famous trial lawyer, given the right kind of breaks. He'd started as assistant district attorney and Sheila had stayed with her prestigious law firm after graduation, working in the commercial law and probate section. Sheila's position had not been by accident. The head of the most lucrative section was Brian Donnelly. The ladies liked him, and he liked the ladies. He'd been divorced twice and was still looking. Mainly at Sheila.

Sheila and her husband were both working fifteen hours a day, she said, and Donnelly made it a point of seeing to it they saw little of each other. Sheila's marriage didn't prosper, but the office romance did. She was flattered and overwhelmed that Donnelly was impressed with her. Sheila mistook the flirtation for love. She found out later it had only been lust on Donnelly's part.

As Hogan listened to her, he understood that she was very naive in worldly matters. Donnelly was thirty years her senior, tall, thin, dignified, very smooth and impressive. Sheila was no match for him. She'd demanded a divorce from her husband. She was enamored, ambitious, determined not to miss what she saw as a golden opportunity.

She'd been sure, she told Hogan, that her actions would lead to a world of prestige and comfort. Then she'd laughed at herself as they sat over coffee, an embarrassed, rueful laugh.

In the society of no-fault divorce, her husband's resistance was pointless. In a few short months, Sheila and Dan were divorced, much to his heartbroken and bitter disappointment. The subsequent marriage between Sheila and Donnelly was soon on the rocks. It lasted five years, but was always tumultuous, the tumults invariably caused by his infidelities. Sheila had never been exposed to such conduct. She couldn't cope. A few drinks every night made things look so much better.

After the few there were a few more, and the few more eventually added up to many. Her employment was terminated when she came back to the office one day, hardly able to walk after a long, leisurely and very liquid Atlanta lunch.

Donnelly said he was compelled to get a divorce because she had become a drunk and an embarrassment. Besides, the excitement was over. Sheila had found work at Legal Aid. But again, drinking had wound up being a terminal employment problem.

In the meantime, the turn of events had not worked to her ex-husband's disadvantage. He'd remarried, had a family, and was the leading trial lawyer in the district attorney's office. It was even rumored that he was in line to become the next district attorney. Realizing all she had lost through her own fault was almost too much for Sheila.

Like most low-bottom serial boozers, she'd found herself drowning in self-pity. She didn't work for months, her debts were everywhere, and her disbarment was imminent if she didn't agree to rehabilitation. She was broke, busted in spirit, and frustrated with fear and anxiety. Only existing insurance allowed her to make the trip to Hazelden.

Hazelden had proven to be magic for Sheila, a refuge of peace and security. She stayed and became a counselor. She'd been sober for two and a half years when she met Hogan. She was a first-rate counselor, one of the best. But beneath her listening skills and her compassion was a deep fear of leaving Hazelden. Anyone close to her knew that. Hogan knew he'd been the only one she'd ever talked to about the possibility of leaving some day. He'd suspected she was offering him an opening, an opening he'd been too afraid to take.

Sheila had seen in Hogan a lawyer with a restlessness, a fervor, and a light. He had the *mark* of great trial lawyers, that striking ability to persuade people to talk to him and be persuaded by him. The light was dim; sometimes flickering like a faulty connection. But, as he walked about the grounds, a stout, broad-shouldered figure with his hands jammed in his pockets, she could tell that it was still there.

Hogan had needed Sheila during those dark times. She was the only one who had faith in his ability to come back. Others didn't see it, and he knew it. His self-esteem was the size of a pinhead where once it had been as big as Mount Rushmore. But Sheila Ryan had looked into Hogan's heart, and seen there a steady glow, a lamp that could not be put out.

She'd given him her telephone number as he prepared to leave, with strict instructions to call if ever tempted to take a drink. He'd wanted her to say, "Call even if you don't want to take a drink. Just call."

Maybe she'd just been waiting for him to do it.

It was two in the morning when he finally picked up the phone.

"Hogan!" Sheila exclaimed, clearly glad to hear from him.

"Were you awake?" he asked, in his slightly raspy voice.

"I am now. It's two in the morning. I hope you haven't taken that first drink."

"I haven't," he assured her. "But I need to tell you what's going on in my life."

Sheila listened to Hogan's tale for nearly thirty minutes.

"What do you think?" he finally asked.

"Just go for it," Sheila told him. "And pray on it. Without God's help, you don't stand a chance."

"I will, if you will," Hogan said.

"What does that mean?"

"It means, I need your help as well. Will you do it?"

"Will I do what?"

Hogan drew a deep breath. What he was about to say scared the hell out of him. "Come here and be my mentor, my confidant, my joint adventurer in a crusade that might ruin us both." He held his breath, scared she'd say no, maybe even more scared she'd say yes.

There was a long silence on the other end of the line, then Sheila's laughter bubbled forth. "Yes," she cried. "Yes, I will."

Hogan sagged with relief. "Thank you," he whispered.

"Jim," Sheila said softly, "I've been hoping you'd call for months."

"What about leaving Hazelden? Are you afraid?"

Again he heard her hesitate. But again she said, "Yes, but I've got to."

"I know," he said.

"It's a big world out there. But I can do it -- if you're there."

"I will be. I am," he assured her. "I'll see you as soon as you can get here. The tickets will be at your place within the hour." He paused, searching for courage. "You . . . you can stay with me."

There was another long pause, then she said, "Oh, Jim, what if your son doesn't accept that kind of arrangement? All your kids. They've had dad to themselves for so many years. And they've looked after you. They're used to the way things are."

"Leave that to me," he said. "All right?"

He heard her sigh. "All right."

Hogan hung up and lay listening to the faint noises of the city night, late revelers on the River walk.

One day at a time, he said to himself. One moment at a time. Now if I can find my pin-striped lawyer's suit and a way to tell the kids. The shit is going to hit the fan, but I'll sink forever if I don't take this damn case and Sheila's help. God knows I probably will anyway, but at least I'll sink trying to swim, and it may be a way back for both of us.

In the past, when Hogan made hard decisions, he was consoled with the view that if he gave his best shot and he failed, it wasn't meant to be. In this instance, he was filled with fear — did he have a best shot left? Would it end with him becoming a disgrace as a public drunk? Was the invitation to Sheila a serious mistake? This was new ground to him, this lack of self-confidence. He wasn't sure what you did with it.

When Sheila arrived only days after the telephone invitation, she was filled with as much apprehension as Hogan. Luggage in hand, she stood in the living room of his large apartment. Her hair and features were as lovely as he remembered.

He took her hand, then they had their arms around one another.

"Two drunks together," she said with a nervous laugh. "This is crazy as hell, but we would never know. The A.A. program is going to get its fullest test to date."

He took both her arms in his hands and stood back to look at her. She was slim, with expressive light-brown eyes, radiant red hair and the telling marks of past alcohol abuse that both added to and detracted from her face. Beyond his gratitude for her skill as a counselor, Hogan hadn't allowed himself to think too much about whether she was gorgeous, attractive, or even more to the point, available.

She was, and Hogan was both shocked and delighted. In a flash it suddenly dawned on him she was beautiful. And incredibly, she was prepared to offer him solace, physical and mental, beyond any expectations. Hogan thought she would continue to help him stay sober until the trial was over. In his mind he felt she could shame him into not taking a drink. Beyond that he had no expectations. And now this. This new world was worth it if all else went up in smoke.

He left word at his office that he was going to Dallas, and they hid out in the apartment. Two days of full-time love-making with enthusiasm Hogan had thought he had forgotten, if he had ever learned. Two marvelous days alone, content with each other's company. He walked with her down the River Walk, and to the two great Plazas at the heart of the city. They meandered and wandered the small streets of La Villita, and Hogan felt he was rediscovering the city all over again.

They talked for hours over coffee at Mi Tierra and lunch at Shilo's and she told him her true task was to keep him sober, no matter what else. They agreed on daily A.A. meetings, reading and meditation. Then, somewhere along the line, she might return to the world of law.

At night, as she stirred in his arms, she felt it just might work. Hogan's breathing was steady and warm and content. She thought about being away from Hazelden as Hogan slept in a tranquillity that seemed to suggest he didn't have a problem in the world. She felt herself drifting away as well and it was the deepest sleep she had had in a long time.

In the next week Sheila discarded her wardrobe of blue jeans and baggy tops and went shopping for dark blue stripes. Then she had to make peace with Hogan's family.

Sheila dreaded the antagonism she felt would inevitably come from Hogan's son, and even the other people in his office. They had been protective of Hogan for so long.

They met for dinner at a riverside restaurant. Paul and Sabine seemed to confer among themselves on an invisible wavelength they'd developed over the years, even as waiters came and went and food arrived on plates. By the entree the silent consensus was *maybe* and by dessert it was a *yes*.

Sheila never seemed to notice any hesitation; she was great company. Her sense of humor about her past misadventures was hilarious. Besides, she had successfully practiced law, and they could sense not only a hesitant desire to return but the potential to rise once again to become a gifted lawyer. In addition, as talk over the dinner warmed up, Sabine and Paul found in Sheila an unexpected ally. They could hardly believe that they'd at last found someone who shared their emotional and intellectual view of the Vietnamese trial.

"You mean you think we could really take it on?" Paul laid his fork down and searched her eyes. "Give me your honest opinion."

"You got it," said Sheila. "My opinion is, go for it."

Sabine smiled politely and said, "I'm just the secretary, Sheila, but I've never seen anything like this. I mean the media."

Hogan watched the two women with interest, pleased at the way Sheila's keen social instincts came into play.

"Well, it's your decision," Sheila said. "I'm brand-new at this and I wouldn't know a fish trap from a set of golf clubs, but count me in." She shrugged her shoulders, then laughed. "I can tell you guys like a good fight. Me, too. So just *count* me in."

Paul smiled and said, "Consider yourself counted."

Sheila knew that wasn't all there was to it, and so the next day she came to the office with Hogan and said to Sabine, "Let me help with something."

"What?" asked Sabine. The Cajun Cyclone sat at her keyboard and it erupted into a letter.

"Typing," said Sheila. "Give me something to type. Or coffee? I make great coffee."

Sheila leaned against the doorjamb. Her thick, dark red hair was cut at neck length, and her dress was a light summer green. To Sabine, she looked too classy to be able to type.

Still hesitant, Sabine handed her a copy of the confession. "Clean copy," she said.

"No problem."

And so Sheila began to join them in their work.

Paul knew she could perhaps help them; or at least help the Old Man. They saw her in that role if the miracle of recovery with all its intensity and drama failed to keep him on the straight and narrow. They watched without seeming to as Hogan and Sheila settled into their new relationship. And they approved.

It was a crusade now. Four against the world.

Chapter Fourteen

August 15th

There were so many things that needed to be done, and all of them immediately. The murder had been committed a month ago. Hogan knew they were far, far behind.

He called them all into his office to map out their strategy.

"Look, it's this way. First, change of venue. That motion has to be prepared extremely well. We've got to get the trial to San Antonio and away from the coastal counties. Secondly, I need to get Big Bob Mitchell to sit in and watch for any chance of reversal on appeal if they do convict. That's his specialty."

"Where is he?" asked Paul. "Didn't I see him in here a month ago? He does a job and then he vaporizes."

"Usually up at the courthouse, I'll go find him right after this meeting," said Hogan. Unable to stand still, he was prowling around the room. "Third, we have to prove self-defense." He held up his hand. "Don't laugh. We have to prove Billy Joe drove him to it —prove Billy Joe Hardin was a bully, that he threatened their lives. Sabine, you are bringing out everything you can on self-defense?"

"Yes," she replied. "Just *rassling* with those great big old law books."

"Better than alligators," said Paul.

"Shows how much you know," Sabine retorted.

"Listen up," said Hogan. "Fourth, we have to work with Lillie May, get her to understand that those boys have to look *likable* to a jury — likable and sympathetic. The way she translates what they say will be of immense importance. Sheila, will you take that on?"

"Happy to," Sheila said with a smile.

"And watch the newspapers," said Hogan. He felt the sudden charge and the lift that comes from starting work on a new case. That shot of adrenaline, planning the attack. "Those guys down there may not have talked to you, but they are talking to the press."

"I'll go over the clippings now," said Sheila.

"We have to get those confessions suppressed, and we have to find that translator. I suspect he didn't know anything about legal terms or what was being said."

"Right," agreed Paul.

"Okay. Let's go. I suspect we're going to lose this one, but at least

Cai and his brother won't be railroaded."

After they left, Hogan settled his glasses on his nose, reached for another cup of coffee, and leaned back to read more of the newspaper clippings. The press was just about to do his job for him.

The Church had referred many people to him for information, but they tended to be scholars of the Vietnamese language, or experts on the Vietnam war, like the redoubtable Dr. Chou, a very knowledgeable gentleman but not productive from an affirmative standpoint of testimony. It did provide a rich background of information that might or might not be developed on cross-examination. But what was really interesting was the way the local authorities in and around San Ignacio were shooting their mouths off.

Hogan looked happily at the morning paper. More quotes from the sheriff and from Cotton Wheeler, the local police chief in San Ignacio. The media was doing a lot of work for the defense. No matter how many times witnesses were told not to speak to the press, some just couldn't resist. What they were saying to the media was that Billy Joe gave the Vietnamese defendants a very hard time for a long time, that he was a bully, that he would get drunk and fight anybody. If he was drinking he'd fight a circle saw, said one fellow.

Hogan got up and found his light summer suit coat, tightened his tie, and left to walk to the courthouse a few blocks away. Knowing he he would have to go past the Esquire Bar, he went to the opposite side of the street.

Some said the old Bexar County Courthouse was ugly. Hogan thought it was beautiful. It had brought him fame and fortune, friends and enemies, good times and bad. It was ponderous, a great stout fortress of red rusticated stone. It had been built just before the turn of the century. It was a total of five stories with a turret on top and large, spacious windows looking out from every floor. It was only a few steps from the San Antonio River, and in front was a large bronze statue of Saint Anthony of Padua, a gift from the people of Spain.

Great live-oaks and palms crowded the front, and under these trees people talked and wiled away the hours as they waited on some legal matter. It formed the south side of the Plaza de las Islas, and San Fernando Cathedral was just to its left on the west side. Where the entrance to the courthouse stood had been the small plot of land of the first mayor of San Antonio, Juan Leal Goraz. It had been the site of his small farmhouse in 1731.

The first floor was given over to administrative offices and lower courts, called county courts, where the civil jurisdiction had recently been increased to relieve the pressure of the fourteen Civil District courts located on the second, third and fourth floors. On the top floor was the Bar Association Library, which was the rent-free home of Big Bob Mitchell. There was not a courtroom in which Hogan hadn't tried a lawsuit, nor courtroom personnel, bailiff, or court reporter that he hadn't known intimately, usually for decades.

At one time the old building housed both civil and criminal courts but as the population and litigation increased, a new building called the Justice Center was built to house all of the criminal courts as well as the appellate court. It was bleakly modern next to its hundred-year-old predecessor, which Hogan regarded as sacred ground. The red limestone was faded and enriched with time.

As he approached the courthouse, Hogan thought, *If I had my druthers, they could bury my bones here and I would be very comfortable.*

Hogan had tried many cases in many places. But the older he got, the more he tried to stay within the confines of this courthouse. It wasn't hard. For years, he had been able to pick his cases. That was why the decision to take the Vietnamese case— an extremely unpopular cause when his popularity and self-esteem were at its lowest -- was so difficult. It wasn't the way he planned to end his career, if that was what it was going to be.

He went in and headed for the top floor, to search out Big Bob Mitchell.

Big Bob was not easy to employ. When he was not disabled from a hangover he could usually be found in the library maintained by the San Antonio Bar Association at the top of the courthouse. It was free of charge, and Big Bob always used the same table.

Big Bob was almost a contemporary of Hogan. He'd never enjoyed material or professional success; the guy had a sad and dramatic story of having married a rich south Texas girl who had left him. Hogan wasn't sure why, but, on the other hand, there *were* those suits of his. A bachelor with nothing in his life except the law, Big Bob was the original raggedy man. The only time Big Bob had a new suit was when he had a case with Hogan. The last time had been three years ago. His coat and trousers and belt rarely matched and his tie was usually soiled from many previous calamities. Bob didn't believe in the necessity of a regular shoe shine or a daily shave.

Despite his less than stylish apparel, Big Bob was a genius in preparing a case for appeal during the course of trial and filing excellent supporting briefs. He did brilliant work when he worked. Sporadic and sometimes unreliable, he still offered two great assets to Hogan. One, he was a genius at his trade. Two, he was intensely loyal to Hogan, who had saved his license when Mitchell was out on a month's drunk and forgot to show up for trial. The client thought it was poor form, and vehemently made himself heard at the grievance committee.

Serving as defense, Hogan got Bob off and earned his eternal gratitude.

Big Bob's skills were legendary. He was fearless and absolutely correct on the law most of the time. Judges knew they would be closely monitored by Mitchell's all-seeing eye. DAs became constrained in their remarks. In short, no lawyer or judge enjoyed appellate castigation and therefore tried to avoid it. Under Big Bob's watchful and zealous eye, deceitful ways were measurably reduced. Hogan's most immediate problem was finding the man.

Hogan walked into the quiet ranks of law books in the Law Library at the top of the old red stone courthouse, thankful for the air conditioning. There were whispers here and there, and the scratching of pens on legal pads.

Spotting Big Bob huddled over a tome on some arcane matter,he shook his head. There he was, as always. He seemed to have set up housekeeping in the place. Hell, this was probably the only place he was happy.

At one time Big Bob had been a handsome man. In his prime, he'd been six-foot-three and an athlete. Now he was gaunt, stooped, bedeviled with an uncertain gait, and his hair was gray and unkempt. He smoked his cigarettes down to the last bit, the nicotine stains on his fingers proof of his incessant habit. He had a tendency to whisper his acerbic comments when they were in trial, and his whisper was as loud as most people's normal speaking voice, but Big Bob was half deaf and nobody could ever convince him his whispers could be heard several blocks away. In the past, he'd generally been faithful to a promise not to drink until court adjourned for the day. Hogan could only hope for the same terms during this case.

Hogan walked over to the messy, paper-scattered table and tapped Mitchell on the shoulder.

"Bob," he said. "Bob, come on and let's talk. I need your help on a case."

"Hogan!" Big Bob's grating voice croaked out in a coarse whisper.

"Sssshhh," said Hogan. "Keep it down."

Mitchell smiled. "What's up, Doc?"

Hogan said, "I've decided to help with that Vietnamese case." He sat down beside Big Bob.

"No contest," said Big Bob. "You'll send those little shits up for life in a second."

"No," whispered Hogan. "I'm *defending* them."

"Of course, of course, what am I thinking of?" Mitchell nodded. "Those poor kids need somebody to fight for their rights, Hogan. You're the man. What do you need, Boss?"

"I want you to write the charge, and sit in on the trial. I think we're going to lose, but we might have a chance on appeal."

"Got a change of venue?" Big Bob patted his suit pockets, looking for cigarettes.

"We're about to propose one, but the D.A. down there is starstruck. He wouldn't give this case up for the deed to the King Ranch." Hogan stood up. "Let's go outside so you can smoke."

They stood under the arched entryway, looking down the steps at the people as they stood and chatted, as they sat on benches. All was slow in the golden liquid heat of August. Much of the talk below them under the trees and around Saint Anthony was in Spanish. Despite the great bank buildings and the new Justice Center across the street, the Plaza de las Islas still retained something of the life of a Spanish village, from two hundred and forty years ago. As they watched, a tall woman and her daughter sat on a bench and unwrapped a lunch of tortillas and eggs and cabrito and began to eat.

Big Bob smoked in the glaring heat and listened.

In all his cases, Hogan first wrote the proposed charge. It would be a compendium of the law of the case that the judge should give before either side gave their closing arguments. Both sides had the opportunity to submit what they regarded as a fair charge, but both sides had to write the charge so both proposals were nothing more than recommendations. In this instance, Hogan was minimally optimistic the judge would give a fair charge to the jury.

"I hope he'll give self-defense as one aspect, and lesser crimes," explained Hogan. "Cai is charged with murder, and his brother Tho as an accomplice."

"Yeah, but there's murder without malice, manslaughter, and self-defense, too," said Big Bob. He lit one cigarette off the end of the other. "All of these have a proper legal definition."

"Which the judge may or may not include," reminded Hogan.

"You let me take care of that," said Big Bob. "You got enough to do to defend those poor kids."

If the judge abused his discretion by failing to write a comprehensive charge within the parameters of the evidence, he could be reversed by the appellate court, and no judge wanted one of his decisions reversed. Big Bob would be waiting on the sidelines, sharpening his legal knives, as always in defense of the client.

"All right." Hogan nodded. "Glad I found you."

Big Bob stuck out his hand. "Good to see you, too, Hogan. I assume I'm hired."

Hogan grinned and shook his hand. The next step would be to get the lanky crane cleaned up and presentable. That would be Sheila's job.

"Of course, you're hired."

"How's the ride on the wagon?"

"Getting by," said Hogan. "See you tomorrow at the office."

Coat over his arm, Hogan covered the two blocks to his office at his usual steady pace. Once again he walked on the other side of the street from the Esquire bar. It made him feel very good indeed.

Hogan spent the rest of the day going over the primary steps. He knew the most important one was the change of venue, removing the trial from the atmosphere of hysteria down on the coast.

He also took time to look over information on how and why the Vietnamese had been resettled in San Ignacio. They were all Catholics, apparently, and almost all of them were from the same place in Vietnam, a village called Ba Lang. It was as if an entire village in Vietnam had been picked up and set down on the coast in Texas. But Cai and his brother Tho were from another village called Vung Tau. Since the fall of Saigon more than three years ago, the Church had been in the business of resettling the Vietnamese in the United States in great numbers, estimated at more than a million.

Father Dominic had given him as much useful information about the boat people as possible. He also had terrifying photographs and stories of starving refugees at sea, floating in tiny cockleshell boats, trying desperately to reach a welcoming shore.

Other churches assisted, but more than sixty percent of the effort came from the Catholic Church. A great many of the Vietnamese Catholics settled along the Gulf Coast. The resettlement began with modest numbers, but soon the Vietnamese immigrants grew to more than seventy-five thousand all along the coast, from Port Arthur to Brownsville. It caused a great deal of criticism, and this criticism was especially shared by Vietnam Veterans — of which there were many. The hostility of local residents, especially in San Ignacio, was immense. There was no government pre-planning or training for the Vietnamese. All of that came from the Catholic Church, and it was modest. The information was fascinating.

It was already growing toward evening. Most of Hogan's employees were leaving the building. From outside came the music of a Tejano band playing *The Tequila Mockingbird* in his bar.

Hogan continued to read until late. Then he went home to join Sheila who was involved with matters concerning the motion for a change of venue. Surprisingly, he felt good. He had not thought of something to drink for the last three or four hours. That was a record.

Hogan smiled to himself. It was the case. His attention had been entirely absorbed by it. Maybe it was the antidote he'd been seeking. Instead of the case driving him to drink, it might drive him from it.

"Put on some music," Sheila said. "And we'd better order something in unless you want to take a chance on my cooking."

Hogan smiled at her. She had changed from her lawyer clothes back to a baggy top and jeans for the evening. "Scott Joplin," he suggested. "And Chinese."

"Yum." She was already back into her research. "Did you find Big Bob?"

He dialed a Chinese restaurant a few blocks away. "Yes, and you've got to get this guy into some decent clothes. And burn the old ones or he'll put them on again without knowing it."

She started to laugh. "I can't *wait* to meet this guy."

Hogan knew he had to settle down, to smooth out. His head was spinning. He lay back in a chair and let Scott Joplin wash over him, the good-heartedness of the music, the joy in it, a sort of calm joy. It was *Sunflower Slow Drag*, and he sank restfully into the melody and the beautiful walking bass.

Chapter Fifteen

They all knew that the Motion to Change Venue could determine the outcome of the case.

"In this case, it's crucial," Hogan said to Sheila. They had walked down to one of the outdoor restaurants on the river for breakfast and coffee. "It's by no means automatic, though often it should be. In this case, it really is a 'life or death' decision. If the judge doesn't at least move this case to San Antonio, in my judgment there is utterly no chance of getting a fair jury."

He pointed out to her that the dangerous thing about a request for Change of Venue is that it often got so political. The popular thing for the judge to do would be to move it to the next county over — not actually in the same coastal county as San Ignacio, but not out of the judge's jurisdiction, either. But the county seat of the next county over, a town called Stillwater, was the worst possible place for the defendant, and yet it would give the legal appearance of fairness. It would unquestionably be the politically smart thing to do, Hogan knew, because the D.A. down there would kill to get this case. A sure win and a big media splash.

"All right," said Sheila, "we file the appropriate motions, accompany them with affidavits, put on the best testimony we can. Who will you get to testify that it should be shifted to San Antonio?"

"Whoever I can," Hogan answered. "I have one guy who takes surveys. And maybe some of the Hispanic political organizations will testify to racism and bias in the area. We can only hope that the judge will do the right thing, not the popular thing. If he doesn't, it's in Big Bob's hands."

By the time they'd gone over the change of venue, the heat was increasing, and they left the river for Hogan's air-conditioned building.

Hogan was now ready to pull out all the stops.

At his own expense, he sent his most experienced investigators to San Ignacio to assist in assembling some evidence or testimony as a predicate for a Motion to Change Venue in the hope of moving the case to San Antonio. From all of the reports, investigation, publications, media, and comments, it was obvious that any town but San Antonio would be a disaster.

San Ignacio was in Scott County, and the county seat was Spanish

Port, thirty miles across the peninsula from San Ignacio.

Judge Charles Barret was the presiding judge of the entire district of four counties, and Hogan had to file his Motion for Change of Venue in Spanish Port. Paul was on the road again down to the coast to file the motion. It stated that the circumstances and the feelings and expressions of the community were such that a fair trial could not be held in either of the three counties over which Barret presided.

Hogan knew, however, that even if Judge Barret allowed a move to a neighboring county, those counties surrounding San Ignacio were of the same mind. The judge wasn't likely to be impressed with testimony from some Catholic priests and Hispanic political groups.

At any rate, he could well understand how it would be considered an insult to tell the people of any one locality that they were incapable of keeping a fair mind, and the judge probably won't do it.

The real graveyard, Hogan felt, would be the town of Stillwater in next-door Potrero County. Hogan had never won a case there yet, and the newspaper there had been extremely partisan.

"Our best bet," Hogan told the group, "is cross-examination of the district attorney's refutation witnesses. We are going to have to catalog the firebombings and the torchings, the comments and meetings, and the protests and the Ku Klux Klan and the Nazi part. We simply ask if they've heard about them and how many times it's happened. Catalogue and chronologize the thing, and hope that it gets so strong that even the judge is embarrassed to do what he's prepared to do, and that, I'm afraid, is to move it to Stillwater."

All of the evidence was easily assembled in affidavit form by Hogan's investigators, thanks to the print media which had not missed one event.

From previous experience, Hogan knew Judge Barret was a solid man on the law and, under normal circumstances, generally ruled with an even hand. He had just never been tested like this. It was also known that the judge didn't view the arrival and resettlement of the Vietnamese with kind and compassionate eyes. Hogan had heard that he blamed the church and the U.S. government for poor preparation, that he felt a sympathy for the American fishermen in the San Ignacio area, who had been there for generations before the Vietnamese arrived.

Barret strongly disagreed with his own Catholic Church, though he was an active and staunch member. He felt the Church had helped cause the problem, as opposed to finding any equitable solution. He had no knowledge of the Vietnamese on a personal level -- but he had lost a son in the Vietnam War.

Hogan didn't know how that might affect them. He'd walked circles in his office trying to figure it out one way or the other. While

Hogan stood and stared out the window, a guest stuck his head in the door.

"What is that smell?" asked O.Z. White, Hogan's survey whiz.

"Ah, the Nutty Professor," said Hogan. He pulled his tie back into place. "That's mint and cinnamon tea. It's horrible. Nothing at all like a good bourbon."

O.Z. sat down and laid out his survey forms on the table.

They proved his point; the feeling was strong against the presence of so many immigrants. And further, the local officials of Stillwater, the mayor, the chief of police, the Chamber of Commerce, all adamantly insisted a fair jury could be selected in the sleepy farm-and-ranch town, and in the surrounding county. The D.A. was also insisting that the people of Stillwater were fair, always had been fair, always would be. He could hardly say much else.

"Thanks anyway, O.Z." said Hogan, resignation strong in his voice. "Sorry."

Hogan had known from the beginning of the intense work that he was on a slippery slope that didn't permit any serious mistakes.

Sheila rested her hand on his arm, papers in her other hand. "We can do it," she assured him.

"All right." Hogan smiled. "Just keep telling me that."

That evening, after long and trying hours in the office, Hogan turned to Sheila and held out his hand.

"Come with me for a walk," he said. "I need to cool down and you do, too."

They walked down Commerce Street, past the large fountain in the middle of the Plaza de las Islas, and on past San Fernando Cathedral, where Hogan attended early morning mass. The evening wind from the Gulf had come up, and Sheila's glossy auburn hair blew around her face. They strolled down the passageway between the Cathedral and the City Hall chambers, into the Plaza de las Armas. They went on, past the Victorian wedding-cake elaborations of City Hall itself and over to the long, low building that was called the Spanish Governor's Palace. It was a stone colonial building from the 1750s, and in front of it, on the flag-stone terrace, stood the booted and spurred bronze statue of a Conquistador.

Behind the restored building was a graceful Spanish garden. Hogan and Sheila sat down on a bench and watched the play of light and shad-ow over the stone lions. Banana trees rattled their long blades in the evening wind, and the sound of homebound traffic seemed remote.

San Antonio was the Mother of Missions and in its old colonial heart was still the stiff-necked pride of the Spaniard and the endurance of the *mestizo* soul.

Hogan intimately knew the history of the Gulf Coast of Texas. There was nowhere in the state he had not litigated. Leaning his stout arm on the bench-back behind Sheila, he told her something of it.

He told her how only the hardiest Anglos and Hispanics had settled down there in the first place. That the great King Ranch had been carved out of old Spanish land-grants by a bought title and main force. The King Ranch cowboys had had to stand off bandits of every persuasion. The counties had been sparsely populated after a while; young men drifting in, young men aggressive enough to make their fortunes with a rope and a running-iron.

After the Civil War, the Confederate soldiers who survived returned, hardened by years of rags and short rations. They'd lived through the worst carnage Americans had ever known, and they did not value human life as they once had.

"It made for a tough people," Hogan said.

Sheila listened intently, her hands clasped around her knee.

He told her how the Union Reconstruction government did not always govern fairly. Local outlaws were often hired as a police force, which merely gave them a license to steal and kill. And so the feuds began. Divisions between those who sided with the Yankee-backed outlaws and those who didn't, but the fights soon descended into nothing but personal vengeance. Law evaporated. Sometimes hundreds of men clashed in private armies, but more often it was death by ambush. It was known as the Taylor-Sutton feud, but it was more like a war. After a while, all reasonable people left the coast with their families and only the most hardened had remained.

"They forgot what law was," said Hogan. "Law was personal vengeance. That history has left its cloud on those counties to this day. Ultimately, all of this morass made for great trial lawyers intimidated by nothing and constantly advocating for the weak and the voiceless."

"When did the feud stop?" asked Sheila.

Hogan said, "In 1876. Captain McNelly of the Texas Rangers was sent down. The Rangers weren't connected to the Reconstruction government, or the Taylors, or the Suttons. There was a trial, and the only way a fair trial was achieved was when six Texas Rangers stood on each side of old Judge Pleasants with cocked carbines. The judge said, 'When you deal with Texas Rangers, you deal with men who are fearless in the discharge of their duty. The reign of the lawless in Dimmit County is at an end'."

Hogan knew the quote by heart. He turned to Sheila with a smile. "All those old-time heroics are passé now, I suppose."

She looked at him and smiled and shook her head.

"No," she said. "And you know it. We're going to recreate them."

Hogan sighed. "Maybe," he said. "Things like that leave a cloud for generations. Objectivity, an unbiased mind, a fair trial — things like that didn't work down there. But for many people, the Klan worked. Not for all, but some."

Sheila thought about it and watched his worn face as she said, "What's the chance for a change of venue?"

"Not good. But we have *got* to get the trial out of the coastal counties."

"How?"

He leaned forward, tapping his beefy left fist lightly into his right palm. I don't know, but we have to. No judge in his right mind would insist the trial be held down there, not with the Klan running around and the firebombing. But then again, maybe this one would."

Sheila shook her head. "If he won't allow a change of venue, well ... I guess just do your best to ask them for a fair trial."

Hogan gave a short laugh. "Me and the Texas Rangers." He thought for a moment. "And also, it's time to start fighting it in the press." He smacked his fist into his palm lightly, again and again, restless and charged up.

Sheila stood up. "We said we'd make that meeting." She smiled and held out her hand.

"All right."

He got to his feet, bear-like and somewhat spent by the heat. So they went back to the office for the car, and then on into the city to a meeting of people like themselves, a club whose membership fee was the costliest in the world.

Chapter Sixteen

August 18th

One of the first things Hogan did the next morning was to call a press conference and take a straight shot at the K.K.K. and all the other related organizations. If there is an Achilles heel, this is it, he thought. It was his gamble at any rate. It wasn't as if he had either leverage or encouragement.

Print and television reporters showed up; the Dallas T.V. station, the Austin and San Antonio stations. He recognized them from their logos. Hogan smiled his good, charming smile and said hello. He knew the reporter from the local station and he even knew his cameraman, a kid called Horse who moved as if the big battery packs belted around his waist weighed nothing. Print reporters held out the small Sony TC-110's, and the radio reporter from Houston was loaded with an old Nagra. Hogan stood and spoke with them in the cool lobby of his building. He told them a story.

The story was this: the Knights of the Ku Klux Klan described themselves as native born Americans and none others, but who were they, really? With the advent of the Vietnamese, the Klan saw a great opportunity. The Klan was reactivated and re-energized all along the Gulf Coast, once again espousing intense patriotism and the superiority of native born Americans. As affiliate chapters began spreading in a few states, the greatest welcome reception was given in Texas.

"They are living on it," said Hogan. "They are fattening on it. They are determined to destroy our system of justice."

They listened as he told them the story of his father. Hogan's father had had his go-round with the Klan in Dallas, because of their anti-Catholic stance. His father had been a dedicated Catholic, and in the late nineteenth century the Klan had attacked the Catholic immigrants coming into Dallas, the Irish, the Italians and Mexicans, and also his outspoken father. For this reason, his father had left Dallas and brought the family to San Antonio when Hogan was very young.

From years past Hogan knew how to fight this kind of battle. He understood the problem and the challenge. They were old foes.

He said to a local television reporter, "If the D.A. fails to criticize the Klan, there's no doubt some of his credibility will fall. He just can't have it both ways. We call on him to repudiate these people. They are disruptive of any civilized society. They trample on the Constitution unless it suits their purposes. They are a disgrace and a menace. They are antagonistic to all that is decent and honorable to our democratic way of life."

Hogan told them the story of the growth of a monster, and they listened. The monster is in your backyard, he told them.

"What keeps these people going?" Sheila sat at the office table beside him, going through the news articles. She held up one, with the photograph of a Klan rally, between thumb and forefinger as if it were a dead mouse.

"Ignorance," said Hogan. "Ignorance and malevolence."

Almost daily Sabine placed more clippings about the Klan on his desk. He sat with Sheila in the evening and watched their activities on the television news. A group of fifteen to twenty Klansmen, wearing masks and bearing arms, paraded around the San Ignacio area and in other fishing towns up the coast toward Galveston.

Hogan kept up his media blitz. He labeled the actions of the Klan as cowardly, brutal, and lawless. He called on the D.A., Roger Davis, to condemn the growth of this thing, knowing all along there were people in the coastal counties that were probably members and had influence in the courthouse. Then he listened in delight to evening news reports as the D.A. tried to skirt a substantive response.

Sheila said, "He's not really saying anything." She bent forward with her chin on her hands, watching the T.V.

"But I am," Hogan replied as his image appeared on the screen. He got up and walked to the window of the apartment and then back again, standing with one hand jammed in his pants pockets, watching the television, electric with energy. He loved a good fight. This was what would qualify as a damn good fight.

He listened to himself call on the United States government to seek out and condemn every Klan violence occurring any where along the Gulf Coast. In the newspapers, the Klansmen and pro-Klansmen complained loudly in letters and otherwise that patriotism should never be squelched. It was their constitutional right, they responded.

Hogan couldn't believe it. He laughed aloud. "Constitutional rights! Violence a constitutional right."

Hogan was sitting at his office table, writing press releases. Maybe he couldn't try the case himself, but he could help Paul with statements to the press.

"Listen to this!" Sheila said as she rushed in. "Read this!" She was walking fast and her long hair was bouncing, and Hogan took a moment to look at her with appreciation, and then he took the clippings. The Grand Dragon of Texas had complained in a letter to the leading newspapers that the editorials were downplaying good news about the Klan and its patriotic work, and playing up every negative story.

"The Grand Dragon himself, Dad," said Paul. "You're stepping out in high company. It's in here, too." He held up an August 25th edition of the *Light*.

Hogan kept providing good copy and the newsmen kept on calling him. His quotes showed up in the Houston *Chronicle* and the San Antonio *Light* and the *Express-News*, and on local and national television.

At their daily conference in the office, Hogan told the group, "This is going to get through to potential jurors." He went through his scribbled notes, putting his thoughts in sequence. "Unless they are deaf and blind and living in a cave."

"Well, there's that, too," said Sabine, with a flip of her head. "Might have some of those down there."

Hogan had the habit of putting his hands repeatedly through his thick gray hair and straightening his tie, whether he had one on or not. In trial, Hogan had been described as a wild cumulus of gray hair, restless beyond description and a deep, ebullient voice that held a jury in a state of hypnosis as his story unfolded. In times of trouble, of which there were many, his preceding reputation for fairness and compassion had created a well of good will that it was difficult to drain. And so the press listened.

The national media was giving him the high ground for his short-lived anti-Klan crusade. But the D.A. had a talent for using the media himself, and now ended up trumping Hogan without fail.

Hogan read the D.A.'s quotes in all the south Texas papers.

"Listen to this," he said to Sheila. "We're in a quote war." Then he read the D.A.'s words. "Of course a fair trial is the aim of every responsible citizen, but let's not forget the rights of the victim. Murder — cold-blooded killing — can't go unpunished in a civilized society. Law and order are our only protection against such killers — particularly those who shoot someone six times in the back. Talking against others to draw attention from the real defendants is an old and untrustworthy trial tactic that should be scorned."

The press coverage now began to shift. Being against the K.K.K. was a given; but here was a murder. What about the murder?

At times Hogan found himself reaching an intensity he knew was not good for him. Sometimes in the middle of the day he would sling his coat over his shoulder and head out of the building to walk along the river, over to the Alamo, anywhere.

He walked past the Esquire Bar, his favorite old watering hole, a bar that catered to the serious drinker. He'd been faithful to it since its opening twenty-five years ago. And now he could not bear to look in there and see his old friend, bartender Tim Carnahan, among the glittering bottles.

As he walked, suddenly Hogan felt a slashing, overwhelming desire for a drink. It was like an electric shock. Instantaneous and pure torture.

He turned on his heel in the middle of the sidewalk, reversed into the stream of people, and took his torment with him he knew not where. He just walked, a solid, beefy figure with his hands jammed in his pockets. God, what a long and lonely walk.

He found himself on the Navarro Street Bridge over the San Antonio River. Below were palm trees and flowers and glinting water. Glimmering in reflection was the old redstone Bexar County Courthouse, tall and majestic, lit by the afternoon sun and shining in the water like a fey palace from another world. Hogan thought it the most majestic thing he had ever seen.

He said 'Leave me alone' to the devils that tormented him with memories of the joys of the Esquire Bar. 'Let me enjoy this sight'. He stood and leaned on the stone railing. Just go along moment to moment, he told himself.

The passing crowd walked around the distinguished-looking gray-haired man as he gazed down at the river, perhaps thinking how content and at ease he must be. Hogan stood and inside himself fought hand-to-hand with alcoholic demons. I'll die before I run, he thought.

In a little while, after he repeated a slow and deliberate prayer, the struggle seemed to lessen. Wait a while longer, he told himself. One day at a time, one moment at a time.

And so it passed, but slowly.

Still he stood. He watched the reflection of the old courthouse waver and break up with the passing barges full of tourists and saw that no matter how turbulent the waters, the reflection steadily gathered itself again and became whole, and so would he.

He understood deeply how his successes meant nothing unless he could gather himself like that and not go to pieces. The bottom line was that he would rather be remembered as a good person than as a great lawyer. Hogan felt it would be a much greater heritage to his family. He wanted to conclude his life with service.

Dignity, pride and respect, which had eluded him over the last years, were his chief priority now. He wanted to do things for the right reasons and the right causes, and he didn't have to study on it long to know what those were. The Vietnamese trial could mean all of that to him.

The doors of life swung on small hinges. The Vietnamese boys were strangers in a strange land which owed them better than they had received. A country which should have befriended them and hadn't. It should have held out a helping hand and an open heart rather than closed minds. He felt the country — his country — owed them something, and he would like to help pay it back by representing them free in this case.

As he leaned on the bridge railing, Hogan recognized defending the Vietnamese would probably be total futility. There was no hope of a reasonable verdict. Perhaps soul satisfaction would be enough. He needed it. He and the D.A. both needed the case, both for their own reasons.

Hogan didn't deceive himself. He knew the task would be unending, the preparation monumentally difficult and of long duration. The cause would be completely unrewarding in any popular aspect. Its value would have to be the good achieved for society and his own spiritual well-being, which at this point needed a super booster shot.

At this stage in his life, money and prestige held little appeal for Hogan. The safe passing to his eternal rest, which Hogan felt was not too far off, occupied more of his contemplation than any future material involvement.

A lifetime of the adversary system dealing with aggressive lawyers, overworked judges, emotionally upset clients, left permanent marks, and he had them. Like what had happened a moment ago. He'd literally been ambushed by the need for a drink. There seemed to be so many ambushes, no matter how much he avoided the old crowd and the scintillating bars.

All he could do was shut the door to the past and recognize that he was powerless over the future. He'd learned meditation. Even for short periods, it left him energized and refreshed, and he made himself give over and watch the movements of the water. It helped him get through the ambushes.

Deep down he felt maybe that's why he'd been given the absurdly impossible task of defending a hugely unpopular foreigner — Vietnamese at that — one who shot an American six times in the back. If he could be of measurable assistance to Cai, it could be the greatest triumph. It would also be an entry back into trial work.

In control again, Hogan turned and began to walk. He was going to be okay. His world *had* changed, and now he had new and sober friends. He could handle his life again. He could take the case himself, not just hand it over to his son. And he'd do his damnedest to win.

Hogan reached his apartment without another thought of the Esquire Bar. Sheila would be doing something with pasta for dinner. She was a terrible cook; they'd both agreed on that. They'd probably end up going out, laughing about it. Another little private joke to add to the new feeling of togetherness.

He would tell her about his skirmish on the Navarro Street Bridge, and later they'd find their way to a meeting in the private, hidden nation of sober alcoholics.

Chapter Seventeen

August 20

"Well, Millford," said Joe Fleming, "I know you lost that boy in Vietnam." They were sitting in Judge Barret's study at the ranch house. Joe Fleming was administrative judge of the area; he'd been on the bench for thirty years. Barret was thinking of disqualifying himself as the judge in the Vietnamese trial, and had asked Fleming for advice. And here he was being almost shamed into accepting the job. He wanted out, and Fleming was telling him otherwise.

Fleming's ranch was near Stillwater, in next-door Potrero County. It was to Stillwater that Judge Barret was thinking of moving the trial.

"You're new on the bench, and if you start dodging things for political or personal reasons which are unavoidable, you'll find your career fairly short. It would be a point of sheer cowardliness if you're doing it just to dodge an unpopular situation. But — if you feel that you simply can't give a fair trial, then obviously you should step aside."

Judge Millford Barret had a district that embraced three counties. He appeared in three different courtrooms, depending on the scheduling of the court session throughout the year. He was largely a stranger in Stillwater, which was why he wanted the trial there. He hoped to make friends and gain some popular presence which would help him in his election, which was only nine months away. He felt it important to establish himself as a figure strong for law and order. But now he was wondering if it was a smart thing to do after all. District Attorney Roger Davis seemed to be running the show and Barret didn't know how to take charge again. He walked past the mantelpiece which held photos of his family and a portrait of his son in uniform.

Judge Barret was in his early fifties, a slight man of five foot ten, with thinning brown hair and a florid complexion. He was soft-spoken, polite, genteel, and knowledgeable in the law. He had been raised in a cattle-and-oil family in the coastal county of Scott. It was a family who sent their sons to Texas A&M and their daughters to Sarah Lawrence, bought their linens from the nuns at Sarita. Everyone in the family had to learn to ride, and to know, at the very least, the difference between an expansion joint and a pump jack. They had been brought up on Grand Baroque and windmills. Local people said they would cross-fence the moon if they could get at it. It was a family with rigorous standards, which is why Judge Barret's son had gone to Vietnam rather than avoiding the draft.

Judge Barret had a strong desire to do the right thing. In this instance, clearly his vision was clouded as to what the right thing should be. So many of his fellow judges had expressed stronger views than Judge Barret, and he knew in his heart of hearts that the right thing to do was to accept the job.

He didn't look forward to a trial with Hogan, whom he didn't know but had heard a great deal about. The judge had paced his living-room floor for several nights over it, and then had called Joe Fleming and asked if he could come over.

"One of the things that gives me the greatest reluctance about the case is this fellow Hogan. I'm told he's not reliable and can't be trusted," the judge confided to Fleming.

"You can trust him to hang in like a bulldog once he gets into the case," said Fleming.

Fleming raised racing Quarter horses as a hobby. They consistently lost, but he felt obligated to keep a few around the place, since next-door Potrero County was known as the home of the American Quarter Horse. Mostly he was interested in the bloodlines. The actual horses were not as interesting, in that they threw people off their backs and were always coming down with some malady. But the bloodlines of Leo and Three Bars and the Billy horses were absorbing, mainly because they remained safely on paper and neither ate nor shat nor broke their own bones. It also made him a 'good old boy.' Stillwater was famous for horses, always had been. He sat his Stetson on his knee and smoked a large, malodorous cigar.

"Go on, I'm listening," Fleming said.

"Well, I've seen some of his statements in the past, and they're almost irreverent about jurors and judges, and particularly so in this case. It's outrageous some of the statements he's made! You'd think he would know better. He's Irish and no gentleman! I suspect he's one of those kind that wants victory at all costs. That thinks any publicity is good publicity," the judge said. "Fleming, why do you think he got involved?"

"Got religion, I guess," said Fleming, and puffed. "Anybody can get it. There ain't no vaccine."

"I don't believe he can possibly be in it for altruistic reasons. How would this case help him?" Barret turned and looked out the study window. It was night but there were pole lights on out at the long barn, neatly painted in white with a maroon trim. Cattle stood under the lights in a halo of mosquitoes. "I've also heard that he's got a drinking problem," said the judge.

Fleming nodded. "Well, it's all in the way you look at it. The problem usually isn't the drinking. The problem is the hangovers."

"Be serious," said Barret, impatiently. He was a mild man under most circumstances, but he felt stressed, even overwhelmed by the case, the media attention, and the terrible violence down in San Ignacio that had put Texas to shame.

"All right, then, Millford, I'm telling you to take the case," said Fleming. He drew on the cigar. "Just take it and do your damnedest. Hogan is supposedly on the wagon, but if this case wouldn't drive a person to drink I don't know what will. It's likely he won't finish it. But he's not a bad fellow."

"Very well," said Barret. "Then I will."

The disaster occurred over an Italian dinner.

Hogan and the rest were in the middle of the preparation of change of venue, late in the evening. Sheila was working with Lillie May, explaining the various charges of murder, murder with malice, self-defense, and manslaughter, so that she could translate them to the two Vietnamese defendants. Sabine and Paul were rounding up witnesses to support their request. They'd been up since early morning and it was now very late.

For decades, Hogan had been known as a favorite of the press. He courted them, and he was always good for great sound-bites and ready interviews. He was great copy.

He knew most of the older reporters from the newspapers and the T.V. commentators on a personal basis and had befriended them on many occasions. Hogan had great war stories about the legal profession and knew all the relationships, the ins and the outs, the amusing stories about famous cases.

Hogan had often spoken off the record to trusted reporters so he could swing a few stories in his direction. But he didn't do that until he was absolutely assured it would be off the record, and he felt he knew the people to whom he was talking.

Paul had met a local reporter, Andy Wharton, who was new to the business of journalism and a stranger to Hogan. When they went out to get something to eat that night, they included him in the group.

They were making their way through a late Italian dinner at Boudreau's on the River Walk. They were eating like locusts. They had missed lunch and they were all starved. Hogan was talkative, and the young reporter seemed flattered to be included in the group. The young man was outgoing and very attentive to Hogan. Hogan felt expansive. The maitre d' had put a tape of Scott Joplin on the background music system because he knew Hogan would like it; the sounds of *Cascades* swirled around them.

"Those rednecks down there are going to kill us if we don't get out," he said.

Sheila looked at the reporter and said, "Are you guys in a drought down here? I haven't seen rain since I've been here."

"They'll sit there with their heads full of law and order and lynch the guy." Hogan took a long drink of ice tea. "Or lunch him, as Father Dominic says. Either way."

Paul cleared his throat. "Yeah, they need rain."

Sheila smoothed back her red hair and said, brightly, "Well, it rains all the time in Atlanta."

Andy Wharton looked at Hogan and started to ask, "You want to get out of--"

"It rains *buckets* all the time in Chicot Switch!" Sabine interrupted. "That's where I'm from."

But nothing would stop Hogan.

"We've worked like hell trying to avoid having this trial in any part of South Texas," Hogan continued. "It's simply impossible to get a fair jury except in San Antonio. Stillwater is known as the purgatory and hell for plaintiffs and criminal defendants. All you have to do is look at their record." He wound fettuccine around his fork. "God, those people believe that law and order means conviction. There's no such thing as self-defense down there in Stillwater, Texas. It's Andersonville."

"Dad," cautioned Paul, but Hogan was up and running.

"They're a bunch of bigots and rednecks, and that's an open secret." He turned to the young reporter. "You understand that all of this is off the record. We can't get stuck there. I'd as soon somebody put us in a cement mixer."

Andy Wharton was a young man two years out of journalism school at the University of Texas. He was determined to make a name for himself and get out of Stillwater and get on with the larger papers as soon as possible. He was prepared to cut corners.

He said good night in an hour or so, and drove home to Stillwater to take notes.

Hogan walked down from the apartment the next morning and saw headlines in the San Antonio paper.

"Oh, my God," he said. He put coins in the slot and drew the paper out. His words stared back at him from the headline of a first-page column.

ATTORNEY BLASTS COURTS, it said.

"Attorney Jim Hogan, defending the Vietnamese brothers accused of the shooting death of a fisherman in San Ignacio, was quoted in an Associated Press story yesterday that 'he held the district court in Stillwater in ill repute.' He called it a 'plaintiffs purgatory.' Hogan referred to the people of the area as 'rednecks'."

Hogan's remarks were printed with even more embellishment in the other San Antonio newspaper. Hogan could see every prospective juror in Potrero County and the town of Stillwater waking up to read his remarks. This was a calamity.

Back in the apartment, Hogan threw the papers down on the breakfast table. "Damn! That kid was a D.A. plant! If we don't get moved to San Antonio, I'm a dead duck." He jammed his hands through his hair. "Jesus."

"Take it a little slower," said Sheila, and put her hand on his arm, but it was as if he hadn't heard her.

Sheila looked at him a moment with great doubt, and then left to go talk to Big Bob. Hogan jerked his tie tight and stalked to the office.

All hell broke loose. His phone at the office was ringing off the hook, and the hearing hadn't even begun. Again and again he told reporters that he hadn't meant 'redneck,' that it had been a private conversation, that it was off the record.

Hogan was infuriated at his betrayal, but the damage was done. The D.A. would never stop exploiting it. Hogan felt most grieved because the Vietnamese were in trouble enough without him creating more.

He could almost laugh at himself; the irony was that it all happened when he was sober. In his drinking days he had gotten away with so much more. Compounding the problem, he had never wanted a drink more in his life. He fought it moment by moment.

Hogan's best intentions had been to keep a low profile and allow the district attorney's own abundant ego to destroy him, if that was possible. Now he was in damage control with the judge, the media and the citizenry.

Chapter Eighteen

August 22

They drove down to Spanish Port, prepared to stay the night. The Hogan group obtained motel rooms near the port, where fishing boats knocked against one another. A light wind came out of the east and before it scudding black puffs of clouds vaulted out of the distant sea-horizon, passed overhead and disappeared.

The courtroom in Spanish Port was not at all like those in the surrounding counties. It was Fifties modern, only three stories and had none of the dignity and pomp of the nineteenth-century courthouses.

The District Courts were located on the second floor, as they always were according to tradition. It seated approximately one hundred people. The ceilings were high with ceiling fans of weak velocity. There was a heavy coat of varnish over that which was once very beautiful wood paneling. The air conditioning was loud and ineffective.

As soon as D.A. Roger Davis and his staff arrived, clambering out of their cars and into the hot, salty air, Hogan and his staff were also admitted and so they all walked in. Big Bob, nattily attired for day one at least, thanks to Sheila, brought up the rear, smiling broadly and scattering cigarette ashes as he went.

When they entered the Scott County Courthouse, an undistinguished little contemporary building, Judge Barret's face was as red as raw beef. He was furious in his choked, genteel way. Hogan put his files on the counsel table, and looked down at the cheap carpeting. Beyond it was imitation tile which was much the worse for wear, but he was looking at his shoes, trying to think. The hearing on the change of venue began at nine, with the Hogan team having the burden. So he would speak first and present his proof first.

The Vietnamese brothers, Cai and Tho, were seated to the left and guarded by deputies. Lillie May sat near them, poised and alert. It was her first day of translating in a courtroom. They boys had clearly spent a sleepless night. They looked terrified, and their hair wasn't properly combed. They looked like they'd been dragged backwards out of a pipe.

As soon as the judge's chambers were opened, Hogan tried to see the judge privately to apologize for his remarks, but the judge didn't give him the opportunity. Hogan returned to his table, trying not to show his chagrin.

Davis gave everyone a great white smile, and laid his files on the

table. He wore a cream-colored tie, covered with black figures of bar-
bells or wrenches, and a light tan suit. He was in top form, handsome
and assured.

Judge Barret seated himself with a swing of his black robes and discreetly touched his damp, reddened face with a handkerchief. He
looked down at Hogan.

"Mr. Hogan, your remarks were the most intemperate that I've
ever seen as a practicing lawyer of 30 years and as a sitting judge," he
said. "They're not only inappropriate and unacceptable, but a damn
lie. People in this area can and do daily afford fair trials. Just because
your chemistry or your views don't mix with them doesn't mean
they're wrong and you're right. I will not accept this kind of behavior
in this trial."

He's as wound up as an eight-day clock, thought Hogan. Paul
looked over at him in alarm. Sheila looked straight ahead, trying not to
show her distress. Lillie May looked at Hogan, wondering if she should
begin translating, but he gave his head a slight shake.

Judge Barret went on. "I thought of holding you in contempt, but
your remarks were not made in the presence of a judge or in the confines
of this courtroom. *However,* it is your sworn obligation and duty and
responsibility to behave properly. If you can't, you ought to give the case
over to more capable people. I want that understood, do you hear?"

"Yes, your Honor," said Hogan.

"You will conduct yourself with decorum. If you don't understand
that, then I suggest you counsel with whomever brought you into this
case and withdraw. Have I made myself clear?"

The judge was obviously very disturbed and was trying to restrain
himself, but doing a very poor job of it. Hogan said nothing. In former
years, he would have.

The district attorney did not smile, but merely sat quietly, enjoying
himself.

Hogan stood up to take his medicine, a wide-shouldered figure in
a light suit. His tie was askew. His wrinkles were even more wrinkled.

"Judge, I understand. I apologize for the remarks. I thought they
were totally off the record. I wasn't quoted accurately or fairly. If you're
saying you feel my clients can't get a fair trial because of my presence,
then I'll withdraw. Perhaps you know, this is a *pro bono* effort on my
part. I did it with the greatest reluctance." He paused and put one hand
in his suit pocket. "It may have occurred to you that there aren't a long
line of volunteers who want to occupy my shoes at this moment."

He waited but the judge said nothing, merely regarding him and
waiting.

"If you know any, I will gladly release this marvelous opportunity
to them. Under no circumstances did I want to get involved. I do feel a

duty, responsibility, and obligation in this difficult challenge. I intend to discharge it, unless you have strong views to the contrary."

The judge was obviously somewhat mollified by Hogan's response. His color began to return to normal.

"Mr. Hogan, I'm not making any recommendations. I'm simply letting it be known that I intend to give both lawyers what they're due. I'm not going to be intimidated nor the victim of any remarks when a ruling doesn't correspond to your sense of accuracy and fairness.

"If you understand, we can proceed. If not, then I think we ought to adjourn until any personality disputes are resolved."

Hogan, however, pressed on. "Judge, I regret terribly what has happened. I'm perfectly prepared to go forward. If that weren't the case, we wouldn't have been involved in all of the very difficult pre-trial work that has brought us here."

The judge nodded, and with hardly a pause, said, "Let's go forward."

Hogan knew that he was at a grave disadvantage. He had to say something positive about the judge and the area in general. Salvaging a public face was extremely critical.

"Your Honor, before we begin with our proof with Mr. O.Z. White as witness, we would like to make a few personal comments."

Judge Barret stared at him a moment, as if to ask, Haven't you said enough already? But finally he nodded and looked away.

Hogan began doggedly, to try to repair the damage. He stood square-shouldered, one hand on the counsel table.

"First, let me apologize to the court for any distress or misunderstanding which might have been caused by erroneous remarks attributed to me. They were published without my knowledge. Those quotes were abbreviated, not in context, and not for public consumption." He looked at the judge. "I feel any community can give a fair trial. What I meant is that the pre-trial publicity has been so great and so slanted that it makes it extremely difficult. The farther from the scene of the publicity, the easier the task becomes to select an impartial jury. Because of the very adverse circumstances, in fairness to the court and to the community, we need to explore every consideration before we agree that a fair and impartial jury can be obtained."

He wondered if this had done any good. He paused and then went on. The D.A. had his hand to his forehead and was staring with great interest at a Rubik's cube he held in his lap.

"However," Hogan continued. "I am very conversant with the judges and the people in the area, and have warm feelings for them. And I have for the past forty years of trial practice. I want to apologize and say that we are going to assist the court in seeing all parties receive a fair trial, especially the defendants."

The district attorney put down the cube and immediately rose. He obviously considered Hogan far in the ditch, and wanted to dig it even deeper. He stated in a flat, angry voice that Mr. Hogan, like Dr. Seuss' elephant, had meant what he said, and said what he meant.

"Judge, Mr. Hogan has been censored in the past and should be now." The D.A. was covertly referring to Hogan's drinking days. "He's no friend of law and order, that's for sure. He would like to escape them but those remarks are indeed his personal views. The court shouldn't tolerate any future diatribe and outbursts by Mr. Hogan and I am sure it won't. We want to assure the court that we are going to do our very best to see that justice prevails in this case."

The judge nodded. He had become cool and diffident again.

He paused and then said, "Mr. District Attorney, I need no counsel on how this trial should be presented. Mr. Hogan, I accept your remarks as well-intentioned. We'll consider the matter behind us and proceed with the hearing."

Well, thought Hogan. He didn't want to hear any grandstanding from the D.A. There's hope.

O.Z. White testified as to his findings and opinions, observations, and background and expertise in the area. Professor White was a short man with heavy glasses, balding and pale. He wore a bow tie in a modest check and seemed like a professor that had been sent from Central Casting.

He admitted he was an expert in such surveys and had vast experience in testifying as to community bias and prejudice. He concluded the only area possible for a fair trial would be in San Antonio. He looked around the courtroom and his thick glasses glinted

The district attorney couldn't restrain his enthusiasm. He shook his head in regret. His black-and-cream tie with its stark patterns seemed to add to his aggressiveness.

"I notice that there are only four hundred interviews. Would you not agree that the margin of error increases with the smallest in number and that a thousand is regarded certainly as more accurate? And incidentally, Mr. White, I know you are a professional witness, but most of these can be answered yes or no."

"Yes," said O.Z. He was rattled. "I mean no."

"Would you not agree that, in the past, you have performed this task for the Hogan Law Firm at least twenty-five times?"

Hogan watched this go on. Sheila, sitting beside him, started to writhe in her seat and push back her red hair, but Hogan gave a brief shake of his head as a signal to cool it.

Each time Mr. White tried to explain, he was cut off by the district attorney insisting that the question could be answered yes or no. Hogan objected that the witness wasn't being given the opportunity to respond, that he was being harassed, and that if need be he should be given the opportunity to explain. It was soon obvious objections were going to be pointless. O.Z. opened his mouth and shut it again as the D.A. fired another question.

"Would you not agree that your fee has gone increasingly up through the years? You began at $150, then $200, and now make the incredible fee of $300 an hour."

"You see, I--"

"Would you agree that you have at least fifty hours in this case and that obviously, therefore, you've been paid at least $15,000?"

The D.A. nodded to himself even before he shot the next question as if he were answering himself. The fans overhead complained rhythmically.

"Mr. White, or Dr. White, which is it?"

"Doctor --"

"You make your living at Trinity University teaching freshman Sociology."

"--White!"

"Is it not correct that you were introduced to this 'trade' in negligence cases by Hogan some ten years ago and that, as a consequence, your income from testifying in court is ten times what you make as a college professor?"

"You said ten --"

"Do you not agree that you retain the college professor responsibility only because it allegedly enhances your probity as a witness?"

"--twice!" the professor almost cried out.

The district attorney continued for some thirty minutes in this kind of castigation of the professional witness, knowing that it probably had little effect on the judge, but it made for great press. He concluded his cross-examination of the witness by inquiring whether White recognized that all of the public figures, the chief of police, the sheriff, the city council, the newspaper publishers, disagreed with his comment that a fair trial couldn't be held in Scott or Potrero Counties.

O.Z. opened his mouth. "They --"

"Do you think it would be fair to say they know more about the feeling of the community than you? Because they've lived here all their lives, do you think it might give them a leg up over you? You probably have seen this area only after you got employed?"

"--might not!" White let out a long breath and looked as if he were about to melt down.

In redirect examination Hogan tried to restore the witness and the credibility of his study. He knew it was futile, but he kept on. He knew he was clumsier and shorter than the D.A. and didn't put up much of an appearance, but he was in the ring now and there was no help for it. He elicited some statistics from poor O.Z. and then let him go.

"We'll take a short recess for lunch," said the judge, and Hogan and his group walked outside. The yielding and tender Gulf wind rattled the fronds of the palms around the courthouse. They walked to a restaurant on the bay shore and ate hamburgers.

"You'd think they'd have seafood," said Sheila.

"They ship it all off," Hogan replied. "Nothing's local any more." He looked out the window to the metallic glinting of the salt water and its vast planes. "I can't believe we're having the trial down here. But we are making no impression whatsoever."

"Yes we are," said Paul. He ate his French fries and brushed salt from his hands.

"I know what kind we're making," said Hogan. "You don't have to humor me. "

Chapter Nineteen

The next testimonial witness for moving the trial was the manager of the crab processing plant, Georgia Cadwaller. The owner refused to appear and they had heard he had advised his manager against it, saying it was bad for business. Georgia, a heavyset woman who had never testified before, was sorely distressed at the idea of being in a courtroom. She knew that her husband also thought it was a very poor idea and she was quickly coming to the same conclusion. She clasped her worn hands. She had a new perm and her head sprouted a crop of wiry curls.

Mrs. Cadwaller testified that the boys and all Vietnamese were victims of severe discrimination and had been for the past three years. She felt it was impossible for them to receive a fair trial.

The D.A. rose and stalked toward her. "Mrs. Cadwaller, wouldn't it be fair to say that you're really no part of the community? You refuse to associate with the others, and your only knowledge of the community is with the Vietnamese?"

"Objection!" said Hogan, surging to his feet.

"Overruled," said Barret. It was obvious the judge was going to permit the harassment notwithstanding Hogan's objections.

"Isn't it correct, Mrs. Cadwaller, that your only interest is that the crab plant prospers? The Vietnamese work for almost nothing? And you're raking in a profit?"

"No, sir, there's more." But that was all she got in before the D.A. handed her back to the defense.

Hogan elicited her opinion on the atmosphere of the coast, but it seemed stiff and rehearsed and he knew he had not done well.

The next witness was Father Dominic. He sat calmly in the witness chair and regarded the D.A. with aplomb. The two Vietnamese defendants gazed at him steadily. They almost smiled.

Father Dominic smiled at the D.A. as if he were a dear friend, and bent forward in his faded black coat and shirt, his white collar in stark contrast, to listen intently to the D.A.'s questions.

He said he personally knew the defendants, but only after his arrival in San Ignacio. He knew all of the Vietnamese who had come to this country and settled in San Ignacio. He testified to the hostility in the community toward the Vietnamese, but only reluctantly, as if he felt his words might make the situation worse. The direct examination followed. The judge seemed unimpressed.

Hogan said, "Well, Father, knowing what you now know, what is your recommendation to the court?"

"Move the case to San Antonio. Then there's no suspicion of unfairness."

"Father, I think the summary of your testimony," said the district attorney, "is that you really don't know American people nor American justice, and, therefore, you only hope that the court does the right thing. Is that not true?"

"I think you've said it very well," said Father Dominic. He smiled warmly at the D.A., as if Davis were a young catechist and had finally got an answer right.

The witness was quickly excused by the district attorney.

Hogan shook his head slightly. He was moved by Father Dominic's humility and truthfulness but in despair over his value as a witness.

Hogan then followed with affidavits from six local priests who had parishes in the surrounding areas. They swore they felt a fair trial could not be obtained and all recommended a move to San Antonio. Hogan thought it advisable not to put them on the stand, to let the affidavits suffice in view of the unfair and harassing cross examination permitted by the court.

The same thing applied to the newspaper men, five in number, who recited in similar affidavits their own familiarity with the area and their opinion that the trial should be moved to San Antonio. One who took the stand as the final live witness was Jess Perkins, a reporter from the *Dallas Morning News*. Perkins was a big man with a loud, booming voice and he was fearless in his opinions.

To Hogan, he identified himself as a reporter who had covered stories involving Vietnamese problems of resettlement for a number of years.

"Yeah!" he said. "San Ignacio and the Gulf Coast area are the hot spots! My God! The *hostility* against the Vietnamese! It's *crazy* to think you can get a fair trial outside of San Antonio!"

He testified at a high rate of decibels that areas like San Antonio or larger cities would accommodate different cultures.

The D.A. approached him. "But you wouldn't expect that you really know the area better than the people who actually lived here all their lives and the generations before them, would you?"

"I don't have an ax to grind and I *do* have great respect for justice in this case!"

The D.A. took a few steps back. "And you're saying, therefore, that the judge should disregard all of the local citizens who have testified by affidavit to the contrary, that he should accept your own view?"

"Why's that so strange?" Perkins bellowed.

"Perhaps you have the view, like attorney Hogan, that we can't accord justice and fairness in this area? The citizens are all rednecks and without any sense of right and wrong?" The D.A. placed a hand on the counsel table and waited.

"Nah! But, *hell!* Look at the trouble and riots, what more reason do you want to move it?"

"I think, Mr. Perkins, you've said about all we need to hear, and therefore, will excuse you," said the district attorney.

Hogan knew additional testimony was pointless. The judge knew the area and the feeling of the community very well. He had to know San Antonio would be a better forum.

After Hogan rested his case, the D.A. quickly put on his large array of prominent authorities, business people, office workers, all unanimous in their criticism of moving the case to San Antonio.

Although Hogan did his best to make his point, he began to feel desperate. "Your Honor, remarks attributed to me, and printed in the paper include: One, that my feeling is that the majority of Americans in rural areas are rednecked and conservative. Two, you have to be a redneck to get justice in this area, Three, that a city this size does not practice fairness. Four, that we hold the district courts in poor repute. Would this not prejudice a jury?"

Judge Barret looked down at Hogan with a slight smile on his face, as if he were saying, *This is called crow, Mr. Hogan, and you are going to have to eat it.*

When Hogan kept on waiting for a reply, the judge finally said, "Yes, Mr. Hogan? You have further points?"

"No, your Honor."

The next morning they left their motels rooms in Spanish Port in a high wind that was coming in off the Gulf and Hogan found himself wondering if the hurricane season was starting already. When he opened the door of the car for Sheila, the wind about took the door off.

"Jesus, it's going to take three people to hold a sheet over a keyhole pretty soon," he muttered.

They drove to the small modern courthouse where the palms in front were blown sideways in the wind.

Judge Barret came in and said, without delay, "The court feels that a full hearing has been accorded, and, therefore, grants the Motion for Change of Venue and moves the matter to Stillwater where it will be tried in a matter of three weeks." Barret looked blandly down at the D.A., and Roger Davis nodded to him in a graceful gesture.

"Oh, no," whispered Hogan.

"The court stands adjourned."

Hogan got up and stalked out of the courtroom. As he passed Cai and Tho he said, "We're dead!"

He saw a look of horror come across Tho and Cai's faces as Lillie May interpreted for them.

The Vietnamese defendants turned and began talking rapidly and in strained tones to Lillie May.

"What is it?" snapped Hogan. He was still furious.

Lillie May said, hesitantly, "You said they were dead. They think the trial is over and they wonder when they are to be executed."

"Oh, for God's sake, explain to them!"

He watched as she tried to reassure them. He saw they were careful only to talk to Lillie May and then only in whispers. They trusted no one.

He saw the relief spread over their faces, and then the deputies herded them out of the room.

Hogan felt whipped. The refreshing wind had passed without rain and the heat and the humidity had returned. It was all he had suspected. This was a defeat and it was the last case he would ever try. He had to face selection of the jury in Stillwater. Those hard faces whom he had called redneck, unfair, bigoted would crowd into the courtroom and stare at him, and he would have to choose which ones would sit on the jury. He asked Sheila if she would mind riding back to San Antonio with the others, and took the other car alone. He made a speedy and unsafe trip to San Antonio and headed for his favorite watering-hole.

Chapter Twenty

The Esquire had the longest bar in town. It was narrow and dark and little went on other than persistent drinking with no intrusions unless invited.

It opened at six A.M. for those favorite customers who daily needed an 'eye-opener' to get started. Hogan had often been one of them. Beer of any brand was the largest seller but anything alcoholic could be obtained. Hogan used to love the place because there was little conversation; it was almost like drinking alone, but not so solitary. The beer was ice cold and side drinks always available.

He had known most of the bartenders since they were young. They knew each other by sight but never had any conversation unless invited, and that was rare. It was a steady crowd. Rarely was a customer lost except by death or cirrhosis. It was just a block from Hogan's office on Commerce Street, west toward the courthouse. A great proximity for celebratory occasions, or defeat, or bitching about judges and justice. On all occasions Hogan had found it to be a true haven.

"Give me a Bud and two shots of Jack Daniels for starters," instructed Hogan as he sat down on his favorite bar stool. The service was instant.

"Just like old times," Hogan murmured. "Enough of this crap. Who am I kidding? I'm not made for sobriety. It's as simple as that." He was ready to settle back for a full day of uninterrupted drinking. "After all, the case got my best shot." And now he was done for. He had shot his mouth off and it was time to pay the fiddler. He could never try the case in Stillwater, and he knew it. He was defeated.

As he reached for his first drink, a strong and burly arm restrained him. The Popeye-sized arm had a Semper Fi-and-anchor tattoo on it.

"Jim, you don't want to do that. This place is closed to you. I'll see you at the meeting tonight."

Tim Carnahan, with his rugged, red face and mass of freckles, was an ex-Marine who had served in the war with Hogan. They'd known each other since grammar school, St. Cecilia's School on Hunstock Street in the south part of San Antonio, a couple of miles south of his current office. Jim had been the brightest and wildest student and Tim the toughest. They later joined the Marine Corps together, and both of them got shot up a lot. Their friendship was deathless. Both were alcoholic and had proven it many times.

Hogan knew Tim Carnahan was strong as battery acid and could probably turn a posthole inside out with one yank. He was fully capable of picking Hogan up and throwing him out if need be. Hogan had been his banker in opening the Esquire a quarter of a century ago. Both had spent untold nights drinking till morning in the bar.

"Ah, let it go, Tim," said Hogan. He felt old, older than dirt. And weak. "It's no use."

"No," said Tim. "Over my dead body." Tim had quit drinking before Hogan had. He had been Hogan's sponsor at the A.A. meetings and he was about to lose another member from the ranks of sobriety. Hogan wouldn't be the first he had lost, by any means.

Hogan looked around. *Jesus, I just about own this place. He can't throw me out.*

"And just who in the hell are you to tell me that I can't have a drink?" Hogan demanded. "I'll foreclose on the joint and throw your ass out of here." His hand was still around the ice-cold beer.

"Here's the little lady who says you're off limits," Tim replied, and watching Hogan as Sheila seated herself on the barstool next to him.

She pushed her auburn hair out of her eyes and crossed those long legs.

"So you got to go down there and talk to the rednecks," she said. "So the judge made you eat crow. Is it worth committing suicide over? Boy, wouldn't the D.A. love that!" She jiggled her foot. "Yep, he's going to love this."

Hogan leaned back and looked at the ceiling. He was tired of fighting it all. Fighting the need for a drink, fighting the trial. Seeing his own stupid comments in the media was a scalding humiliation, and he was tired of fighting the media. The cool, calm bar was a refuge, a sanctuary, and drink was medicine for his wounds.

"Leave me alone," he said.

"All the people depending on you and you turn tail and run. Don't you know we'd all like to have a drink? This won't be the last time, but if you take that drink it'll be the last time you need to think about quitting. If you take that drink, I'm out of here for good."

"God, Sheila, I'm tired. We're beat before we start. Don't you understand that?"

"You're the one who wanted to be the captain of the ship, Hogan." She put an elbow on the bar so she could look into his face. "So if the ship's sinking, you're supposed to be the last one off, not the first. Or haven't you heard it that way?" Sheila retorted. "You're supposed to go down with the ship."

Hogan crossed his heavy arms in and put his forehead on them.

Sheila didn't let up. "We're all feeling lower than whale shit, and our great leader tails it out of the court house leaving us all out in left field. You're supposed to be our commander, not a damn coward slipping out the back door. Shit, this is just the opening round. It's going to get so much worse.

"If you take a drink now, I promise you you'll never, *never* recover. There will be no return. We knew this was the last chance for you and me, and you're throwing it away in the first round. I thought you would at least wait for the verdict."

"Right," came Hogan's weary answer.

Sheila smiled slightly. "What?" She paused and held herself in suspended silence.

"I said all right."

She sat and said nothing, waiting. Tim leaned over the bar, staring at Hogan with his lined, gray eyes. The fans overhead whirred. All along the bar glasses clinked and there was a murmur of conversation.

Hogan reached into his pocket and extracted his wallet, then shoved a hundred-dollar bill onto the counter.

"Give me a glass of ice tea," he said, and in a second Tim had it on the counter.

"Thanks, Tim," said Hogan.

"Any time."

He took the glass of ice tea with him and left straight for the office.

"That's the best drink I've ever had. I think I'll stay with it," he told Sheila when they were behind his closed office door. He put his arms around her and held her for a long time.

Finally they sat down across the table from each other.

"Don't think about it," Sheila told him. "Let's get to work."

Hours later they turned out the lights, fully prepared to attempt the impossible -- select a fair and impartial jury in Stillwater, Texas.

Hogan was besieged by thoughts as he and Sheila fell asleep. They weren't very organized, but they needed to be expressed. Sheila listened.

"I have to stick it through," he told her

"Good," she said. She was wearing a pale green nightgown and looked beautiful. "I'm listening."

"This is going to be humiliating."

"It's worth it."

"Yeah, I know." He lay back and looked at the ceiling. "I believe in the law. I always have. I believe it orders human life. It stands between us and chaos. I've seen chaos, Sheila. It's called war. The Vietnamese kids have seen it. It allows nothing for the young or for beauty or pity.

The law is a gift. To uphold it for every human being is something that has formed my life."

He stopped and looked at the glow of the bedside lamp. He knew this was a fork in the road that really was life or death to him, and now he finally understood. He had it straight. He couldn't, no matter the provocation, take that first drink. It was not even an option.

"The very worst day ahead will be better than any day with a drink in my hand. I've tried it both ways. This is not only better, it's the only way for me if I'm to survive. I'm glad I'm the last best hope for those little Vietnamese bastards; they are mine too."

Both of them were betting their love and careers on two Vietnamese killers who may or may not have a worthy cause. If it failed, perhaps what they had between them would still survive.

Sheila lay back and sighed. Feeling as if she'd been wrung out, she turned out the light.

She knew a bridge had been crossed but there were so many more to go.

Chapter Twenty-One

August 30, Stillwater

Potrero County High Sheriff Harold Fellows sat drinking beer with the D.A. at the Five Bar Lounge. Roger Davis was fondling an Old-Fashioned, rolling the short glass around in his hand while the ice melted. Sheriff Fellows considered an Old-Fashioned a sissy drink.

"I expect that they may end up in my jail," Fellows said. "Assuming the judge does the right thing and sends them here for the trial. Hell, we can make them as uncomfortable as possible, and if there's an attempt at escape, it'll be their last one."

The sheriff was the kind of law-enforcement official who thought it was probably better to be feared than liked. He had succeeded.

"Well, that's not going to make me look very good, is it?" Davis waited for an answer but Fellows went ahead and drank his beer. "If we could just get some jurors to agree that they deserve life in prison, it would be the best way to deal with this situation."

"Yeah. For you," said Fellows. He was one of the few men who could rival Billy Joe Hardin in stature and weight -- and volume. The D.A. hadn't known Billy Joe, but he'd seen the photos supplied by Judy, his widow. Sheriff Fellows looked more like him than Billy Joe's own brothers did. He was about two hundred and fifty pounds, over six feet, and he wore a ten-gallon hat that looked like it could contain twenty gallons. It was laying upside down on the floor beside the sheriff's enormous booted feet.

Fellows was known to consume enormous amounts of beer, probably a case a day, but he was still very effective. He wore a forty-five revolver, a massive badge and chewed tobacco with wide yellow teeth. Even to the D.A., his eyes seemed cold and penetrating.

"I think it's fair to say we run a tight town," the sheriff said. "I don't think any prospective juror is going to disagree with that very much. Although it might take a couple of visits."

Roger Davis knew Fellows liked being called the 'High Sheriff.' His father before him had been a sheriff for thirty years.

"I've been meaning to get back at that smart-ass lawyer Hogan, and this is my chance," Fellows said. He finished his beer and the waitress was immediately at hand with another. "I've waited for a long time. He accused my dad of perjury in a case in which he was defending a bank robber. He said me and Dad were trying to fix the jury. It damaged us both here in our community. A lot. Of course, he lost the cases. But it's still payback and in spades."

"I remember that," said the D.A. The local rock band was just beginning to do a sound test. It was about time to get out of the Five Bar lounge. It seemed like there weren't any good country-western bands any more. Everybody wanted to hear songs by the Grateful Dead and Twisted Sister.

"That's when me and Dad were just doing our duty as we saw it— helping our friends. That loudmouth Hogan has been popping off ever since."

"What goes around comes around," the D.A. declared.

"Yeah, he thought he was talking off the record," Fellows continued. "Then he's all over the papers, calling us a bunch of rednecks and bigots, saying this is no place to get a fair trial. That man is dancin' with the devil."

The D.A. nodded impatiently. "Just get up there and tell people who Billy Joe really was. Hogan's going to try to trash him. Going to say he ran the Viets into a corner. You stop that. Barret is going to do the right thing and seat twelve impartial jurors and then immediately proceed to give those boys the max. Don't worry about Barret. We just need the right jurors."

"Well, I'd be pleased to testify," said Fellows. "As a matter of fact I can't wait. And don't worry about the jurors."

When Cai and Tho arrived from San Ignacio to the Potrero County Jail, Sheriff Fellows watched as they were booked in and their few possessions transferred from the Scott county deputies to his own. He followed behind when they were shown to a cell. They were absolutely silent, and did not even speak to the young Vietnamese interpreter, a slim man almost as silent as they were, as they went to their cells.

The sheriff explained the rules to the boys through the Vietnamese interpreter. He leaned forward, towering over them. "Boys, this is going to be the last home you will have. It ain't exactly your home away from home. You can make it pleasant or unpleasant. You make it pleasant by doing what you're told."

The speech kept the frightened interpreter, who looked much like Cai, at a desperate verbal gallop, trying to keep up. Clad in a white shirt, maroon pants and dirty runners, he was too intimidated to ask him to wait. After a while, he just spoke a few short phrases.

The sheriff continued. "You are not guests, but dangerous prisoners who have committed the worst crime in the book — cold-blooded murder. It's twice as bad because Billy Joe was my friend. There is never a suggestion around here, always a command. Get out of line the slightest bit and you'll never forget it. I don't know whether you are Vietcong or not. Try to escape or step out of line and you get six holes in the back, just like you did with Billy Joe. If you stay here very long, you may decide it's not a bad way to go. Be my guest."

Afterwards, at the office, Fellows said to the interpreter, "You're the one that interpreted when they got the confession, right?"

"Ah, yes," said the man.

"What the hell is your name?"

"Nguyen Van--."

"Here, spell it." Sheriff Fellows handed the man a pen and a legal pad. The interpreter carefully spelled out his name, then Sheriff Fellows took up the legal pad, put it on his scarred desk, and looked up at the man. "Nguyen Van Muon? Huh? Is that how you pronounce it?"

"Yes." The interpreter nodded.

"Did you tell him exactly everything I said?"

"Yes."

Outside, the town of Stillwater and the main square with its great courthouse lay crinkling in the heat-waves.

"Well, it damn well better be. And the D.A. wants to make sure you say exactly what you're supposed to say. All right? You hear me?"

"Yes," the man said.

Fellows counted out three ten-dollar bills and handed them to him with a receipt.

"Sign here. That's your pay so far. Show up on time and do as you're told."

"Yes, sir. Yes." The small man took the money, walked out of the jail and to the bus station. There, later in the day, he took a bus for Houston. His plan was to never be seen again.

Reporters came to talk to Sheriff Fellows at the Stillwater jail, now that the Vietnamese defendants were in his lock-up. He was happy to speak with them. His face crinkled into a great grin.

When questioned about Billy Joe, he was enthusiastic. "He was my friend and a loyal one. I circulated a lot of his petitions about the Vietnamese and throwing them out of this country. I believed in what he was doing."

The print reporters looked at him doubtfully as their pens raced across notepads.

"Billy Joe was a real patriot. When those little bastards shot him, they declared war. The only way to end it is by the maximum conviction under the law. I just regret that we can't give them more than a life sentence, but you know, nowadays the laws are so screwed up that they always protect the criminal."

The District Clerk of Stillwater Courthouse was the person who normally sent out at random the notices to the prospective jurors for attendance at the trial. The sheriff was a cousin to the District Clerk. They knew exactly which names they wanted on the jury list.

"What do you think?" asked the D.A. He walked up and down the carpet of his Stillwater office, staring out the windows at the heat.

"We'll get who we want," assured the sheriff. He sat in the DA's office with a list of names.

It was just this activity at which Hogan had caught him and his dad years ago. Hogan had tried to get Sheriff Fellow's father indicted. Now his son was running into Hogan once again. Memories were long in south Texas, and as sharp and spiny as the cactus that embellish the landscape.

Hogan knew that Sheriff Fellows was not above shifting over to the civil side and assisting the defense lawyer who paid the highest fee for his jury selection. The higher or lesser the "award," depending on the source of his employment, the higher the sheriff's fee. It was not an unattractive bit of moonlighting for the sheriff. Sort of a fringe benefit of the job.

Hogan thought about it as he took a few moments to stroll down to the River Walk early in the morning. He needed to walk and think, cool out. The atmosphere in the office was intense, and he needed to stay away from it from time to time. In the old days, he would have hit the Esquire Bar and stayed there till he drank himself into a stupor.

The sun glinted off the placid San Antonio River. The graceful promenades alongside were populated by tourists who seemed to have not a care in the world.

"We'll manage," Hogan told himself as he passed a newspaper vendor. The papers were full of the trial.

It would be great, he mused, never to have to return to Stillwater, to simply languish in civilized San Antonio. But it was not to be.

He stopped for coffee in a little cafe near a waterfall and took out his notepad, planning strategy.

"Dad?" Hogan looked up from his coffee, his notepad.

It was Paul, walking down the riverside sidewalks, looking for him. "We need you. You have to help us with the suppression."

They discussed Tho's confession, sitting around Hogan's office table. They had two weeks before they had to appear in court in Stillwater. The confession was the only thing that tied Cai's brother to being an accomplice. It contained his admission that he assisted and encouraged Cai in the shooting. All of the other evidence, Hogan knew, was to the contrary. Without the admission, the D.A. would have no evidence whatsoever against Tho as an accomplice, and the judge, as a matter of law, would have to direct the jury to render a verdict in Tho's favor.

Lillie May sat with them.

"They say that the sheriff and the investigator intimidated them when they were first arrested and put in jail in Spanish Port," she explained. "They made them sign a confession. The interpreter who was supposed to tell the investigator what they said didn't speak English very well."

"Which interpreter?" asked Hogan. "How many are there?"

"Just the one," said Lillie May. "He interpreted in Spanish Port, and then just recently, they asked him to come to Stillwater when they were moved to jail there, and he did some interpreting for the sheriff there."

"Where is the interpreter?" asked Hogan.

"He left," said Lillie May.

Hogan looked at her doubtfully. "Left the area?"

"That's correct," Lillie May said, in her precise voice.

"Why? Where did he go?"

Lillie May tipped her head to one side and thought about it. "I think he was frightened, like most of the Vietnamese people there." She paused. "And I am not sure where he went."

Hogan frowned. "We have to get that confession suppressed when the D.A. attempts to introduce it. The D.A. knows the importance of finding that interpreter, or he damn well ought to." Hogan shook his head. "I don't know; maybe he doesn't know how important it is. Maybe he's just all good teeth and great hair."

Restless again, Hogan got up and got a drink of water from the cooler and came back again. "He has to prove the boys knew what was in the confession, and that they understood their rights. Otherwise, the prosecution will have failed as a matter of law. We have to file the motion to suppress those confessions A.S.A.P. Because, if Cai is found guilty, then the judge will have a very difficult time directing the jury to find Tho *not* guilty. That's why timing is so important."

Hogan sat down again and tapped a pencil on his legal pad.

"Lillie May," he said, "let's go down there and talk to them."

"I'll come with you," said Sheila.

"No, I need you for something more important," said Hogan. "We've got to find that Texas Ranger." He flipped through material on suppression of confessions.

"Okay, if that's what you want," Sheila agreed. It pleased her that he trusted her with so important an assignment.

Chapter Twenty-Two

August 29th

The Stillwater jail was similar to the jail in Spanish Port, the same gray-painted steel bars, concrete floors, and concrete-block walls that wept dampness. The sheriff's deputies inspected the packages that Hogan and Lillie May had brought for the boys, and then escorted them in.

They found the brothers waiting for them in the visitor's room, in a fog of cigarette smoke. Cai's face was puffy from jail food and pale. Tho, younger but slightly taller, looked particularly depressed, but they both broke out into excited Vietnamese when they saw Lillie May and Hogan.

She smiled and handed them their packages of chocolates, cigarettes, comic books with simple English phrases, playing cards and hard candy. She spoke happily to them, evidently spreading good cheer and optimism.

Hogan looked over at the deputy who stared back, rocking back and forth on his heels.

"Ask them --" he began.

Lillie May held up her hand.

"I know what to ask them, Mr. Hogan," she said. "Leave it to me." She glanced up at the deputy.

Hogan smiled. "You're turning into a lawyer, Lillie May," he said.

"Thank you," she replied.

When they returned, Lillie May went over her notes with Hogan and Sheila at the office.

"They said the interpreter didn't know what the sheriff was saying except that they were supposed to sign something. The interpreter just said, 'Say you did it and maybe they won't shoot you.' They were frightened for their lives, they said, and they signed. The interpreter said a lot of things that the sheriff didn't say, they know for sure."

"Like what?" asked Sheila.

"Like, he was telling them that the boats were being burnt and people were throwing firebombs and so on." Lillie May looked up from her handwriting. "And he was just talking about his wife in Stillwater --"

Hogan leaned forward, his thick hand around a pen.

"What?" he said. "His wife was in Stillwater?"

"Yes. Cai said that the translator didn't really know what the sheriff was saying at all. He just said things so the sheriff would see he was talking. The translator would say, '*Ma*, he is talking too fast and he makes me nervous'."

"What's *ma*?"

"That's just like saying, 'well'." Lillie May lifted a hand, indicating it was of no importance. "But Cai says, the investigator was angry and threatening. They think he said they were going to be shot by the people."

"Jesus," said Sheila. "That's outrageous."

Hogan nodded. "We've got to get this thrown out. In due time, though. In due time. Right when the D.A. tries to introduce it before the state rests its case. He'll have to find this interpreter and get him up there and get him to tell what he said. If he can find him. If he can't — who knows? The judge just might follow the law, one time."

Hogan got up and went to his office door and stuck his head out. He saw Paul coming down the hall with a sheaf of surveys in his hand.

"Paul," Hogan said. "Can you find out if the D.A. is looking for the interpreter that first translated for Cai and Tho when they were arrested?"

Paul paused in mid-step. His expression was bleak. The surveys were so overwhelmingly against the Vietnamese that they had no value, they were meaningless as an aid in helping the Hogans select a jury.

"How am I going to do that?"

"Look on the police records and get his name, and then get Father Dominic to help you look."

Paul did his best, but the interpreter, whose first name was Muon, was nowhere to be found.

Lillie May smiled when she heard the news. "Too bad." She shook her lovely head. "Too bad, Mr. Hogan."

With the help of Sheila, Paul, and Sabine, Bob Mitchell prepared a Motion to Suppress Confessions of Cai and Tho Nguyen, requesting the court to conduct a preliminary hearing out of the presence of the jury toward the end that the illegally obtained confessions be suppressed. Big lanky Bob, his bony wrists thrusting out of his frayed suit, always seemed to be drowning himself in paper, but he was never so happy.

It was clear the alleged confessions were not the product of a free and voluntary decision on the part of the defendants, but were obtained in direct violation of their privilege against self-incrimination of the United States Constitution, the Fifth Amendment, and the Texas

Constitution. They were garbled, the sentences didn't logically follow one another, and the language was often that of police procedure, not that of a Vietnamese peasant-fisherman speaking through an interpreter.

"By Jesus, my old shanty-Irish grandfather could have done a better job of confessing to a murder than this, and made it all up on the spot." Hogan laughed. "This has no more truth to it than a pig has feathers."

Hogan wrote out his argument; the defendants were not immediately taken before a Magistrate and given a legally sufficient warning of their Constitutional and statutory rights as guaranteed by the United States Constitution and the Code of Criminal Procedure of the State of Texas by the person to whom they allegedly gave the written confessions. He wrote on. Their confessions, he argued, were taken without counsel, when they had not and could not intelligently and knowingly waive their rights to counsel since they didn't speak or write English.

They were deprived of the opportunity to read and understand the confessions they were signing because no interpreter was present during the Magistrate's warning or during the warning given by the persons to whom the confessions were made. No valid waiver, therefore, transpired, when, in fact, they couldn't and didn't understand the warning given to them, if it was given, and the confessions, therefore, were inadmissible and could not be read to the defendants.

The preparation for the trial went on. One week passed and the next began to fly past, day by day, hour by hour. Hogan felt himself becoming tense. They sat down with Lillie May and Father Dominic and once again reviewed the laws of self-defense, manslaughter, murder, and murder with malice, so these terms could be translated for Cai and Tho.

"Okay," Hogan said. "Let's see. God, it has been so long since I tried a criminal case! Any other lesser charges, Sheila?"

Sheila looked up out of her shock of shining auburn hair and said, "Homicide in a No-Homicide zone?"

Hogan laughed. "That would do it." He turned to Lillie May. "Lillie May, can you somehow translate for these boys so that the jury sees things from their point of view?" He explained that her dignity, clarity, expression, and appearance, must transcend the moment and so that she, in effect, become the defendant and not the defendant themselves who were the focus. It was no small assignment.

"Can you interpret for them, say their words, so the jury'll see that they're likable, that they aren't killers? Can you be their voice and --"

Lillie May held up her small hand.

"Leave it to me, Mr. Hogan."

He nodded. "I guess I will. Do I have a choice?"

As the days went past, as they pushed toward the trial, Hogan noticed that the D.A. didn't show any apparent enthusiasm for Vietnamese interpreters.

"He's paranoid on the subject," said Big Bob in his grinding, hoarse voice. "He feels they can't be trusted."

Hogan smiled. "Maybe he's right."

One morning, Sabine dropped a note onto Hogan's table. It was from Paul. She hurried out again, bent on some task that involved a Houston telephone book. Hogan didn't ask. He read the note.

P. and Fr. Dominic says original interpreter nowhere to be found.

Hogan nodded. He liked it. They would have to use Lillie May and probably didn't even realize it.

The Vietnamese who was currently being used by the D.A., according to what Hogan had heard, was both surly and reluctant. He was an older man with close cropped hair, from Houston where there were a great many Vietnamese in the community since it was so close to the fishing ports of Galveston and Port Arthur. The translator, Thoai Con Cai, sensed the D.A. disliked and distrusted him. He had heard criticism that the D.A. felt he had put the best spin possible on the testimony in behalf of the defendants, and so the older man simply refused to put out any effort whatsoever.

Hogan knew that the D.A. had been unsuccessful in seeking out an American who could interpret Vietnamese, so he had to let it go. He felt he could get along without one, that he was not vulnerable in this area. His only accommodation thus far was to use his new Vietnamese interpreter as little as possible, and the man showed up and said as little as possible.

The judge accepted both Lillie May and the man from Houston as interpreters, examined them, and was visibly impressed. Lillie May and the older man bowed to one another, Lillie May's bow a little deeper in respect to his age.

The district attorney was still resting in the glow of having had the trial moved to Stillwater instead of San Antonio. The matter of interpreters, though perplexing, was not of major importance to him.

Chapter Twenty-Three

September Fifth, the Beginning of Trial

They drove to Stillwater in the familiar heat. It was a forty-five minute drive. They went in two cars, dodging the torn-up places and the gravel trucks, slowing down again and again for the flagmen.

Hogan had never had much success in the Stillwater courthouse. However, he was determined to be a model of deportment and gentlemanliness, a new resolution for him. The judge would find it incredible, but Hogan was certain it was the only thing that would work. No matter how unfair the charge or contention, he would answer with civility and fairness. Hogan was absolutely determined to be a contrast to the conduct of the D.A. Roger Davis was on full charge, convinced he was racing toward victory.

Hogan was eager to face the wolves, the hostile reception from the media, even the surly judge. He felt the courthouse personnel, still rankling from his remarks on rednecks, were the most fierce antagonists he had ever experienced. He told himself he would cross that bridge, no matter the barrier. Hogan's trust in Sheila was complete after the incident of the Esquire Bar, and he was grateful to have her solidly at his side.

As they drove toward the courthouse, Hogan started describing for them the scene, as if he were opening a novel.

"Outlined against a hazy November sky, the four horsemen again rode this ill-fated day. You know them: Pestilence, death, famine, and this courtroom."

Sheila laughed.

"Okay," he said. "We'll take it and pretend we are glad to be here, and grateful for the circumstances."

The Potrero County courthouse stood up above the rest of the buildings of Stillwater, solidly brick. A relatively small group of architects had designed most of Texas' historic courthouses during the period the Potrero County courthouse was built.

Most of the nineteenth-century courthouses were built after the state, in 1881, authorized counties to issue construction bonds. The County's prosperity often was reflected in the grandeur of its buildings. No building was more important than the county courthouse. It was the center of activity and its appearance reflected the vitality of the community.

As they walked up to the old building, they knew they were in a prosperous county. The courthouse itself was a three-story brick and limestone structure, with limestone columns and porticos.

The Goddess of Justice atop the courthouse was a nine foot tall statue, blindfolded, holding out her scales of justice over the rolling grasslands and horse pastures and cotton fields. Sheila gazed at statues to the fallen heroes of wars of yesteryear. The names of the fallen were carved in the stone, sad and reticent. They walked up into the shadowed entrance, still cool at eight-thirty in the morning. Their heels clicked on the original mosaic tile where it still outlined the lobby, but it was in bad need of repair. In the middle of the rotunda floor was the Lone Star of the state.

The courtroom, as always, was located on the second floor. Hogan trudged slowly up the steps. The atmosphere seemed heavy and endless. The elevator was old and creaky and nobody ever took it without a feeling of imminent disaster. Lawyers and courthouse employees knew to take the stairs. It was a trip Hogan had tried desperately to avoid, but now that he was here he was prepared to do his damnedest.

Most of the furnishings of the courtroom were antiques, beautifully and sturdily built. Inside they found old wood courtroom railings, staircases and benches on the inside. They put their briefcases on the floor and the files on the counsel table. Where it had not been painted over, the original wood finish was still extraordinarily beautiful, glowing; in contrast to the banal modern additions.

In front of the railing separating the spectators from the inner area, there was more of the original wood floor, which would have been better served without the stained and worn carpet that covered a portion of it.

Hogan stopped and looked at the familiar interior. Any courthouse held the highest respect in his heart. He believed them still to be the high temples of justice, and he wondered how many of his younger colleagues were beginning to find his beliefs old-fashioned. But as always, Hogan felt a thrill of pride to be among those present in any court trial. Pride, and the electric charge of the challenge. He knew he was both lucky and smart. He never quite believed his good fortune and so he tended to think it was more luck than anything.

He had been a Private First Class in the Marine Corps -- three times. Every liberty he'd gotten drunk and into fights and ended up busted. The only success he'd achieved had been on the battlefield. The same with lawsuits. Hogan felt they, too, were a kind of battle.

The achievement of monumental verdicts on behalf of his clients had come one after the other. They had to recognize him as one of the best trial lawyers there was, but there were a good many who thought him too unorthodox and flamboyant. He was in the headlines as often as in the courtroom, which was not, as he had recently learned, always to his advantage.

The raised bench loomed over all. The judge was paramount, and in his hands rested the administration of justice. Hogan knew that Barret, this genteel and mild mannered man, however, was consistently bullied by the district attorney. Hogan tightened his tie, readying for the conflicts that were coming.

To the immediate left, enclosed by a jury rail, were fourteen seats for the jury -- twelve seats for jurors and two for alternates in the event that something happened to any of the twelve during the course of trial. Hogan and his team had to fill those places with as much advantage to their clients as they could. Even though Hogan knew the process was going to be grueling, he was somehow looking forward to it.

To the rear of the room, there were approximately fifteen rows of twelve seats, places for the prospective jury panel during *voir dire* examination. After they had come up with a jury, spectators would occupy those same seats. Overhead were ceiling fans which no longer functioned; they had been replaced with sporadic air conditioning.

Hogan looked up. Along the walls were photographs of deceased district judges who had presided for the past century over that particular court.

Sheila leaned toward him and whispered, "What do you say, Hogan?"

Hogan shook his heavy head. "The trouble I've seen."

In a few minutes, with hostility so thick in the room you could cut it, he would be compelled to announce ready for the Vietnamese defendants. He then would begin the process of selecting a jury under circumstances he deemed impossible. The only hope he had was that, as the days wore on, even the judge would concede he had made a mistake.

The process of selecting a jury was known as a *voir dire* examination. It means 'to speak the truth.' The prospective jurors were supposed to be truthful about whether or not they could look at the evidence presented with an open mind.

Hogan leaned over to Sheila. "If ever there was a dichotomy, this is it. If the jurors spoke the truth, we would have a courthouse lynching on the front lawn, and that's a fact." Hogan already had spoken the truth, and he was damn lucky not to be in jail himself.

"I hope they do," said Sabine. She was now crisp and efficient, bringing out the files. She wore a short skirt and jacket in navy blue, her pointed collar fresh in blue and white stripes. "I mean, I hope they just speak right out about how they feel about the boys."

The two Vietnamese defendants had become 'the boys.'

"We're going to get a fair trial," Hogan said. "I mean it."

He'd spent four decades of his professional life opposing those courts and jurors who would allow corporations to kill and injure for profit, who would refuse to acknowledge responsibility. Now he was in a criminal trial, but nonetheless he had always felt up to any challenge. A trial by an impartial jury; that was Cai and Tho's rights under the Constitution. At one time Hogan would have charged in, sure of victory. He wasn't so confident now. He restlessly shifted in his seat and flipped through his notes on the legal pad as Sabine sat quietly beside him.

"Tell me about this," Sabine said. She was watching the D.A. and his staff arrange themselves at their table on the other side of the courtroom.

Hogan smiled at her. She was so young and determined, so eager to make it to law school. She made him feel old and wise and so he gave in to the temptation to pontificate.

"Like it or not, it's the best system ever devised. Our system is based on it. Judges and legislators face the temptations of money, power, and fame. The jury system, on the other hand, has no equal. These are ordinary folks, a part of the system, equal to the judges and lawyers and legislators. That's why the selection of the jury, which we're going to have here in a minute, has such great importance. If they will just be truthful about their biases and excuse themselves, we'll have the kind of fair trial the system means us to have."

Big Bob Mitchell leaned over and said, "What they're going to say is, 'We are going to really lynch those squint-eyes from the nearest tree'."

Hunched over his legal pad, Big Bob looked uneasy this morning, but that was nothing unusual. He always looked like he was hungover, but no matter the circumstances he refused to be intimidated. Mitchell militantly protected the appellate record against any onslaught to prevent his right to do so.

"You're not going to be able to select a fair jury. The judge is going to come up with erroneous explanations, and the sheriff is going to go around to prospective jurors and tell them what to say so they can qualify, and they'll salvage twelve people who will say they can and will be fair. We will use our pre-emptory challenges, continue to challenge for cause, show on the record that the challenge is good, and let the judge overrule us. I can almost guarantee a reversal because these guys want a hanging, not a trial. So let the hanging begin. We're ready. Seize the opportunity." With that, Big Bob shoved himself up and ambled to the far end of the counsel table.

Paul watched Big Bob draw an untidy stack of papers from his enormous briefcase. He was outfitted in a greenish tweed coat and oversized blue pants. Sheila had not gotten to him in time.

"He's the St. George of the damned," said Paul to his father.

"You got it," Hogan agreed.

The moment of truth was now upon him as Judge Barret took his seat and asked "Mr. Hogan, what is the plea of the defendant?"

"Not guilty, your Honor."

Judge Barret was calm and assured.

"Mr. Bailiff, call the jurors. Gentlemen, I intend to get a jury this week and would expect to conclude the case by the following week. The matter of suppression of confession and motion to dismiss has received my attention and there will be a ruling at the appropriate time. Let's proceed to try this matter with dispatch. Is that all right with you, Mr. Hogan?"

"Yes, your Honor."

They returned home, having said the words — *not guilty* — that would plunge them into the fray. Not guilty. Hogan felt they had set up a banner, planted it. They had to stand firm around it now, and there was no backing out.

Chapter Twenty-Four

September 7th, Stillwater

The next morning at the courthouse they were met by a tall, gangly six-and-a-half foot, half-bald man in his mid-thirties, who introduced himself as Steve Kendrick. He was pale and soft-spoken, an unassuming man, seeming almost insecure at first glance. It was a misleading impression. He wore a pale gray sharkskin suit that was glossy for being over-worn, over-cleaned and probably slept in. From the wedding ring on his hand, Hogan figured he was a young lawyer with a young family.

He stepped forward and put his hand out with a shy grin and said, "Mr. Hogan, I know you don't know me, but I've heard a lot of good things about you that I admire. I've seen you try lawsuits and heard you at seminars."

"Thanks," said Hogan. He wondered which seminars. Some were better than others and Hogan's sporadic memory loss made him cautious.

"Look, sir," said Kendrick. "I've just been practicing law for ten years, but I've lived in the community here all my life. I know a lot of the people here personally. Consensus has it your chances in this lawsuit are negligible to nil. People are asking why they don't just plead guilty and forget it."

"I figured," said Hogan.

"I've had the jury list for several days. I've gone over it in great detail. I've graded each name by number. I want to review this with you as to why and who might be all right, considering the circumstances. In five hundred there are twenty-five possibles. It's that bad."

Hogan nodded with a small smile. He immediately connected with the young man, who appeared sincere. Hogan did momentarily wonder at the man's offer to help, since doing so wouldn't be a popular or prudent thing in the town of Stillwater, but he quickly dismissed the thought. Kendrick's information was extremely intriguing, and heaven knew they needed all the help they could get.

"I can tell by the faces that I am not their favorite guy at the moment," Hogan said, pulling his thoughts back to the list under discussion.

"They certainly regard you personally as an asshole," Kendrick said. "But, you know, a few of these people want to do the right thing. I think they're just waiting for somebody to stand up against the D.A."

Kendrick shifted his beat-up old briefcase to the other hand. "I'll tell you something else. The high sheriff has prepared the ground for jury selection like a master. He tells them to say, 'I can set aside all I've seen and heard and give the boys a fair trial'."

The young lawyer looked a bit embarrassed. "And another thing, Mr. Hogan. The judge is my uncle. He does his best to be fair. He *will* be fair, but maybe later rather than sooner."

He paused. "If you can tone down your own style, it will help you with this judge. Some show of genuine concern for this system will go a long way with him."

"I appreciate this," Hogan said. "I'm still listening."

"I remember at one seminar you said, 'The story from the head to the heart is a long and difficult journey but you have to take it if you want to prevail. Lawsuits are decided on emotion, not logic, and you have to talk heart to heart if you are going to win'." Kendrick paused. "I bet you've wondered dozens of times how the hell you got into this case."

"Just lucky," said Sheila before introducing herself. She had come walking up the steps from the dusty blue Ford. It was almost nine and already it was nearly ninety degrees, and light tendrils of auburn hair were sticking to her temples.

"Happy to meet you," said Kendrick. "You're on the case as well?"

"Just another volunteer," Sheila answered. "I'm working with Jim on this case. I'm the file manager and a member of the Esquire Mutual Aid Society."

"She's also a lawyer," explained Hogan.

"Right!" Sheila said with a snap of her fingers. "Sometimes I forget."

Hogan smiled at her, admiring her glossy red hair and her neat blue suit.

Kendrick knew there was some kind of a private conversation going on but what it was he didn't know so he laughed and looked agreeably confused.

"Just how do we do this?" Hogan inquired.

Kendrick turned back to Hogan. He seemed hesitant and embarrassed to be telling Hogan how to conduct the trial, but he plunged on.

"Let your son do the opening argument. Let him do those prospective jurors where there is some hope of successful cross-examination. You take those that are insensitive and hopeless. Paul is presently fresh in this thing, and he'll at least have a receptive juror's ear. Maybe they'll give him some attention."

"That's not half bad," said Hogan. "We'll sleep on it." He gestured toward the courthouse door. "I would ask you to sit with us at the council table but that's asking too much. This is your hometown, after all."

"Hell, I'd be honored."

Surprised, Hogan accepted Kendrick's offer, and they went inside.

Hogan knew that a very young lawyer like Paul could be effective simply because of his youthful appearance and demeanor. Next to somebody with the D.A.'s abrasive style, it might make a great contrast. But he also knew that a young lawyer often failed to professionally recover from a bad defeat. And this case was a sure loser. He felt strongly that he was assigning Paul to a professional disaster which might be his undoing. But where was the alternative?

In many respects Paul was his mother's son. He was a gentleman, and far better looking than his father; taller, thinner, and not all used up from past debaucheries. They were very good friends and Hogan could never understand why. They were so different. Paul was kind, respectful, considerate, and he had a face designed for trust. His courtly manners in the courtroom often rendered him bulletproof.

Hogan, on the other hand, was passionate, insistent, often a messenger that overwhelmed the message. Hogan knew it but he was too long in the tooth to dramatically change.

Hogan wondered what the hell he would have done under the same circumstances thirty years ago.

Monday, September 7th, at nine in the morning at the Potrero County Courthouse, the restless crowd of prospective jurors shifted in their seats.

The judge had called five hundred prospective jurors, the most in the history of the county. Outside, the media camped on the courthouse steps. They were hot and disgruntled. The cameramen shifted their heavy cameras around from one spot to another on their shoulders, heavy battery-packs sagging at their belts. Print reporters collected in small groups under the live-oaks with iced tea and sandwiches.

In the courtroom, Judge Barret said, "Call in the first prospective jurors." He paused. "Gentlemen, are you ready?"

"Ready for the State of Texas!" the D.A. rang out.

"Ready for the defendants," said Hogan, in a far more sedate voice.

The judge was brisk. Hogan could tell the 'redneck' remarks still rankled.

"Gentlemen, the D.A. will start first. You'll be permitted a general statement to the panel, response to any questions it might provoke, and individual examination. The defense will follow. I'll expect to impanel a jury by the end of the week. Any questions? Let's get started."

They were silent and watched as the jurors were being seated and given a number for identification.

The judge greeted the prospective jurors. He explained carefully, in his mild voice, about the hours and permissible exemptions from jury duty, and went over the selection process. He then heard from those with a legitimate excuse.

Hogan listened and watched. He had been practicing the art of jury selection for four decades. The villainy of the defendant was the usual focus of the prosecution. The defense leaned heavily on the vulnerability and the truthfulness of the accused.

But the rules of the past simply didn't apply in this case.

Hogan had always relied on luck and his gut reaction to prospective jurors. Then he would carefully develop a narrative, a theme, a story with a point of view he hoped the jurors would accept. A dramatic story, one that built up to the denouement of the closing argument. But now he had to get through jury selection and for a moment he feared that, in order to find unbiased jurors, they would go through the entire population of South Texas.

Hogan tried to keep his expression pleasant and interested as the prospective jurors filed in, probably every one of them fresh from reading his remarks about rednecks in the local paper.

The D.A. had gone nautical with his tie. It had ship's wheels and compass roses in bright yellow and green. The Blue Peter waved jauntily from his tie knot.

"May it please the court and you prospective jurors." Davis smiled at the crowd. His hair was perfectly styled, sprayed into place. "I was born and raised in this area and this has been my proud job and privilege for almost ten years. I can think of no higher privilege than preserving law and order in this community, making people safe in their own homes. In their own kitchens. In their own garages. In their own trailers and boats. I will never forget the rights of the victims of crime. That's why I became a lawyer."

Hogan objected.

The judge said, "Sustained. Let's proceed." But it did little to cure the harm that the D.A. was causing. Hogan weighed simply not objecting, but he knew he had to get his objections on the record even if it made him look like a yammering jack-in-the box.

"Does our friendship or acquaintance prevent you from serving as fair jurors? Does anyone on the jury panel think they can't base a verdict on the evidence?"

The district attorney walked back to his table. "The judge will submit to you the definitions of elements of murder in this state. What we have here is a cold-blooded, savage killing. Murder carries with it what is known as murder in the first degree punishment and murder with malice. Any of you feel you can't inflict the maximum sentence in this case, a case where an alien blasted a patriotic American by the name of Billy Joe Hardin six times in the back?"

The D.A., tall and resplendent in his tie, stood square and faced the five hundred. Hogan groaned to himself. There were no hands.

"When you shoot someone in the back, and he falls face down, and you walk up and fire five more bullets in his back, *bang! bang! bang!* a plea of self-defense in our eyes is a joke and an insult."

Objection to these remarks was overruled. Hogan noticed that when Barret overruled him, he would not look Hogan in the eye. He said to Paul, "You take over. Barret is so mad at me he won't even look at me."

Paul nodded. Nervous, he looked at Sabine. She smiled at him.

"*Sois fret,*" she whispered.

"What's that mean?"

"Go rassle your alligator."

Davis turned to address the prospective jurors again. "You have a range of punishments to chose from. If you find them guilty, you have to decide the punishment. Anyone here have any reservations about your ability to assess punishment?"

No hands. The five hundred people seemed to be sitting quiet, alert, suspicious. Maybe they agreed and maybe they didn't, thought Hogan, but not a one of them was going to distinguish themselves from the crowd by raising a hand. Threatened, they were silent and herd-like.

The D.A. nodded, taking silence for agreement. He was dynamic and broad in his gestures. He calmed himself down and smiled, showing his superb teeth.

"I don't believe it's necessary to ask you good citizens any personal questions. I'm satisfied you qualify as good jurors and can be of great service to your community. We'll take the first twelve, your Honor."

The judge nodded agreeably and started to say something, but the D.A. spun on his heel and continued talking. Judge Barret was left with his mouth slightly open but he sat back and listened without objection.

"I was outraged and indignant with what Hogan has said about the good folks of Stillwater," said the D.A.

Paul shot to his feet.

"Objection, please!"

"Overruled." Barret stared steadily down at the D.A. as if mesmerized.

Roger Davis continued. "But we have to lay all of that aside and give these accused a fair trial. I'm sure we can all weigh the evidence presented and listen to what the accused has to say. As for myself, I have taken on this trial as part of *my* duty. Money has never been my goal, only justice. Stillwater is *not* a community of bigots and rednecks, and I'm outraged that any member of the bar would say such things to get this case removed out of this community where it really belongs."

Paul's many objections were promptly overruled by the judge. But Hogan noticed he did so with a greater show of courtesy. He even gave a soft admonition to the district attorney to carry on with the examination.

The D.A. nodded one curt nod, impatiently, as if to brush the judge and Paul aside.

"I'm sure you folks can give these boys, accused of killing Billy Joe by shooting him six times in the back and standing over him and continuing to shoot him to make sure that he's dead, a fair trial. And he *was* dead. Very dead."

The judge told the prospective jurors to disregard such remarks. The D.A. ignored him.

"You will be the judges of the facts. You must not be inflamed by the fact that the defendant has been indicted and you must recognize that he is entitled to reasonable doubt. We ask you to give them all that and then begin your deliberations. You can all fairly do that, can't you?"

At this point even the judge seemed taken aback at the D.A.'s cavalier attitude, staring at him and his bright tie in amazement through his glasses, but he continued to overrule the defense's objections.

He turned toward Hogan, looking down at him, seeming a bit stunned.

"Mr. Hogan, you may proceed."

"Go on, Dad," whispered Paul. Sabine sat back. Looking disappointed, she turned her great round dark eyes to the floor.

Hogan did so with greater reluctance than he had ever begun a *voir dire* examination. He couldn't see a single receptive person who wanted to hear what he had to say. Nonetheless he had to try, and so he began.

In the pleasantest manner he could manage, he walked slowly toward the crowd in his deceptive shamble, a smile on his weathered face with its whiskey lines, and his thick tumble of silver-gray hair slightly tousled. And they saw he was not as trim and athletic as the D.A., nor did he have his height, and they looked at his nose which had once been straight but was now listing slightly to port from some long-ago brawl on liberty in the south Pacific.

In his deep voice, Hogan began to tell them the story that he would tell throughout the trial.

"May it please the court and you prospective jurors. This is my one chance here to talk with you before the business of this trial begins, a trial where a life is resting in your hands. I want you to know that. And the only reason we're here now, is that I want to hear what it is you all think about this. It's a tough case. We didn't want to be in this town trying this lawsuit. How many of you are aware of that?"

Every hand went up.

Hogan nodded and looked down at his shoes, pondering it, as if he had just received some vital information.

"How many of you resent that?"

Again every hand showed their displeasure.

"How many of you resent me serving as a defense lawyer in this case?"

Again Hogan was scoring 100%. He would be on a roll in the appellate court but, in the trial court here, it was even worse than he expected.

Hogan then decided to shift the ground. He paused to introduce each member of his team at the council table, and quietly explained he had taken the case without a fee, and, more importantly, that the D.A. had not mentioned to them that a plea of manslaughter or self-defense was possible.

"The judge will so instruct you as to the definition of manslaughter. How many of you feel you can't listen to such evidence in this case?" Again a showing of at least half of the hands.

Then Hogan asked the general question. "How many of you, based on what you have read, heard, or believe from any source, including the questions we have already asked, feel you cannot give a verdict based just on the evidence here in the courtroom and the instructions given by the judge?"

More than three-quarters of the panel indicated they couldn't.

Hogan got their individual names and moved to have those people excused for cause.

The judge was in a dilemma because he recognized that Hogan would continue to throw his hard-hitting, truth-seeking questions at the remaining prospective jurors. He could see no way out but to grant the motion. The judge could clearly foresee that his calling of five hundred prospective jurors had been wise.

Hogan continued with his examination, confident that most of his questions would establish bias and prejudice. That might not do any good in this trial, but it would serve Big Bob well in his efforts to seek a reversal.

"The judge will tell you also that adequate cause means cause that would commonly produce a degree of anger, rage, resentment, or terror in a person of ordinary temper sufficient to render the mind incapable of calm reflection, and throw him into a desperate struggle for his life. How many could give any credence to this defense?"

Hogan looked into the faces of the people of Stillwater — ordinary people who would have a life in their hands. The reaction was the same.

Almost sixty prospective jurors had been eliminated for cause by the time the morning was over. The estimate of one week to select a jury had been too optimistic. They might have to spend as much as two or three weeks on the relentless task.

Hogan ground determinedly on. He shoved his hand through his hair and then tried to smooth it down again.

"The judge will also instruct you on the law of self-defense. This is the reason why these defendants are pleading not guilty. The judge will tell you the defendant is justified in using force against another and the degree of force he reasonably believes is immediately necessary to protect himself against the other's use or attempted use of unlawful force against him. How many feel you can't or won't listen to law and evidence of self-defense in this case?"

Almost universal, the group refused to entertain such defense regardless of the evidence. Hogan had just discovered his biggest weapon yet for elimination of jurors.

Speaking carefully in his low voice, Hogan explained the law on self-defense, and asked if there were any who could not consider it. There were many. Like most of the people in the room, whether they raised their hands and admitted it or not, they agreed with the D.A. that the idea of self-defense was laughable.

"If you have a reasonable doubt as to whether or not the defendant was acting in self-defense," Hogan said, "then you should give the benefit of that doubt to them and acquit them and say by your verdict not guilty."

Most of the prospective jurors indicated they could not and would not. Very few jurors remained.

Then Hogan told the ones that remained that the law allowed the D.A. to present his evidence first, but despite this, they must withhold judgment until they had heard the other side.

They listened intently.

"Can all of you promise to do that? Those that can't?"

Fewer hands this time.

Then he asked, "Because the D.A. says these boys are guilty, how many of you will accept his judgment without further evidence?"

Many did. Now there were less than seventy left.

Hogan turned and pointed to the Vietnamese brothers, Cai, who had held the gun in his hand, and his younger brother Tho.

"These boys as they stand here before you are simply not guilty under the law. That's the presumption of innocence. They are presumed to be innocent, not guilty. It's the duty of the district attorney to tell you that. He didn't. He should have. The judge will charge to that effect. The district attorney should have told you that the fact they've been indicted is absolutely no evidence of guilt. He didn't, and should have. You need to know that's the law. The question is how many feel you can't or won't follow that law?"

Other hands went up and the number qualified was less than fifty.

Hogan watched as more people got up from their seats and walked out of the dark courtroom into the blazing light of day, back to their lives in Potrero County.

"These boys like to fish. They've done it all their life. That was their occupation. It's the occupation of the Vietnamese who are presently in San Ignacio. There is competition in the waters between the Americans and Vietnamese. Perhaps there shouldn't be, but there is. And that's what precipitated the shooting.

"With that as a predicate, are there any among your number any who feel like they can't give a fair trial under those circumstances?"

Eight more jurors disqualified themselves.

"How many of you were in the Vietnam war? Based upon that premise, can you give these Vietnamese boys a fair trial?"

Four more jurors disqualified themselves.

The judge interrupted the questions. "Gentlemen, we'll discontinue for the day. We have gone through more than four hundred jurors. More will be impaneled overnight and we will continue until a jury is selected."

Chapter Twenty-Five

It had been an exhausting day. They all walked across the street to Steve Kendrick's tiny office over the drugstore across the street from the courthouse. It was becoming their home away from home, tiny as it was.

It was clearly the office of a struggling young small-town lawyer, and they were all jammed in knee-to-knee. Steve Kendrick's inexhaustible enthusiasm made up for the lack of space. A roaring window unit struggled to cool the air.

"If we went to a restaurant around town, we'd probably get mobbed," remarked Sabine.

"Yeah, maybe," said Paul. They all felt better where they were.

"Mr. Hogan, they will go out tonight to see if they can find more people for the jury?" asked Lillie May.

"Yes, and that's when the sheriff is most dangerous," said Kendrick. "At night time, when fresh jurors are assembled. He'll drop by and get them to say, 'Yes, I think they're probably guilty but I can put aside my prejudice and listen to the defense'." Kendrick gulped a cold drink. "The judge should admit he's made a mistake, but he won't. I know him. But he knows this is wrong, and I think he'll loosen up."

Kendrick, they found, rarely spoke at such length, but he was furious at the way justice was administered in his home town and his home county. His long thin frame was slumped. He was discouraged and angry, but he looked over to Hogan with admiration.

"You're killing yourself in a losing cause," he said. "I hate to see it."

"Not yet," Hogan responded. "You never know. What about that missing interpreter?"

Kendrick smiled. "You know, we have a Vietnamese maid to help with the kids. She knows him, it turns out. He's the husband of a cousin of hers. She said he's gone, and gone for good."

Hogan looked over at the young man for a moment.

"I see."

Steve shrugged. "Scared of the system. He's an immigrant, too, and it's a murder trial. I guess he thinks it's safer not to be involved."

That night, as the group stayed late at the office in San Antonio, working on the *voir dire*, they stopped to watch the television reports.

They saw that a strange thing was happening with the media, particularly the television reporters. The media were beginning to see what was happening and the tone of the coverage was changing. Media accounts of the Vietnamese trial were beginning to reflect for the first time that perhaps the defense did have a tale to tell. They had ordered in a meal and Hogan scarcely knew what he was eating.

"Is that really true? What the rest of those jurors are claiming?" asked Sabine. She paused to take a sip of coffee. "Are they really presuming the defendants are innocent? Or can any juror?"

"I hope," Hogan answered. "The way our system works, the presumption of innocence is the legal codification that man is fundamentally good. This presumption stops police or anyone else from smashing in your front door and taking you away. You've studied the Napoleonic Code. It's the code used in France and Mexico, and you don't like it and I don't either. It's abusive. We have another way and it works."

Paul and Sabine bent forward over their plates, listening intently.

"Ordinary people can do extraordinary things when they are called upon sometimes. They can drop their biases, they can keep a fair mind. We have to ask it of them. Otherwise, we expect nothing. I'm going to tell these people I expect everything. And you know, sometimes ordinary people can rise to great heights."

Paul loosened his tie and sighed. Discouragement could be read in the sloping shape of his shoulders. "We've lost two motions for change of venue, all the evidentiary hearings, and probably have had as bad a press and media attack as possible. How are we going to get past this barrage of crap?"

Hogan shook his head and said he hoped it was temporary. Then he looked over at his son and smiled some encouragement.

"Basically, there's nothing wrong with the system, Paul," he said. "It's just people who can screw it up, as always."

There was a long silence. They were all tired. Sabine arrived with more coffee. Outside the windows, in the night-time streets of San Antonio's downtown, were the familiar sounds of an ambulance screaming its way up Navarro to the Nix Hospital.

"Be prepared," Hogan cautioned. "The judge is probably going to qualify jurors by the simple mechanism of saying, 'even though you feel you have a fixed opinion, you can set it aside, can't you?' The prospective juror will be ashamed to say no, most likely. And so they're on. The judge will have the assistance of the sheriff, who will have told them what to say."

"You can't get a fair jury like that!" Sabine protested.

She had left off her jacket and now she pulled the tails of her blouse out of her skirt, looking more like the Sabine they had known for four years. It occurred to Hogan that, today in the courtroom, the young woman had looked like a lawyer. And now, indignant, she was talking like one.

"I know it." Hogan sighed and shifted around in his chair. Restless, he reached for his coffee. "The short answer is we do the best we can under probably impossible circumstances."

"So what do we do?" Sheila leaned far back in her chair and grasped her elbows, her long beautiful legs crossed at the knee. "I'm not from south Texas."

Hogan smiled at her. "You aren't used to the ways of our fair state."

Sheila smiled back. "Hey, it's the same in Georgia."

"You know, people become as attached to their prejudices as they do to their material possessions. I think we'd rather give up our bank accounts than our stereotypes. People are afraid there are too many immigrants in this country, too much crime in the streets, and that maximum punishment is the answer. They think if you're hard on criminals, if you're hard on crime, it will cure the underlying ills of society. This overlooks the problem of poverty and broken homes as things that spawn crime in the first place. We're called on to care for the needy and the deserving and the downtrodden, but it seems our country is more convinced of the importance of warning people against welfare cheats. We have become a vindictive, racist society," said Hogan.

"Dad, that's good," Paul rebutted. "But we're in the here and now. The folks down there are probably making voodoo dolls of you." Paul was impatient. His thin frame was hunched over his coffee cup. "And they think Cai and Tho are some kind of Chinese tong gangsters."

"Okay," said Hogan. "Don't remind me. But maybe we can convince them that the boys and their lawyers are unpopular, *but* not guilty beyond a reasonable doubt. What Cai and Tho did can be explained by their cultural differences, if anyone will listen. Somewhere along the line, we are bound to get some good breaks, guys, because so far, our luck has been so damn bad."

They all nodded and looked at their coffee cups or the carpet and fell silent again.

Hogan finally said, "It's late. We've got to wind this up. I need some down time."

"Give me some wisdom on this judge before we go," said Paul. "We need it."

"Well." Hogan pulled his tie completely out of its knot. "A lot of judges want to clear their dockets and complete the case. I don't know the track record of this one, but so far, I'd put him in that category."

Paul shook his head. "I think my course in life is going to be trying to pick my cases, and stay away from ones like this one."

Hogan laughed.

"Cai and Tho are like most criminals. They commit crimes they can't afford to commit. So here we are, at no fee. But I've been going on and on most of my life about how we all have to give back for what's been given us, and now here's my chance. I just didn't intend to give *this* much."

"I think we have a chance," Paul said. "The system is, you don't have to prove your innocence, but the state must prove your guilt."

"Yeah, but you'd better come up with a good story anyway," replied Hogan. "A damn good one."

Sabine shook her head. "The things I've seen go on in my county over in Louisiana. In Chicot Switch! Mr. Hogan, sometimes I think ordinary people means ordinary bigots."

"Sabine ..." Hogan pushed his papers together and slid them into a file folder as a prelude to leaving. Sheila noticed. She reached for her shoulder bag while still listening intently. "All of my life in the legal profession, I have said the ordinary people who sit as jurors in this country, sometimes for as little as six dollars a day, are hard-working folks. They're retired people or still active, people who gained wisdom through experience, as school teachers who care for and understand children, factory workers who work with machinery and have experienced the trouble of strike, and small businessmen who fight for survival and know about the harshness of banks." He sat up, energized again by the expression of one of his profoundest beliefs. "These are people who know something about America and life, and right and wrong, and pain and guilt and fear and anger and love."

They all sat spellbound, hearing something they already knew was true but needed to hear again. They needed to hear it spoken with passion to bring that fundamental belief back to them once again in all its power.

"And when people like that are assembled together, think of the years of experience they've gone through. They know more than any judge or lawyer in this country. Even with all the crap we've run into, I still say you want a jury of ordinary folks. If you are in difficulty or charged with a crime, if you had a choice between a group of intellects who've led very protected lives and a motley group of ordinary people, take the advice of an old man and pick the ordinary ones."

Sabine smiled. "Okay, *bien sure,* Mr. Hogan, I'll keep on going on faith."

"That a girl," said Hogan.

"Well, gotta get back to my office and start on that motion to suppress confession," Sabine said, gathering up her papers and heading for the door.

"Thanks, Sabine," Hogan said. "I appreciate your dedication."

She smiled. "You are sure back and running again, Mr. Hogan."

"I guess I am," he said. "It's those peach-and-mint teas you've been pushing at me."

"I knew it," she said with a big grin. "And I haven't even started on my Cajun voodoo brews yet."

"Don't work too late," Hogan told her.

"I won't."

Hogan took Sheila's hand and they walked past the receptionist's desk and out the door. It was a hot night, but misty clouds were rolling up in ranks from the southeast and far overhead the grackles flew past, as if running from a coming storm.

Chapter Twenty-Six

September 8th

Early the next morning, Hogan slipped out of the apartment and headed for early mass at San Fernando Cathedral. He walked down Market Street to Plaza de las Islas and crossed the Plaza. He happily entered the portals of the old cathedral.

It was the oldest sanctuary cathedral in the United States. In a small recess reposed the remains of the heroes of the Alamo. At the front was the baptismal font used in the baptism of Jim Bowie. From the time of its opening until the present time, the City Council met in the old Cathedral in a special ceremony to begin their term of office. It was the spot from which all geography was measured in San Antonio. It was the place where Santa Anna had set up camp, unlimbered his cannon, and shelled the Alamo. It was on the tower of this Cathedral that the Mexican commander had run up the red flag of No Quarter.

The apse of the cathedral had been built in 1731, the first Spanish settlers giving freely of their labor and what money they had in order to build it. The front part, with twin towers, had been erected in 1875, the carved stones fitting in perfectly with the ancient apse behind. It was done in the classic Gothic style, nothing showy, nothing modern either, and tall stained-glass windows were added. The light came through the windows in long shafts, bearing with them the heat of the south Texas day, shining with dust-motes.

In the very back, men were buried in the wall in the medieval style, Hispanic and Anglo alike. Beneath his feet was the old *camposanto*, whose bodies had never been removed, and so beneath him slept the very Spanish founders of San Antonio, in their long cool dream of peace, awaiting a final awakening.

Drunk or sober Hogan had been going there for almost thirty years. The only times he missed were when the hangovers were just too much. When he was drinking, he came because he couldn't sleep. When he got sober, he came because he'd gotten too damn much sleep.

It was a place for early mass, for silence and peace, for a moment of reflection before the pressures of the day. At five in the morning it was cool and every stone seemed to be filled with potential light.

Many years ago, Hogan had given his pledge to his mentor in the Marine Corps. If he made it out of Iwo Jima alive he would attend daily mass. He'd survived Iwo. The chaplain, Father Mahoney, hadn't

Hogan had kept his pledge. Well, almost. There'd been gaps in his observance, but he'd always returned.

Like his daily exercises in the gymnasium of the basement to his building, he missed it terribly when he couldn't make time for it. Hogan found peace and serenity in this two-hundred-and-sixty-year-old cathedral as he did nowhere else in the world. He seemed to shuck off the cares of the world as soon as he walked in the door.

He often attended an early mass where there were no celebrants except himself and four or five down-and-out alcoholics and street people, and the priest.

The seats were wooden and hard, but Hogan found them just right. He loved to light a vigil candle, think of all his departed family and friends, count his blessings, and review the events of the coming day. No matter the problem, in the solitude and quiet of the cathedral he could gain a degree of tranquillity like nowhere else.

Through the years he had met many priests coming and going, parishioners old and young, nuns and postulates, and the drunks and derelicts and down-and-outers for which the cathedral was known. Hogan's patience for the oddballs of life seemed infinite, and he thought of them as friends.

Over the years he had always come alone and left that way as he walked back to his office two blocks to the east.

Throughout the Vietnamese trial, the others occasionally came, too, without a word of encouragement from Hogan. Sheila first, then gradually the children, and later even atheist Big Bob Mitchell. Each in their own way found peace and comfort within the old walls, and then they could rise to fight another day in Stillwater.

New prospective jurors were present as the judge told Hogan to continue with his examination. As always, Cai and his brother Tho sat without expression. Lillie May's quick tonal murmur was a running commentary in Vietnamese.

Hogan began again with all of the questions which had disqualified so many the previous day. This continued until late Friday night.

Fifty jurors survived after the first days of questioning. Hogan held individual examinations, aiming at further disqualification and also trying now to put forward his point of view, his story, as he questioned them.

Then Hogan addressed the prospective jurors once again. A superb storyteller with a mission.

"Okay. Here is something that is very important." He leaned a hand on the counsel table and spoke to them in conversational tones. "Upon arriving here in the car this morning, I heard on the radio about this trial and about what the chief of police down in San Ignacio feels you ought to do. In effect, lynch them."

"Objection!" shouted the D.A.

Judge Barret looked at Davis, flushing slightly. With obvious reluctance, he said, "Now just a moment, sir. Now just a moment. It was on the radio. Overruled."

Hogan began to feel good; he went on. "And there is a great deal in the local newspaper about this trial. Now, is there anything on the radio, or the television, or the newspaper that would prevent you from giving a fair trial?"

There was no response this time.

"How many of you have lost sons or daughters that served in the Vietnam War?"

Several of the prospective jurors were Vietnam veterans or the spouses or parents of Vietnam veterans. Hogan knew that the victim deserved consideration, but so did the Vietnamese defendants. A terrible war had been fought with the premise that their voice and rights were important, and this was the time and place to prove all was not in vain.

"In all of the publicity about this case, did you read or hear that these brothers were in the war fighting for and with American Marines? That they lost everything, mother, brothers, sisters? Is that something that might give different insights into those matters if you have heard about them?"

"Of course," said a few. Hogan found that some were at least listening for the first time in five days.

"How many of you know these brothers had to leave Vietnam or be killed by the Communists because they fought alongside of the American Marines?"

"Objection!" cried Roger Davis.

"Well, let them respond," said Barret in a mild and reasonable voice. "Overruled."

The reaction from many of the prospective jurors was affirmative.

"How many of you have heard that the Vietnamese don't pay taxes; that they live on food stamps after they get here?"

All hands were raised.

"The truth is, they do pay taxes and they refuse food stamps. Did you know that?"

The prospective jurors sat with dubious looks on their faces.

Hogan asked how many of them knew Judge Barret, senior judge in the community?

Most of them did, and favorably Hogan could tell.

Hogan took a moment's pause and then told them that Judge Barret agreed that the media had misquoted him, and then, most important of all, Hogan felt, he told them something to stiffen their spines against pressure; any kind of pressure.

In his low, rumbling voice, now crisp with urgency and conviction, he laid before them the fact that none of them should ever give way against their own personal beliefs.

"You should never relinquish your rights as a juror. If you believe something, you hold onto it no matter whether the others are for you or whether it's popular or unpopular. You never surrender your will to the rest of your fellow jurors. Hold on to what you believe," he admonished. "No one can ever force you to give up what you believe. Do you understand that it is the right thing, not the popular thing, we will be asking you to do? How many can do that?"

Hogan saw something in their faces then, a small nod of agreement. He smiled. There it was. That Lone Star look. Fierce individualism. It was a two-edged sword, he knew, that cut both ways, but for the moment he and they were in agreement. And then the moment passed.

"The judge will tell you something else that's very, very important. Nobody — the sheriff, the media or the D.A. — have any right to talk to you after you become a prospective juror. Has that happened to any of you?"

Great quiet seemed to visit the small number of people left. Some said they had said hello to the sheriff and just visited, and the same with the D.A.

"Do you know that after you are selected — if you are — absolutely no one is to visit or talk to you about this case? If they do, you report it to the judge. Such conduct is wrong and illegal, did you know that? On your oath as jurors, will you promise you won't permit that to happen?"

The judge listened with interest and waved away the D.A.'s objections.

Several more jurors were excused for various reasons. One man stubbornly maintained he just didn't like the defendants. Rudolfo Saenz was middle-aged and looked like a solid, hardworking citizen.

Surprised, Hogan asked, "Why not?"

"Well, I just don't like them."

"There's almost no one here in this room that likes them," Hogan said. "But, I mean, is there a serious reason why you don't?"

Rudolfo Saenz said stubbornly, "No. It's just that I don't like them. Period."

Hogan persisted. "And not liking the Vietnamese, you couldn't give them a fair trial?"

"Right."

Saenz was excused.

Another woman seemed intimidated by the highly-charged atmosphere around the case. "Well, it's sort of like there's politics involved in it, and so it'll be kind of hard to get a jury to perform the right thing." She looked out at the courtroom through thick glasses. "In my opinion, if they could have half of them Vietnamese and half American, it would be a better deal to me."

"Because they are Vietnamese ...?" Hogan began.

"If I would get picked," she interrupted, "and say that way, by God. I would do it."

Hogan said, "But God isn't doing the picking. I am."

"Well, there's politics involved in it." She scanned the courtroom again, huge behind the thick lenses. "If it was an innocent verdict, they might find out who was on the jury and you might get something done to you."

Hogan frowned. "You mean, politically you might be hurt?"

"Well, I heard a lot of things, like they shouldn't even get a trial. I mean, either way, it could hurt me or my family."

Hogan turned and said, "We would challenge for cause."

Barret said, "I'm going to sustain the challenge."

Two ex-military men, both colonels, were faultless in their replies and remained on the jury.

Once again, Hogan explained to the remaining jurors.

"Do you understand each of those rights to a fair trial are constitutionally the right of each of us? If it is wrongfully taken from the least of us — Vietnamese fishermen and former Marines — then we are all in jeopardy." Satisfied that he'd done all he could do for the moment, he nodded his head and turned back to his counsel table.

Then, even though they knew it was hopeless, Big Bob put forth his case as to why the challenges for cause to the remaining jurors should be granted because of their prior answers. The judge refused his motion for mistrial, and seated and swore in twelve jurors and two alternates.

Over coffee at Kendrick's small office, the young lawyer said, "Do you know you're going to get two retired colonels who served in Vietnam?"

Hogan nodded while the rest listened.

"Yes. I don't know why in the world a man can't be fair just because he fought in Vietnam and made colonel," said Hogan. Just being back in the courtroom again, when he thought he would have to leave it forever, had fired up his boilers. He gulped his coffee. "These kids were on their side. Are we ready to go?"

The highway back to San Antonio was dusty and crowded with machines and workmen laying the new, wider pavement. They were glad to see the towers of the city in the distance. The case had become a cause, a mission, a crusade, a philosophy. It was firing up everybody's boilers.

In composition, the jury consisted of six men and six women. The composition broke down like this:

The first juror, whom the judge admitted over objection as they all were, was Jack Sheppard, retired for three years. He worked as a roofer, bricklayer, janitor, and mechanic.

The second, was Charles Mayes. He'd previously served as a jury foreman on a criminal case. He was a pressman for the local newspaper.

Next was Sam Washington. He was a retired Lieutenant Colonel. He was an infantryman in Vietnam for two tours, and then later an attorney with the JAG for ten years.

Fourth, Sam Wright was a Staff Sergeant in artillery before retirement. He served in Vietnam and then served twenty-one years before retirement. He was in the aircraft control after retirement at Kelly Field.

Fifth was Mrs. Joyce Chapman, an elementary school teacher whose husband was retired from the Air Force. He had been a pilot.

The sixth juror was Mrs. Eunice Benjamin. She'd retired from civil service seven years ago. After that she did upholstery work and her husband was also retired because of medical reasons. He worked in civil service.

Seventh was Charles Down, retired. He was a fireman in the emergency flight-line fire department in Corpus Christi Naval Air Station.

The eighth juror was Mrs. Sue Rector. Retired, she'd been an English teacher in junior high for thirty-two years.

The ninth was Loyce Harris, a military wife, with a husband in the Air Force. He would be retiring the next month as a chief master sergeant. Mrs. Harris had worked in the civil service for fifteen years.

Tenth was Mrs. Guadalupe Rosas. She worked for Santos Valley Mills and her husband was a trucker.

Number eleven was Lionel Richardson who had retired as a full colonel three years ago. He was twice in Vietnam, twice wounded, and subsequently given disability retirement.

The twelfth juror was Joshua Taylor who was a retired colonel, who'd been a tactical fighter pilot.

The first alternate juror was Virgil Crews, a retired electrician. He'd worked at Brook Air Force Base for twenty-six years.

The second alternate was Ralph Norwin, an accountant with a masters degree from St. Mary's University.

Hogan had been praying for the one juror who would champion the cause of the Vietnamese, but in this group he couldn't find one.

The two who were an absolute terror in Hogan's heart were the retired colonels. Both of them had fought in Vietnam, had strong opinions about the war and the Vietnamese, and felt that law and order was slack in this country and jurors needed to be of stout heart and noble minds. They both wanted to serve to see that justice prevailed, and they had both said they would be open-minded about the evidence.

Their answers were too unbelievable, for Hogan, in view of their background. After all, they were Vietnam veterans. In his judgment, they were just waiting to inflict the maximum penalty. They were the leaders and the others would follow.

The jurors were impaneled, sworn to do their duty, given instructions by the judge, and the trial was to begin the following morning with opening statement by the D.A. and then the defense, if they elected to do so at that time.

But Hogan had decided to hold out. He would not give an opening statement until the D.A. rested his case. He would simply lay in wait for the D.A.'s witnesses and get facts out of them through cross-examination. Then, later, when he had established some credibility for the fact that Billy Joe had driven Cai into a corner, Paul would give an opening statement.

At the office, Hogan once more sat down with Lillie May to go over her interpreter's role. Despite her assurances, he knew that Cai and Tho both tended to look furtive because they were so terrified. Sometimes they looked absolutely sinister. Hogan knew this jury had to be made to like them somehow.

"They look fairly unsympathetic," he explained. "In all lawsuits, you can never dismiss the power of likeability. The jury needs to like our clients. A jury will find a reason to convict a defendant they don't like. It's not fair, but that's life. Lillie May, you, on the other hand, are one of the most likable people I know."

"Thank you," she responded. "I understand what needs to be done." She smiled reassuringly at Hogan.

"If you don't, if you can't, we are walking a minefield that is going to blow. We are back in Vietnam— you have to go carefully, carefully."

"Yes," she said. "I can do this. I have been in many minefields. So have they."

There was no break in her confidence, no breach in her alertness and optimism. She amazed Hogan. "The jury will listen to me," she promised.

"But Cai never seems to say more than two words at a time," Hogan complained. "He never explains himself, never gives details, offers stories."

"But *I* will." Lillie May smiled again. "I know what he means to say."

She was alert, sensitive and beautiful. She was five feet of fierce determination. Her English was excellent, a reflection of her penetrat-

ing intelligence. She was a good listener. Hers was a heavy responsibility, but Hogan believed she could be formidable as she stood beside Cai
and translated, if only Cai would just say something, explain. He
hoped Lillie wasn't thinking of making it up. She would never get
away with that. But he had no better advice.

"You'll just have to get across to the jury, somehow, that these guys
aren't all that bad."

Lillie May nodded once, smiling confidently, and said, "Leave it to
me, Mr. Hogan."

Hogan shrugged and then nodded. He wasn't sure she really
understood just how bad things were. They couldn't have gotten a
worse trial if they had been back in Vietnam.

Chapter Twenty-Seven

September 9th

At the jail in Stillwater, Cai and his younger brother, Tho, languished in their gray-painted cells, smoking incessantly. Every day Sheriff Fellows advised the boys that their attitude had been surly and uncooperative. As a result, they couldn't expect full meals or any meals, if it continued. They regarded him with their black eyes and nodded and said nothing.

He also told them that they might want to change their plea from self-defense to guilty to save a lot of time.

Fellows leaned against the bars. "Throw yourself on the mercy of the court, and you might have a chance," he recommended. "You are in deep, deep shit. That lawyer from San Antonio you got is nothing but trouble."

The boys nodded again and looked at one another. The sheriff was convinced that they understood English perfectly well. How long had they been in this country anyway? Three years. That was long enough.

He suggested that they might want to make complaints against Hogan to the Bar Association for his poor preparation and lousy remarks about Stillwater.

"Damn show-boat. He popped off about our town being full of bigots and rednecks. You boys are going to have to pay the penalty for him being a big shot and stupid," he told them. "Lawyers like him believe they go to the movies while the clients to the slammer. It's a cinch you boys are going to the slammer for the rest of your life. Now if we could just figure out a way to send him with you."

The two Vietnamese were perfectly silent. The only movement was when they lifted a cigarette to their lips.

Fellows laughed at the thought of Hogan in the slammer.

"Boys, we've got a hostile crowd out there. It might be that some of our citizens feel they should lynch you, and not have to go to all of the time and expense of this trial."

He returned to his office in front of the building, thinking they might not have understood a word he said. Where was the Vietnamese interpreter who'd done the translating for the confession, when they were first thrown in jail down in Spanish Port? The chief of police down there, Cotton Wheeler, said the guy had evaporated.

The district attorney went first, and he was even better than Hogan thought that he would be. Hogan had a high regard for the district attorney's ability, if not his integrity, or his ties. Today's masterpiece was a wild mixture of magenta and mauve.

The district attorney obviously felt confident and relaxed. He looked good, a man who could work hard and play hard, and to top it off, he was a moderate drinker.

Moderation was not that usual among prosecutors because of the nature of their business. The work was repetitious, Hogan knew; the opposing lawyers not the brightest nor highly motivated, and the dismal, incompetent petty criminals that were the prosecutors' daily diet as defendants was hardly inspiring.

The opening statement was for the purpose of outlining the evidence to be presented and how it was to be accomplished. Its purpose was not to argue or motivate, but rather to make a presentation which better enabled the jurors to follow the testimony.

This district attorney rarely followed this pattern. Even though he was prematurely arguing the case, the objection, if granted, would be a rebuke from the bench in the mildest of tones. Over the years the judge had become very respectful of the D.A. and the D.A. appreciated this.

Roger Davis began his remarks, as usual, by pausing to look each juror in the face for about five seconds. He was looking them over, and drawing attention to himself because of the pause.

He began, "I've been your district attorney and prosecutor and leader for law and order in this community for many years, and this is one of the most important cases I have ever been involved in. It's not just that one of our more popular and lovable, contributing citizens of the community was shot six times in the back, mercilessly, by a Vietnamese, whom the defense attorney — who doesn't like us very much anyway — will identify as a foreigner in a foreign land. Well, nobody dragged him here. He came voluntarily. No, he just couldn't wait to get here.

"To top it off, the Vietnamese would excuse it by saying it was done in self-defense. It's hardly self-defense when you shoot a man in the back. It's hardly self-defense when you walk over to him and load five more shots into him after he's on the ground dying. That may make sense in Vietnam, but not here in America."

"Objection!" Hogan stood. "He's arguing the case!"

"Overruled," said the judge.

The D.A. went on as if nobody had said anything.

"You know that Billy Joe left a loving wife and three children, and that he had been a citizen in San Ignacio all his life, and his family before him for generations. The Vietnamese, on the contrary, didn't want to get along. Billy Joe was the one man who insisted they *fit in*, act like the rest of us if they're going to come to this country. Is that too much to ask? To abide by the laws of the land they wanted to adopt? He was the one man who stood against the killer. So Cai Van Nguyen ambushed him, shot him in the back once to drop him, and when he was trying to crawl away he walked up and put five more shots into his back. No mercy, ladies and gentlemen; he showed no mercy. Five shots in the back when Billy Joe Hardin was down."

The D.A. paused to let this sink in. Hogan could tell it was sinking in, very well and very deeply.

"Objection!" Hogan said.

"Sustained," said Barret. Then in his mild voice he said to the D.A., "Please keep to presentation of the evidence."

The D.A. paced the courtroom, and finally began to talk about his presentation of the evidence. He would show the jurors that Billy Joe was shot in the back at a distance of two feet; that Cai had fled the scene after throwing the murder weapon into the bay.

Then the D.A. concluded with, "We know what life is like without law and order. The law clearly states that somebody who shoots someone in the back six times is a murderer. There is no other possible viewpoint."

At the conclusion, Hogan could have sworn the jurors, almost to the person, nodded their approval and agreement.

"That was one hell of a performance," Big Bob whispered in his loud voice. Hogan flinched, and looked up at the judge.

Judge Barret inquired of the defense whether they intended to make an opening statement.

Hogan said, "Your Honor, if it please the court, we will reserve opening statement until after the district attorney has made his presentation of the evidence."

Judge Barret looked at the D.A. for a few speculative moments and then nodded. Addressing all of them, he said, "Mr. Hogan, I expect the prosecution will complete its case within the week. And so we will see you at nine in the morning."

Sheila had bought tickets for the symphony at the Majestic Theater, and they made their way through the lobby at seven Saturday evening. It was a weekend and Sheila was determined that they would not work through it. They would go to the symphony, to the McNay Art Museum, even the zoo.

Hogan held her arm as they wound their way through the crowd. It was supposed to give them some relaxation, something other than the obsession with the trial, with law. That narrow obsession had been one of the wellsprings of Hogan's long descent into alcoholism, and he knew he must avoid it, so he decided he would enjoy the evening.

Sheila wore a slim-cut dress in dark brown crepe. Hogan noted it had sequins on it and a slit up one side. Heads turned as the tall red-head made her way ahead of him, up to one of the boxes on the right-hand side. He was properly starch-fronted and black-tied, and told himself this was part of the regimen. They made their way into the box.

"What are we listening to here?" he asked. The lights dimmed and he pushed his glasses back on his nose. "I'll bet the damned high sheriff isn't sitting around soaking up culture. He's out visiting with prospective jurors."

"Don't think about it," Sheila instructed.

"And we have *got* to find that Texas Ranger! He's the only credible witness we've got. He's off fishing in the Arctic or ..."

"Ssssh," said Sheila. She laid a finger on his lips. "No trial, just music."

"Well, then, what is it?" He felt himself becoming impatient.

"Mozart. *Eine Kleine Nachtmusik.* The pianist has come all the way from Boston."

The pianist sat down at the Yamaha grand and flipped his coattails out behind him in a rather flirty motion. His teeth and the piano keys were ablaze in the footlights.

"Cute," said Hogan.

"Sssshhh." Sheila bent forward. "He's supposed to be very, very good."

The opening bars poured out from the pianists' hands, the clean, almost otherworldly purity of Mozart. "Oh, I love it." She leaned back, and the sequins glittered.

"I'm Irish," grumbled Hogan. "All we know is fiddling and whiskey. And I'm Texan, too, so throw in Bob Wills."

"Hogan, for Gods' sake!" Sheila said in a harsh whisper.

He put his arm around her shoulders, sighed and tried to listen. But his mind was on the high sheriff, and the D.A., and Tho's confession, which he had to get suppressed. He suddenly realized people were applauding, so he began to applaud as well, feeling like a trained seal.

Next was something from *The Magic Flute*, the program said. He put one hand to his face and leaned his elbow on the armrest. It was lively and spirited orchestral music, and the arms and leaping fiddle-bows in the string section were fascinating, moving together as they did, like preying mantises, but he found himself beginning to think about Judge Barret.

When was the Judge going to wake up and realize the D.A. was going to win this case by stampeding the jury with all this law-and-order rhetoric and by walking all over the rules, and leave the judge to be reversed on appeal, while the D.A. went off covered in glory? The D.A. didn't give a damn if the decision was reversed. It would land on the judge. A reversed case could dog a judge for years. The D.A. would be up to his garish tie knot in a political campaign.

Damn! If he could just get the confession suppressed. It might at least free Tho, who really was no accomplice at all, who was innocent in both fact and intent.

"And that depends on the interpreter," he muttered.

Sheila looked over at him.

"Hogan," she chided. "You are talking to yourself about the trial. This is amazing. Right in the middle of *The Magic Flute*." She started to laugh. "Do you really need me?" she asked.

He looked at her intently. Now, all of a sudden, she wasn't laughing.

"I love you," she said. "Or I guess I've fallen in love with you." He listened as she qualified herself. "But do you really need me?"

Hogan was so taken aback. He was, for a moment, speechless.

"Yes," he said, finally.

"For what?" She looked at him intently.

"For everything."

"I don't know." She turned back to the performance and her eyes were on the orchestra. "It's possible all you really need is the courtroom." Her lovely auburn hair glinted in the subdued light.

"Where is this conversation going?" Hogan questioned.

Sheila let out a long breath.

"I was thinking maybe Hazelden is the place for me, after all. I'm watching you disappear into the courtroom and nothing but the courtroom."

The music filled the air around Hogan with its invisible structures and he knew she was right. He had to be able to turn it off. He closed his eyes briefly and ran his hand through his thick mass of gray hair.

"Don't make up your mind right this minute," he said. He hoped it sounded like a joke.

"I'm not. We'll go on to the end of the trial, whatever it brings, and then we'll see."

Her took her hand and they sat there in silence through pieces from Hayden and, to his complete surprise and delight, a full orchestral arrangement of Scott Joplin's *Solace: a Mexican Serenade.*

"That's wonderful!" he exclaimed. He leaned forward as if to catch every note. "Ragtime! I would never have imagined."

They made their way out with the black-suited, sequined crowd. His mind was working furiously — it never seemed to work any other way — as he held Sheila's arm. They were out on Houston Street and the crowd was dispersing in the hot night, cars driving up to take on passengers.

"Listen," he said, "I have a really weird idea." They walked across the street to the Gunter Hotel, looking for a coffee shop.

"Yes?" She seemed more distant than before; maybe what she said had been on her mind for a while.

He said, "That ragtime piece was the best thing I've heard in years. Maybe it's time I looked into some other world than law. Music. Hell, I bet I could learn to read music myself."

Sheila laughed delightedly. "I can't believe you! Isn't it late to be starting? Could you really?"

He stopped in the lobby of the Gunter Hotel and put both hands on his hips, making himself look even beefier than he was.

"Damn right. You know what? I am going to learn to play the piano, and by God I will play Scott Joplin. Name your favorite piece, madame."

She stood looking at him, smiling. A little doubtful.

"All right," she said. "*Weeping Willow.*"

"That's your favorite?"

"Yes."

"All right."

Two days later a second-hand Holloway upright appeared in the Casino Club apartment, hauled in from the freight elevator by four sweating movers.

After that, instead of thinking for hours about things he couldn't change for the moment, and if he and Sheila weren't in a meeting, Hogan often plinked away with his stout fingers on scales and exercises. He suddenly found it comforting and intriguing.

Chapter Twenty-Eight

September 11th

It was Sunday night. They had gathered in Hogan's office. In the the distance, from St. John's church, they could hear the bells chiming eight o'clock. Hogan hated to work on a Sunday, but the next morning was the day the D.A. was putting on his witnesses, and he knew the D.A. and his minions were not resting on their laurels down in Stillwater.

"If you don't mind me asking, why the hell didn't we give an opening statement?" Paul asked, obviously disgruntled.

"Because we have so damn little to say," answered Hogan. "We are playing for time, for a break of any kind."

Sheila was working very hard on proposed cross-examination. She had unconsciously stepped back into her role of defense attorney without knowing she was doing it. She and Paul and Sabine had come up with good cross-examination which Paul was going to conduct on the state's witnesses. All of them were trained as lawyers and they'd fallen into step with one another easily.

They gave their extensive review to Hogan for comment.

"This cross-examination can be effective if you do it, Paul," said Hogan. "Something may come out of this case for all of us. Cases have a way of taking on a life of their own. Tomorrow we announce 'ready,' and Paul, it's largely your show." He picked up his files. "Sheila, what's on for tonight?"

"*Weeping Willow*," she said. "We've had enough meeting for this Sunday night."

Hogan laughed.

"What?" said Sabine. She looked over at Hogan curiously.

"Dad got a piano," Paul explained with a shrug.

"*What?*" Sabine repeated. "Why, Mr. Hogan, I didn't know you could play."

"He's learning to play it." Paul opened the door for Sabine. "I'm not kidding. He'll do it, too."

Hogan and Sheila left out of the front doors, and he stood for a moment to look up at his office building.

"You want to know how I came by this?"

"I know your personal history," said Sheila. "Not your business."

"Want to hear?"

She nodded.

As a boy in grade school he'd sold newspapers in front of this very building in downtown San Antonio. At that time it was the First National Bank and to him it was the most beautiful building in the world. It was three stories with a basement and a sunroof, made of limestone with a stately cupola on the turret and large pillars of limestone as the front archway.

Sheila looked up at the curious little alleyways beside it, and the slope to the river walk behind it.

Hogan told her that it was the first national bank chartered after the Civil War. The founder was a friend of Abraham Lincoln and had made a fortune running contraband and smuggled goods through the weak southern blockade. The bank had been an immediate and continuing success for more than a hundred years. Among the old Colonel's bank customers were Charles Goodnight, the greatest trail-driver of them all. There was Shanghai Pierce, Mifflen Kennedy, Captain Richard King of the King Ranch, and San Antonio trail drivers John and Ab Blocker. They'd walked in fresh from the trail with bank drafts or letters of credit and, often enough, satchels of gold double eagles. Though many later customers were more gently reared, as they said, the old bank still sometimes seemed to contain a faint echo of the ring of their spurs.

It had been the most prestigious bank in San Antonio, but the population of the city had begun to head north, and then the last owner died. The director decided to close the bank and move north too. It remained closed and sad for seven years.

After his return from the war, Hogan explained, life had taken off like a rocket. Marriage, kids, lawsuits, all-night drinking parties. He was Pecos Pete riding the tornado. Sheila laughed. His Irish gift of language could always make her laugh, no matter what. They strolled down Navarro street, toward Shilo's restaurant.

Hogan told her he had gone to the University of Texas in journalism, then he became a sports writer, and then a lawyer. The first twenty years involved low verdicts, tough judges, unfair legislation and laws favoring the corporations and wrongdoers. But suddenly the favorable legal skies had opened for him -- for the next two decades. Hogan became one of the outstanding lawyers in the country.

One day in a small neighboring town he got the largest verdict in the history of the United States — twenty-five million dollars for a young boy terribly burned in a truck-trailer explosion when the truck overturned and exploded.

Hogan had immediately purchased the building of his dreams, the building he'd fantasized over all of his adult years. He restored it, keeping the old teller's cages intact, the cathedral ceiling, and the wainscoting. He tiled the lobby walls with paintings and sculpture. It became known as the Hogan Building and its clientele were the poor, weak and unrecognized, in contrast to the influential, the rich and the opulent, who had supported it for a hundred years. Hogan had shared his good fortune, contributing to every good cause that came along. He had, like most Texans, supported the Democratic party.

"That's quite a story," she said. "When you were selling newspapers, did you really ever imagine you would own it?"

"I don't know," he answered. "All I knew was maybe I'd work there. Be in it, if nothing else. Be dressed in a suit and tie and be somebody."

"You are somebody," Sheila said, and smiled up at him.

"Yes. Just ask the jurors in Stillwater."

She poked him in the side. "Ssshhhh. We have a meeting to go to."

He hailed a taxi and they were off to a meeting at the Oblate Seminary.

Chapter Twenty-Nine

September 12th

They drove down in their two cars, the five-year-old blue Ford and the dark metallic-green Buick. Sheila kept her window open, enjoying the fresh morning air which would soon dissipate in the heat of the day.

The judge began the trial promptly at nine. The crowd was dangerously overflowing, in and out of the courtroom. Surprisingly, the court had refused T.V. cameras. Like a Greek chorus, the Hardin family was in attendance, crowded into the front rows along with other spectators from San Antonio, San Ignacio and Stillwater. The Hardins watched with avid interest. The media from throughout the country was camped out around the courthouse, resting in the shade of the live-oaks and running to the various cafes and restaurants in town for doughnuts and coffee.

The air of the second-floor courtroom was stale from the overworked air conditioning.

"Mr. District Attorney, you may proceed," said Judge Barret.

The D.A. responded, "The state is ready."

"And what says the defendant?"

Paul responded with much less confidence.

"The defendant is ready."

The defendants were dressed in modest clothes provided by Lillie May and Sabine. They had had fresh haircuts, and looked as if they had been skinned. They were pale from their incarceration, and Cai looked around with furtive glances.

Hogan had entered Billy Joe's fish-knife, the one he had cut Cai with, as evidence, and it lay on the counsel table with its paper tag, looking as if it were for sale in a junk shop.

Lillie May was seated on Hogan's right, interpreting each time the district attorney asked a question, and then interpreting the response. Cai's brother, Tho, leaned forward to hear her.

The first witness called by the district attorney was the pathologist, Dr. Clint Lyons. Hogan listened as Dr. Lyons began with a thorough description of the injuries. The doctor concluded with the opinion that the first shot was fatal and the additional shots no more than an expression of the malice of the defendant, and a sure bet that Hardin was dead.

He described the trajectory of the bullets, indicating that the first shot went in the back and upward through the heart. Dr. Lyons explained that Billy Joe was dying almost immediately.

He described the other five shots as a downward trajectory. It was his opinion that Billy Joe was lying face down and back toward Cai when the other five shots were fired from mere inches away. Dr. Lyons testified that the distance was not greater than two feet at the time of the first shot and much closer with the additional shots.

The pathologist's testimony was considered crucial by the district attorney, as he knew Cai's testimony was to the contrary.

As the D.A. drew him out, the doctor said there was no evidence that Billy Joe had been advancing toward Cai, nor any action that could pose a threat to Cai at the time of the shooting.

"Billy Joe never saw Cai draw the pistol or fire a shot," the doctor said. He said it firmly and looked down at Cai.

The D.A. nodded, respectful of another professional man. He asked for a physical description of Billy Joe and Hogan felt a flash of hope.

"About six foot one," said Dr. Lyons, "and approximately two hundred and twenty pounds."

Nothing was said of the size of Cai but Hogan would get to that himself, and with relish.

Paul got up to cross-examine the pathologist, clearing his throat and looking up anxiously. He knew the witness was hostile and anxious to do even more damage. However, the theory of self-defense was in desperate need of repair.

Paul began ever so lightly. "Doctor, I suppose you agree that your knowledge wouldn't extend before the shooting itself?"

"I'm not sure I know what you mean."

Paul gestured with his hand as if he were at a loss for words to explain himself. Hogan looked over at the jury. First impressions were often indelible. Mrs. Chapman, the elementary school teacher, was looking with a kindly and interested expression at Paul.

"For instance," Paul said, "whether Billy Joe had stomped Cai with his boot and broken his fingers just before the shooting would be a matter beyond your knowledge?"

"I didn't examine anyone other than the deceased! Why should I?"

"Well, that's why it's fair to say you don't know whether, immediately before the shooting, Billy Joe stomped and broke Cai's fingers with his boot?"

"Of course not!"

"Cut him with his knife?" Paul paused and the doctor shook his head in a disgusted gesture. "Beat him physically? Threatened to kill him and throw him in the ocean? These events are all beyond your knowledge?"

"Objection!" cried the D.A. "Duplicitus and irrelevant!"

The judge instructed Paul to break it down, which he did. Each time, the witness was compelled to say, "I don't know."

Finally Dr. Lyons said, angrily, "There were six shots in the back, and he was retreating. He wasn't coming at this Vietnamese man."

Paul tried to soften the effect of testimony, which obviously was harmful. In a polite voice, he asked, "You are aware of the immense difference in weight and size of the deceased and Cai Van Nguyen?"

Dr. Lyons was furious at being pushed into describing the difference in physical size, at being asked to testify about previous fights.

"No, sir, I am a pathologist. I don't examine the accused."

Paul felt well advised to quit with the few compliant responses he received, and backed off, thanking the doctor as he stepped from the witness box. As the doctor walked out, Hogan saw him nod to several of the jurors in a friendly way. Obviously, he knew them.

The next three witnesses were high school students who had seen the actual shooting while on their way home after a basketball game. Hogan quickly saw that their major weakness was their eagerness to testify, and to go beyond the bounds of the questions. They had an exciting story to tell, and woe to any lawyer who tried to guide their answers. Freshly scrubbed and dressed in their Sunday best, they wore white shirts and slacks. The oldest even had a tie.

The D.A. got up, walked toward them with a man-to-man smile and began his questioning.

Gene Byford was a handsome, sturdy, blond young man of seventeen. He'd obviously spent most of his young years outdoors. He gave great, energetic affirmative nods as the D.A. asked if he had seen the shooting.

The jury leaned forward in concert, eyes on the young man.

"I saw Cai creep up on Billy Joe. He kind of looked like a creeping Indian. He could almost touch him when he fired the first shot right in his back. Billy Joe fell face down. And then Cai kept shooting. Man, there was smoke and bangs ... I didn't hear him yell or anything but I saw the blood. His pistol was inches away. I think he quit because he ran out of bullets."

Paul, in cross-examination, sensed that the young man was not antagonistic, simply well-coached.

"Gene, you were there when Billy Joe cut Cai with this knife?"

"I didn't see a lot of that, because I ran when I saw the knife."

"But it did happen. Cai was bleeding from the chest when you ran away?"

"Yeah. I think so. Billy Joe was cussing at him. He yelled something."

Paul listened intently, then asked, "What did he yell?"

"I couldn't hear him so good. I was running too fast."

"In the past, you'd heard about Billy Joe beating up on Cai?"

"I don't know how many times. I guess I heard it, but I can't remember."

Paul nodded, and paused for a minute. Hogan knew that this was where all that newspaper clipping was going to pay off. Paul looked up, his face all innocent. "But didn't you tell the reporters that Billy Joe had cut Cai's tires?"

Gene sat stone-still for a minute, startled, caught in the light of his own past words. Talking to the reporters had been such fun. What had he said? "Uh . . . that's just what I heard." His voice was low and less sure.

"And didn't you say he tried to run him down in front of Flores' saloon?"

Paul's face was sympathetic as the young man tried to remember what he had said to the reporters.

"Well, I didn't see that. I just heard it."

"How about Billy Joe stomping Cai fingers and breaking them?"

The witness shrugged, and looked at his fingernails. "I didn't know any of that. But, yeah, I did say I had *heard* that."

Paul felt he had gotten so much more than expected, and something told him to quit.

"Thank you," he said abruptly.

Gene started to get up but the bailiff signaled him to wait.

The district attorney went back for a concluding question. "Would you describe this as a cold-blooded killing?"

"Oh, yeah, man. Billy Joe didn't have a chance. It was like a firing squad."

The witness was excused, and Gene gratefully left the stand, feeling as though he hadn't done as well as he was supposed to.

Hogan watched as the D.A. called Jerry Curtis. The eighteen-year-old was possibly the brightest of the eyewitnesses. Roger Davis was becoming cautious with the young men, realizing that the importance of being an eyewitness was leading them into dramatic recitations that might go anywhere.

Jerry Curtis was slim, nearly six feet, red hair, freckles, bright expressive face and eyes and a definite Texas drawl. The young redhead told the court that he had seen some kind of a fight between Cai and Billy Joe at the dock, and had hung around to see what was going to happen next.

"Cai was mad enough to kick a hog barefooted. He jumped in an old car, and they took off as fast as it could go," Jerry Curtis said. "They came back in just a few minutes. Man, I knew there was going to be trouble. I saw Cai jump out with Tho trying to hold him back."

The next portion about Cai was unexpected, but Jerry was a difficult witness to contain. He was an athlete and leader in the classroom.

He had been counseled by the D.A., but he had a mind of his own.

"Cai had a pistol in his right hand. He kind of crept up and then ran toward Billy Joe. He shot him while his back was turned. He was probably three to six feet from him the first shot. He was close enough to where he couldn't miss, and Billy Joe yelled this kind of big yell. It was awful." He paused and sighed. "Then Cai ran over to Billy Joe after he fell with the first shot in his back, and pumped about five more shots into his back while he was face down. It's like he wanted to make sure he was dead. Cai took off after the shooting. That's all I know, but it was brutal, man. Brutal. Cai looked to me like he planned it all, including the escape."

A smug look on his face, the D.A. sat down. He was clearly interested in seeing what Paul could do with that one.

Paul began cautiously with little expectation. "Jerry, didn't you sign a statement for the investigator that said you didn't actually *see* the shooting?"

Jerry said he thought he had. He said it shamefaced, obviously embarrassed to be caught out on his dramatic testimony.

The district attorney denied any knowledge of any statement, surprised and indignant.

Jerry said, "You know, I think I did. I may have. But I talked to the other guys and the district attorney, and I guess I'm wrong. But I sure remember them typing up something for me to sign."

Patiently, in his mild voice, Paul said, "So when you say you thought Cai was kind of an expert at what he was doing in firing the pistol, it may be that you never saw him at all?"

Hogan saw several members of the jury frown, including one of the two colonels.

Jerry showed every sign of confusion. "Yeah, but I think I did. I know that sounds crazy, but I've probably talked to too many guys. Like reporters and everybody."

"Were you told not to talk to us about what you knew?"

"Yeah. I thought that was crazy, because I've got nothing to hide."

"In this statement, which the district attorney says he doesn't have, did you say Cai and Tho were pretty good guys? You certainly told the Houston papers that."

Jerry smiled with a wry twist to his mouth. "I may have, but you know, I didn't really know them. I probably meant that was their reputation."

"And didn't you in this statement say Billy Joe could be pretty scary when he was drinking?"

There was a long silence. Finally, Jerry said, "Well, you know, he was so big and he liked to yell a lot and drink a lot. I mean, that guy could drink enough to float a bass boat."

"As a matter of fact, he was yelling at Cai that he would cut his throat and throw him in the water?" Paul asked.

Jerry considered, turning his head to one side. "Ummmmmm ... not in those words."

Paul continued with no sign of impatience. "What words do you remember?"

"Well ... something like 'ocean,' but I think he was just threatening and didn't really mean it." Jerry looked up at Paul. "Billy Joe was more talk and show than action."

Paul nodded agreeably, then he asked, "Would it be fair to say that the district attorney and sheriff helped you to review the whole thing before you testified?"

"They just helped to refresh me. I've never done this before. But, yeah, they told me how to act."

"And did they do this with the other two boys?"

"Sure, so we could help each other."

"Kind of get your stories straight?"

"I guess you could put it that way."

"In other words, so that you could all pretty much not contradict each other?"

"I guess that's right, but they always reminded us to be sure everything was the truth. And that's what I've done, you can be sure of that. I ain't going to lie for nobody."

"To the best of your ability, but you remembered it better at the time you made this statement we don't have?"

"Yeah."

"Last question, Jerry. If Billy Joe threatened to kill you, would it scare you?"

"You better believe it. He was one big dude."

Redirect by the district attorney, obviously irritated with his witness, was brief.

"Jerry, you are certain, aren't you, that Cai slipped up on Billy Joe and shot him in the back and five more times after he was laying on the ground?"

Jerry looked suspiciously at the D.A. It looked to Hogan like he was thinking how he'd had been caught out on the matter of the statement and was feeling somewhat betrayed.

Without enthusiasm, the young man replied, "I'm sure about the shooting, but not the number of times."

The witness was excused.

The next witness called was Dudley Smith, age sixteen. Dudley was small for his age, and shy and not very talkative. He was the most nervous of the three. On direct examination by the district attorney, he testified that he knew nothing of any threats or violence, but he did witness the shooting.

In a low voice, he said, "The best way I can describe it would be that it was like an assassination or a drive-by shooting. Boy, it was cold-blooded. Billy Joe was just walking away, and he never knew what hit him."

With a barely concealed smirk, the district attorney turned to Paul. "You may inquire."

Paul walked up toward the boy. Dudley was staring at him wide-eyed. Paul asked, "Was Billy Joe related to you, Dudley?"

"Not me. Just my mother. Cousins or something, I guess."

"And he was a good friend of the family?"

"Kinda. He wasn't over at the house a lot. Billy Joe and Dad drank a lot of beer together at the Flores Lounge after fishing part of the day. He wasn't no friend of mine particularly."

"Were you at Flores bar when Billy Joe chased Cai and Tho around the bar and they escaped through the back door?"

Paul shook his head. "I wasn't there. I just heard about it."

"Did you hear that he was threatening to kill them?"

"Objection! Hearsay!"

The objection was sustained. The jury was watching the witness, silent and attentive.

"Did you also hear about the knifing that happened just minutes before the shooting?"

"I didn't see that. I might have heard about that, too. I think I saw the knife. Big one."

Paul felt he had gotten all he could and so the witness was excused.

The judge interrupted after the witness was excused.

"Gentlemen, it is near noon. Let's adjourn until one."

Chapter Thirty

"What do you think?" Paul asked Hogan. They were reviewing the morning at Kendrick's office. As usual, they were packed in tightly, with Paul even sitting on the floor. Lillie May had come this time too. Often she went back to the jail to visit with Cai and Tho and reassure them that things were going well.

Kendrick's young wife came to the office, to make coffee and hand out something to eat. "Keep your blood sugar up," she said. Today it was chips and salsa and sandwiches. There were soft drinks in a cooler and the old air-conditioner wheezed and roared.

"We got much more than could be expected," Hogan said. "The boys were well coached but difficult to control. The judge was amazingly easy in letting in all of the hearsay about what others had heard."

"Boy, all those quotes from the newspapers, they are saving us," Sabine remarked.

Hogan nodded. "I think we're done with his witnesses who are telling everybody about the actual shooting. From here on, I think it's just hearts and flowers as to how good a guy Billy Joe was."

"The sheriff is real pissed off because he still can't find his Vietnamese interpreter," Kendrick remarked. "And somehow the rumor got around that he was being taped when he was talking to the boys."

"Oh, dear," said Hogan. "That's unfortunate. Now, how did that rumor start?"

Kendrick's small dark-haired wife smiled. "Like we told you, our housekeeper is Vietnamese and the interpreter is her cousin's husband. She says the interpreter at the confession is nowhere to be found. So we spooked Sheriff Fellows by sending word that his talks to the boys were taped." She smiled again and lifted her hands. "What do I know?"

"So, where *is* the mysterious disappearing interpreter?" Hogan asked.

"We heard he's gotten another job out of town, and the sheriff is near panic trying to find him," Kendrick answered. "I don't know if the district attorney will call Sheriff Wheeler to testify in behalf of Billy Joe's character, but I think he will, because the sheriff has a lot of friends on the jury."

"What about the man he has now?" Hogan asked. "You know, the elderly man?"

Kendrick laughed. "The D.A. thinks they're all moles."

"Let's hope he's right," Big Bob added. "I think I can help with the sheriff's scenario when the time comes. By that time Hogan will be so pissed off that he'll revert to his true character; revolting." Big Bob lit one cigarette off the end of the other and the blue smoke drifted in layers about the room. He wore a pair of ochre-colored polyester slacks with a wide belt and a Nehru jacket in bright blue. He puffed, and said, "Imagine thinking Hogan could go through all of this stone cold sober. The day of miracles is still with us."

Hogan shook his head. "If you just want an easy life, you're missing most of the important things. Until you give yourself to some great cause you haven't even begun to live."

"Is this the cause?" Paul asked.

"It's the only one we've got," Hogan replied.

That afternoon, District Attorney Roger Davis was looking forward to his best witness, Chief of Police Cotton Wheeler of Stillwater.

Cotton was a 'good old boy' down to the core. He was built like a sparkplug. There'd been a bartender prize fighter back in the old days named Tony Galindo, and Hogan thought he and Cotton Wheeler looked exactly alike.

Cotton walked confidently toward the witness stand, and turned to sit down. About five-eleven, and well over two hundred pounds, he settled himself easily in the witness chair. He looked over at the jury with eyes that were dark and small; his narrow mouth was set in a stern line. He shrugged his broad shoulders inside his coat, and his chest expanse was vast and his hands looked like they had great strength. He was all muscle, hard and tested by many brawls and fist fights to prove it.

For the ten previous years, Cotton had been a homicide detective in Houston. When the job of chief came open in San Ignacio, he grabbed it.

Chief Wheeler had bought a special uniform for just these kind of occasions; solid blue pants, skin-tight light blue shirt, with chevrons on the blue uniform coat. There was a lot of gold braid on the epaulettes. He wore on his Sam Browne belt a pair of handcuffs and a forty-five magnum, with a holster and bullets in their cases all around. His white hat was embroidered on the top and sides.

Hogan shook his head. Cotton Wheeler could easily have passed for a full general or admiral, if adornment meant anything. And Paul knew he was in real trouble when neither the audience, jury or judge seemed to think Cotton was dressed funny.

Cotton was sworn in and his testimony began. Like most law enforcement officers, he knew what he was doing in court testimony. He was very attentive and polite, and talked mostly to the jurors.

First, the D.A. went over his record. He had been a cop on the beat for five years in Houston, then vice, then drugs, then homicide. With that and his present job in San Ignacio, he had twenty-five years of total service. Cotton had also been to many FBI sponsored seminars and schools.

Nearly an hour was spent on this dialogue between Davis and Cotton, establishing his record and credibility. Hogan rolled a pencil between his fingers, put it down, picked up a paper clip, tried to keep a straight face and listen.

Finally the questions began.

"Chief, how did you find out about this killing?" The D.A. leaned forward, as if he had never heard the answer before and was intensely interested. He wore a tie of black and white and red, the red bits were like loose piano keys and the black and white was scattered in star formations. It was a startling tie. But it was, after all, the late 'Seventies and men were being encouraged to be daring, break out of the old sartorial mold, and the D.A. had taken it to heart.

Cotton coughed to clear his throat before answering. "I was having a cup of coffee. A kid came running and told me to get down by the boats as Billy Joe had been shot and that one of the Vietnamese did it. I left without even paying for my coffee."

"What did you find when you got there?"

"A bunch of people. Billy Joe was laying on his face. He'd been shot in the back, big holes. I cordoned off the area and notified Doc, our medical examiner, and the forensic team."

The D.A. said, "Tell the jury if you found any weapons or ...?"

"I looked in Billy Joe's pickup and there were no weapons, rifles, knives, or anything in that pickup. There was blood on the back of the truck close to the tailgate. I think he grabbed hold of it when he was falling. I took pictures."

The pictures were introduced for the jury.

Cotton continued. "Then I started rounding up witnesses. We didn't find the gun, but we got the killer."

"Did you know Billy Joe?"

"Yes, I did," Cotton said, gravely. "There was nothing wrong with the man. He was a great American. He had a marvelous family, and he didn't deserve to be cut down at the age of twenty-eight."

"Objection," said Hogan.

"Overruled," said Barret promptly. As usual, when he said it, he refused to look at Hogan.

It became obvious that the judge didn't intend to curtail Cotton, even though Hogan saw he was being largely irrelevant and non-responsive. This was Cotton Wheeler's day, and the judge was going to let him have his full say.

"Did you recover the murder weapon?" The D.A. stood relaxed now, as he had a good witness on hand and no surprises lurking in corners. His black-and-red-and-white tie stood out in the dim courtroom like a comet.

The chief shook his head. "No, we didn't. We dragged the bay, where they said he threw it. But it was never recovered. Then both of the boys ran. It took us only days to re-capture them. They were picked up in Port Arthur." He shrugged his wide shoulders. "Only guilty people run. That's twenty-five years of experience speaking. If it was self-defense, he would have gutted it out and stayed to prove it."

Hogan got up. "Objection," he said.

"Overruled," said Barret, looking out across the courtroom.

The only person happy about the situation was Bob Mitchell, even though he was dying for a beer. He was thrilled with the record of error he felt was being created by endless objections and endless overruling, for no reason other than the judge didn't want to offend Cotton. Big Bob felt Hogan might not prevail, but he damn sure was going to have a lurid record of complaints for the appellate court when they appealed what was surely going to be a guilty verdict.

Hogan seemed reconciled to the inability to be heard, but, in truth, he couldn't have felt worse. Each nail was driven harder into maximum sentence and Cotton was the hammer.

"Well, Paul." Hogan looked over at his son.

Paul took a deep breath and stood up. Chief Wheeler watched him approach with an interested look.

"Chief, have you been accused of pistol-whipping 'the Viets,' as you call them?"

"Very few times. There wasn't anything to it."

Paul frowned as if he were confused. "You mean you only pistol-whipped them a little?"

Hogan looked over at the jury. The schoolteacher and the fireman and one of the colonels were looking doubtfully at Cotton.

"No, young man, I mean the accusations were exaggerated. If guys get into a fight and I have to separate them, I occasionally have to knock somebody on the head a little. It has a calming effect."

Paul, smiled. "I see. So there have been times when --"

"I clipped one of the Viets over the head, yes. They got into a tangle with some of the crabbers."

"In other words, Chief, you feel there are those times when you need to take the law into your own hands and mete out justice as you see it."

The chief of police crossed his arms and stared at Paul. "I don't think it has anything to do with these boys killing Billy Joe Hardin."

Paul nodded and walked back toward the counsel table, down at the end where Cai and Tho sat, listening to Lillie May translate. She stopped, and all three of them looked up at Paul and across to the chief.

Paul said, "Chief, you mentioned several times about these boys killing Billy Joe. Which boy did it?"

They were dressed similarly in cheap, but new, polyester slacks in a dark color, and neat white shirts. They looked so much alike, their faces both frightened and stoic, that there was really no particular identification. The brothers peered out of their taut masks of faces with expressionless black eyes.

The chief picked out the wrong one.

"Chief, what's the name, in your judgment, of the man who did the killing?"

"Uh ... that one. Cai did the killing." Again he pointed to Tho.

"Now, of course, you don't know that because you weren't there. All you know is what you've been told, isn't that correct?"

"I was there immediately afterwards."

Paul didn't know how this was going to help him, but the chief had misidentified the accused and he felt that was some small gain, so he went on.

"Chief, you've identified Tho as the killer. You just identified the wrong man."

"Well, there they are sitting together," the sheriff answered. He was exasperated. "They look exactly alike."

"But that's just proof that identification by eyewitnesses can be very misleading."

The chief was obviously getting furious.

Big Bob whispered, "Paul's doing a great job, even if it's not going to do any good. He might as well have fun."

"Sssshhh," said Hogan. Hogan wondered sometimes if Big Bob had learned to whisper in a sawmill.

But the chief had also talked freely to the newspapers, and Paul went to the counsel table and came back with some of the clippings in his hand, bending over them for a quick look.

"Well, Chief Wheeler, you told the Houston and Dallas papers that Billy Joe had cut Cai and had stomped him one time at the dock, and that there was bad blood between them. Let me give it to you exactly as you said it. 'I do know that Billy Joe had been quick with his knife and had cut the boy, and I do know that he had threatened to shoot Cai and throw him in the ocean'." Paul looked up and smiled.

The chief snorted. "The media makes things up. Those reporters have got to have something controversial. If you read it correctly, those are misquotes. You ought to know about misquotes. Mr. Hogan has had a bunch."

"But you said it, sir," Paul said stubbornly.

The district attorney complained, by objection, that the witness was being badgered. The court granted the objection and said, "Let's proceed. If there is a point, perhaps you've made it. The matter is now argumentative."

Paul went on, but it was grueling. Chief Wheeler had had far more experience in testimony and cross-examinations than Paul, and Hogan, back at the counsel table, felt as if he were slowly being wrung out. Chief Wheeler maintained again and again that Cai and Tho were known as the troublemakers among the Vietnamese, that they had pulled up traps and crowded the other crabbers. He said again and again that Billy Joe was a good family man, and if he occasionally got into a fight or drank too much, it was no more than any other man had done. Yes, he had the knife with which Billy Joe had cut Cai on the chest, but Cai had preferred not to press charges, probably because he was in too much trouble himself.

"Cai had been living in San Ignacio for two years," said Paul, desperate to make a positive point. "The only one with a police record was Billy Joe."

"Yeah, but Billy Joe is the one who's dead."

The chief left the stand larger than life, and even more like General Patton than when he first went up.

Paul sat down, looking, as Big Bob said later, as if he'd just pumped a railway hand car clear across Texas.

The Ford started and then died with all the indicator lights on. The temperature gage ran up as high as it would go and they stood fainting in the heat while Kendrick called a local garage.

It was the water-pump.

"Go back inside," said Kendrick. "In my office, and we'll have it going as soon as possible."

They had it towed to a garage on the highway, and Hogan stayed to watch. He wanted to talk to the garage man. Kendrick stayed with him.

There was some racketing noise as another mechanic used an automatic bolt-puller, and the place was full of fumes.

"You all working on that trial?" the mechanic asked. He had his head down in the bowels of the engine.

"Yes," said Hogan. "What do you think of it?"

"Boy, I don't know." The mechanic laid his cigarette down on the edge of an axle hub on the floor. He blew out a stream of smoke. "I think it's the heat. I think they're goin' to find him guilty because of the heat." He bent to the engine again with the water-pump in one hand.

"The heat?" Hogan and Kendrick looked at one another. Hogan's tie was pulled loose and he carried his suit jacket in one hand.

"That jury's goin' to want to get out of there as fast as they can and get back to their lives, and it's hot and everything," the mechanic explained. He began to put the water-pump into place. "So it's real simple to do a guilty. It'd take some thinkin' to do a innocent." He stood up and reached for the cigarette and took a drag. "That's what I think."

Hogan took a long breath. One discouragement after another.

The Ford was repaired and they drove back to San Antonio a bit more hopeful. They had begun to establish their story. At the office in San Antonio that evening, Lillie May and Sabine were working on the format for Cai's questions. Sheila was still trying vainly to get in touch with the missing Texas Ranger, whom they felt would tell the truth about Billy Joe if she could find him.

They had finally prevailed on Georgia Cadwaller to give them Lambert's home phone number in Rockport, on the coast, a favorite spot for retirees. Slim Lambert's wife told them he was up fishing in the Canadian wilderness, near a town called Vermillion River, and he usually flew on a bush airline called Blue Arrow.

"It's not too late to call," said Sheila. She looked at her watch and began to dial. Although the rest of them were busy, they were half-listening.

Sheila looked up from the telephone and said, "Well, thanks, let us know."

She clapped it back down and brushed a strand of hair away from her light-brown eyes. She had a short silky dress on in autumn colors, and it showed her legs to advantage and made her auburn hair glow.

"Any luck?" Hogan paused, his shirtsleeves rolled high on his arms. He had a sandwich in one hand and a brief on another case of self-defense in the other.

"No. That was Vermilion Bay, Ontario, Canada. A bush-plane outfit. Supposedly, he's gone fishing in a place called Slate Falls."

"Hmmmm." Hogan looked at his sandwich and realized he was probably not going to be able to eat it. "Can you call this town, this Slate Falls?"

"First of all, it's not a town, it's some very remote Indian village. And then, they don't speak English there, this guy said. Just the Indian language, and he's gone with a guide."

Sheila sighed. Then she suddenly snapped her fingers, picked up the phone again, looked at a notepad with telephone numbers scribbled all over it. She dialed again.

"Hello? Yes, can you refer me to a bush-plane line? Or outfit, or whatever you call it?" She was silent for a moment. "Yes, and that goes into Slate Falls? Um hum. Thanks."

She pressed down the button until she got a tone and began dialing again.

"It's called Blue Arrow Airlines. Yikes." She listened. By this time Sabine and Paul had also drifted in. Paul sat on the edge of the desk.

"Hello? May I talk with one of your pilots that flies to, uh ... Slate Falls? To the fishing camp there. Okay, there *isn't* a fishing camp, there's just lakes all over. Right. But don't you have a flight into there?"

She listened, and looked up, and saw them all watching and listening. She put her hand over the mouthpiece. "They go when somebody wants to go. It's not a regular flight or anything." She took her hand away and said, "Okay, we're looking for a man named Slim Lambert, he's from Texas ... okay, a couple of days ago. Well, can you call there?"

She listened for several more moments. "Wait," she said. "I have to explain this."

Sheila looked up at them, her hand over the mouthpiece and said, "They have a radiotelephone connection, but he says — get this — the radio-telephones don't work when there's a lot of northern lights. He says it's high-frequency radio and the northern lights interfere, and there's a lot of northern lights right now." She turned back to the receiver, and said thank you and goodbye.

Hogan shook his head. The man had just disappeared into a northern wilderness.

"I know!" Sheila said. "Let me just go up there and get him."

"Are you out of your mind?"

"Do I sound like I am out of my mind?" Sheila snapped back. "Am I doing anything else around here worthwhile? The man has disappeared into the bush, and half the time you can't get through up there. The nearest place is an Indian village that only has one telephone and that's not even a telephone. It's some kind of radio that doesn't work if there's an aurora borealis. I'll just go up there and rent a plane and pick him up. Bingo."

"Bingo, my ass!" Suddenly Hogan felt a quick constriction around his heart.

The thought of Sheila going off into the northern wilderness left him feeling abandoned. She was talking about jumping ship when he needed her. Maybe he hadn't told her that enough. Maybe he hadn't given her the challenging, lawyerly work. But he was too proud to get humble, and especially not in front of everybody. He stood with both fists on his hips and his suspenders askew, glaring at her.

"We need him *now*," said Sheila. She slammed her pencil down.

"Absolutely not."

The rest of them were perfectly silent. Sabine looked at Paul and at the office boy who stood with his mouth open and a stack of papers in his arms.

"Since when did I join the Marines?" asked Sheila.

"I'm captain of the ship, Sheila. Somebody has to be in charge in this madhouse."

Sheila crossed her arms over her small breasts, and the silky dress pulled into tight creases. Her brown eyes sparked as she glared back.

"Do I have anything really important to do? Maybe I could run to the supermarket and get some brie and wine? Or maybe I could come in a tutu and sell cigarettes."

"Stop!!" yelled Hogan. He took a breath. "Everybody stop. Let's quit for the night."

At eleven that night, Sheila was rolled up in a comforter with two pillows on the living room couch, brushing her hair out. She heard, from the dining room the first tentative phrases of a Scott Joplin rag, first the melody and then two more bars of the walking bass. Then she heard his gravely, raspy voice.

"Still mad?" Hogan called.

"Yes!" she flung herself back down in the pillows. "And don't come in here!"

"Shall we have breakfast together?" Seductively, she heard him play the melody again. It was the lovely *Solace.*

"No." She picked up her hairbrush, and began stroking out her hair with such vigorous angry strokes that it crackled and flew.

"Try to look at things from my point of view," called Hogan. "I need abject slaves, a red-hot sex partner, a full-time housekeeper and a skilled secretary. Is that too much to ask?"

"I'm not joking. And I'm not going to Stillwater tomorrow."

There was a long pause, and then his voice was sadder than ever as he said, "All right."

Sheila spent a sleepless night, mainly counting money. She had not depended on Hogan but had brought her entire savings with her and she was calculating the cost of a ticket to the Canadian wilderness.

Chapter Thirty-One

September 13th

The D.A. again called Sheriff Fellows as a witness to testify as to Billy Joe's character, despite the fact that the man had the two Vietnamese defendants in his jail. Some of the print reporters frowned slightly, and a television reporter, sitting in the spectator's area taking notes for a later report, seemed taken aback. She frowned and wrote something quickly, then looked up again to listen.

The big man lumbered up to the stand. He was clearly pleased and confident. He even winked at one of the jurors. Hogan and Kendrick looked at one another and then looked away, shaking their heads.

To the preliminary questions he explained that he was born and raised in Stillwater, was a high school football hero and had succeeded his father, who for thirty years had been sheriff of Potrero County. Hogan could sense the silence behind him among the spectators.

The D.A. nodded respectfully as he listened to the sheriffs credentials, and then asked, "Did you know Billy Joe Hardin?"

"I sure did. He was a close friend, a patriotic American and a good family man."

Hogan was sure he was once again dragging himself to his feet for nothing, but he did it anyway. "Objection."

Surprisingly, the judge said, "Sustained." But he still wouldn't look Hogan in the eye. "Sheriff, just answer the question," said Judge Barret. His disapproval of the sheriff was obvious.

Hogan listened to the catechism. Sheriff Wheeler had known Billy Joe since high school, Billy Joe had been in Vietnam and felt the Vietnamese ...

"Objection!" Hogan was on his feet again, feeling old and weary and depressed. Sheila had refused to come, and he had seen her in the living room packing a bag. She had refused to speak to him. He had been wrong to treat her like a personal counselor only, when the girl was a talented lawyer, but how in hell was he supposed to think of everything at once?

The objection was granted. It was apparent that the judge was going to allow some leeway, but not much. Hogan was beginning to think it wasn't a good idea to keep on objecting; that he would let matters take their course, because an idea had just occurred to him as to the course to take on cross-examination. Hogan tried to keep from moving restlessly in his chair. This egotistical witness just might dig a hole for himself.

Hogan heard murmurs behind him. It was the Hardin family, complete with Billy Joe's two sons, three brothers, and one sister, crowded onto the front seats of the spectator's gallery. They were there every day, usually with loud comments, and occasionally exclamations to the 'Almighty.'

"Sheriff, was Billy Joe a violent man?" The D.A.'s voice was genuinely questioning, searching.

The sheriff took on a firm expression.

"I've heard those lies being bandied around. There's not a damn bit of truth in that." He nodded toward Hogan. "This defense lawyer would make up anything if he felt it would help his clients. It's a damn shame to try to wreck a man's reputation after he's dead."

The defense's objection did little more than to give Hogan the opportunity to give a short speech of outrage and indignation.

"Sustained," said Barret, avoiding Hogan's eye. He too was becoming weary of it but still could not face Hogan. "Jury, disregard."

"What about threats or beatings by Billy Joe of the defendant before the shooting?"

"Never heard anything about it on Billy Joe's part. Now the Vietnamese did — circled his boat and threatened him and his wife and his kids."

"Sheriff, we have no more questions," the D.A. said. Hogan watched with a wry expression as the D.A. went back to his counsel table. The only point of the sheriff's testimony was that he had close personal friends on the jury.

Hogan began slowly, but with an end in sight. He lifted his leonine head, stood up, and walked in his deceptive shamble across the floor to the witness stand. He stood before the man, as rumpled as some scholar from the dusty stacks of law books, apparently rather humble before this man of action.

"Sheriff, would you say you are almost identically Billy Joe's height and weight?"

"About." He stared suspiciously at Hogan.

Hogan stood back and looked at the sheriff, and then at Cai. Then he said, "Sheriff, you mind coming down from the stand and standing next to Cai?"

The big man shrugged and got up and walked toward the counsel table, his heels clicking on the tile floor.

Cai stared up at him and Hogan could tell he was so frightened of the man his lips were stuck together, dry as leather. He could see Cai's hand was shaking. Next to him, his brother Tho looked even more alarmed.

"Lillie May, would you tell Cai to come and stand by the sheriff?" He heard the rapid, low murmur of the tonal language, its singing quality, and Cai got up and walked toward the sheriff, visibly leaning away from him. The young Vietnamese man measured below the sheriff's shoulders as they stood together in front of the jurors. Cai was quaking although the sheriff was simply standing there with his arms crossed.

Hogan said, "Would it be fair to say that you are at least a foot and a half taller and probably one hundred and twenty-five pounds heavier?"

The sheriff said, "Oh, hell, yes."

"And, sheriff, if you struck him with your fists, do you believe you could easily kill him?"

"You better believe it," the sheriff answered.

Cai looked on in terror. It was as if someone had reincarnated Billy Joe. Hogan could tell several jurors had dubious looks on their faces, thinking of the Vietnamese defendant in this man's jail.

"Now, Sheriff, take Billy Joe's knife and advance toward Cai. If you threatened to kill him, do you think you could put him in fear of his life?" Hogan's gray eyes were suddenly alert, not very scholarly at all, but with the brightness of a raptor. He pinned the sheriff in his gaze and leaned slightly forward. Astonished, Lillie May watched the transformation.

"No question about it. But I wouldn't need no knife."

The sheriff walked over to the counsel table and picked up the fish-knife with the tag on it. He advanced toward Cai, knife in hand. Cai looked behind him toward the courthouse doors. He was measuring his options.

Hogan nodded. "And, Sheriff, if you stomped his hands with your boots, you reckon you could break his fingers?"

"Yeah," said Fellows. He nodded.

"And, Sheriff, if you threatened to kill this boy and throw him to the fish, you think it would put him in fear of his life?"

"I expect so." The sheriff looked down at Cai speculatively. Cai looked as if he were going to faint as Lillie May kept translating the sheriff's responses.

"Thank you, Sheriff."

Hogan turned to Cai and indicated he should take his seat again. He didn't wait for Lillie May's translation but slipped back into the wooden chair beside his brother instantly. Tho turned to him and made some small, almost inaudible comment in Vietnamese. Cai nodded quickly and they were silent again.

Hogan said, "Sheriff, we appreciate your cooperation, you've been very candid. If you'll take your seat again ..." As soon as he was seated, Hogan walked forward, his arms crossed across his chest, his head cocked to one side, looking at the sheriff intently. "Sheriff Wheeler, presume your best friend Billy Joe did all of this to Cai. Would that have put this young man in fear of his life?"

"I guess if Billy Joe really did, it would." The sheriff leaned back and glared at Hogan realizing how much he had helped the defense. "But there's nothing says he did."

Sabine took an audio tape cassette out of her briefcase and laid it on the table. Hogan turned and restlessly walked back down the jury rail.

"While the Vietnamese brothers have been in your jail you talked to them daily through a Vietnamese interpreter, have you not?" Hogan nodded as if he already knew the answer.

"I sure do. When the interpreter shows up. I understand you have a tape of the conversation."

"Maybe there'll be no need for that, Sheriff. Let me ask you specifically about what you said to them. Did you tell them they would be better off pleading guilty and saving the county a lot of money and a useless trial?"

"I probably said it." He shifted his large boots and sat up again. He cleared his throat. A shaft of sunlight came through the windows of the courtroom and the plastic of the audio tape glinted.

"And, Sheriff, did you tell them there wasn't a chance in hell of them going free, and it's a damn shame they couldn't be hung on the courthouse lawn?"

The sheriff began to feel less secure. Hogan read slowly, loudly accusatorily, and there seemed to be no escape.

"You've got it all there. I damn sure ain't going to deny it."

The jurymen looked at the sheriff with blank expressions. Jack Sheppard, the man who worked as a bricklayer and roofer, stared steadily at him. Lieutenant Colonel Sam Washington shook his head very slightly. He'd been the one who had worked for the Judge Advocate General, the Army's legal department.

Hogan felt that he had gone as far as he dared. The tape on the table behind him was blank. Sheila had prepared the questions.

"Thanks, Sheriff Fellows. That'll be all."

He ambled away like a slightly perturbed giant.

Big Bob whispered to Sabine, "That jury looks like it's pissed off at *Hogan*, for the love of Mike."

"He's down," whispered Sabine.

"Where's our beautiful redhead?"

"They had a terrible fight last night at the office. She said she wasn't coming today."

"No wonder he looks like he's been run over by a switch engine."

The D.A. watched Sheriff Fellows sit heavily down in the spectator's section.

For the rest of the afternoon District Attorney Davis called the mayor of San Ignacio and city council persons to testify that Billy Joe was peaceable, law-abiding, and had an excellent reputation for law and order. Some had heard of prior threats. None believed them. Most had not heard anything. They knew nothing of the actual shooting, nor did they know Cai or Tho.

On cross-examination, Hogan brought out that the witnesses' prior quotes to the media contradicted the testimony, but the consensus was that little had been done to hurt the credibility of the officials of the little town of San Ignacio.

In Minneapolis, Sheila Ryan got off the afternoon flight from Dallas. She threw her sports bag over her shoulder by the handles and walked across the gleaming concourse to the small desk of Keewaytin Airlines on the far side of the airport. She was wearing khakis and a dark green polo shirt, a pair of boating shoes, but even these casual clothes couldn't hide the long slim legs and square shoulders, and a model's easy walk.

"Round trip," she said.

"That's return," the flight attendant said as she ripped off one of her tickets. "We're Canadian." She smiled. "We say return."

Sheila boarded the small two-engine King air Beechcraft and sat back with only a small tremor of nerves as they lifted above the city in what to her was a tiny aircraft. The other passengers seemed to be used to it and most of them promptly fell asleep.

Within two hours she had been borne aloft through the clear air over miles and miles of a relentless pine forest, over the invisible Canadian-American border, into a world of rolling hills and the occasional glassy blue gleam of a lake. They suddenly banked downwards, arrowing toward a small town with a pulp-mill smokestack and boxy company houses. Sheila closed her eyes, thinking it would be better if she didn't look.

At the small airport at Vermilion Bay, northern Ontario, she found the air suddenly crisp and sharp. A man in a brown uniform with a yellow stripe down the side asked for her identification.

"Of course." She offered her passport. She had never been without it for the last ten years, and she watched as the official checked through it. The airport was hardly more than a waiting room, and outside the runway cut its way though sandy soil and banks of tall pine. "You're the border patrol?"

The man shook his head and handed her passport back. "Mounties," he said. "We gave up on the Eddie Arnold hats and red coats."

She smiled her good smile. "Shucks," she said.

"I know. Disappoints all you Yanks."

"Listen," she said, "give me a hand. I'm a lawyer working on a case down in Texas." She saw a spark of interest in his eyes. "And there's a witness we need. There's no subpoena out for him or anything, it's completely voluntary. But he's come up from Texas to fish. Comes up every year."

He stared at her blankly, listening. It was a policeman's look, reserved, giving away nothing.

"Comes up to fish," he repeated. He reached up and shifted his billed cap. It was banded in yellow as well. "No subpoena?"

"No."

"Where does he fish?"

As the Mountie spoke he turned and automatically swept the airport with his gaze. Nothing was happening. The other passengers, mainly native people, were picking up luggage and greeting relatives. Sheila heard the Indian language being spoken, and from outside came the clean scent of pine.

"At a place called Slate Falls."

The Mountie nodded. He pointed outside. "Right out there," he said, "are a lot of taxis. Get one of them into the Blue Arrow water base."

"Water base?" Sheila shifted her bag.

"That's a sort of bush airline that has planes that land on water." His eyes sparkled with amusement. "And the place where they all are parked on their pontoons, at a dock, is called a water base. It's just outside of town."

"All right." She smiled back at him and laughed. "So I'm from Texas."

The Mountie grinned. "Hire one of those planes. Be prepared, it's expensive. Get a pilot to fly you to Slate Falls. The pilots can probably tell you when the guy came through and where he is. They get word through a special communications device."

"Which is?"

She almost knew the answer before he said it.

"Moccasin telegraph."

Sheila took a taxi into the pulp-mill town and spent the night in a Best Western motel. It wasn't long until the wind shifted and she realized the frail, clean pine scent was being swept away in the dense and foul odor of the pulp-mill stacks. When she woke up in the morning she almost felt her resolution fail. She was far from anyplace or anyone she knew. She felt as if some crackling glaze might shatter around her heart at any moment. Her love affair with Hogan held so much for her. She was risking it all. What if it turned out to be just another failure? What would she do then?

Suddenly she wished she had a cool glass of white wine to start the day with. Champagne and oysters. Temptation was strong.

Don't think of it, she said to herself, pushing the traitorous thoughts away. She had begun, and so she would finish.

By ten in the morning she sat in the co-pilot's seat of a Cessna 185, hanging on to the door handle as the pilot shot the little plane down the lake. The surface was alive with whitecaps and she shut her eyes while the big silver pontoons, like enormous galoshes, ripped the tops off and then the plane shot into the air.

Chapter Thirty-Two

The district attorney next called Charlie Hardin, Billy Joe's older brother. Paul and Sabine recognized him from their conversation with him in the Flores Bar in San Ignacio. He was dressed in a sports coat and tie, his shoes shined.

He identified himself as a crabber, married with three children, and among the generation who grew up in the San Ignacio area. He was smaller than his brother, slimmer, but just as sure of himself. He testified adamantly that he had never known Billy Joe to threaten anyone in his entire life. He maintained that Billy Joe had held a lot of meetings and passed around petitions for people to sign to ask for the removal of the Vietnamese, but he had never lifted a hand to any of them.

The district attorney passed the witness and Hogan recognized the virtue of brevity at this point. "Mr. Hardin, did you make the remark that the only safe thing for the Vietnamese was to put them on reservations like the Indians and make them live there until they learned American ways?"

"I said it, and I believe it. It's the only civilized thing to do."

"Were you the one who printed up and sold the T-shirts with the slogan 'Kick the Gooks Out of San Ignacio'?" Hogan turned suddenly and stared at Hardin, as if daring him to admit it. His gray eyes bore into the young man, expectant and demanding.

Defensively, defiantly, the young man said, "I helped Billy Joe do that, and most of the people were very glad to get them."

"You identified Cai by describing him as a 'damn Vietcong'?"

"I believe that he is. You don't shoot a man in the back without mighty good reasons, and Billy Joe certainly never gave him any."

Hogan was a bit startled to see that the young man's eyes were glassy with rage as he looked over at the defendants. He had lost a brother, and, Hogan knew, his killer was alive and well sitting here in the courtroom. It was obvious that he didn't feel it was fair. It was a difficult moment, and Hogan knew that the statue of Justice on top of the courthouse carried not only a pair of scales but a sword. Justice was often hard, and her sword had a terrible edge.

"We have no further questions, your Honor," he said.

Roger Davis seemed smooth and confident, and he lifted his movie-star handsome head to address the judge with a smile.

"The state calls Lieutenant Sam Jordan, deputy sheriff. He was the investigating officer who took the confessions of Cai and Tho. We now have the confessions as exhibit number twelve, and we tender it as evidence in the case."

"Objection." This was what Hogan had been waiting for, with such high hopes. "Judge, we have a motion on file to suppress that document outside the hearing of the jury. We want to argue the law which we have given in our brief, but first we want to put Cai on the stand to prove they had no idea what they were signing because the interpreter didn't either."

Hogan paused for a moment. Barret looked at him blankly, and then looked away.

"The Investigator couldn't speak Vietnamese and the interpreter couldn't speak much English, so there was never any adequate communication between the investigator and the defendants to warn them of their rights before they signed the confession." He saw Big Bob was poised with his files in front of him as if holding six-shooters.

"Very well," said Barret. "I will see you in my chambers."

The jury was excused, and in a few moments Hogan was sitting in front of the judge, with Roger Davis, his assistant, and Big Bob Mitchell to one side.

"Your Honor is aware this very well could be a crucial part of the trial," said Hogan.

The D.A. was looking toward the courtroom door, thinking of something else. Hogan noticed it and said, "We have extensive motions to quash the confessions of these two boys because of the lack of an appropriate warning, the lack of legal representation, and the obvious impossibility of communication between the interrogator Jordan and the defendants. Apparently their interpreter is missing and this is vital in proving the legality of the confession."

He paused and saw that, finally, Barret was looking directly at him. He went on. "Your Honor, did the defendants know what was being said? If not, they couldn't be properly warned. We insist upon putting the defendants on the stand to make a record to again fortify the motion that the confessions are incompetent, inadmissible, and very prejudicial."

Judge Barret pressed his lips together and looked away, down at his papers and then over to the D.A. The D.A. was apparently looking for some missing document, shuffling papers and whispering to his assistant. He obviously felt so certain that the motion to suppress the confessions, already heard, and this motion to direct a verdict in favor of Tho were so doomed to failure, they merited little of his attention and, based on the judge's past actions, his attitude was probably justified.

Barret knew this was extremely sensitive ground for reversal, especially if there was a missing interpreter. Yet the judge was loath to strike the confessions. He assumed it was vital to charging Tho with being an accomplice.

For purposes of appellate record, Hogan needed the testimony of Cai outside the presence of the jury to show that there was no proper translation, nor offer of counsel nor recitation of his rights, and to clarify whether or not his brother Tho was an accomplice. Whether the judge could be persuaded was a different matter, but it had to be done. Without the confession, Hogan knew, Cai's testimony could stand uncontradicted.

The D.A. finally looked up and said his interpreter was not immediately available and waived the necessity of his presence. The D.A. was convinced that there was nothing Cai could say that would have any credibility or significance.

The judge responded. "Mr. Hogan, I'm not impressed with the necessity of this testimony at this time. However, I suppose you are informed by Mr. Mitchell that it is necessary for the purposes of the appellate record." He looked badgered, caught between two fires. "With this in mind, let's be prepared to do it in the morning at eight with the hope that it will be brief and limited to just the vital areas under discussion as they relate to the undesirability of the confession. In the meantime, Mr. District Attorney, I would think it would be well to have the interpreter who was present at the confession in court for examination."

"Excuse me, your Honor?" Roger Davis looked up quickly from his search for whatever he was searching for.

Barret repeated what he'd said, in his mild voice, which had suddenly grown firmer by a hair. "I said, counselor, find the interpreter so we can substantiate that these confessions were properly taken."

"Yes, of course." Davis nodded impatiently.

Barret said, "The court stands adjourned until such time. I presume Judy Hardin, the widow, is your last witness. We can conclude with her this afternoon, and let you rest your case after the court's ruling on this motion to suppress the confession."

Hogan's beefy, strong shoulders seemed slightly slumped as he scooped his papers into his briefcase. Sabine, as always sympathetic, smiled and shook her head at him as if to say, 'It'll be all right.' She looked over for Paul and then pressed her curly dark hair back from her forehead. Then they all walked out to the car, avoiding the reporters as much as possible, and ready for the long ride to San Antonio.

Kendrick was waiting for Hogan outside of the courtroom with what he obviously thought was important information

"I've got to see you right away in my office," he told Hogan. When the Hogans and Big Bob arrived shortly afterwards. Kendrick welcomed them in. His one-man office was crowded with any number beyond three. His secretary was his wife who served those mornings when she could get a baby-sitter for the two small children. To say that Kendrick's office was modest was being charitable. They sat and thought, smoked and drank coffee. Nobody mentioned Sheila's absence but the air was thick with tension.

Big Bob rubbed his long thin hands together. "Even this judge can't admit the confession if there's no one to testify otherwise."

Big Bob lit one cigarette from the end of the other and pulled a flask from his briefcase. His suit jacket was new, thanks to Sheila, and already generously sprayed with cigarette ashes down the front. He had discarded the matching pants, however, for his favorite maroon polyester slacks that were two inches two short.

"All right," Hogan said with a smile. But prior defeats caused him to remain cautious. He didn't entirely share Big Bob's confidence. "I hope." He dropped his head into his hands. "This is so crucial, and here I've lost my best researcher." He wanted to say my best friend, my lover, my rescuer, but he didn't. "Hell, I ought to fire her for taking off like that."

"I'll hire her," said Big Bob.

"The hell you will," said Hogan.

"Are you ready to proceed with your hearing, Mr. Hogan?" the judge asked as he took the bench promptly at eight a.m.

There were few in the courtroom as the hearing was apparently only housekeeping, tidying up the raveling ends, and the results of admitting the confession seemingly foregone. Hogan presented his arguments, and the D.A., in a rather languid manner, presented his own. It was over quickly, too quickly, and Hogan was now free to bring Cai to the stand to testify as to the manner in which the confessions were taken in the San Ignacio jail.

Hogan and others would have been amazed to learn that, after the hearings on the motion to suppress the confession, the judge had worked with the two law clerks to review that which was furnished by the defendants until a late hour the previous night. He now looked troubled and overwrought.

The D.A.'s review led them over many considerations, particularly in the review prepared by his clerks. But he said nothing about producing the interpreter, and said nothing by way of refutation of Hogan's charge that the interpreter was himself incompetent. It was this that troubled Judge Barret the most. He thought this was fatal to the admission. He did not want to be reversed. He desperately wanted to be fair, and to be seen as being fair. But it was apparent the D.A. would be happy to see him be the sacrificial lamb.

Barret was also becoming even more irritated with the D.A. Roger Davis seemed only too willing to commit the most egregious error as long as the maximum verdict for both boys was obtained. It was finally sinking in with Barret that the D.A. didn't plan to be around if the case was reversed; he obviously thought he'd be well on into a political career by then.

The judge felt differently. He expected to be on the bench the rest of his life. He did not want to be excoriated by the appeals court for reversible error.

Chapter Thirty-Three

The jury was still out, and in the presence of only the officers of the court and the silent spectators, Cai took the stand. He raised his hand for the oath and then sank down in the witness stand as if taking cover from enemy fire. Lillie May, demure as always, sat near him. If she was nervous, not a tremor crossed her lovely, porcelain-clear face.

During the trial Roger Davis, as district attorney for three counties, had been served by the first assistant D.A. The local county attorney had two assistants from his own staff as additional counsel. Davis had apparently left his assistant to do the cross questioning because he had a television interview to give.

Strangely, not only did he allow an inexperienced assistant to do the cross, but he proceeded without his own interpreter. The D.A. had not bothered to find another interpreter, but had accepted Lillie May. He was satisfied that the judge would support the home team regardless of the circumstances. Reversal was the last thing on Roger Davis' mind. It would take a year and he planned to be in Congress by then.

Hogan tightened his tie and rose to his feet to begin his questioning of Cai. He knew it was vital to get the confessions suppressed, first of all, because Cai's brother Tho was in no way guilty of being an accomplice, secondly because Cai had been bullied into confessing. Hogan had read the statement many times, each with disbelief. It was a travesty of a system of justice he deeply believed in.

He smiled at Cai, so small and still in the witness stand, in what he hoped was a comforting way. Lillie May sat beside him in a prim little dress of pale green with a jacket to match. The spectators looked at her with interest. They had seen her often at the counsel table, but it was the first time they had heard her speak.

"Cai, were you told you could have a lawyer before you said anything about the incident?"

He heard Lillie May's quick translation, the lilting tones. She listened to his brief, whispered reply and then lifted her head and said, in clear, precise English,

"It is not true that I was told I could have a lawyer. Of course, I would have, had I known."

Even Hogan was momentarily surprised by her perfectly audible voice, its crisp intonation, her confidence.

"Yes," he said. "Now, tell the jury, were you advised that you did *not* have to say anything if you didn't want to?" He jammed his hands in his pockets, bending forward slightly at the waist to hear her. He did everything in his power to direct the attention of the court toward Lillie May.

Again the quick, whispered exchange; then Lillie May turned away and spoke to the judge.

She said, "I was never advised that I didn't have to give a statement. I wouldn't have done so, if I thought I could refuse. They said I had to sign something, a written statement they put in front of me." She gestured slightly with her small hand, as if indicating a piece of paper in front of her.

"Was the interpreter clear about all this?"

The judge leaned forward, gazing at this drama before him, leaning forward as if to hear Cai's low, brief whisper whether he could understand it or not.

Lillie May shook her head. "I didn't know what it said and the Vietnamese interpreter told me he wasn't sure either."

Hogan glanced up to see that the judge was leaning forward and listening with rapt attention to the young Vietnamese woman. My God, thought Hogan. She is hypnotizing us all. Her silky, pure-black hair in its bobbed cut swung slightly as she turned to hear Cai, then turned back to the judge.

The D.A. seemed to be the only one who escaped Lillie May's magnetism or the seriousness of the situation. In the brief time he was in the courtroom, he was scribbling on a legal pad and then became irritated with a pen that had run dry or clogged up, and was pestering one of his assistants to go get him another one, one of the kind he liked especially. A Pentel. The assistant was looking through his pockets and finally got up to go get him one from the office.

Then the D.A. glanced at his watch and got up and left as well. The assistant returned with the pen, looked around, saw the D.A. was gone, shrugged and sat down. It was several minutes before the D.A. returned. He busied himself at the table, seeming to pay little attention to Hogan's questions.

"I was so afraid. This man threatened my life if I didn't sign where he told me," Lillie May said in her clear, light voice. Her black eyes were alert. "I had no idea what it was that he wanted of me or why I must sign."

It was as if the small, elegant woman herself had been badgered by the police for a statement.

"I never denied killing Billy Joe, but I told him again and again. I only did it because I was afraid he was going to kill me. I don't know yet what's in the statement. I can't read or understand English. The Vietnamese interpreter didn't seem to know any more than me what was going on. I know nothing of American law or rights or justice, nor was it ever explained to me."

The more that Hogan went on with his questions, the more the judge realized how compelling the record would appear if not refuted. Lillie May had transformed the situation. The testimony had taken on a life of its own; it was no longer just regarded as a formality. The judge was increasingly troubled by the lack of apparent interest or refutation by the D.A. Why did he keep leaving? Why had he let the assistant take over?

Hogan continued. "Were you ever told that you had the right to remain silent, that you didn't have to give a statement, and that it would be used against you?"

"I never heard those words. He told me I had no rights and that probably I'd be lynched and killed if I didn't sign where he told me. To this day, I don't know what's in the statement. No one told me."

Lacking the interpreter who had done the translating at the time, there was no one to refute Cai's statement.

Hogan began to read the statement to him and the denials by Cai, through Lillie May, were completely at odds with the confession that the sheriff's investigator had witnessed and vouched for its verity. Hogan read slowly, pausing for the translation, and he and Lillie May's voices followed each other like chant and response.

"Did you say this?" he asked her. "My brother Tho urged me to get a gun and go back to the bay to find Billy Joe?" Hogan unconsciously asked questions, not of Cai, but of Lillie May. It was almost as if they were matching wits and she was on trial. Cai became inconsequential.

Only the district attorney didn't sense what was happening. He was occupied with his pending cross-examination of Cai and not the testimony given by Lillie May. Although the atmosphere in the court-room was changing, he was too busy bustling in and out of the court-room for interviews with the press to notice. He was even oblivious to the fact that the judge was no longer the castigating, opinionated jurist he'd been the past many weeks.

Behind his back, Hogan heard murmurs from the Hardin family which was sitting, as always, on the front row.

"No. Tho tried to stop me. He said, 'no, don't,' and he went with me to try to take the gun away from me." Lillie May barely turned to Cai to listen again before she said, "He told me not to get the gun, not to go find Billy Joe. But I am older brother, in Vietnam younger broth-er obey older. He only begged. I am ashamed in front of all the Vietnamese people."

Hogan knew he had better stop where he was. It was clear Lillie May had evoked some response where before there was none, and he didn't want to push it. Something told him, 'stop right here.'

The cross-examination was conducted by the assistant D.A. and to say it was indifferent was charitable.

"Didn't you say in your confession that you and Tho acted together?"

"I don't know what was written in that confession," said Lillie May for Cai, in her clear voice "I can't read English and it wasn't translated for me. I never told those men that Tho helped me. He didn't help me. He told me not to go down to the dock, and I am ashamed."

"But that's what the confession says," the assistant D.A. insisted.

"Like I have said, I don't know what it says. My brother Tho is completely innocent. He had no part in any of this except to try to stop me."

At this moment, Cai through Lillie May testified that the Vietnamese translator told him that he could be shot or lynched and that his best bet was to plead guilty and leave it up to the judge, that this was what the investigator had said.

The D.A. walked in as Lillie May was translating with her precise clarity. He listened for a moment and seemed flustered at best, but grew livid with what Lillie May just said. His face got red. It was one of the few times he let his anger show.

"*Just a moment!*" he shouted. "You are trying to convince this court that one of our peace officers would threaten you?"

"Yes, sir, they did," Lillie May shot back almost before Cai could whisper.

The D.A. looked furious. He said to the assistant, "I'll take this." The abashed young assistant sat down. The judge watched with marked attention, and looked at Lillie May again. Her skin was as light and smooth as porcelain in the faintly damp heat of the courtroom. In the midst of conflicting personalities and tension, she sat unmoved, a slight smile on her face. She looked up at the judge, nodding politely.

"Is he trying to say the confession is false?" the D.A. asked.

She listened and turned again. "I don't know," she said. "I don't know what is in it." Judge Barret seemed to nod in sympathy for the young woman, the first indication of any sympathy Hogan had seen from him.

Something marvelous was happening, one of those moments in a courtroom when events had taken on their own power, their own trajectory, and woe to the unwise lawyer who stood in their way. It was like a drama whose players were utterly unrehearsed but following some script that had come out of nowhere.

"Who was in the room at the time?" demanded the D.A.

Lillie May turned her head slightly to translate and then hear the undertone of Cai's one-sentence response. She turned her face back to the D.A. without expression. "Only that one man, very big, very loud. I was alone and afraid of him."

"Why didn't you turn to the interpreter for help?"

"He was as scared as me."

"You did sign this confession? That is your signature?"

"I would have signed anything I thought I had to. I think that's my signature."

With the thought that the hearing was nothing more than an irritant, the D.A. abruptly concluded with the witness.

"I presume you have refuting evidence, Mr. D.A?" inquired the judge.

"Sure, Judge, the officer in question."

The investigating officer, Lieutenant Sam Jordan, was a young man with a mustache and a thick head of light-brown hair. In contrast to the other lawmen who had come in, he was soft-spoken and diffident and replied in short sentences. The D.A. grew irritated with him for his moderation, as he had with Cotton Wheeler for his arrogance.

"You had a good translator?"

"I don't know, sir. I don't speak Vietnamese, but I was as clear as I could be. I read him and his brother their rights. The Vietnamese man said something in their language. Then I asked both of them how they got mixed up in it and what they did and everything, and then the Vietnamese guy said whatever I said, I guess. How do I know, sir? Nobody threatened them, I'll tell you."

After his testimony refuting Cai point by point, the judge interrupted. He was clearly disturbed and preoccupied. He had a habit of tucking down the sleeves of his judicial robes when he was in a quandary, and in the present circumstances the judge was working overtime.

"Mr. D.A., I presume you are going to present the interpreter for corroboration of what the defendant did and said?"

"No, your Honor, I'm not. I'm told he has fled the scene and no longer is in the state. We don't expect to have him available before this hearing or trial is concluded."

The judge looked troubled and trapped. "Mr. D.A., I view this matter very seriously."

But the district attorney still wasn't getting it. "Well, here's the confessions," he said, stubbornly.

"I will withhold my ruling until tomorrow. I don't mind telling you I'm extremely troubled. Let's proceed. Are you resting at the time, subject to my ruling?"

"We are, your Honor."

The court adjourned until the following morning with the request of the attorneys to be in at 8:00 in order that the ruling on the admissibility of the confession could be discussed as well as any remaining prosecution witnesses.

Chapter Thirty-Four

September 14th

A thunderstorm was growling around at the edges of the sky, and squall lines of fat dark clouds came forward in ranks as they drove down toward Stillwater.

Hogan was so charged with anxiety over the judge's upcoming ruling he was drumming his fingers on the wheel and impatient with the delays for road work on Highway 10. Sabine sat beside him, separating papers into their proper files and juggling a Styrofoam cup of coffee. In the back seat, Paul lay back in the corner, half asleep.

"And so, Paul, she didn't say anything to you either?" Hogan said.

"Dad, don't get me mixed up in this."

"Why did she have to pull this now? Why now?"

"Put it out of your mind, Dad," said Paul. "Just for now. We have to win this case."

"We're not going to do it without a good witness for Cai and that means the Texas Ranger. And we can't find him."

"We'll do okay, Mr. Hogan, if we can get the confession suppressed." Sabine tried to be cheerful.

"Maybe she just needed a little rest," said Paul. It sounded stupid even to him.

Hogan thought of her sleeping on the couch, all that gleaming hair on the pillow and her light satin pajamas and mentally kicked himself. After he wished kicking himself, he cleared his throat and shifted his shoulders inside his jacket, head down, ready to charge into the courtroom.

When they went inside, Hogan felt that somehow there had been a change in the atmosphere of the old Stillwater courthouse, just like the air was changing outside. But it was lost on District Attorney Davis. Davis apparently had a new haircut, a blow-dry affair, and was sporting one of his flashiest ties yet; a paisley affair in lemon-yellow and scarlet. Outside, the air darkened as the storm bore down on them.

The judge ponderously reviewed the record.

"Gentlemen. I have spent the night reviewing the testimony, the evidence and the arguments of both sides. Short of serious evidence to the contrary, which I haven't seen, I have no alternative but to suppress the confessions, and direct a verdict in favor of Tho Cao Den of not guilty as an accomplice to murder in the case."

The courtroom was deadly quiet. Stunned.

The district attorney was utterly still for five seconds, and then he went ballistic. He vaulted up out of his seat behind his counsel table and strode forward. His yellow and scarlet tie flew free of its clasp.

"This is an impossible ruling! It would mean the defendant would go free because of a ruling of this court! Such action is not only absurd, it is intolerable!" The D.A. was shouting at, not addressing, the court. The man was actually yelling. The bailiff and judge were bewildered and outraged and Hogan speechless. "This is the worst ruling I have ever heard! I cannot imagine the reasons behind such a breach of justice!"

Hogan heard voices from the spectator area, exclamations and murmurs. Whether they were over the ruling or the D.A.'s conduct, he couldn't tell.

The D.A.'s reaction was so violent the judge had to respond to protect his own dignity. Judge Barret's face had flushed beet red. The color rose to his hairline and he was aware of it, and it made him even more angry and embarrassed.

"One more word!" he said to the D.A. "One more outburst and you, sir, are in contempt of this court and will be remanded to jail." His tones were measured but strong. He pointed to the D.A. "This is the most intemperate and inexcusable conduct that I have ever witnessed. We are going to take a ten-minute recess. I want the testimony, and I want Mr. Hogan to begin. Mr. D.A., these remarks are mild compared to those you will hear if I ever witness such attitudes or remarks again in this trial. The court stands adjourned."

The D.A. stood silent with his mouth open. He was a shaken man, stunned with disbelief. For the first time in ten years, the D.A. had been threatened with sanctions by the court.

Two forces which had been one were suddenly divided. It was almost as if for the first time the judge seemed to sense how far he had traveled in allowing the D.A. to take over his courtroom. His face was so red, it would take hours for him to return to his normal color.

All the years before, and at the start of this case, the D.A. had made it appear that he was just terribly bright and the judge awfully wise. Hogan had resigned himself to his fate, to losing before the jury and calmly building a case for a strong appeal.

That was then, and now was now. It appeared that the facade was gone. Cai was to be the recipient of a fair trial. Whether it would influence the jury's verdict was an entirely different matter.

They stood outside on the steps with cold sodas. Big Bob smoked.

"For the first time since we got the case I can't wait to get back to the courtroom." Hogan was looking and feeling ten years younger.

Promptly at 2:00 P.M., the judge took the bench. His face was still slightly flushed. He twitched his shoulders inside his robe and stared mildly down at the D.A., once again self-contained.

"Mr. District Attorney, have you found the translator?"

"No, your Honor. He's missing and I can't predict that we will ever find him. The whole thing is quite sinister, and I don't presently have an explanation."

"Under these circumstances, my ruling stands. The motion for directed verdict of not guilty in favor of Tho as an accomplice is granted."

The spectators, including the press and the Hardin family, broke out into exclamations, groans, and a few cheers. All of the Hardin family — and Billy Joe had a lot of siblings and relatives — as well as the press and the media had expected the judge to take a recess and then change his mind upon his return. He hadn't done so.

With much gavel-pounding and shouting the judge restored order. He warned against future outbursts. The D.A. recognized his best interest was to get the maximum jury verdict against Cai and put the blame squarely on the judge for Tho's release. He had regained his cool. All was well. He was still the people's champion. He strode out with a smile for the press.

The assistant D.A. who had blown the testimony at the hearing for suppression of confession sat silently. Humbled, he was left to gather all the Pentel pens and extra legal pads and go running after the D.A.

Roger Davis and his assistants lugged their briefcases into his office.

"Don't worry about this confession shit. We have it wired," the district attorney said. They were extracting Cokes from a small refrigerator. The tall windows were blocked with heavy dark-green shades, for the morning cool had passed and the sun bore down with ferocity. He was prepared to call his final witness. "We proved the murder. The confession business got a little sticky, but we are going to put the final nail in with the widow."

"She's so believable," said one of the staff. "Great presence."

"And the interpreter?" Roger Davis looked around. "Where the hell did *our* guy go? Why wasn't he there?"

"He isn't anywhere," said the assistant D.A. "Besides, I never liked him." He poured his Coke into a glass of ice sitting on Davis' leather blotter pad and watched anxiously as it nearly foamed over the top. Roger Davis glared at the soft drink as if he dared it to run over. The assistant took out his handkerchief and wiped delicately around the glass even though it hadn't.

"Why not?" the D.A. demanded.

The assistant D.A. shrugged. "He's somehow related to some other Vietnamese here in Stillwater. They all talk together. We don't need one, and it's my opinion that we steer clear of all of them. They may be going straight to Hogan with information."

"Yeah." Roger Davis drummed his fingers on the blotter. "So his brother isn't guilty, so what? What can Cai say — I wasn't aiming at him? I just washed my pistol and I couldn't do a thing with it?"

His staff laughed.

"Yeah, you take some of the cross if we ever get to Hogan's witnesses. Like he has any worth listening to."

The assistant brightened up. "Thanks!"

"That's all right, son," said Davis. "You're young. You're probably still thinking about truth and justice and the American way. I'm thinking about bigger things."

They all returned to the courthouse. There was the usual small bustle of men in suits and papers and the bailiff refreshing the pitchers of cool water. Barret's color was almost normal.

"The state calls Mrs. Billy Joe Hardin."

Judy Hardin was dressed appropriately in black. Her dress was slightly above the knee, her stockings black, worn with small black high heels. Her face bore the marks of the recent tragedy and long periods of tough Texas weather and hard work, but her features were regular and she was obviously without guile, and this made her attractive. Her hair was bleached blonde from the sun and contrasted with her black dress. A slim woman of about 5'3", she could have used ten to fifteen pounds. Hogan couldn't help but have great sympathy for her. She, too, was a creature of circumstances she didn't create. He heard beside him a small murmur, almost inaudible, from both Sabine and Lillie May.

"Please give us your name." The tall, handsome D.A. bent toward her, condescending and smooth.

"I'm Judy Hardin, Billy Joe's widow. "

"If you will, give the jury your background leading up to marrying Billy Joe."

"Well..." She was hesitant. Being so exposed in a public place had flustered her. She looked out at the spectators with apprehension and then said, "I grew up in the bay area. We have been around shrimpers most of our life."

The district attorney slowly and with good effect went through Judy's history. It needed no embellishment. It was sad and difficult. She met Billy Joe when she was a waitress at the Flores bar. They were married a year later. His family disapproved. Her family lived in Georgia, too far away to help. Ten years after the marriage, she had three small children, a trailer home, debts as much as the credit cards would allow, and a future crowded with the same insecurity that had plagued her all her life. Her voice was soft and her manner appealing.

"How long were you married to Billy Joe?"

"We were married ten years and have three children, one, two and four."

"Was Billy Joe a good husband?"

Murmurs from behind, as the Hardin family commented. You bet. Damn right. Yeah.

"He was kind and considerate and a good provider. Like there are those people, not knowing our ways and customs, who might think Billy Joe was a bit loud and harsh, but he was really kind. Her voice quavered. "And decent and he loved us ... he loved his children ..." Her voice broke, garbling the words. "... very much."

"Did you ever know Billy Joe to threaten to kill any of the Vietnamese?"

"No."

"Tell us about your husband." The D.A. nodded to her to encourage her.

She cleared her throat before replying. "Billy Joe was a good man. He didn't have a lot of education. He just loved fishing, is all. It took seven years to pay for our boat, and then the Viets came." Her eyes were red, and she wiped them with a tissue and looked over at Cai and Tho, who looked back, briefly. Then Cai looked away at the judge and Tho looked at his hands.

"Maybe it wasn't all their fault, but they were just taking all the crab harvest."

"Why did he want the Vietnamese out of San Ignacio?"

"Objection!"

"Overruled."

"There were too many of them. There wasn't room for us and them, and not enough fish. They didn't know our ways and traditions and laws and customs, or care. They had no interest in doing anything other than invading the waters and ruining our fishing. Billy Joe fought in Vietnam, and he felt the country should stand up for its own citizens. He said if the government wouldn't, he would."

Hogan had tried in vain to stop it. Over and over again he objected that the testimony was hearsay and unresponsive, but this was drama and tragedy and Barret was going to allow it no matter what.

"And what was Billy Joe's attitude?"

"Well, he formed a lot of organizations, contacted all of the authorities, and had meetings urging the Viets to leave."

"You say you have three children. Would you point them out for the jury?"

The two oldest children stood up from among the spectators as planned. A relative held the baby up. All were dressed in cheap but proper clothes. Judy then said that she had no one to support her young family, and that she was all alone. She explained her only job had been as a waitress ten years ago, and that she hadn't graduated from high school.

"Did the Vietnamese ever threaten you or your children?"

"Yes. They surrounded our boat one time. This one Vietnamese had a knife in his mouth; they looked like pirates. They banged into our boat. I was frightened to death for me and the kids. There were a lot of them. They kept circling and getting closer. We got out of the bay and out of our boat as soon as we could." She was fighting against tears again. "Billy Joe wasn't going to stand for that kind of stuff with his family. The Viets weren't going to back away. Someone was going to get hurt bad. I didn't know it was going to be us." Tears dripped down her face.

Hogan could hardly bear to look at her. He was as tender as an open wound, with Sheila gone and no word from her, no call, no note, and his own rage making him feel tense and flustered.

After a few moments Judy seemed to take control of herself. Her face was swollen from days of crying. The bailiff offered her another tissue.

"That was the worst time. All of us were hysterical. We thought they meant to kill us, and I think they would have but for the Coast Guard stopping them. They always seemed hostile whenever we saw them on the street. They pretended they couldn't speak English, but usually they could. Billy Joe never shot anybody, never killed anybody, never threatened anybody."

"Judy, did Billy Joe smash up any of Cai's equipment, or any of the Vietnamese fishermen's equipment?"

"They said he smashed up some pots."

Roger Davis nodded, frowned, and asked, "Flowerpots?"

"No, like a crab trap."

"And what is it like? Is it easy to smash up?"

Judy held out her hands. "They're about this big, and they're made out of plastic-coated chicken wire. They have a hole on either side for the crabs to get in. Called eyes."

"And they crumple up easily?"

"Yeah." Judy wiped her nose. "We've run over them with the car there in front of the house and had to spend hours getting the kinks out."

Davis said, "So Billy Joe stomped ..."

"They said he stomped their traps, but likely he just stepped on one by accident."

Davis nodded and smiled at her, as if to tell her it would not be much longer. She gave a small, shy smile in return.

"Now, Judy, the jury needs to know whether Billy Joe was a violent man. Was he a bully and a brute as Mr. Hogan insists on describing him? You heard about the knifing and threats and beatings. You believe them?" The district attorney, with his low-key and sympathetic manner, kept the tone gentle and moderate.

Again Hogan stood. He felt that the jury was growing weary of him. He was growing weary of himself. "Leading. Calls for speculation."

"Overruled." Barret would not look at him.

The jury, looking as though someone had tried to turn off their favorite soap opera, glared at him.

He sat down. Sabine leaned close to him. "Mr. Hogan, everything will be okay. You'll see. Sheila will be back."

"Be quiet," he whispered harshly.

She bit her lip and looked away.

Judy Hardin was saying, "People will tell you Billy Joe was not a violent man. I never heard no threats, no beatings. I've got to believe that's made up. The Viets were the ones that got violent. It's my husband that's dead."

"The state passes the witness," Davis said. He walked back to his counsel table with a jaunty stride, sat down, and leaned back in his chair. It was his courthouse and he was at home in it. He felt made for this moment and this case.

Hogan unsuccessfully asked that her testimony be stricken as unresponsive, and when this was denied he paused for a moment to gather his thoughts. Then he stood up and smiled at the widow. He knew his cross-examination needed the greatest sensitivity and brevity. He tried to convey to her his sympathy and had told her as much several times during the recess. She hadn't replied.

"Judy, may I call you that? I think Father Dominic was a friend of yours."

She looked up suspiciously at Hogan. "He was."

"You attended his Catholic Mass when you could?"

"I'm Catholic. I go to church."

"You knew he was working for a peaceful settlement with the fishermen, and he often talked to you about it." Hogan smiled at her encouragingly. Among the spectators, Father Dominic looked at Judy with a deep sadness on his face, his round glasses reflecting light.

"We couldn't find no solution short of the Viets leaving."

"I think he finally agreed and told you that even Cai and Tho had agreed it was hopeless and that they were ready to leave?"

She nodded. "That was the last conversation we had just before the news that Billy Joe had been killed." She suddenly drew in a hiccuping breath that was the beginning of a sob. She swallowed. "A kid come running through the trailer park, he was yelling that Billy Joe had been shot. I was hoping he was only wounded ..."

"That must have been terrible," said Hogan.

"Yes," she said. She straightened in her seat and squared her shoulders. "It's okay, I'm all right."

Hogan waited, polite and attentive. Then he said. "They were just about to leave town, Cai and Tho?"

"Yeah, they were."

"That doesn't sound like two men plotting to kill Billy Joe, does it, Judy?"

"I don't know what they had in mind."

"Do you know, Mrs. Hardin, if the Ku Klux Klan and the American Nazi Party had active chapters in San Ignacio?"

"I heard that they did."

"Billy Joe was a member of those organizations, wasn't he?"

"I don't think so. I heard that, but I don't believe it." She shrugged and looked away.

"There were firebombings of the Vietnamese homes before the shooting and burning of their boats before the shooting, were there not?"

"Yeah, that's true."

"Did Billy Joe carry a rifle in his truck?"

"Not all the time."

"Was it loaded?"

"I don't think so. It wasn't there after the shooting. The deputy found nothing in his truck."

"Do you know if this is Billy Joe's knife?" Hogan turned back to the counsel table and picked up the fish knife with its tag, held it up and put it back down again. He made sure the jury had a good look at it.

She shifted her neat black high heels and pushed her hair out of her face. "It looks like it. All the crabbers had knives like that. They needed them in the fishing."

Hogan knew and felt she was a devastating witness; she certainly wasn't helping his cause. She hurt a lot without even knowing it, just by her compelling appearance of sadness and helplessness. Hogan knew he was digging a dry hole. It was time to quit.

Hogan turned back to his counsel table. "No further questions."

Judy Hardin left the stand.

The state had finally concluded its case against Cai and Tho. The district attorney acknowledged Mrs. Hardin with a wry smile and a touch on her elbow. Hogan watched her go and in his mind he knew he had no defense.

Chapter Thirty-Five

September 15th

The next morning flights of grackles crossed the early-morning sky as the five of them, in two cars, a Ford and a Chevy, drove east out of the city toward Stillwater. The sun came up from behind the buildings at St. Paul's Square, over the old ice plant on the east side, and then they were in the countryside. Great thunderheads were rising up out of the northwest, from the Hill Country, but they sailed on over without rain. They were the great desert-country thunderheads, like galleons, setting sail for some distant land.

In the grassy pastures of Potrero County, mares stood in the shade with half-grown foals at their sides, whipping their tails at the flies. The cactus fruit made crowns of blood-red on the prickly pear, and on the mesquites the bean-pods hung in vermilion and cream. The two cars passed the small houses at the outskirts of the town, and then turned into the main square.

Sabine chatted animatedly with Paul, trying to cover an absence that stood out like a great empty space. Hogan leaned back as Paul drove, trying to settle his mind. They parked, dodged the reporters, and went up to the second floor.

"Are you ready for the defense, Mr. Hogan?" the judge promptly inquired as he greeted the jury and called the court into session at nine in the morning,

"We are, your Honor, but first Paul will give the opening statement which we reserved until this moment."

"You may proceed."

Paul put his hands behind his back and spoke directly in his sincere voice to the jurors, taking a few minutes before beginning, visiting with each juror as he eyed them individually.

"We commend you jurors for your service," he said. "It's not a popular thing to do. You'll soon see there are two sides to this case even though the D.A. has tried to hide that fact."

"Objection!" The D.A. sprang up vigorously, objecting that the limits of opening had already been violated, and that a closing argument was improper at that time.

Judge Barret considered, finally agreed, and instructed Paul accordingly.

Paul nodded, and then said, "We reserved the right to give our opening statement at this time rather than customarily following the D.A.'s remarks. Because we did, we are in a better position to show you where we have been but also and, more importantly, where we are going.

"It is not to his credit that Mr. Davis, your district attorney, is so zealous in prosecuting the guilty that he is unmindful of being equally responsible for protecting the innocent. He has, as you have seen from the evidence, been quite ready to sacrifice these young men on the altar of bigotry and prejudice to further his own worldly gain and unabridged ambition."

"Ob-*jec*-tion!"

"Sustained. Mr. Hogan, please."

Paul nodded and then looked at the jury directly, standing square in front of the jury rail. "It is not a pleasant or popular thing to say Billy Joe was a bully, that he beat up these young men half his size, that he helped organize groups that burned down their homes and their fishing boats. We don't enjoy it, but the facts dictate it. He forced Cai to take his life to defend his own.

"It is our painful duty to say things against Billy Joe Hardin. We would rather not, particularly in the face of a wonderful family and a widow for whom we grieve."

Again and again the D.A. tried to interrupt, claiming that Paul's statements were argumentative, but he was overruled. He was probably correct in his objections, but the judge now apparently felt so much had been permitted in the D.A.'s opening remarks that he'd better balance the other side.

This trial, thought Sabine, is wild. I *know* I want to be a lawyer.

Paul had been taught not to get distracted and to gain advantage to repeated objections by such statements, "As I was saying" or "To start again where I was before the interruption," and he did so, doggedly.

"A short time ago, Cai and Tho fought side by side with the Americans in the mountains and deltas of Vietnam. Cai and Tho fought with the 104th Marines in the highlands of Quang Tri. Both were wounded in the Battle of Chu Lai. In '75 Saigon fell and they fled from the Vietcong and brought their hopes and dreams, which they had earned, to this promised land.

"San Ignacio and the waters of the Gulf of Mexico looked good to them. It was delta country and reminded them of home. They worked as machinists, fishermen, and laborers, put their money away, and bought a boat. Together they harvested San Ignacio Bay. In the morning before the sun came up, they'd steer out through the channel and cast their nets into the water. They worked the Gulf fishing grounds in a boat that had been the fruit of their labor. Then people began to resent them, and asked organizations to come in that said, 'America for

Americans.' Others said 'You want them out, you got to burn them out.' Then they brought in the Texas Klan."

Paul held out both hands wide, as if laying out the simple facts.

"Billy Joe resented and hated the Vietnamese. He threatened them, slashed Cai with his fish knife. He took every method except peaceful ones to settle their differences. And I assure you, ladies and gentlemen, he was a big man and these two young men were in fear of their lives. We will show you that all the facts converge on one thing—it was kill or be killed. Cai didn't want that in Vietnam nor in San Ignacio. He got it both places. Self-defense was not only appropriate, but the only thing to do."

He paused and took a breath. "Thank you for being here. Duty is difficult, especially in this instance. We have every confidence you will do the right thing."

Paul concluded in a silent courtroom. It was the first time Hogan had heard the place silent since the case began.

Because of other pending matters the judge recessed the trial early, giving the attorneys the opportunity to review the charge he had given them. In Texas state courts the judge reads his charge before arguments and it can be of great advantage if tilted to either side in instructions given or omitted. In this instance, it was simply fair to both, pure and simple.

Hogan read it with an increasing sense of relief. To his surprise and pleasure, it was almost identical to that requested by Big Bob and Sheila. The D.A. was furious but there were no outbursts. He, too, was finally beginning to feel the change in the air.

Chapter Thirty-Six

Sheila Ryan was about eight hundred feet over the lengthy, slate-colored surface of Slate Falls Lake. The air was very cool, for it was the middle of September and at latitude fifty-four north, the season was advanced. It was splendid weather, however, and below her the poplars shone in lemon-yellow banks against the dark pines. She instinctively lifted her feet away from the floor, as if to avoid being bumped by the earth so close below. She felt as if she were aloft in a kite.

"Put those earphones on!" the pilot shouted at her over the noise of the engine. He pointed at a pair of earphones on a hook just under what appeared to be a radio dial. Sheila nodded and reached down and put them on.

She couldn't hear anything. She leaned forward to look out the front windscreen and her hair flew in sheaves around her forehead. She took them off again, untangling them from her hair.

"I can't hear anything!" she yelled.

The pilot, a young fellow with a thick rusty moustache and blue eyes and a day's growth of beard, shook his head. He looked out his side window, pulled the stick toward himself to lower flaps, and then picked up the cut ends of the wires dangling from the big cup-shaped earphones.

"Keeps your ears warm!!" he shouted, and then they were dropping down all those eight hundred feet, as if they were bumping down steps foot by foot, toward the lake.

At the end of a bay was a tiny Indian village with a long dock thrust out into the lake. Sheila felt like Indiana Jones. She jerked the useless earphones off and let them encircle her neck and clutched the door handle once again.

They seemed to be rushing down through the air, the blue, clean, perfect Canadian air of the wilderness which resisted them with such force. The lake was lightly white-capped but, as they drew closer, every one of those foaming daisies of whitecaps looked to her like a mountain top.

They smashed into the whitecaps, rebounded several feet, and then plunged down into them again and at last the tiny plane dipped its big silver pontoons deep into the blue water and they floated, bounding lightly, toward the dock. Sheila's hands were wet with sweat, and she watched as an Indian man in jeans and down jacket took the rope the pilot flung to him. They were tied on.

Sheila grabbed her sports bag and jumped the four feet to the dock. There was a light wind, and it smelled of wood smoke and other things she could not identify. The village houses were small, they looked busy. Woodpiles outside replete with saws and axes, there were furs laced to hoops and the loud snoring noises of chainsaws at work somewhere. All around, the thick forest stood at attention.

The Indian man shook her hand. He stared at her gravely and said, "Miss, you are looking for a fisherman, that Texan, Slim Lambert?"

"Yes, I am." She shifted her bag, dropped it between her feet. Her dark-green polo shirt was not enough, and she got a heavy yellow sweatshirt out of the bag and pulled it over her head. As soon as her head appeared out of the neck-hole, she shoved back her hair and asked, "Do you know where he is?"

The young man continued as if he hadn't heard her. "And you are a lawyer and you want him to come and speak in a murder trial."

"Well, yes." She was astounded. She crossed her arms. "Anything else?"

"Yes. He is an important witness and you never flew on these little planes before and you want to take him back right now." He made a downward motion with his hand, as if to say, 'that is the end of all the information I have.'

"Pretty good," she said. "This was all moccasin telegraph?"

He nodded. "Yep."

"I think you could give AT&T some lessons."

"Yep. Now, you want to talk to Slim?"

Sheila smiled and said, "Yep."

Half an hour later, balancing carefully, she stepped out of the six-teen-foot canoe with its loud little motor on the stem, onto a weathered dock. She hadn't done gymnastics in high school for nothing. Wood smoke streamed out sideways in the light breeze. A man was sitting on the dock in a canvas chair carefully attaching a leader to a large hook. He was a long man with a full head of hair and his hat was far back on the his head. The light frail sun buttered his khakis a warm color and the tall pines behind him stood like sentinels in the morning light.

Sheila felt like Stanley approaching Livingstone.

She walked toward him, her hand out.

"Mr. Lambert, I presume?"

He looked up, took in her slim figure and the red hair lightly blown by the northern breeze, and her hand stretched out to him.

"Yes?"

"We need you," she said. "At a murder trial in Texas."

He put both hands on the wooden arms of the canvas chair and stood up. Slim was a man of about six foot one or two. He had a face that had seen a lot of combat, and a lot of weathering

"Well, I'll be damned," he said. "You come a long way."

Judge Barret sensed Hogan was stalling.

The judge's suspicions were correct. Hogan was waiting to see whether the former Texas Ranger, Slim Lambert, was going to appear. They seemed to have been hunting him for weeks.

Billy Martin, the first witness called, was a smart young man but very self-effacing. He was over six foot tall and was darkly handsome but extremely retiring and modest. He also knew he shouldn't be there. He was a young man of flexible convictions and apprehensive he would suffer serious consequences if it appeared he was on the side of the Vietnamese. He was recently married with a young family and he needed to keep his job at the chemical plant near San Ignacio. He had been advised not to testify.

When he looked at the scowling D.A., he fervently wished he wasn't in the courtroom. He had on a blue work-shirt and jeans. He had to go to work at the chromium plant as soon as he got out of here, back to the noise of the bashing ore bins and stink of the chrome, and he wasn't dressing up for some situation where he had been dragged in. He was under subpoena and was told he had to tell the truth.

"Yeah. I saw Billy Joe stomp on Cai's fingers at the dock. I left before there was any shooting. I don't know anything about arguments or fights before the shooting — only what I heard. That's all I've got to say. I'm not here because I want to be." Billy's replies and the questions came in short order.

Strangely enough, Billy Martin was stronger on cross-examination than on direct. He couldn't understand why he was being battered and accused by the district attorney when he knew he was telling the truth so far as he knew it. D.A. Davis, with his glossy hair and striding, self-confident manner seemed a tiny bit baffled. His movie-star looks weren't doing him any good with this witness.

Several times Billy said, "Mister, you know I don't want to be here. I tried to get excused. That's all I know about the situation, what I saw."

"But you're not here to say the shooting was justified?"

"No, sir."

"Or that it wasn't a cold-blooded, premeditated murder?"

"No."

"When you shoot a man in the back it speaks for itself?"

"I guess the jurors would know best. I guess the judge does, too. All

I know is Cai was howling and holding his bloody fingers when I left. That Billy Joe was one big dude."

Davis sighed and turned back to his counsel table, his lips pressed together. He concluded he had pushed enough — maybe too much.

"No further questions."

Still Hogan held out and dragged the trial out, waiting and hoping for the Texas Ranger. He could not do this much longer or he would lose all the good will he had won through Lillie May. The tension in the courtroom was growing, as if someone were playing one tune over and over and over. Judge Barret had finally begun to look Hogan in the eye. Now, he was staring at him with iron resolution, waiting. The two defendants sat and looked straight ahead, mainly at the witnesses, and, lacking a witness, anywhere but at the judge or jury.

Hogan could tell the jury had never once slackened their interest, but whether it was because they were looking forward to sending Cai to prison for life, or were wondering just where justice lay, he could not tell. Mrs. Martinez and the fireman, Charles Mays, were the only ones who showed any emotion, and it had been they who seemed slightly impatient with Hogan's seemingly pointless witnesses. The two colonels sat without expression, the picture of stern justice.

Hogan wondered if they were afraid of a long, tedious trial. After all, it was now September in Stillwater, and high school activities had begun, and the racing stables were preparing for the racing season. There were cheerleaders every day out on the high school football field, leaping and screaming in blue and silver, Stillwater's colors. The teenaged boys ran at one another in heavy padding and helmets. Streams of dust rose from the fields as the cotton stalks were plowed under, and long eleven-horse vans pulled out for the tracks in Louisiana and Florida. Life was going on out there and, as interesting as the trial might have been initially, the violence and excitement of the Klan, of riots in a small town, and the buzzing, fly-like media, they were stuck in a dark courtroom listening to endless and often irrelevant testimony.

With reluctance, Hogan called his next witness. He had reservations because he just didn't know when this man was telling the truth.

Nguyen Duc Bang was a cautious, reticent man. He talked very softly. The judge had to admonish him several times to speak up as the court reporter and others couldn't hear him. He lacked credibility simply because he was so nervous. Bang looked like a man in desperate need of a cigarette. He was tall for a Vietnamese, very thin, almost emaciated, much the appearance of the defendants themselves, except that he was about a foot taller. His English was poor and halting and on the whole, he was extremely defensive. Though he was put on by the defense, for the lack of other witnesses, he probably hurt more than helped. The sheriff had been seen talking to him just before he took the stand. There was strong evidence the conversation was disquieting to Nguyen Duc Bang.

On direct examination, Bang said he saw Billy Joe cut Cai about twenty minutes before the shooting. He said he saw Billy Joe chase Cai around the Flores saloon on one occasion and beat him before Cai could get away. "Billy Joe, he yelled he would blow his head off if Cai didn't leave town."

Hogan concluded his questions quickly. In print, his testimony would look very good. In reality, after the district attorney was through, it was much weaker. His responses were so helpful to the district attorney, it was almost as if it had been rehearsed.

"You'd do anything you could to help these boys, wouldn't you?" the D.A. asked.

"Yeah, sure." He looked furtively over at Cai and Tho. They looked straight back at him.

"And that means, of course, that you would invent stories to suggest that they were being bullied by Billy Joe?"

"What?"

"I mean you know nothing about Billy Joe's threats, but just what you have been told."

"Yeah."

"It's my understanding that you left immediately, and that you drove Cai out of town in your car after you saw him kill Billy Joe?"

"Yeah, he want to go, man, real bad. He pay me."

"You've shown up only for this trial and refused to reveal where you live. Is that true?"

"Yeah."

"You refused to talk to the investigators?"

"Yeah."

"What is it that you have to hide that would make you be so afraid?"

"I been run out of my home. I just don't want trouble. I don't want to be here."

"You know the killing was in cold blood?"

"Yeah."

"We have no further questions," the district attorney said. From his smug look, it was clear the D.A. felt Hogan was helping rather than hurting the prosecution.

He was quite content to let him use up time before putting Cai on the stand. He felt it was just a matter of getting this case to the jury for the inevitable verdict.

"It's all over but the celebration," he assured his lawyers.

Chapter Thirty-Seven

Stillwater baked in the September heat. Air-conditioners in the old courthouse labored to keep the heat at bay, and the countryside, studded with cactus and mesquite around Stillwater, was turning droughty brown. They came back after a short lunch and made their way through the usual gaggle of reporters, some of whom they were coming to know well. Hogan's friends seemed to be returning.

The Hardins were as always packed on the front row of benches. Nothing or no one escaped their attention.

Hogan was fishing desperately for help. He called Georgia Cadwaller again.

"This is absolutely the last witness we are going to call if the Ranger doesn't show. It looks like filler and it's hurting more than helping," Hogan whispered to Paul and Sabine and Big Bob.

They were glad to see Georgia again. Though neither conventionally attractive nor engaging, there was something so essentially honest in her attitude that people liked her. She was Ma Kettle, the salt of the earth, the great Earth Goddess with a whiskey voice.

The crab processing plant Georgia ran was the only real home she had. She didn't want to jeopardize her job. She had appeared as a witness in the motion for change of venue, and now was here only by subpoena as she was fearful that it might hurt her position at the plant if she volunteered.

Hogan began with the usual background questions and, once again, Georgia came through as the hard-working, honest person she was. "Georgia, do you know Cai?"

"I sure do."

"Tell the jury about him."

"He's honest and hardworking. His hours were about four in the morning until midnight. Worked his butt off."

"Does he seem to like the area of San Ignacio?"

"He loved it and wanted to make it his home for life."

"What was preventing him?"

"They were harassing him to death, especially Billy Joe."

"Would you say Billy Joe was a peaceful man?

"Peaceful!" Georgia laughed. "If he was twins, his parents would have killed theirselves."

"We have no further questions," concluded Hogan.

The D.A. came up, looking at her with distaste. "Georgia, you know nothing about the shooting, do you?"

"No, sir."

"Nor do you personally know of any threats or abuse by Billy Joe?"

"Not personally."

"The only thing you *are* sure of is that the Vietnamese are great cheap labor and that makes your boss a nice profit. Isn't that right?"

"Didn't we go through this before?" she asked. "Didn't this man ask me this whole damn thing before?" She looked around. Several members of the jury laughed. But it was a good laugh. They liked her.

Judge Barret smiled. "That was on another aspect of the trial," he explained in a kindly voice. "On whether it should have been moved. Now you're here to tell us if there was a conflict between Billy Joe Hardin and these defendants."

"Yes, sir, there was." She nodded. She turned back to the jury. "Billy Joe said he'd get them all out of town if it took all day. He'd usually say it when he was toilet huggin' drunk. Then he was as mean as a acre of snakes."

"Mrs. Cadwaller ..."

But the jury's eyes were sparkling. It was, at last, some entertainment in all the long boring testimony. Even the judge was smiling.

"You never *saw* any fighting between them with *your own eyes*, did you?" The D.A.'s tie was decorated with fish in brilliant colors.

"Mister District Attorney, you sure got some ties," she said. "That one would about wake the dead. That's a *coonass* tie."

Sabine let out a small shriek of uncontainable laughter before slapping a hand over her mouth. Hogan just smiled. He knew *coonass*, which had no racial significance and no known etymology, meant a Louisianan, and specifically a French Cajun from Louisiana.

The D.A. stood tall and gathered his patience. "Mrs. Cadwaller, I said ..."

"I know what you said. No, I never seen him actually whip up on little Cai there, but I seen Cai's hand ..."

"That'll do."

"But I tell you, them organizations that come in, they had ol' Billy Joe stirred up. He wasn't bright. He couldn't pour rainwater out of a boot if the instructions were printed on the heel ..." The courtroom was reaching a dangerous level of hilarity.

"That'll *do*, Mrs. Cadwaller."

"And he'd fight a circle-saw if he were drunk."

"Judge ...

Judge Barret bit his lip but his eyes sparkled with delight. "Mrs. Cadwaller ..." he said, forcing sternness into his voice.

"All right, all right," she muttered. She lifted her heavy frame up onto her feet. "So long, Mr. D.A. I hope all your kids are born nekkid."

Several of the jurors laughed outright and then tried to cough and cover it up, but others were subsiding in helpless, if silent laughter.

"Mr. Hogan, we are going to adjourn for the day. I assume that you plan to conclude your testimony tomorrow so the case can be argued the following day?" the judge asked Hogan.

"Yes, your Honor."

Father Dominic had driven down to San Ignacio the day before, to stay the night there with a family of his parishioners. He had gone down to walk the streets of the little town again before he was called to testify. He walked down Matagorda Street, nodding to all he met as the hot Gulf wind came up from the steel-gray water.

He had never imagined himself becoming involved in a matter such as this. We must not become isolated because of this, he thought. So he walked through the streets of town as if they were all friends, as if nothing had happened, as if anything that indeed had happened was not beyond repair.

In his deep faith, Father Dominic assumed that Billy Joe was before a greater judge. He knew that Cai would someday be before that great judge as well. He nodded cheerfully to an Anglo housewife who was walking back from the grocery store with a paper sack of groceries. She looked at him dubiously and then nodded back. Just these simple things, he told himself. A simple nod, a stroll down the street, all could have a calming effect. He looked at the paper bags. In Vietnam, that heavy brown paper would be precious. Here, they threw it away.

At the docks, he stood and looked out over the sea, and knew why so many men of all races and ages fell in love with it. It was something so much bigger than mere human beings. And in its enormity it relieved people of their petty, endless, pompous strivings. The evening wind combed through his hair. He watched a crab boat come in, a small sixteen-footer, a man standing at the forward wheel, cutting through the still bay water. The man stood still and straight at the wheel and his reflection preceded him in the glassy water, and then broke up in the waves winging away from the boat.

He calmed himself and watched rolling, foamy clouds build on the southern horizon, heard the shouts of children and the *whap whap whap* of a basketball. San Ignacio was tiny, but here a great change had begun. He turned and walked back toward the center of town where he had parked in the grocery-store lot. A car full of young Anglo men in ball caps drove past, and they looked him over, but none of them said a word. He nodded to them as well, and gave his most cheerful smile.

Hogan called Father Dominic to the stand. He probably wouldn't hurt and might help. Besides, Hogan needed the time. He'd left one message after another with the bush-plane company but none had been returned.

Father Dominic was impressive because he was a man who seemed to radiate calm. He seemed at peace with himself and showed no dislike or resentment of anyone. But Hogan knew that he could never predict what the man of God was going to say. His was an old-fashioned wisdom and education, and his honesty was rigorous. He was small in height, probably five foot four, soft of voice, wide and large of frame but not fat. His face was unlined, untroubled and his glasses were large in heavy frames.

"Would you state your name?"

"I'm Father Dominic."

"And if you would give the jury your occupation?"

"I'm a Roman Catholic priest and have been for the last ten years."

"If you would give them your chronological history before becoming a priest?"

"I was born and raised in Vietnam. My family were all killed in the war. I was ordained at a Catholic Seminary in Vietnam. It was my hope to remain at the monastery and be a cloistered monk. God ruled otherwise."

With little interruption, Father Dominic explained that he worked among the resettlement camps. He told the jury that most of the people were from the same villages, Ba Lang and Vung Tau.

"Like many immigrants, they cling together in family groups," he explained.

The D.A. was energetic with his objections. Repeatedly the court overruled. It was obvious the defendants were being given increased latitude. The D.A. was quietly but obviously furious.

"They are a traumatized people. Presently they are trying by hard work and education and loyalty to this country to fit in as best they can. If ever they reach the mainstream of America, I'm sure my countrymen will make proud and productive Americans."

Hogan let that sink in, then stuck his hands in his pockets once again and walked back, as if thinking.

"What about the killing, Father Dominic? Is that any way to fit into the mainstream?"

Father Dominic looked down. His eyes were round and guileless behind his glasses. "I pray for them daily and for the victim's family as part of my evening devotions."

In a quick glance, Hogan could tell that there was not a member of the jury who doubted it, but then again, it wasn't Father Dominic who was on trial. At any rate, he seemed to have brought an eloquence and understanding to the plight of Cai that Hogan could not. Hogan had intended to use him only as filler, but he turned out to be more like heartwood. He calmed everyone, he brought everything down to a reasonable level, he seemed to hold a key.

But it was possible that Hogan was kidding himself. There was no key to be found in minds that were closed. At any rate, Father Dominic fortified his belief that he was on the right side for the right reason.

"Tell the jury about Cai and Tho particularly." With that question he again sensed coldness from the jury.

"I've known them for a number of years. They are prepared to take whatever is just and fair. Beyond that, I can't say. I don't know what happened at the time of the shooting or what caused it."

Again the objection that the testimony was unresponsive and irrelevant was overruled. Clearly the judge and D.A. were no longer singing from the same sheet of music. The D.A. went to some lengths in remarks and body language to show that.

"Tell the jury what you know about Billy Joe."

"I knew his wife much better because she came to Mass when she could. I would say he was obsessed with the thought that the Vietnamese must leave. Perhaps at times he over-reacted. I cannot say because I saw no abuse nor heard any threat. I did share his view that the Vietnamese were unwelcome and they needed to leave, and find a better place to settle."

"No further questions," said Hogan.

The district attorney could hardly wait. He rose, straightening his brilliant lavender and green tie.

He strode up to the small priest. "Father, when Cai slipped up on Billy Joe and shot him in the back and then five or six other times while he was laying on the ground dying or dead, I don't think he was just being a nice peaceful fisherman, don't you agree?"

Father Dominic shook his head sadly. "It was a terrible act. I can only believe he must have taken an awful beating to make him behave that way. That is not the kind of person that I know him to be. Yes, I agree, it is a terrible act."

"And as to threats and knifing and beatings, you know nothing about that of your own knowledge, do you, Father?"

"No, I don't and am not prepared to repeat any stories I merely heard."

The priest sat resolute, refusing to retail slander. Hogan gave a small, low groan. Couldn't he have seen just one threat, one waved fist?

"We have no further questions," the district attorney said. He felt sure Hogan was reaching, stalling, knowing that he soon had to put Cai on the stand. That's when the district attorney expected to move in for the kill. To him these delays and all else, including the missing Vietnamese interpreter, were inconsequential.

Outside, several print and television reporters pressed forward. Paul and Sabine went on ahead, anxious to get out of the heat and into an air-conditioned car.

"Are you concluding?" asked one reporter.

"Probably," said Hogan. Head down, he strode past the mob. He felt they certainly had not done him any favors and that he owed them little time. The harm they could cause had long since occurred, and repeatedly.

Big Bob followed close on Hogan's heels. As soon as they climbed into their car, the reporters fell back like a wolf-pack giving up. They had no prey this time.

The defense team headed for San Antonio, with no plans other than Cai's examination. They all knew the cross-examination would be merciless. It had been put off as long as possible. Hogan looked out the windows at the familiar countryside rolling by, the grasslands with grazing horses and cattle, and in the far distance, the towers of San Antonio -- the Tower Life building and the big tourist hotels crowded around the small building called the Alamo.

All those grand, modern buildings, and the most important one of all was a tiny stone chapel in the midst of the humming city. No one came to San Antonio to gaze at the superb architecture of the Hilton or the Sheraton. They were only places to stay while the visitors went, hat in hand, to the small, one-story, precariously preserved limestone church where more than a hundred men had died in a desperate last stand against thousands. Hogan thought about it. It gave him hope. He told himself, people will always respond to what truly matters, as opposed to what is flashy, a thing of the moment. That's what he hoped, anyway.

He knew the D.A. would take the reticent, shy Cai apart on the witness stand. Then he remembered Lillie May, and he held out a small, lambent glow of hope in his heart that he had not been too boorish, too hard, that by some miracle Sheila would come back to him.

God, he missed her. He hadn't realized how much she'd come to mean to him until she was gone. But he could do nothing to find her, to bring her back. He felt clumsy and lost and lonely, and the feelings infuriated him, and so he kept silent.

At the office, Hogan opened the door to his large room and then stood stock-still when he saw Sheila sitting in his chair, behind his desk, dressed in khakis and a royal blue polo shirt and boating shoes, drinking a cup of coffee.

Sabine and Paul said, at the same time, "Sheila!"

"Hi," she said. "Go away," she told Paul and Sabine.

They did.

Hogan stood with one fist on a hip and stared at her.

"Thought I went off on a tear?"

"No," he said, but his breath was going short and he could hardly trust himself to say anything else.

"Want to fire me?"

"No," he said.

Then Hogan walked over and took her by the arm and she stood up to meet him and he put his arms around her and held her very close. Outside, another siren was shrieking its way to the Nix, and the bells at St. Joseph's could be faintly heard ringing seven at night.

He held her long slim body to him as long as the bells rang, as if they were ringing out some magical affirmation. He felt her relax, finally and hold him as well.

Then he said into her hair, "Why'd you go?"

"I went to find Lambert," she said. "Someone had to."

"You smell like wood smoke. Engine oil."

"You won't believe it. I haven't been out of these clothes for three days."

He stood back and took both her hands. "Sheila, are you going to come back here and be a lawyer?"

"Are you going to have me acting like an office boy?" She smiled. "Office person?"

"All right. I'm an insensitive boor. You, on the other hand, were A.W.O.L. You can't walk out of a trial like that! At least, not without clearing it with me first."

She waved a finger in front of his face. "I didn't walk out of the trial. Technically. I was on an investigative mission."

He shrugged, laughed, and put his arms around her again.

"Wait!" She reached behind her and took his hands. "Come down to the coffee room."

She almost ran, pulling Hogan behind her. "Come on. I've got someone I want you to meet."

His long legs were stretched out in front of him; his polished Lucchese boots gleamed. He looked up from his cup of coffee, rose and held out his hand. "Mr. Hogan." His voice was rough from whiskey and cigarettes, deep and low and laconic.

"I'm glad to see you, sir." Hogan pumped the man's hand. Whether all this trauma had been worth it or not, he wasn't sure, but Lambert was the only good witness he had. "We'll put you up, and I really thank you for coming."

"Thank Miss Ryan here." The retired Ranger was courtly in his manners as he nodded toward Sheila. "When she walked up to me on that dock, I had to look twice. I couldn't believe it."

They sat up late in the dining room of the apartment, while Sheila, still reserved, listened to Hogan tell her the events of the trial that she had missed.

"He did?" Sheila lost all reserve in a bout of laughter, listening to Hogan's description of Davis' outrage at the suppression of the confessions. "By God, we have a chance!"

"We?" Hogan looked at her up out of his wrinkled face, wrinkles which seemed to get deeper as the trial went on.

"Yes. We." She smiled happily. "There's nobody like you, Hogan. There never was. I have to take the good and the bad both, but I just don't want to sit around for *all* the bad."

"Yeah, yeah, I know. I know." He reached over and took her by the shoulders. "It's going to work," he said.

They sank into the bed and he felt that silky auburn hair beneath his forearm, and later on when he felt she was asleep, he went into the dining room and sat down at the piano. He looked carefully at the score, and to quiet himself, he began to play.

Chapter Thirty-Eight

September 17th

It was six in the morning. Sheila knew Hogan always left very early for his walk across the still, cool cityscape to San Fernando Cathedral. She listened for the sound of his key in the lock and his whistling.

She was up, had coffee made, and this morning she was stripping the plastic film from a recently cleaned suit. She studied the summer suit. It was made of linen and silk, a pale blue with beige turned-back cuffs on the jacket and a sleeveless dress underneath. Yes, it would do.

As she dressed, Sheila followed Hogan's movements about the apartment. Clinking sounds from the kitchen. Then the plinking of piano keys as she fastened the bone necklace around her neck. She heard a few bars of some old exercises, and then he picked out the melody of the beautiful old Irish hymn, *St. Patrick's Breastplate*. He played it twice, and then once again with the left-hand accompaniment.

Then, slowly, the opening bars of *Weeping Willow*. She stood and listened until the music stopped.

The morning breeze had blown in and whisked away all the muggy air. The sky overhead, over the rooftops of downtown San Antonio was as clear as glass, and the pigeons flashed like sprays of confetti from the roof of St. Joseph's to the broad live-oaks of the Alamo Plaza.

He walked in and looked at her.

"There's a lawyer if I ever saw one."

She smiled, and they said nothing but only looked at one another. He reached for his briefcase with one hand and held the door open for her.

Hogan watched as Lambert greeted nearly everyone in the courthouse as a friend — the bailiff, the district attorney, even one or two of the older reporters.

Sheila and Hogan had spent an hour with Lambert the previous evening, asking about his background, checking out what kind of guy he was.

Slim had spent twenty years with the Rangers before retirement, and for five years thereafter he was a constable in San Ignacio, while ranching near Victoria on a few thousand acres willed to him by the bachelor uncle who had reared him. The land had been in the Lambert family for two hundred years. It wasn't a big living, but a good one.

"Besides that, I don't want to do all that much ranching at my age," he said. "Neither does the wife." They found he had received a Bronze and Silver Star in Vietnam and had known Billy Joe.

He was impeccable, Hogan thought.

Sabine and Paul greeted Sheila happily, shaking her hand and congratulating her on finding the Ranger. They seemed greatly relieved. There were low murmurs between them, and once Sabine kicked Paul's ankle under the table.

When they had set out their files, Hogan turned to Sheila and, much to everyone's surprise, said, "Take the witness." He was handing her his ace in the hole.

When he was called, the lanky Ranger walked to the stand, slow as molasses and completely unflappable.

Sheila looked at him for a moment, and then smiled, and stood up and walked, still smiling her broad good smile, toward the Ranger.

Barret looked at her with a little surprise and Davis leaned back and stared at her long legs, then finally leaned forward as if to take her seriously.

In a clear voice, she quickly established Lambert's credentials, his service records and combat awards, and his retirement. Lambert went through it all easily. In his years as a Ranger he had testified many times.

Finally Sheila tipped her head toward him and said, "Mr. Lambert, would you describe Billy Joe?"

"He was a rough, big ol' stout boy who was capable of smashing most people if they got in his way," said Lambert. "I've put him in to cool down a couple of times. He could be pretty mean." Slim's voice was calm and smooth, deeply accented with south Texas inflections. "Billy Joe had a reputation for fighting, that's for sure."

"And describe his general ..." Sheila paused, looking for the word she wanted. "Lifestyle?" She stepped slowly near the jury rail in her neat beige heels, turned, and said. "Did he hunt? Shoot birds?"

"I think he hunted," said Lambert. "He carried a rifle in his pickup anyhow, at least every time I saw him driving around town."

"What were your conversations with him??"

"Objection!" Davis came to his feet. "She's asking for hearsay!"

The judge said, "Mr. Davis, he is allowed to say what he *said* to Mr. Hardin, telling about your own words isn't hearsay unless you have a split personality."

There were titters from the spectators as Davis sat down.

Lambert looked out over the courtroom and said, "I told that boy, I said, 'I've heard of your threats to kill some of these Vietnamese boys, but you want to make sure that the killing isn't on the other side.' He said, 'What do you mean?' and I said, 'You know, this is going to keep on until some of these Vietnamese boys might do the killing. If the corner gets too tight, they stand their ground'."

Lambert looked at the jury. "That's why I told Billy Joe to back off and cool it before there was real trouble."

Sheila had gotten all she could and there was no point going on. She thanked Lambert and he nodded to her, and stepped down. Returning to the table, she sat down by Sabine, who reached over under the table and squeezed her hand. Hogan scribbled *'just right'* on a note and shoved it down to her. Sheila read it and smiled happily.

On cross-examination, Slim acknowledged that the incident was two years ago, that he knew nothing about the killing, that he certainly couldn't testify that the shooting was in self-defense. The Hardin family generally had a good name, he said. Billy Joe had a good wife and two lovely children. Mr. and Mrs. Hardin contributed a lot to the community, and he had known them as friends for decades.

Then Sheila, with a nod from Hogan, stood up again.

"Mr. Lambert, have you ever heard of the legend of a seven-year-old girl named Kim?"

"Sure, anyone associated with the 104th Marines, like me, has heard of it." It had already been established that Slim Lambert had been awarded the silver star and bronze star for his Vietnam service.

"Objection! Not relevant!"

"Wait," said the judge. "Let's see if it is or if it isn't."

"Your Honor, it will be connected with testimony from Cai himself given the opportunity." Sheila stood poised in her powder-blue suit, and Hogan wondered what the hell she had gained from Lambert on the flight home. She had kept behind some surprise. He laughed quietly.

The jury listened, frowning, as Lambert went on to explain that he knew a Hispanic Vietnam veteran by the name of Raul, who still lived in Oklahoma City. "He's badly disabled because of a nervous breakdown and his life's in ruin because of something that happened long ago during the Vietnam War. Raul's squad befriended Vietnamese village children who would visit them daily to try to get candy from them. Raul became very friendly and paternal to a seven-year-old girl named Kim. She was the same age as his daughter."

"Objection!" Davis shot up.

"Be quiet, Mr. Davis," said Barret, impatiently. "Overruled."

"One day, Kim was used by the Vietcong as a kamikaze. She showed up alone at the soldiers' camp, wired with explosives. Before she got too close, she unbuttoned her blouse to show the soldiers the bomb. What she was saying," Lambert explained, "was 'take me out now, because if I get any closer, I'm going to take all of you.' Raul was one of the men who shot her and, to this day, he is in torment, anguish, a shell of a man. He was never able to get over the experience. It was as if he had shot his own daughter."

"She gave her life so he and his fellow Marines could live," Sheila said.

The district attorney again asked that his testimony be stricken as irrelevant, and the jury was instructed to disregard it.

"It was the bravest thing I've ever seen," Lambert said.

"Mr. Lambert, who were the 104th Marines?" Sheila asked.

Lambert explained that they were a rag-tag outfit of young Vietnamese boys who served under the tutelage of several Marine Corps sergeants. They called themselves the 104th Marines for the lack of a better title. Largely they served as scouts for the Marines, but they'd been thoroughly trained and were immensely helpful.

"They had the dirtiest and most dangerous work in that miserable war. But for their abilities we would have been killed a dozen times."

Sheila nodded and turned in a light, graceful motion to the jury, regarded them, and then back to Lambert.

"Mr. Lambert, is there anything you can add?"

"Well, that's about all I've got to say. This jury has a rough problem," he volunteered. "I've always been for law and order but with even-handed justice."

The retired Ranger was excused, and he strode out of the courtroom in the same long slow walk he had entered it. He paused outside, looked at the reporters and their cameras, put his Stetson back on his head and walked out of everyone's life the same way he had walked in.

Chapter Thirty-Nine

At noon recess, Hogan and Sheila had driven to a good barbecue place south of Stillwater, and then got caught in the highway construction as they returned. The expressway was under construction and traffic was so slow that progress was impossible. He waited while the earth-moving machines rumbled and the flagmen signaled lines of cars to stop and then start, stop and then start again. When they got back, they'd call their last witness. The thought was a great relief to Hogan.

Exasperated, they arrived just as the judge was calling for Mr. Hogan and the next witness. Sheila and Hogan quickly slid into their places.

The next witness would be Cai.

When he'd first met Cai Van Nguyen, the young man was only a little over five feet. It now looked like he had shrunk to four-and-a-half feet. He appeared to have lost twenty pounds, and he couldn't have weighed much more than one hundred to begin with. His clothes looked like they belonged to a much larger and older man. They had reasonably fit him just weeks ago when the trial first began. His color was chalk-white and he spoke in whispers. Hogan could have bet good money that the boy had lain awake all night in the jail.

Lillie May was fresh and keenly aware of the importance of the moment. Her previous success on the stand must have given her confidence. She wore a pale gray suit with a shell-pink blouse, and a small string of pearls. Her hair had been newly cut in a cropped bob that fell to just below her ears. Her shining black hair shook as she turned her head one way or the other. Sitting beside Cai at the counsel table, she looked over at the brothers with her tilted black eyes, and gave them a confident smile.

Hogan hurried to take his place at the counsel table and said to Sheila, "I'm not entirely sure where all of this legend of Kim and 104th Marines was leading, but you did a superb job of getting it out of him. Right now, we have absolutely nothing to lose. We are that far behind." He turned to Lillie May.

"Are you ready?"

She smiled and he detected only the barest edge of nervousness.

"Yes, Mr. Hogan."

"All right."

"Good, then."

He sounded resigned, and he was walking with his head down now even more as if studying the old wooden floors of the courthouse for a solution. His hands, as always, were jammed hard in his pockets.

Cai walked over to the stand as if the floor were a minefield.

Hogan nodded to him comfortingly. It had little effect, so he just went ahead. He began with general questions as to the age, origin, occupation, and antecedents of Cai in order that he could quickly follow up into the effective testimony, if any.

"What is your name?"

He saw Cai bent to Lillie May and whisper.

"Cai Van Nguyen," said Lily May, her face serious and composed.

"And who are your brothers and sisters?"

"I have only one brother, and that's Tho. The rest of my family is still in Vietnam. They were held."

"How old are you?"

"I'm twenty-one."

"And what is your occupation?"

"I have been a fisherman all my life," said Lillie May after a low murmur from Cai. As she turned from Cai back to Hogan her shining hair swung.

"Where was your home, then, Cai?" Hogan looked at the young man but Cai avoided Hogan's eyes, instead looking down at his hands, responding again in that almost inaudible voice.

"I come from a village in central Vietnam which was a fishing village. Vung Tau. And I have always fished for a living, except for the time I was fighting with the Americans."

"Were you involved in the war?"

Lillie May listened, and then turned to Hogan and said, "Yes. We were always on the side of the Americans."

"You've heard Texas Ranger Lambert's testimony about Kim and the 104th Marines. Did you know her?"

"She was my cousin."

The atmosphere was tense, and even the jury was listening intently with puzzled expressions as to the connection between the legend of Kim and the defendants. The D.A. seemed preoccupied with his preparation for cross-examination and failed to object. Both colonels both seemed particularly interested.

"Did you know the 104th Marines?"

"I served with them for almost a year with my brother, Tho."

Surprised murmurs swept the courtroom.

"What did you do?"

Cai seemed about to sink away as he whispered his replies. Lillie May was the focus, and it was to her face the jury turned when the time came for an answer. She seemed to be on trial, not Cai. The attention of both the judge and jury were riveted on her.

"We served as scouts finding the enemy and trying to locate land mines, detecting ambush traps and snipers. Then we got ambushed."

"How did that happen?" Hogan couldn't stop himself from asking the question. He was an old infantryman, a Marine, himself. Ambushes were of almost hypnotic interest to any grunt.

"Objection, your Honor. I mean really, this is ..."

"Overruled.."

"This is utterly irrelevant."

"I repeat, overruled. I feel it has some bearing on Mr. Nguyen's abilities with weapons."

This mollified Davis somewhat, and he sat back down grumbling.

"We had been betrayed. The 104th was mostly Vietnamese young guys with a few American Marines. All were destroyed except two American survivors—and me and Tho. We were at Gigidinh when we were overrun. We were surrounded and cut down by crossfire and mortars."

Lillie May looked at the jury, speaking in her clear and resonant voice. She said, for Cai, "We were fighting a war we didn't understand but supported." The room was in total silence.

"What happened after the 104th Marines were destroyed?"

"Me and Tho were taken to the hospital. We stayed there for many weeks and were discharged only days before the fall of Saigon in May of 1975."

"How did you leave Saigon?"

"We were on the last boat out. A colonel who knew of the 104th got us aboard." Cai's replies were muffled and short but they came to the jury through Lillie May, with a voice that was resonant, credible, sincere.

"We left Vietnam six days after the fall of Saigon. We left in a small boat; it had the capacity for eight people but we were with twenty other people. For eight days and seven nights, we were on the open sea moving toward the Philippines. We had little or no food or water during all that time. The rains were drenching us. We arrived at Manila but were told to stay in the bay. We stayed in the boat, again without food and water, for eleven days more until they finally moved us into the camp."

Hogan couldn't understand what was happening. The questions were his, but the responses were all Lillie May. It was a moment he had never witnessed in a courtroom. Even the judge was spellbound by the diminutive lady and her resolute, clear voice. He was silent as she listened first to Cai's whispering and then turned and gave what was apparently his replies; although Hogan could not be sure. He was never sure. But he felt like he'd just spent a Confederate dollar and got back American change, and he wasn't going to argue with his luck.

"How were you recruited into the 104th Marines?"

"We volunteered, and they took us. We formed our own group as guides and scouts, and gave ourselves the title of the 104th because the Marines trained us."

"How old were you?"

"Fifteen, when all this began."

"What was your education?"

"Eighth grade."

"What happened to your family?"

"They were separated all over Vietnam." The jury looked at Lillie May. It was as if she were saying it was *her* family that had been scattered and lost — and perhaps they had been. The fate of all Vietnam seemed to be reflected in her black eyes.

"After you got to this country, did you ever receive any food stamps or welfare aid?"

Lillie May shook her head and her hair swung out in a fan and then fell back into place. "We never received any money from the government at any time, or food stamps either. They did not help us try to buy our boats or with any living quarters or any necessities. We thought that was okay and still do. All we want is a chance to work."

Hogan smiled slightly, then asked, "How did you get a boat when you moved to San Ignacio?"

"I saved $300 as a welder in Louisiana. I bought a very old boat and saved my money to overhaul the engine. The man who owned the crab plant gave me the traps initially or lent the money so that I could pay him back. Nothing was given to me. I worked for three months to pay back for the traps. Many of them were lost or taken or destroyed by the American fishermen."

"Who was it that didn't want you in San Ignacio?"

Hogan had the habit of turning and then walking toward the witness when he wanted to draw attention to the testimony. Sometimes he would drift over to the far end of the jury rail and from there put his inquiries. He himself was enchanted, mesmerized by the story that was unfolding in front of him, this epic journey across dangerous seas, the arrival, the wandering, the search for a home. He felt like a stage manager, standing in the wings with his rumpled hair and favorite old jacket, while in the spotlight was this lovely woman and what was becoming her story. She was becoming not only Cai's voice but Cai himself, while the Vietnamese fisherman faded more and more until he seemed to disappear.

"Wasn't there a complaint that you did not follow the customs and traditions of the local fishermen?" Hogan asked.

Lillie May listened briefly, then shrugged. "I know nothing about their customs or traditions. We worked day and night all the time. It was

August and this is when the crab harvest is the best, and the season doesn't last that long. We had to work hard when the time was right."

Hogan continued to shift his position in front of the jury, drawing attention to Lillie May, though she needed little help.

"When did you first start crabbing in San Ignacio?"

"We started in the San Antonio Bay where the crabs were pretty rare. We decided to go back up the river which was the most popular spot. The Americans said we were crabbing in waters that belonged to them."

"When is the first time you met Billy Joe?"

Now Lillie May began to speak more slowly, and directly to the jurors. Sheila had done a superb job in coaching her, Hogan saw.

"He came up one day to our boat and placed a gun on top of the crate of crabs and threatened that, if we didn't leave the waters, he was going to kill us. He said he would shoot us on the open ocean and throw us overboard and no one would ever know."

"Were there any witnesses? Did you make any complaints?"

Lillie May shook her head. "We were too scared to make any complaints. There were only Vietnamese. This happened three or four weeks before the shooting."

"Did you continue to fish in the waters that Billy Joe said were his?"

"We did not. We went to the least desirable spots. Even then Billy Joe would not leave us alone, and he was threatening to put bullet holes in our boat if we didn't leave San Ignacio."

"But didn't you earlier threaten Billy Joe and his family?"

"We did circle his boat. Trying to get him to leave our pots alone."

"Did you make any threats toward him?"

"No. Never." She said it with great firmness. Hogan nodded.

"But it was said that you had knives and were circling his boat while his wife and children were aboard," said Hogan. He tried to make his voice sound firm, as if he were not going to cover up anything his client had done.

Lillie May listened to Cai, then looked at Hogan and said, "We wouldn't do that. We heard that story, but it didn't happen. We don't know why this man hated us so much. His wife is a very nice lady. We would see her at Mass. We respect her." Lillie May had slowly turned again to the jurors and was looking at them with her black eyes. "And I would say, as translator, 'respect' is very important word in Vietnamese."

"Go on," Hogan said, quietly.

"Three weeks before the shooting, Billy Joe approached me and my brother and two Vietnamese with me while we were crabbing in the mouth of the San Antonio River."

Lillie May listened intently to Cai, to his quick fluid tones of Vietnamese. Her translation —if not his, thought Hogan — was elo-

200

quent. The D.A., across at his counsel table, was making notes for cross-examination, and he seemed to have every confidence he was going to deal the finishing blow.

Lillie May said, "After destroying our crab pots, Billy Joe started waving his knife and saying he would cut our throats if we continued fishing in his waters. After that, Billy Joe slashed the tires on my car, and a few days later, he threatened to use the same knife on my throat. Billy Joe said he would shoot all of the Vietnamese in the open sea and throw their bodies in the ocean if we didn't leave. We finally decided we had no choice; he was not going to let us stay."

Lillie May listened to Cai and once again turned to the jury. "We tried several times to make up to him and told him, through others, that we wanted only peace and to make a living in San Ignacio, but he wouldn't listen. He didn't want peace. We finally saw we would have to leave."

Lillie May sighed and pushed back a lock of her crow's-wing hair. Her hand went briefly to the pearls, and then she clasped both hands in her lap again. Hogan paused and then looked straight at the jury. Both he and Lillie May seemed to understand that the moment of truth had arrived.

With some hesitation, and in a lower voice, Hogan said, "Tell the jury about the day of the shooting."

Turning slightly to Cai, Lillie May listened, and then replied. Her voice was strong and without hesitation. "On that day, me and my brother had gone to the boat dock to check on our boat when Billy Joe arrived. He stomped on my hand very hard and broke my finger. He pulled out a knife and began chasing me. I tried to get into my car, but the doors were locked and he began beating me. He slashed me several times on the chest."

Hogan handed Cai the knife and told him to show the jury how Billy Joe had slashed him. Cai made a slight, embarrassed slashing motion as if carefully parting the air in front of him into two halves. Then he handed the weapon back to Hogan. The long fish knife made a clatter as it was laid back on the table.

Cai held his bruised and crooked finger on the rail and the jury leaned over to see. The Hardin family murmured and stared in disbelief. Some of Billy Joe's kin looked at one another and then down at their shoes.

"I was getting out of my boat. It was late afternoon, and I was just putting my hand on the dock to pull out of the boat. I'm still not sure what set him off. I think it was because it was the biggest catch we had ever made." Lillie May paused and took a breath, then leaned forward and drank delicately from a glass of water.

"I ran away from Billy Joe to a friend's house, got a 38 caliber pistol and a rifle and came back. I knew where a friend of mine kept the pistol hidden in a closet. I knew it was Billie Joe or me. This time he had come to make good on his threat. There was murder in his eye. I had to return to protect my friends and my boat. I was scared for my life and I know he intended to kill me and them. This time I didn't know any way out."

"What happened next?" Hogan adjusted his glasses and looked intently at the judge first, and then the jury. Judge Barret was sitting perfectly still, listening and watching Lillie May with a rapt expression. So was the jury.

"Billy Joe began beating me again as soon as I came back. He hit me with his fists many times, and his fists were like a big hammer. He turned and walked toward the truck. I knew he carried a loaded rifle in the truck. He bragged about it all the time. One time he pointed to it and said, 'The gooks are going to find out about this'."

Lillie May took a breath and looked at the jury again. "I pulled the pistol and fired. I don't know how many times I fired. I was very frightened and wouldn't have shot except I thought he was going to kill us all. The cops or anybody else wouldn't stop him. They always looked the other way. He was bigger than the law."

For a second Lillie May's voice seemed to break slightly and she cleared her throat and went on. "I'm very, very sorry about what happened. I tried my very best to avoid it. He wouldn't let me. I ran, but he always found me. He never would let me just run away. Very sad. Very sorry."

Hogan didn't need a reminder that he had come to a good stopping place. He pointed to the witness with his glasses. He turned to the judge and then the jury again. "That's our story, your Honor, jurors."

Hogan slowly sat down, using his handkerchief to wipe the palms of his hands. He realized for better or for worse it was over now. It was now in the hands of the gods and Lillie May.

Chapter Forty

Afternoon, September 17th

The D.A. was so eager with his cross-examination that he allowed Lillie May to serve as the interpreter without objection. Hogan noted that his tie was much more subdued now, after Georgia Davis had brought attention to his taste. It was a regimental stripe in muted colors.

"You accept Lillie May as translator?" asked the judge.

"Yes, your Honor," said Davis. "She's better than the translator we had that didn't show up." He turned to Cai

"You say he had murder in his eye, but you didn't see his eye, because you shot him in the back."

Lillie May's face was expressionless and polite, but there was a tautness to it, Hogan saw. Her slim hands were clasped tightly in her lap. "I never saw him *without* murder in his eye. The man hated me from the minute he saw me. I still don't understand why."

"But he was going away from you, not toward you?"

"I knew that he intended to kill me and my brother. I never did him any harm."

"Well you did him the harm of shooting him in the back, and then standing over him and firing five times more as he lay dying. I guess that's harm enough, wouldn't you say?"

When Lillie May did not immediately reply, the D.A. repeated himself. He had not the sense to wait for her to relay the question to Cai and listen to the answer. He walked toward Cai.

"Would you answer, please?"

"I was so afraid," said Lillie May. "I blanked out in the terror of the moment. He had just threatened me too many times, and beat me once too often, and cut me, and told me many times he was going to kill me one time too many."

"Do you speak English?" Davis asked Cai. This time Davis did wait, gazing on with interest, while Lillie May translated.

"He doesn't speak English."

"Then how does he know what Billy Joe said?"

Lillie May said, "A friend told him what Billy Joe was saying."

The district attorney seemed not to be able to separate Cai from Lillie May. Cai was giving such whispered and brief replies, he seemed to have vanished from the courtroom.

"So you went down to the dock with a gun and you were afraid of him?" Roger Davis leaned forward for the answer. "He had no weapon and he couldn't possibly have meant you harm if he was leaving?" The D.A. seemed incredulous.

"I thought he was going to his truck to get the rifle. He was big enough to kill me with his hands or his knife or his rifle." Lillie May sounded desperate. "I saw him going to the truck --"

The D.A. knew when to interrupt. And that was whenever he thought Lillie May was making a point. He talked to the jury, and not to Lillie May and Cai.

"But you heard the policeman say there was no rifle, no knife, nothing to show there was anything harmful to you in his truck."

"If that was so, it would be the first time he ever showed up in a truck without a rifle," Lillie May replied.

The D.A. turned on her, angry and indignant. "Are you saying our police are lying about what they found?"

Lillie May translated in her quick, low musical tones as fast as the D.A. spoke and then she returned quickly, "I am only telling you what I know from times past."

Again the D.A. interrupted her, and his voice was raised. "But that didn't happen. The point is, you shot a fellow human being in the back, and there's no defense for that. Don't you agree?"

"I hate what has happened. I'm very sorry for his wife and children. I cry daily over what happened. I would give anything to undo it, but I did kill him, because I was so afraid he was going to kill me." Lillie May's voice was strained, but she sat up straighter than before, her shoulders braced. Her dark eyes regarded him fearlessly as she sat prim and unmoving in her pale suit and her pearls.

As Hogan bent forward, listening, he understood that the interrogation by the district attorney centered entirely upon the fact that Cai shot Billy Joe in cold blood and that Billy Joe was unarmed. The jury obviously got the point, nodding in agreement with the D.A.'s questions. Hogan knew they were not really questions; they were statements.

"There was no one who witnessed the shooting that said Billy Joe was doing anything to put you in danger. Are you saying now that all the young men here who say you shot Billy Joe are lying?"

The D.A. moved toward Lillie May while he talked to the jury. In his passion and enthusiasm for a slashing cross-examination, the D.A. suddenly seemed to want to destroy Lillie May herself, but he had struck the rock bottom of her resistance. Her replies were rapid and unflustered, her expression calm. The D.A.'s growing dislike for the elegant Vietnamese woman became almost as strong as what he felt for Cai.

Hogan watched; it was surreal, the way the scene became transformed. Roger Davis was certain he was winning, but more and more it seemed he was on a slippery slope rather than familiar ground, and Hogan watched with growing amazement as he began to slide down it.

To the D.A., Lillie May suddenly seemed to be the lone wall of resistance. He had to destroy her as well as Cai. In his haste and zeal, he wasn't even sure why. Nor was he considering how productive his behavior was. He only felt he was being manipulated and he was furious. The district attorney moved closer.

"You got the gun for the specific purpose of killing Billy Joe and shooting him in the back. It was just a matter of going looking for him and waiting till he was unarmed and his back was toward you."

"No, I did not want to kill him. I wanted to return to the dock, get our boats and as much material as I could, and leave --"

Again the D.A. stopped Lillie May.

"But you didn't have to come back." He walked away from her, looking at the jury. His voice rose. "The only purpose of returning was to kill Billy Joe. You could have gone your own way!" He was almost shouting.

"You have it all wrong," she said without hesitation. "You seem not to want the truth."

The D.A. again brushed her aside, hoping to make her seem small and insignificant.

"Where did you get the weapons that you used to shoot Billy Joe?"

"A close friend of mine had a pistol and a rifle. He had bought it from a Black man about two years before and said they shouldn't be taken out of his house."

Again the D.A. stopped her. "So you knew you were wrong."

Lillie May went on as if she hadn't heard him. She had suddenly learned that this was the only method of getting anything said. "I took both weapons and headed back for the dock. My brother got in the car, telling me I shouldn't go near Billy Joe. He tried to get me to turn back."

The D.A. became incredulous. "No one could stop you? Even your own brother? Or your friends? You were bent on murder and nobody was going to stop you?" He shook his head and gave a short laugh and walked across the room to his chair at the counsel table to hear her replies. He crossed his arms.

Lillie May was undisturbed. "I got out of the car, went to the dock. The only reason I returned was to get my boat. It cost me $3,000 to fix it, and everything I had in the world was involved in that boat. He said he was going to sink it with bullet holes. I couldn't let that happen."

The D.A. rose again, feeling sure he had Cai trapped. But he pointed his finger at Lillie May, not Cai, and he did it without thinking.

"But when you came back there were no bullet holes in the boat. Billy Joe was just going about his normal business. He had a boat there, too; he was a hardworking man with a family to support." He marched toward Lillie May and his voice rose almost to a shout. "You are not only a killer, but a liar!"

For the first time Lillie May seemed shaken, or perhaps angry.

"How dare you!" she said.

Her eyes flashed and Hogan smiled to himself. They will like her better for that, he thought.

The D.A. was delighted. He had broken through Lillie May's armor

But Lillie May immediately smoothed down again, becoming inscrutable and self-contained once more. She went on as if she hadn't heard him. "When I arrived, I saw Billy Joe had shot several holes in my boat. It was sinking down into the water. It seemed like everything was going down with it. I knew he was not going to let me escape."

This time she didn't stop, even though the D.A. tried to jump in again, she simply kept right on her in light, clear voice.

"When he turned toward his pickup and his rifle at the dock, I knew he would kill me."

"But how did you *know*?"

For the first time the strain of incessant translating began to tell on Lillie May. Perhaps also the emotional stress was beginning to tell, the fact that she held a man's life in her hands. Hogan could see her slim hands shaking ever so slightly and his heart went out to her.

"Objection!" He was on his feet before he knew it. Anything to give her a moment of respite. Beside him, Sheila's hands were so sweaty she was clutching a blank piece of paper beneath the table and wiping her palms. "Badgering ..."

"Sustained," said Judge Barret. "She ... uh ... *he* has told you how he knew or his reasons for surmise."

"You didn't need two loaded guns to go get your things." The D.A. shook his head in disbelief. "You've been a soldier; you know how to ambush somebody. So you got your weapon and went down there and literally ambushed him."

"No, I went for my boat --"

"The fact is, you stalked him like a professional killer!" The D.A. shouted loudly enough to stop her, and this time he did throw her into confusion. "Weren't you trained to kill?" he demanded.

"I don't know," Lillie May said. She paused for breath. "I don't know, I don't know."

The D.A. moved even closer. It was as if his hands were around her neck. She was so small, and the D.A. was so large.

"You talk too fast," she said. She paused and took a breath. She said something to Cai and listened to his brief reply. "Before I fired the first shot, I remembered what he had said about throwing me in the ocean, I remembered him breaking my fingers, and I remembered the blood coming down on my chest from the knife wounds. I remembered my trailer going up in flames, I remembered the holes in my new boat. I remembered Billy Joe saying he would kill me one day out on the bay and he would throw me in the sea and throw his gun after. I remembered he said no one would ever know or care. That's why I shot." Lillie May was quickly recovering her balance, and somehow she stood her ground.

The courtroom was utterly still. Cai had begun to cry. He briefly put his head in his hands and smeared away tears and looked up again. It was the first emotion Hogan had ever seen him show. The D.A. was furious with Lillie May's ability to stand between him and the defendant.

"I don't understand why you just didn't leave San Ignacio if Billy Joe was such a problem. Just leave! Isn't that better than killing a family man, a man with a wife and two children?"

Lillie May edged closer to Cai to hear him. He was crying silently into his hands again and lifted his wet face to answer. "I only wanted one more week of the good crab harvest, so I could have money to leave and start over somewhere else. My brother still begged me to run away. But everything was there, my boat and everything. When I started shooting, I went crazy. I think I shot him some more, I'm not sure."

"And after you *shot* him, six times, you ran for it!" The D.A. turned and smiled at the jury with an incredulous look. "He ran for it." He turned again to the two Vietnamese. "Isn't that what you did?"

Lillie May answered. "I took off my watch and gave it to my friend's wife, and I told him that I knew I would have to go to jail for a long time or maybe I would be shot. On the way home, I threw the gun into the bay and became very, very afraid. I knew it was the end. Yes, I did run. It was a mistake. That's why I gave myself up.

"My brother went back to our home. It was a trailer in the trailer park. It was burnt out from bombs. He said he would wait there for the police. He did nothing wrong —only tried to stop me. I was not going to wait around."

Lillie May now asked for a brief recess as Cai seemed to be getting weaker. She could hardly hear him. The judge agreed to the recess.

In the brief recess, Hogan drank a Dr. Pepper and stared at the stone steps of the courtroom, blazing white limestone in the autumn heat. Sheila sat staring out at the brick storefronts, the dusty streets. How much longer? Hogan thought.

After far too short a time, they returned to the intensity of the interrogation and Lillie May continued.

"I got a friend of mine to drive me to Houston, where I spent Saturday and Sunday. I contacted a man by the name of Dr. Chou. He persuaded me to turn myself into the police. The police said they would send a police car right away, but the wait was too long. I saw a police car drive by and stop at a light. I ran up and knocked on the window. Dr. Chou had someone write a message that I had killed a man in San Ignacio, and that I was turning myself in. The policeman took me to jail in San Ignacio."

"Tell the jury how you got from San Ignacio to this jail."

"We had a hearing as to where the trial was to be held. I think the judge said it was here. The next day, I was taken to this jail. Every day we were questioned and threatened by the sheriff through a local Vietnamese interpreter."

Hogan listened to her clear, unshaken voice, as entranced as the rest of the courtroom.

"How can you expect the jury to find this as anything but cold-blooded murder?" asked the D.A.

He loomed over both of them, hoping the incessant repetition would get him back on the high ground. He had lost it, somehow, and since he did not know how he'd managed to lose it, he couldn't figure out the way to get back. His statement was beginning to sound weaker and weaker.

"I believe in self-defense, everyone does, but how can six shots in the back be self-defense? The man had no knife, no weapon!"

"I expect the jury to find only the truth," Lillie May replied for Cai. "That doesn't seem to be your intent."

The D.A. glared at her. "I will decide myself what my intent is, young woman." he said sharply, and Hogan saw one or two of the women jurors frown slightly. "You are trained as a killer, and expect to come to a country whose justice system has become far too lenient and get away with it."

"I was chased by that man until I had to fight."

The D.A. nodded and then said in a reasonable voice, "Everybody who commits a crime always has a great story, and yours is no exception."

Then the D.A. turned and walked straight at Cai, a sudden change meant to throw him and Lillie May off. The D.A. demonstrated with both hands holding an imaginary pistol. "Were you holding the pistol in a trained police grip? And the Mazurik boy tells us Billy Joe threw out both hands and said, 'No, man!' Begging for his life!"

"Objection! Not a question!"

Hogan's intervention had allowed Lillie May to find her balance again.

"I tell you, it was not like that. I didn't want to." Lillie May paused and bent her head to Cai. "The jury should do that which is just."

"I'm sure they will." The D.A. put down the imaginary pistol. He smiled. "I have no more questions."

The D.A. turned his tall frame to the jury and smiled at them in confidence, gave a short nod. Then he turned back to the counsel table and sat down, shifting his shoulders inside his striped suit and patting down a surprisingly subdued tie.

Hogan got up, determined to repair any damage.

Once again he asked Cai about his experience in the 104th.

Through Lillie May, Cai replied, "Father Dominic talked to us often at the church in San Ignacio. He taught us to memorize things, things from American writings. This one especially."

Cai began to recite from memory, in a shadowy whisper. Lillie May said in her perfect, lightly accented English, "Give me your tired, your poor --"

The D.A. was on his feet and doing his best to dilute the emotional content of the moment. But Lillie May turned her head away from him and continued to talk to the jury. Her voice grew stronger.

"Objection," said the D.A. "Poetry has no place."

"Overruled," said Judge Barret.

"-- your huddled masses yearning to breathe free, send me the wretched refuse of your teeming shores. Send these --"

"Objection!"

"Overruled."

"-- the homeless and the tempest-tossed, to me. I lift --"

"Your Honor!"

"Overruled."

"-- my lamp beside the Golden Door.'"

Cai gestured slightly with one net-scarred hand. Lillie May was misty-eyed, trying furtively to wipe away her own tears without anyone seeing her. She pressed her eyes quickly with the palms of both hands. The tip of her nose was bright red. Then she looked up again and her eyes were sparkling with unshed tears.

Hogan could recognize the crescendo of the moment and promptly advised the court, "The defense rests."

Lillie May smiled, nodded, and stepped down. Then she stood, her small hands clasped against her skirt, and bowed formally, first to the judge and then to the jury.

Hogan was shaken out of his contemplation of the small woman and Cai as they left the witness stand. With surprise he heard the D.A. agree to rest the state's case. Hogan knew Davis was so convinced that the cold-blooded killer now belonged to the Texas penal system that he was choosing not to put on the vast array of rebuttal witnesses he had waiting in the wings. Davis marched across the floor, smiling at his assistants.

Big Bob leaned over close to Hogan and said, "He's the only guy I've ever known that can strut sitting down."

Looking tired, Hogan closed his briefcase. He gathered the last papers as he heard the Hardin brothers tell the rest of the family, "That's the end of that murdering gook." Hogan just shook his head.

As Lillie May left the courtroom behind Cai, Hogan smiled at them. He knew she would visit with Cai and stay with him at the jail during the extremely tense hours of jury deliberation. He saw Father Dominic step out of the spectator's area and follow as well.

Sheila fell in beside Hogan. She pressed her eyes with a handkerchief quickly, and then walked out gracefully, her head held high. They had gotten through. There was hostility everywhere around them, but she walked through it as if it were nothing.

They were all headed for Kendrick's tiny offices over the drugstore.

Hogan took Sheila's arm. "Oh, God, I'd like to have a drink. Oh, for the days gone by. I feel like I've earned a barrel of whiskey and I could drink it overnight."

They walked up to Kendrick's offices, Sheila was taking the stairs like a gazelle, laughing.

"Oh, Hogan," she said. "There's nobody like you."

"Hell, if I had known I was going to live this long, I guess I would have taken better care of myself."

Chapter Forty-One

The judge set arguments to begin promptly at one, after lunch. "Do you want me to give the first half of our argument?" Paul asked Hogan. Sabine sat on the floor with her hands around her knees; the rest of them were in the few available chairs. Kendrick sat on the corner of his desk and handed around Styrofoam cups of coffee. It was tasteless coffee, but they were beyond noticing what anything tasted like.

Outside, the flights of pigeons, fat from the feed stores and small local grain mills, flew in shifting planes toward the courthouse, and the grackles argued and disputed in the trees. The sun slid slowly down toward the horizon, losing none of its power to scald and burn. It would not cool down until long after dark. The little air-conditioner made sawing noises, pouring out its inadequate stream of cool air. They all felt like they'd "been rode hard and put away wet."

"Hell, yes," said Hogan. He laughed. "Of course!"

"It's ready."

"I know."

"I did just a little bit more work on it the night you guys ran us out of the office." Paul glanced over at Sabine. "Then we went out."

"Okay." Hogan looked up, suddenly aware he'd been so absorbed he'd missed important things, like realizing how close Sabine and Paul had become. "You guys aren't going to go elope or anything are you?"

Sabine sat straight up, as if somebody had shot her in the back with a B.B. gun. "Mr. Hogan!"

"No, Dad," said Paul. "Um, not yet."

"Well, let me know," Hogan said with a grin, and he sank back against his chair back, thinking, trying to remember what he'd been like when he was twenty-five. He shook his head. Bone-weary, he felt he couldn't have faced all this at such a young age. "From now on," he said to Paul, "you're first chair, and I'll occasionally whisper to you from the second chair."

Sabine squealed in delight and Paul simply grinned.

Hogan was glad to be at the end of it. Glad to conclude with a judge who seemed to view him with respect rather than with contempt. Oh, yes, the ending was far, far better than the beginning.

Young Kendrick was right. Judge Barret did have integrity and respect for the law.

"We all owe a huge debt of gratitude to Lillie May," Hogan said. "All of us, including the judge. She brought a kind of reality to this case which it wouldn't have had otherwise."

"Yeah, she did," Paul agreed. "And when she bowed, I about choked up."

"You did choke up," said Sabine.

"I know it." Paul ducked his head and drank his lukewarm coffee. "I about bawled."

"If it hadn't been for her, Cai would have been slaughtered," Hogan added. "I choked up, too."

"Okay," said Sheila. "Everybody choked up."

"Mr. Kendrick," said Hogan. "We are forever in your debt."

The young man bowed slightly. "My pleasure."

Sheila and Sabine went into the other room to wash faces, restore makeup, and brush hair. Sheila pulled her hair back tightly and clasped it with barrette as if she were folding a flag. She saw Hogan watching her and smiled; she had faced the enemy and had not retreated.

Judge Barret looked at both of the lawyers before him. He looked Hogan directly in the eye, nodded and turned to his notes. He cleared his throat and spoke with a calm and serenity new to his previous posture. The air-conditioners hummed in the background.

"Gentlemen, I wanted to say a few words before I read the charge to the jury."

"Each side gets forty-five minutes. I understand the D.A. intends to use thirty-five minutes in opening and ten minutes in rebuttal. Mr. Hogan, I understand you will divide your time with Paul. He will take twenty-five minutes and you will have the last twenty. Is all that correct?"

He looked from one to the other, and the two men glanced at one another and then back to the judge and nodded.

"Before we call in the jury, let me commend both sides on a job very well done in an extremely difficult case. It has been remarkably free of side-bar remarks. Perhaps you used them all outside the court."

Hogan's worn Irish face broke into a rueful smile.

"Mr. Hogan, I know you've had some heavy guns after you, including mine. I know it's been short rations as to evidence and encouragement on your side. All of you have behaved in the finest traditions of our profession, and I commend your diligence and inspiration. You are welcome to my court at any time."

"Judge, I think that's going a little too far," the D.A. said. "But I must say, for an impossible defense and case, they put up a hell of a facade."

In one of his stage whispers, Big Bob said, "Is this the same judge who was going to throw all of us in jail?"

The judge had finally learned not to be startled by Big Bob's stage whispers and raw comments. He merely glared at him over his glasses and then returned his attention to Hogan and Davis. "Gentlemen, let's get started. At least one of you should remain during jury deliberations because I want all of the lawyers here when the verdict is received."

The district attorney, who as a matter of law had the burden of proof, always got two shots at the jury, and Hogan prepared himself to sit it out, listening, taking his arguments apart in his mind, finding the weak places.

Roger Davis was excellent, as always. His voice was pervasive and his presence was firm. His oratorical style, voice, and the organization of his address were superb. He thanked the jurors for joining him in the great effort to maintain a peaceful society. Then he made mincemeat of the theory of self-defense.

"We have a life that was lost forever. A man on whom depended a wife and three small children. We have here the defendant who believes the way to settle your differences with someone is to wait until his back is turned and then empty a revolver into him. I thought we abandoned that kind of a solution a long time ago in south Texas. Those days are behind us. We don't need that any more. What we need now is law and order. The defendant is a coward, a killer, and Billy Joe was unarmed. Those are the facts."

It was a scenario from which the D.A. never varied.

"This man stood and shot five times, firing away over Billy Joe's dying body ..." Sobs could be heard from the family in the audience. "That man's life meant nothing to him." Davis' voice rose. He tucked his now-modest tie discreetly in his suit jacket; energy and outrage seemed to make him even taller than he was.

"Not a shadow of a doubt, not a reservation to the contrary. You have heard the experts, you have heard the witnesses. Mr. Hogan tried to paint Billy Joe as a man who needed killing, but we don't have the death penalty permitted in this case." He paused. "*Even though* it is deserved — for the defendant. You see, Cai Van Nguyen decided that Billy Joe needed killing, and so he became judge and jury and executioner all in one and took a good man's life as he was throwing up his hands and saying, 'No, man!' We bent to the rules of society and gave this man a fair trial, and now this terrible crime, this murder of a good patriotic American, deserves the maximum penalty."

Davis paused just a moment. "This isn't Vietnam," he said. "This is America. We don't, we can't, we never will permit a murdering coward to go free. He and Billy Joe may have had their differences, ladies and gentlemen, but we don't allow disagreements to be settled that way any more. *Murder is not an option!"*

He stopped and looked at the jury, looked at each one of them. "Murder is not an option. It isn't an argument. Cai Van Nguyen took a life, and he took that life for eternity. Cai is still here living and breathing. What we do in *this* country is give people life in prison for doing that.

"I know you will do the right thing. Do it now — fairly — justly — quickly."

The D.A.'s argument was powerful. Several jurors nodded when he demanded the maximum sentence. The D.A. used up the balance of his time talking of law and order, necessity of punishment and rights of victims. It was a twice-told tale but the D.A. did it so well and this community never seemed to tire of hearing of it.

At his conclusion the D.A. expressed his profuse thanks for the opportunity of once again serving the people in the interest of truth and justice. Then the court acknowledged Paul for his portion of the argument.

Chapter Forty-Two

"So you too must befriend the alien, for you were once alien your-selves," began Paul. "Deuteronomy 10:12-22."

The words of the D.A. were burning in Paul's mind. Roger Davis' superior experience and competence would, Paul felt, reduce his own efforts to a pale shadow. He closed the Bible and turned to face the jury.

"Much that needs to be said is as old as the earliest Biblical admonition we have just given. The hard truth is, you may not like me or Cai or the message of not guilty that we bring. But when you examine the evidence, your heart will tell you it is the right thing to do.

"Just as life has never been easy for Cai and his family, not during the months of death and dying when he slugged it out as a fighting Marine side by side with Americans, or when he crossed an alien ocean in a leaky boat to get to these shores, so we bring you a hard truth. The verdict of not guilty may not be the one you want to render, but under your oath it is the one you must render."

Paul cleared his throat nervously, eyeing each of the jurors, testing to see how well these hard truths were registering. They told him nothing.

"Self-defense is not a mockery. It is the truth. Billy Joe just cornered Cai too many times. Cai had to turn and fight. Billy Joe made him. It will not be a popular verdict for the district attorney, either, because he has political aspirations and he needs this trial and the media attention to get him onto the fast track. He would sacrifice this defendant for his own purposes."

Hogan sat at the counsel table and pressed a pencil between his fingers until his fingertips were white. *Attack, attack,* he said silently to his son. *Attack.*

"Our system demands you give Cai the benefit of the doubt. Look at it from his point of view. It was one of terror, ladies and gentlemen. Even now at this late hour the state refuses to recognize the beatings, the knifing, the threats which caused this killing. They choose to ignore all of this. All of the eye-witnesses in effect admitted to it, and yet the D.A. tried to suppress it. The sheriff should be prosecuted, not praised. He conspired in every way possible to see that the defendant not receive a fair trial. You know it and we know it. It is a disgrace to your community."

Hogan smiled slightly. Paul was indeed on the offensive.

"If suppression of evidence and twisting the rules and perverting the truth is permitted, then protection of the innocent vanishes."

The jury stared back at him. They were listening to every word and reflecting nothing.

Paul continued. "You know Slim Lambert's reputation for truth and fairness. He told you Cai was threatened shamefully. He told you, 'Law and order without truth and justice is impossible.' In contrast, the message of the prosecution has been conviction at any cost!

"What we ask of you is hard, but especially men of the military who have so valiantly served your country know that no one ever said the concept of duty would be easy. That was so in the terrible war in Vietnam and it is true now. We haven't had it easy, and neither will you now that the responsibility is yours. For months we have fought this lonely but necessary battle for justice. When you find this defendant not guilty under the evidence — as you must — you will have done that duty, hard as that may appear when you first consider it.

"The privilege of serving as a juror has another side, as a coin has two sides. The other side is responsibility and that duty can't be shirked or covered up because the path of truth and justice is sometimes difficult. Yours is a great moment of opportunity. Don't neglect or miss it. This can be your finest hour. Thank you and God speed!"

Paul turned from the jury, grateful that they had at least heard him out and he sat down again, glancing over at Hogan.

Hogan gave him a warm smile and a nod. Then he stood up and walked to the jury rail where he took time to look at each juror.

"I'm too old, and this case has been too hard to talk to you in pious platitudes," he said. "We have taken a great deal of abuse from the district attorney, who is determined to have a conviction regardless of truth or justice or fairness. He is making the most of the media attention in this case, only for political gain. Justice is not his pursuit."

He walked a few steps and then turned to them and said, "I know all about law and order, and this isn't it. My education began when I joined the Marine corps at age seventeen and served until I was twenty-one. I was wounded in action twice and served in five major campaigns. The responsibility for law and order in this world was my full ration at a very early age. I respect it and understand it."

Hogan paused, reflecting.

"My education in law and order continued as I worked as assistant D.A. and chief prosecutor of Bexar County for four years as soon as I graduated from the University of Texas Law School. Perhaps you can now better understand our position that this case has two sides that must be heard for justice to prevail. Maybe you understand that more so now than when we started this case. We hope so. It couldn't be worse."

216

Some of the jurors smiled and Hogan began to relax, thinking that some measure of acceptance might have come about. He paused for a drink of water. Then slowly he continued.

"Let's talk straight about our system of justice. Our justice system is a structured way of discouraging violence, *but also* protecting the right of self-defense. Billy Joe wouldn't back off. He wouldn't relent. The most timid and peaceful of men will turn and fight when there is no escape, as Cai had none. Texas Ranger Lambert explained that to Billy Joe one day. 'One of these days you may push too hard,' he told him. But Billy Joe was as deaf as a cow skull. He wouldn't listen. And he pushed too hard. Cai ran as hard and fast and as often as he could, but Billy Joe cornered him."

Hogan turned toward the whole of the courtroom, waving his hand in a slow sweep. "He left Cai no place to run. No place to hide. He's little, isn't he, ladies and gentlemen? He's skinny and he doesn't weigh a hundred pounds and he doesn't look like a threat to anybody, so Billy Joe just had a great old time, whupping up on him. And you know what? In fear of his living, and his life, finally this little skinny guy turned, in terror, and fought back.

"Judge Barret has instructed you on the law on self-defense, and you must know by now that it fits this case. The charge will be given to you when we conclude our remarks. Read it and you will see that it is *written* for this situation."

Now, instead of the shambling, slightly rumpled man they had heard for the past two months, Hogan stood straight before them, his shoulders squared and his face alive with determination. His voice grew passionate.

"Ladies and gentlemen, you *cannot* let the rights of the weakest or the most unimportant or unpopular among you fall through the cracks and expect the system will work for the *next* person looking for justice and fairness! It is the torch of justice you pass on to the next person seeking justice under the law, and it is viable only if it remains so after your verdict."

Hogan continued to talk directly to the two retired colonels — not with the expectation of success, but with the certain recognition and knowledge that the verdict was going to lay with them. He didn't see a single sympathetic face, but he at least wanted to make it hard on them. They didn't seem to give him any encouragement. Often they looked away from him, as the judge had at the start of the trial.

"Who is running our system of justice? The high sheriff, remember him? The same size and weight as Billy Joe, a good friend of Billy Joe. Remember as he stood beside this young man, Cai, towering over him, Billy Joe's knife in hand, and said 'I know I could put the boy in fear of his life and then some.' Imagine Billy Joe towering over Cai with that in his hand." Hogan picked the knife up, turned it over and then laid it down again.

"A hundred pounds heavier. A giant versus a dwarf. A Goliath against a David. Slashed him across the chest, put holes in his boat, smashed his traps, and smashed his fingers. What kind of a man does that to someone so much smaller, an immigrant who can't even speak English, who is poor, desperate, alone?"

Hogan heard a short outburst from one of the Hardins and then the judge violently banged the gavel for order. Barret grew red in the face again and told the bailiff to clear the courtroom if it continued.

Hogan didn't let up. He was renewed. He crossed his arms and looked at them with a slight smile.

"Indeed the only preposterous thing about self-defense is that any fair juror under the evidence could reject it. For you see, it is now *your* responsibility—not the district attorney's. It is *your* verdict, not the D.A.'s, nor the judge's. You can't shift the responsibility. It will always bear your name. It is something for your grandchildren's children to see — how you behaved in the moment of extreme challenge. We know what we ask is hard, but in the long run you will never regret it. For you will have done your duty. It will be as proud a moment for you as any soldier that comes to bear arms for his country. It will be your finest hour."

Hogan decided it was time for emotional forensics whether they worked or not. It was the truth, and the truth should set his client free. That's the way it was supposed to work; even if it sometimes didn't. He glanced at the clock as he moved to a conclusion.

"Cai's constitutional right to a fair and just trial were jeopardized before we even started. It is your collective responsibility to see that justice without fear, favor or prejudice accompanies your verdict."

Hogan, with his tousled gray hair, the deeply-cut wrinkles, and the rumpled suit, seemed a tower of strength as he walked the distance of the jury rail.

"Protection of the least among us is the only method whereby we create a justice system that brings fairness and justice to all. Many a soldier went to Vietnam, not because he thought the war was right, but because it was his duty. Many a Vietnam veteran fought, not because he wanted to, but because his country beckoned. He didn't create the war nor understand it, but he served. That's just the way it was. Cai did all of this, serving with the 104th Marines, seeing his cousin Kim killed, fleeing that devastated country for a new life."

Hogan looked at them all again, almost with affection.

"Time is now growing short and I will conclude. You have been generous with your patience as has the judge.

"Our own responsibilities are shifting to you. It is a fearful ordeal, and the project upon which we have all engaged is now resting with you, the people, the wisdom, conscience and judgment of this community. To his credit, Judge Barret has already done half your job for you in directing that Tho be found not guilty. You take only the second step by finding his brother Cai not guilty.

"You now know the story of the fright, the fear, and the desperation that these young men, and twenty others, underwent in that small, tiny and tempestuous sea for eight days, trying to get to the land of their dreams. Our Armed Forces directed them toward the Philippines. They lived in a camp and only then, after week upon week upon week, they finally reached these shores. Seven of them, living in a two bedroom trailer with few comforts or encouragement or a helping hand. The challenges which met them were as threatening as those cruel, thrashing seas.

"You must view these circumstances through their eyes as to how and why this tragedy took place and what compelled this young man to take the life of a man who otherwise would have killed him, who said, again and again, 'I will shoot you and throw you overboard.' Cai, ladies and gentlemen, had seen people shot. He had seen people go overboard. And when Billy Joe said it, he believed it."

Hogan paused, letting it sink in.

Then, in an almost conversational tone of voice, he said, "Many years ago, there came to the shores of this country a small little Irishman who was both insignificant and unheralded. He came filled with stories of democracy and its ways of freedom and opportunity for all the people. He never did very well in life, but he raised three children, sold shoes, and rose to the prestigious rank of $150 a week at best. He taught his children that the most sacred place in the United States, as a pinnacle of freedom and democracy, was the Statue of Liberty and the most sacred words in all of this democratic land, as taught to Cai by Father Dominic, were these:

"'Give me your tired, your poor and huddled masses; yearning to breathe free. The wretched refuse of your teeming shore. Send these, the homeless, tempest-tossed to me. I lift my lamp beside the golden door.'

"That little Irishman was my old man, and the inscription is from the Statue of Liberty. That man was my father, and those words were his credo for the greatness of America. By your verdict of not guilty, you can show that democracy is available to all — to the lowliest, to the most forsaken — that it works for the protection of all of us."

Hogan stood and faced them, looked at the jury, and said, "You have received our best efforts and our prayers that you will be guided to a just and fair verdict of not guilty. Thank you and God speed."

Chapter Forty-Three

The D.A. was outraged by the personal remarks made against him. But he'd sat at the counsel table listening to them with an unruffled air. He cleared his throat, pushed his legal pad away from him, and rose once again. He took out his handkerchief and tapped his forehead with it. The air-conditioners were not cooling the place well enough. Then he slowly stepped up to the jury rail, pausing for a few seconds before beginning his bid for the jurors' attention as he'd been taught.

"You have just heard outrageous remarks against me and your public officials," he said, shaking his head regretfully. "We knew it was coming, because Jim Hogan has expressed himself openly and publicly as to how he feels about this community. He has said it is a defendant's purgatory, and that's one of his milder expressions."

Davis threw out both hands. "It's this simple. Do you want to live in a community where a fellow citizen can be shot six times in the back and his murderer go free? Neither do I. That's why I have spent all of my adult life withstanding the trickery and deceit and chicanery you have just witnessed. Our streets will not be free — nor the law have the ability to protect you — if the result he suggests is permitted. It is an outrageous thought to even suggest that you turn this man loose on our streets. When will he kill again? Hogan doesn't live here, but you and I do. He doesn't care. He's going to pick up and go back to San Antonio. Which is in the best interests of your neighborhood and homes? Lock him up or let him go free to kill again?

"As always, I'm proud and privileged to serve as your district attorney, to be the voice and protector of law and order."

Dramatically he pointed to Hogan and then Cai.

"When Cai put six shots into Billy Joe's back, it spelled a murder of the severest kind—a cowardly, merciless act permitting no excuse. Billy Joe died at the hands of a man who decided to be judge, jury, and executioner. That's what he thought about the American system of justice. We have run the defense's charade of fair trial and level playing field to the last drum-beat, and it's just that—a cruel hoax manufactured for this case to free a dangerous criminal on your streets among your children.

"He would receive a life sentence or death if he were in his own country of Vietnam, and he deserves the maximum in this country, which offered him so much. It offered him freedom, self-respect, opportunity. He turned his back on all of it as he pumped lead into Billy Joe's back. We don't want him as a citizen of this country. Felons, cowards, killers, don't belong here. Nobody ever said, 'Send me your criminals, your murderers,' did they? The maximum penalty of life is the only appropriate response. If the law permitted, it should be death."

The jury always seemed to relax with the D.A., Hogan noted again. They seemed to be at ease with Davis, but Hogan drove them crazy with demands. He saw this clearly, and knew it was too late to change anything he'd done.

"I'm proud to deliver this case into your competent and fair hands.," the D.A. said. "I know justice in its most severe terms will be served. You have my admiration for a difficult job well done."

There was a nearly tangible feeling of release when the arguments were ended. The jury sat back, their bodies became less tense. There were audible sighs from behind Hogan from the Hardin family and the spectators in general. The reporters capped their pens.

Judge Barret said, "Gentlemen, we will retire the jury and begin deliberation. Mr. Sheriff, please escort the jurors to the jury room until they have reached a verdict."

The two alternate jurors were excused and the remaining twelve went to the jury room to decide the fate of the Defendant.

The courtroom suddenly seemed empty and cavernous, almost ominous.

The town square, Hogan saw, was filling up with cars and with people on foot, despite the heat. There was a crowd around the stone front steps of the old courthouse, and they weren't all media, either.

There were at least four media panel trucks with television station logos on them, and cables running in all directions. It looked like the carnival had come to town. Hogan didn't like the look of it. Preparations for their covert departure, he decided, needed attention. He took off his jacket and slung it over his shoulder, then took Sheila by the elbow and hurried across the street to Kendrick's office above the drugstore.

They sat, tired but wildly energized. Paul and Big Bob smoked one cigarette after another, nearly driving everybody out.

"Jeez," said Kendrick, "my office has never been so popular or so full. I sure wish you guys were clients."

Everyone was in high humor, mainly out of relief that it was over. Although Kendrick had suffered immense local criticism for getting involved, it didn't seem to bother him.

Hogan turned a chair around backwards and sat on it, leaning his arms on the back. "At least it's over. I'm proud of every one of you. I've

221

never seen it tougher from judge to jury to district attorney to evidence than this. Any trial in the future will be a cinch for you guys, compared to this."

Hogan saw that Paul and Sabine seemed hopeful, full of affection for him, and expectant.

"You'll grow up, and fast," he said.

Sheila disagreed. "Let's not grow up," she said.

Kendrick turned on the radio to the country-western station and they listened to Willie Nelson's *Redheaded Stranger*. Sheila drank a cold soda; in different circumstances she would have had a celebratory drink and then some.

"What do you bet?" Hogan asked Big Bob, whose lanky form was doubled up on the floor, in a corner, his bony knees in his hands.

"Three hours, and max," Bob answered.

Three hours seemed like thirty. Speculation as to what the jury was doing, how they reacted, and what the verdict was going to be ranged from pessimism to cautious optimism as five o'clock came and went.

"The jurors were so cold. I couldn't read a damn thing except 'We don't believe a damn word you say'," Hogan said. "What the hell, it's now four hours. Bob predicted three and I said two. Shows you how much I know."

He leaned his chin on his forearms, thinking. Sheila and Sabine were talking about Lillie May's wonderful translation, and Paul and Big Bob were still smoking steadily. Veils of cigarette smoke drifted through the air like airborne nooses and Hogan was becoming stifled with them. The country-western station Kendrick favored was now playing *Take Me Back To Tulsa*.

Hogan stood up. "I'm going to go have a chat with the bailiff," he said.

He went down the stairs and into the hot air of the September night. He threaded his way past the camera vans, through knots of people, over to the courthouse and to the stairs.

The bailiff tipped his head at him. Hogan had known the man for years. "Mr. Hogan, it's hot and argumentative in the jury room, and the colonels are the loudest in the group."

Hogan said, "I appreciate it. Thanks."

The bailiff looked both directions, then said, "Probably one or two for your gook and they have to whip them into line."

Hogan nodded. "It's about what I expect."

Hogan went back outside and across the street, and the bailiff went back to guarding the jury-room door.

Judge Barret sent word to the lawyers that the jurors intended to continue to work until they got a verdict. They didn't want to go for dinner.

The jury sent several notes to the judge with reference to clarification of lesser sentences that accompanied premeditated murder. The judge wrote back to review the legal definitions he had given and they would find appropriate answers. Other notes wanted a fuller definition of self-defense. One note later asked how parole worked in this case.

Hogan couldn't stand it. The wait was torture. He walked over to the courthouse yet again.

The bailiff shook his head. "Some guy was talking about Kim and the 104th Marines. What the hell does that have to do with this case? We should have shot the bastards. No offense intended, counselor."

Hogan went back to Kendrick's .

Suddenly, shortly after midnight, there was a loud knock on the door of the jury room. The judge was informed that a verdict had been reached, and the messenger, the assistant D.A., came knocking at Kendrick's door to announce it. They all jumped. The door opened, and the assistant said, "Come on. We got a verdict."

Hogan's long experience told him that plans for a rapid departure down the backstairs were both prudent and necessary. He had a few friends to help with protection to escort them out of the courthouse and into waiting cars, if it proved necessary. Hogan had the feeling that it would, no matter what the verdict. Hogan's sixth sense, as he watched a swelling and potentially dangerous crowd, was on the alert. He stood for a moment before going over, with his jacket slung over his shoulder, his tie loose. The crowd was nearly as big as it was at five o'clock, and a line of traffic snaked around the square and down the side streets. Then they all walked over to the old courthouse, and the statue of Justice glinted under the courthouse lights, metallic and ominous under the great stars.

Inside, the courtroom was jammed with more people than it should have properly held.

As the jurors returned, their expressions were the same as they had always been throughout the trial; cold and indifferent toward Cai, cordial and hospitable toward the district attorney.

Chapter Forty-Four

September 19th, Midnight

"Mr. Foreman, have you reached a verdict?"

Colonel Washington, who was the foreman, replied, "We have, your Honor." He handed the verdict to the clerk who gave it to the judge.

The judge adjusted his glasses and read it aloud. "We the jury find the defendant not guilty."

Hogan's group was speechless. There were murmurs throughout the packed courtroom and shouts from the Hardin family. Lillie May put her hands to her face, and then almost shouted to Cai in Vietnamese, who simply stared at her.

"No! No!" It was someone from the Hardins in the front.

In horror and indignation the D.A. jumped to his feet. "Is that your verdict?" He stared at them. "Your Honor, I ask that the jury be polled!"

Each individual juror was asked if that was his verdict. They each agreed it was. The D.A. was chalk white, and perspiration stood out on his forehead despite the air-conditioned air.

Hogan felt his shoulders slump with relief, and he put his head in his hands. "My God," he whispered.

Sheila and Lillie May threw their arms around one another, Paul and Sabine were laughing with astonishment and delight, and Big Bob slapped his files, laughing.

The judge tried in vain to restore order in an increasingly noisy courtroom. The bailiff ran from the courtroom to call for the sheriff's deputies.

The conduct of the jury was even stranger. When they were dismissed, they walked past Hogan with expressions of contempt. He held out his hand to shake hands with them and was stunned when they refused. They passed Cai and Hogan without a word or any recognition or sign of friendship.

Hogan stood for a second with his hand out, and then put it back into his pocket and looked at the few remaining jurors quizzically, but they too walked on by.

Each one of them, on the contrary, shook hands firmly and enthusiastically with the D.A. Hogan heard several of them congratulate him for standing up for law and order. Hogan listened in astonishment.

Leaning back against the wall with his hands now in his pocket instead of held out, Hogan heard the colonel who was the foreman, with tears in his eyes, tell the district attorney, "That was the hardest damn thing I ever had to do. You were superb."

Suddenly the district attorney took hold of himself, and turned with a wide smile to all the people who were congratulating him. Once again he was the hero. He was the people's lawyer -- despite the fact that he'd lost the case.

In the past, when Hogan was presented with a not guilty verdict, he'd always prepared himself for the compliments, the congratulations and the accolades, the embraces and cries of triumph. He'd always tried to present a sense of humility, even if he didn't feel it. But in this instance, he was completely floored. There were no warm words of praise, no congratulatory slaps on the back, no show of admiration. Only scorn.

"Let's get out of here," said Hogan. "Cai, come on — you're free."

Cai stood in a blank puzzlement until Lillie May took one hand and Hogan the other and hurried him off.

Hogan knew the route of escape -- through the judge's office, and down the back stairs. The disheveled judge encouraged their rapid departure and instructed the bailiff to watch until they were safely in their cars.

Fighting hard to hang on to their briefcases, they shoved their way through the crowd clustered at the exit. Hogan muttered a fervent "Thank God" when the appearance of the district attorney drew the mob's attention. Grateful to leave the blinding flashes of cameras and television lights to the D.A., the defense team hurried to the cars they'd parked at the far back corner of the lot.

As Paul tried to hustle Cai into a car for a fast get-away, Hogan embraced Lillie May and asked her to give the boys his best.

"We'll try to figure out later what happened," he told her. Despite his assurances, Hogan had the feeling he'd never know what had swung the jurors. It could have been Lillie May, the selection of the jury, the challenge to the jury to do the right thing, maybe even Hogan's own input.

"Thank you for what you've done," Lillie May said.

Suddenly escaping Paul's grasp, Cai turned and stuck out his hand. With a wide grin on his face and tears in his eyes, he gripped Hogan's hand. Then, in perfect English, he said, "Old man, you were great. Thank you."

Too astonished to reply, Hogan, mouth open, simply stood there holding Cai's hand. The rest of the Hogan group was in as much shock as their leader.

Releasing Hogan's hand, Cai reached into his shirt pocket, drew out a package of Lucky Strikes and lit one. He shot the crowd at the courthouse a quick glance, making sure no one but their small group could hear him.

"Well, we figured our best shot was to keep our mouths shut and trust in Lillie May," Cai explained.

"Jesus," said Hogan.

"But--" Paul began.

"I don't believe it!" Sheila interrupted.

Sabine and Kendrick just stood there gaping.

"Yeah, I know it wasn't your game plan," Cai said. "But we knew he'd kill us on cross-examination. We gambled that he couldn't lay a glove on Lillie May."

Cai puffed as the group kept standing and staring.

"I'm getting too old for this," Hogan finally said.

"But they were right," said Lillie May. She smiled proudly.

Cai shrugged. "The son-of-a-bitch *needed* killing. Maybe that made a difference. Who knows?"

Hogan felt shell-shocked. How would he have played the defense if he'd known the truth? He couldn't imagine. "Get out of here," he finally said. "Get in the car and go."

Cai hopped in, small and sprightly. "I'm on my way to Houston to some friends."

As the car drove away into the night, Cai leaned out the window and yelled, "You will always be in our prayers! God is good!"

"I don't know how much God had to do with it," muttered Hogan. He took off his jacket and slung it across his shoulders, then turned and reached for Sheila's hand. "Let's get out of here," he said.

It was over. This time there was not the same kind of jubilation as in other cases, just a kind of mystery. But it was over -- and they'd survived. That's all that mattered.

Paul and Sabine paused by their dusty Chevrolet. "Dad, when are you two going to get married?" asked Paul. "This is embarrassing. You can't just be an old hippie all your life."

Ducking inside the car, Paul and Sabine quickly clunked the doors shut, leaving Hogan open-mouthed again. Sheila couldn't stop laughing as she watched their car pull out and head back to San Antonio.

Hogan sat at the piano in the apartment, the windows were open and the late evening breeze slid over the city, as it did every evening, up from the Gulf's cooling water. It was finished now, and Cai Van Nguyen was released to make his way in America as a fisherman or a mechanic or schoolteacher, and his children to perhaps become astronauts or go to Harvard or MIT. And Tho and Lillie May and Father Dominic as well would all become ordinary Americans. The ordinary people who sat on juries with the majesty of the law in their hands; the juries that almost always, somehow, did the right thing.

Hogan sat at the old upright piano and slowly, cautiously, began to play *Weeping Willow*. His thick hands moved hesitantly but without error, and the piece flowed out as Joplin meant it to be played — with grace, with hesitation. Hogan's tie was loose as always and his hair fell forward on his forehead. He had a toothpick in the corner of his mouth and a glass of ice tea sitting on top of the upright.

Sheila stood in the door and looked at him. She was wearing a silk dress in fall patterns and a small string of pearls.

She said, "You're doing a Hoagy Carmichael."

"I know it." He smiled but didn't look up, keeping his eyes on the score. "You should have a little hat, and a cigarette. What's the line?"

She said, "Just whistle."

He smiled ever more broadly and kept on playing. She walked over and put her arms on top of the piano and her chin on her arms.

"Are you staying around for the next hopeless case?" he asked.

"Depends," she said. "One day at a time, just like the Steps say."

"All right."

He played the piece to its finish and got up and put his arms around her and stood holding her a long time.

"What's next?" he asked.

"*Solace*," she said. "A Mexican serenade."